Has The Idol Gone Crazy Today

james

Published by james, 2024.

This is a work of fiction. Similarities to real people, places, or events are entirely coincidental.

HAS THE IDOL GONE CRAZY TODAY

First edition. November 8, 2024.

ISBN: 979-8227154668

Written by james.

Table of Contents

Synopsis:

Zhi Chang is a low-key dance cover artist with hundreds of thousands of followers on her channel. Known for her graceful movements and cool demeanor, she has always preferred to stay out of the spotlight, letting her art speak for itself.

But one day, her peaceful world is turned upside down when she discovers she's been edited into a viral "meme remix" video. Her carefully crafted elegance is now paired with chaotic beats, wild effects, and a level of absurdity that leaves her mortified... and unexpectedly famous.

As the video spreads like wildfire, Zhi Chang finds herself in a strange twist of fate—brought closer to the creator of the remix, an enigmatic yet charming video editor. Known for his witty humor and mischievous spirit, he never imagined that the girl in his edits would one day become the woman beside him.

"When I first chose you as my video material, I never thought you'd become the one sharing my pillow."

With humor, unexpected romance, and the clash of creativity, *Has the Idol Gone Crazy Today?* is a lighthearted story of fame, love, and the unpredictable power of the internet. Can Zhi Chang keep her life grounded while her online persona spins out of control? Or will this unexpected fame lead her to the adventure—and the partner—she never saw coming?

Chapter 1 Tang Zhi

Another summer has arrived, and the southern cities are still active after the dragon boat race.

The rain outside is cheerful, but the scene inside is completely different.

In the spacious dance studio, incandescent lamps clearly illuminate every corner. The black and white decoration is simple and fashionable. The three walls with a wall of mirrors are a unique scene in the dance studio.

At this time, the speakers in the corner are playing bright and lively music. There is only one girl wearing hot pants and short T-shirt in the spacious dance studio.

Chang Zhi, the owner of the Internet celebrity "Try" milk tea shop, is also a well-known dance cover up master on B station. She has 470,000 followers on B station and 500,000 fans on Weibo.

The young and promising Chang Zhi has a middle-parted curly hair, delicate eyebrows and eyes on her small face, a high nose bridge, and a heart-shaped mouth of just the right thickness and size. She is a typical beauty. If you ignore the haggard feeling brought by the dark blue due to staying up late, I am afraid that she will be pulled into the entertainment industry to be an actor without makeup.

At this moment, Chang Zhi is practicing her next cover dance that she is going to release.

She routinely updates at 7:07 pm every Saturday night, and today is Friday. Because it is summer, the milk tea shop is booming.

She was forced to go to the shop to help a few days ago, and she started practicing today.

Time is tight. In addition to the recording time, there is also post-production. Chang Zhi is very glad that she just hired another employee to replace her position in the milk tea shop yesterday, otherwise she would really have to stay up until dawn today.

Among the many dances, Chang Zhi loves to cover the dances of Korean groups in Kimchi Country. After all, it is a country with extremely developed entertainment industry. Naturally, this aspect is becoming more and more strict. There are also some high-quality dance songs. Chang Zhi picked a song that she thought was pretty good and the dance was also okay yesterday, and she started thinking about it this morning.

Chang Zhi's eyes were focused on her movements in the mirror at this time.

Because she really likes the composition of this song, she couldn't help humming along with the rhythm of the music.

Twisting the waist, shaking the head, circling... the small movements connected smoothly and naturally, in line with the rhythm of the song, the speed gradually increased, and the state was getting better and better. But not long after, looking at herself in the mirror, Chang Zhi frowned slightly and slowed down her movements.

I didn't keep up with this part again... It's always here.

The music in the speakers continued to play, but Chang Zhi had stopped moving. She ran to the mirror and picked up her phone to open the practice room version of this music again. She put on headphones and pulled the progress bar to the part before the wrong part with her slender index finger. She listened to the beat of the music bit by bit with her little head and stared at the video.

Three, two, one...

Chang Zhi followed the movements of the video with her empty hands unconsciously. She silently replayed the clip in her mind. She took off the headphones, put the phone back in place, ran to a corner of the dance studio, took out the camera from her backpack and positioned it, ready to try recording it once and compare it with the original song.

Keep improving.

The music started, and she started to move again to the beat. She danced until the evening, and Chang Zhi, holding the camera, breathed a sigh of relief.

Go home.

Chang Zhi went down to the front desk on the first floor, and the receptionist asked her spontaneously: "Miss Chang, will you come tomorrow?"

As usual, Chang Zhi booked the entire dance studio every Friday and Saturday morning and afternoon.

But today she was fast.

Chang Zhi thought about it and shook her head: "Not necessarily, I'll see the weather tomorrow, if the weather is good, I'll go to the outdoor scene... Well, anyway, I'll call you at 8 o'clock tomorrow morning to tell you."

The dance studio opens at 9 o'clock.

The receptionist smiled and said hello.

Before Chang Zhi walked out of the building, she had just said a few words to the receptionist. The rain outside, which had stopped for a while, started again. Chang Zhi stopped and looked at her newly bought thousand-yuan AD sports shoes on her feet, and then looked at the long water that was about to merge into a stream under the three steps at the door.

She saw the car splashing water nearly as high as a person on the road not far away.

"............"

She sighed.

It hadn't rained when she went out in the morning, but it started to rain heavily when she was about to go back in the afternoon. She had only worn these shoes for two days, and they were going to be ruined again.

It was obviously a first-tier city, so is the drainage system really that bad?

Resigned to her fate, she held up her dark green umbrella, moved her bag in front of her with one hand, and went down the stairs to the platform to hail a taxi.

She didn't dare to drive, so she didn't buy a car even if she had a little money.

There was an outdoor parking lot here. As soon as Chang Zhi went down two steps, she saw a black Land Rover coming from not far away. With the sound of the car's horn, it quickly drove to one meter of the stairs, and the "stream" she had just sighed about was now splashing one meter high with the rolling of the wheels-

Chang Zhi subconsciously closed her eyes.

All this happened so quickly that she forgot to raise her umbrella forward to block it.

Cold water drops instantly stuck to the legs and arms, flowing down the texture and bringing waves of discomfort, and the originally dry clothes instantly became wet.

m...mp!

Chang Zhi, who was soaked like a drowned chicken, opened her eyes angrily, and at the same time heard a sudden brake sound.

The car stopped, and Chang Zhi took a deep breath and swallowed the discordant words that almost blurted out.

Because Chang Zhi saw a person coming down from the main driver's seat.

Wen Yanxing just came back from abroad a few days ago. After staying at home for two days, he finally adjusted to the time difference. In the afternoon, when he was tinkering with the video at home, he received a call from an old classmate asking for a get-together.

Wen Yanxing has always been a punctual person. He hurriedly released the video and went out. Who knew that it would rain heavily when he was about to reach the destination. The ground was slippery, and the wheels slipped and almost lost control. Fortunately, he controlled it in time and didn't hit anything, but-

The water stirred up by the car wet a woman.

Chang Zhi saw the man walking quickly from not far away, and in an instant he came to her.

The man was holding a black umbrella. He was slender under the umbrella, wearing a light gray shirt and casual pants. He was about 1.84 meters tall, with broad shoulders and narrow waist, and a very good-looking figure... At this moment, he looked at her with his dark eyes, his thin lips slightly parted, and his cold voice was a little apologetic: "Miss, I'm sorry, the tire slipped just now, I didn't mean to splash you, you see...?"

Chang Zhi swallowed all her complaints immediately.

Originally, this kind of thing might not be intentional. If the man just drove away like this, she could still complain about the decline of morals, but now he stopped to apologize...

The tire slipped.

She also heard the particularly loud brake sound.

Chang Zhi had nothing to say. She shook her head and said, "Forget it. It's nothing."

Wen Yanxing was already very sorry. It was the first time he encountered such a thing and he didn't know how to deal with it. He also heard the other party say that it was okay. He didn't know how to compensate him, and...

The woman in front of him also had water drops on her face. Her face was incredibly small. After apologizing, Wen Yanxing looked at her seriously, from her eyebrows to her lips and then to-

Legs.

Proportionate and slender, some muscles in the calves made the lines of the legs more beautiful... Wen Yanxing estimated that the woman was about 1.65 meters tall, but the proportions were particularly good and almost familiar... A face suddenly appeared in his mind, and a hint of surprise flashed in Wen Yanxing's eyes.

No wonder he felt familiar, this is not...

Chang Zhi didn't know what the man in front of her was thinking. She looked down at her body and felt a little worried.

A light cough came from above, and then the man spoke. At the same time, a pack of tissues was handed to her -

"How about wiping it?" There was a hint of guilt in the voice, but Chang Zhi didn't hear it.

She just felt embarrassed now, too embarrassed, not sure if it was because of embarrassment or cold, and felt goose bumps on her arms.

But Chang Zhi still took it and said thank you.

Thanks to the rain, although Chang Zhi became a drowned chicken, she still managed to escape the strange eyes of passers-by and got home.

When she got home, Chang Zhi threw her bag on the sofa, kicked off her wet shoes, and hurried to the bathroom to take a hot bath.

It was half an hour later when she came out of the bathroom.

She walked to the sofa while wiping her hair and sat down. She habitually took her phone out of her bag to see if there was any message. Before she unlocked the screen, she was startled by the message prompts that almost filled the entire lock screen interface.

What the hell?

There are WeChat and QQ. Her fan group and fan management group have reached 99, and there are several private chats from □□.

Chang Zhi first clicked on the message from her bestie Deng Jiadai at the top of the message notification.

This guy is said to be very busy recently, why did he suddenly send her a message?

Subconsciously, Chang Zhi had a bad premonition.

In fact, her intuition was quite accurate.

[18:20]

[Your Jia]: Are you there?

[Your Jia]: I heard that you were edited into a ghost video haha ... With a premonition from nowhere, Chang Zhi exited and looked at the Moments.

[Moments]

[Your Jia]: A wonderful dinner [Picture] [Picture] ——1 minute ago.

Chang Zhi: "................."

Is he a human? He didn't reply to her but posted on Moments. Is he a human?

Not a human.

[Tang Zhi]: Damn, you have the guts to post on Moments, you have the guts to eat, you have the guts to explain it to me, reply to me, reply to me! ?

Chapter 2 How can we know

Chang Zhi is facing the biggest challenge of her life at this moment.

As an excellent dance up master on Station B, Chang Zhi has been practicing dancing since she was a child. She has been well-known since she released her first dance cover video. In her previous life, the word "ghost" was not related to her.

What is a ghost video?

In the official words: a ghost video ghost is a kind of material that is highly synchronized and quickly repeated with the rhythm of the background music to achieve a brainwashing or funny effect.

As an excellent dance cover up, the word "fun"... should not appear on her

On the other side, Deng Jiadai has not replied to her.

Chang Zhi knows with her toes that Deng Jiadai is definitely enjoying herself now. She has always valued love over friendship and loves to tease her the most. If she didn't respond to her crazy question marks, she might be laughing at the phone screen in private.

No longer bothered to care about Deng Jiadai, Chang Zhi clicked on the QQ message, and a bunch of unread messages jumped up one after another. Chang Zhi glanced at them quickly. There were administrators, fans, and friends. After thinking about it, Chang Zhi clicked into the management group first, intending to ask the administrators first.

<Twenty-four Yamen>

[Yin En]: Pu, just online, did you see the video recommended on the homepage?

[Liu Fang]: I saw it, I saw it, Yan Zhi's new work released in the afternoon... My sister Tang is in the picture.

[Yuzi]: Hahahaha, so excited and happy, my husband is a ghost goddess, hahahaha

——This is someone who knows about this. .

[Liu Fang]: Forget it, when did Yan Zhi become your husband? He is the father of my child.

[Fu Da Miao]: ....[Black Question Mark Face.jpg]

[Fu Da Miao]: What the hell is this?

——This is from the masses who are unaware of the truth like her.

For some reason, it felt like everyone around knew about this. It was rare to meet someone who also didn't know the truth. Chang Zhi was a little relieved.

Tang Zhi's fingers quickly clicked a few times on the nine-square input method.

[Simple and hardworking Tang Zhi]: ... What were you talking about just now?

[Yin En]: Sister Tang, are you online? I chatted with you privately but you didn't reply to me.

[Simple and hardworking Tang Zhi]: I was outside just now, and I was soaked by the rain. I just saw your messages after I got home and took a shower. There were too many messages and I didn't have time to read them, so I posted them here first. What's going on?

[Liu Fang]: Sister Tang, you don't know yet? ? ?

[Yuzi]: This, link //.bi

Chang Zhi raised her eyebrows. Before she clicked in, the introduction appeared below.

[All Stars] Let's dance and find the place where the ghosts and animals belong. up: How can we know

...This name has a slight rhyme effect, which is a good reference to the theme. Chang Zhi, who has a little knowledge of ghost videos, has almost determined that the background music of this video must be "Let's Dance".

Facing the dark video interface waiting for her to press the play button, Chang Zhi felt a little bit of collapse. .

The beat of "Let's Dance" is a passionate and old song with a sense of age. Chang Zhi had heard this song in small shops on the street several years ago. The lyrics are simple and easy to remember. She can hum it after listening to it two or three times.

The song is very popular, but it concerns herself. Chang Zhi is ready to treat this ghost video with a cold face throughout the whole process.

Chang Zhi puffed up her cheeks and nervously clicked the play button.

The rhythm of the beat sounded, and Chang Zhi couldn't help holding her breath.

The barrage filled the screen almost instantly. She vaguely saw something like [Tang Jie's fans come to watch (≧≦)/] [Dance area enters ghost animal area celebration~] [Landing time——]

She still has fans to brush the barrage?

Chang Zhi: "???" Fake fans, is she so happy to be ghosted?

The prelude lasted 20 seconds. At the 21st second when the lyrics and voice came out, as *Ge Ping's face appeared in front of her, Chang Zhi's mouth twitched.

Do you still remember the fear dominated by *"The Legend of the Seven Heroes of Rainbow Cat and Blue Rabbit" in those years?

"I am confused about what you are talking about, only *Jin Ke La makes me think clearly——"

"Reason will no longer work from now on, only Jin Ke La will lead me out of the lost path——"

"Jin Ke La Jin Ke La wheat yields one acre and eight——"

What the hell... what words rhyme so well? ?

Chang Zhi felt that she could not remember the original lyrics in a trance.

The barrage in front of me quickly slid [Kneel down when I open my mouth] [Full score for lyrics, draw your sword in the music section]

[This is just an appetizer] [Songs with Jin Ke La are good songs]

[Mom, I can't go out] [This song is not good at all, I just listened to it 38 times]...

At 1min40s of the video, with the angry "I want Jin Ke La, no Jin Ke La scum" from the *Father in "Downfall of the Empire", Chang Zhi propped up her chin and began to shake her legs unconsciously while listening to the song, probably because she hadn't seen herself yet.

At 2min, the barrage began to brush words like [High energy ahead] [Fake high energy, get out of here]

Chang Zhi sat up unconsciously, and the speed of shaking her legs gradually slowed down. She picked up the water cup on the table and drank the water slowly to suppress her inner anxiety.

At 2min24s, when the phrase "Let's dance" echoed in her ears, the barrage that had been slightly reduced came out again——

[Strong onlookers. �

�Guide to the video of this girl with a.v. number ******�

�Congratulations to the ghost animal area for entering the dance area! �

�What's the matter with the previous one? It's a strong advertisement for our dance area! �

�Red letter popular science: The girl is the dance area up Tang Zhi�

�Contract this pair of standing legs��Don't even think about it! �

There is even a considerate counter——

�Tang Zhi Fan Club counter starts counting below↓�

�Rotate x1��Rotate x2��Rotate x3��Rotate x4��Rotate x... Hey! ��Sorry, I'm dazzled. I'll do it again! See you all for 2min24s! �

The voices of Zhuge Liang and Wang Situ were in my ears: "Keep dancing, it's better to dance than to be a ghost animal. Let's get along in this way and find the way back to the ghost animal..."

"Puff, cough, cough..." Suddenly choked by the cold water, Chang Zhi coughed and tears came out. In the video, she was wearing a black suspender skirt, which was repeatedly edited to have a repeated rotation effect, and the skirt also rotated with her body intimately.

2min24s, 2min31s, 2min36, dancing twice appeared eight times in total, so Tang Zhi's repeated rotation picture card appeared exactly eight times, and with the editing of other ghost animal stars, there was no sense of disobedience.

After drinking a big sip of water to stop coughing, Chang Zhi stroked her chest to calm down. The video had already ended.

It was terrible.

Chang Zhi temporarily pressed her right hand that wanted to hold the mouse to replay the video, and her fair face was stained with a layer of red.

Calm down - take a deep breath.

She dragged the progress bar back to where she appeared, turned off all the barrages, and watched it again for the second time.

I can't bear to look at it, I can't bear to look at it.

Although the picture quality is terrible for some reason, I can still vaguely see her face.

Chang Zhi opened the QQ management group and started typing.

[Simple and hardworking Tang Zhi]: ... I've finished watching it.

[Simple and hardworking Tang Zhi]: What can I do? I'm also desperate.jpg

... The despair that can be felt across the screen.

[Fu Da Miao]: I just finished watching it too... I haven't seen the ghost animal, but this is quite fun, hahaha? Sister Tang, are you going to delete it?

[Yuzi]: No, I think it's pretty good. Free advertising in the ghost animal area, it's not ugly, it's beautiful.

[Simple and hardworking Tang Zhi]: How can you see the beauty of the high-blur quality that only the eyes and mouth can be seen?

[Yuzi]: Temperament, even if you turn 666 times a second, you are still beautiful.

[Simple and hardworking Tang Zhi]: Then you can only see the temperament of my corpse.

[Liu Fang]: Didn't that Pipa sauce get ghost-made before? And it became even more popular. It was even used as the cover of the video. I think this is great. This wave of advertisements will probably boost my sister Tang's dance career!

[Yin En]: 2333 I also think it's good and funny to keep it.

Chang Zhi looked at the dog-headed military advisors on the screen indifferently.

Oh, is it really okay to just leave it alone? She is also a girl!

[Simple and hardworking Tang Zhi]: I'm just a low-key up master, why do you treat me like this?

[Yuzi]: Because you dance, it fits the theme.

[Simple and hardworking Tang Zhi]: There are so many dancing up masters!

[Yuzi]: Because you... you dance well! Be optimistic, baby, what if they are your fans?

[Simple and hardworking Tang Zhi]: What kind of fans would ghost-make their idols?

[Yin En]: Who knows! Hahahahahahahahahaha

Chang Zhi: "..."

I give her full marks for being clever, she's very strong.

[Simple and hardworking Tang Zhi]: Don't joke around, if you were my fan, I'd chop off my head for you.

[Yin En]: Don't be so silly, Sister Tang

[Yuzu]: If I could make a ghost video, I'd make a ghost video of you, too, after all, I love you deeply.

[Simple and hardworking Tang Zhi]: Then the day you finish making the video will be the last day of your life, and I'll burn incense for you on that day next year, and you can pay me in advance today for the money.

[Yuzu]: Wish you good fortune! Good luck!

Chang Zhi subconsciously clicked on the red envelope.

"0.01 yuan has been deposited into the wallet."

Then her administrators all said "666" in a row

[Simple and hardworking Tang Zhi]: ...

[Simple and hardworking Tang Zhi]: So naughty, so naughty.

She! Just! Say! There! Is! No! Serious! Person! In! This! Group! of! People!

[Yin En]: Actually, Sister Tang, I think, if you are really uncomfortable, why don't you join Yanzhi Penguin to chat?

...

Hmm?

Are you serious?

Chapter 3 Huai

Chang Zhi looked at the messages about Yan Zhi on the screen of her mobile phone, and thought about recording and posting videos tomorrow, and paying rent the day after tomorrow... With so many things piled up, her head was almost broken.

"Ah—" A sneeze shook her internal organs.

Chang Zhi sniffed her nose, and her eyes were moist.

Well, I caught a cold again after being drenched in water today.

Touching her still wet hair, Chang Zhi reluctantly turned off the air conditioner and turned on the fan, then sat in front of the fan and blew her hair with a hair dryer.

Otherwise it was too hot. It was pure hot when it didn't rain, and it was... a little humid and hot when it rained.

Disgusting weather.

After her hair was dry, Chang Zhi slowly turned on the computer.

Add Penguin to chat... Thinking so in her mind, Chang Zhi first clicked on Yan Zhi's up homepage on Bilibili, and saw the Weibo address in the introduction, so Chang Zhi crawled over there.

As soon as I entered Weibo, I saw Yan Zhi's avatar was a very cute hedgehog, so cute, but the high-definition and composition showed that it was found on the Internet.

Then I looked down.

Chang Zhi was shocked to see that the number of fans was 2.5 million.

2.5 million fans...

Could it be that they bought zombie fans?

You should know that among the popular game area ups, dance area ups, and music area ups on B station, the up with the highest number of fans is the anchor of a certain platform in the game area, and the fans are only a little over 3 million.

She, a newcomer who has just started out and has a good momentum for less than two years, has only more than 500,000 fans. Yan Zhi has doubled his number several times. What the hell is this...

Chang Zhi drank a sip of cold water to calm down, looked at the number of reposts and comments on Yan Zhi's original Weibo, and tried to analyze the reliability of the number of fans.

...The conclusion is that it is very normal and reliable, and Yan Zhi's fans are extremely active.

Chang Zhi took a quick look at the comments and found that most of them were female fans. Some said, "Will the male god post a video today?" "Yan Da has a nice voice, I want a good morning alarm clock..." "Let's make a sound mad in the next issue." "It's okay, husband, I don't have any inspiration. I'll think about it slowly. The video posted today is enough for me to watch for a month."

There are even some -

"What could be happier than my husband having sex with a goddess? I'm probably the winner in life."

Chang Zhi: "..."

Chang Zhi felt that after today, the attributes of her fans would probably start to become a little abnormal.

After a quick look on Weibo, Chang Zhi found nothing. She had to go back to Yan Zhi's B station homepage. She clicked on the video list and found a video about a horror game in a bunch of videos. She clicked on it and it seemed to be quite popular. Chang Zhi tried to play it.

The screen was still black, but a light cough entered her ears, followed by a slightly magnetic and low voice——

"Okay, today's video is a continuation of the xx game recorded last month. I've been busy returning to China recently and don't have much time to play games. I haven't done much in other videos..."

Chang Zhi was stunned.

This voice... is very nice.

The pronunciation is clear but not rigid, and the voice is very good and charming.

Well, she seems to know why Yan Zhi has so many fans.

Hearing this voice, she also wants to follow him.

Before watching the video, Chang Zhi directly clicked on the private message on Yan Zhi's homepage.

She hesitated for a long time in front of the computer, not knowing where to start. In fact, this matter, if you say it's a matter of settling accounts, it doesn't seem to be a big deal, but it feels a bit weird psychologically. This contradictory mentality made Chang Zhi only send four words and two punctuation marks in the end——

[21:30]

[Tang Zhi]: Hello... are you there?

Because she had to record a video the next day, Chang Zhi went to bed early.

When she woke up, she habitually checked B Station, but Yan Zhi didn't reply to her.

Chang Zhi breathed a sigh of relief.

It was okay that she didn't reply, she hadn't thought about how to speak or what she wanted to do.

Today was a sunny day. She first called the receptionist who had an appointment yesterday and told her that she didn't need to order it. She also prepared two sets of clothes and equipment, and then called her photography friend Jiang Huai.

Jiang Huai has known her for two years. At first, Chang Zhi met him on the photography forum on the Internet. At that time, she had just started to make flip videos, and she bought a SLR and prepared to shoot. But to be honest, maybe she didn't have talent. Chang Zhi looked at a lot of teaching materials and the effect of the recording was average.

And she didn't know how to do post-production...

Then she met Jiang Huai from the same city, this magical man who was good at photography and post-production...

The call was very slow, and the music sounded for a long time. Just when Chang Zhi thought the music would stop, the call was connected.

"...Hello?" The voice on the other end of the line was a slightly hoarse male voice, with the sleepiness of the early morning.

Chang Zhi couldn't help but lower her voice: "Jiang Huai, are you awake?"

"...Ah," Jiang Huai was still a little stunned, as if he had just regained consciousness, "Chang Zhi?" His voice was also much more sober.

Chang Zhi smiled: "You just recognized it was me?"

"I'm not awake yet," Jiang Huai sat up from the bed, half of his sleepiness dispelled, "...I stayed up late to edit a video last night and went to bed after one o'clock. The alarm I set for eight o'clock hasn't rung yet, so why did you call? Um, wait—" The voice was a little farther away from the microphone.

Chang Zhi: "???"...It's nine o'clock now, right?

"I guess I didn't save the alarm I set yesterday??" Jiang Huai's tone was full of surprise, "I just woke up, Chang Zhi, you won't have gone out, right?"

"No," Chang Zhi looked at herself in the full-length mirror with her bag on her back and shoes on, and told a white lie, "I just woke up not long ago."

"Well... then I'll hurry up and try to finish the shooting early and leave two hours for post-production."

"Okay."

"Then I'll go wash up and change clothes first, hang up."

After hanging up the phone, she made an appointment with Jiang Huai on the phone for the time and place, sat at home and browsed Weibo, and it was almost time, so Chang Zhi was ready to go out.

As soon as she opened the door, she was startled by the movement of the door opposite.

By the way, the house Chang Zhi lives in is rented, because it is close to her milk tea shop and there are no houses for sale nearby, so she had to rent the house across the street from the milk tea shop.

Because it is in a first-tier city close to the city center, Chang Zhi rents a three-bedroom and one-living room for 7,000 yuan a month, which is also acceptable.

By the way, Chang Zhi remembered that the room opposite her was empty and no one lived there... What was going on?

The door was wide open, and there were several furniture pieces in the corridor, and then several workers kept carrying these furniture in.

So early in the morning... Chang Zhi looked at the time and it was only half past eight. Was it moving?

Passing through the gap between the pile of furniture, Chang Zhi just caught an elevator.

Who knew that the person she saw when the elevator door opened was the landlord.

The landlord's surname was He, and Chang Zhi could not remember his full name. Anyway, she usually called him landlord. He was only about 28 years old. Because they lived on the upper and lower floors, he would greet Chang Zhi when he saw her in the elevator.

"Good morning," Chang Zhi greeted casually, "What are you moving so early in the morning? Is someone going to live opposite?"

Chang Zhi had lived here for three years, and no one had ever lived opposite her, and it had not been rented out.

He Shengbi also saw Chang Zhi. Chang Zhi tied her hair into a ponytail today, and put on a very fresh makeup, looking very youthful. Looking down, oh, these legs - He Shengbi immediately looked away.

At this time, he also heard Chang Zhi's question, so he said: "Yes, I seem to have told you before, this building was bought by me and my friend. His kid was abroad before, and now he is back. He has no place to live but insisted on living here. He bought a few more pieces of furniture last night, and they were delivered this morning. Aren't they moving in?"

Speaking of this, He Shengbi was also depressed. He was fine at the party last night, but after returning home, he was woken up by a phone call at three o'clock in the middle of the night. He said he was moving in without saying anything, and said that someone would move furniture in at eight o'clock in the morning - isn't this crazy?

Chang Zhi didn't know much about it, and she didn't feel anything after hearing this. She just knew that someone was going to live across the street. After saying hello to the landlord, Chang Zhi went downstairs to take a car.

The time to meet Jiang Huai is ten o'clock.

Chang Zhi has already arranged the schedule for this afternoon. Actually, it is a bit rushed. There are two scenes in total, but they must be shot before 4 pm because she has to go back to check the business in the store. Well... she has to hurry up.

Chang Zhi stood at the gate of a park waiting for Jiang Huai. Her phone vibrated. It turned out that Deng Jiadai, the heartless guy, replied to her message.

...She dared to reply to her after all the tricks she used last night? ? Aren't you afraid that she will scold her?

I'm afraid she replied because she has something to ask her.

[10:23]

[Your Jia]: Did you watch the video?

[Tang Zhi]: You are not ashamed to say that, did you have fun last night?

[Your Jia]: I had a lot of fun. I didn't expect there would be such a night show

[Tang Zhi]: Wow, didn't you think that I didn't know anything and looked confused? Wouldn't your conscience hurt?

[Your Jia]: I believe that with your intelligence, it will be no problem~ little girl.

Humph—Chang Zhi sneered. This guy is just talking nonsense.

[Your Jia]: ...Oh, right.

[Your Jia]: Meng Xi contacted me.

Chapter 4 Yanxing

Chang Zhi was stunned when she saw the name at first glance.

Before she could react, she heard someone calling her name.

"Chang Zhi, here."

It was Jiang Huai.

Chang Zhi hurriedly put the phone into her pocket, then looked up and smiled and asked naturally: "Did you have breakfast?"

Jiang Huai was dressed in a white T-shirt and casual pants, with a black schoolbag on his back, dressed like a big boy. Hearing this, he replied: "I did. I came across a newly opened breakfast shop on the way. The soy milk and fried dough sticks there are delicious... Did you eat?"

Chang Zhi joked: "I got up earlier than you, so I must have eaten."

"Okay, okay," Jiang Huai spread his hands, "It's not my fault, it's the phone's fault."

"Let's go, let's go into the park."

Chang Zhi chose two places for shooting. The scenes were quite close. One was an ordinary park here, and the other was the mangroves near this park.

The two took their equipment and chose a lawn with few people. The weather was good and it was morning, so Chang Zhi was quite satisfied. Jiang Huai set up a tripod on the spot, and placed a small speaker next to it, the sound was neither too loud nor too small, just enough for Chang Zhi to hear.

After all, it can't be too disturbing, right?

The video started recording, the music started, and the two began to get busy.

Several videos should be recorded for easy editing.

A whole morning was spent like this, but Chang Zhi was not in good condition today and made several mistakes. Even Jiang Huai asked Chang Zhi what happened. The video was not really recorded until 4:30 in the afternoon.

I said goodbye to Jiang Huai at the station and agreed to send her the post-edited video via Penguin at 6:30. After watching Jiang Huai get on the bus that went directly to his residence, Chang Zhi was the only one waiting for the bus at the station.

There were very few cars here. While waiting, Chang Zhi found that the sky was gradually getting darker. Looking up, she saw a dark cloud floating towards her not far away, dark and overwhelming, with a depressing atmosphere.

Chang Zhi was a little anxious. How could she know it would rain today? She didn't bring an umbrella when she went out because she thought it was cumbersome.

But after waiting for a while, the car finally arrived. As soon as Chang Zhi got on the car, raindrops hit the car window.

Chang Zhi arrived at the "Try" milk tea shop at around five o'clock. As soon as she got off the car, she put her bag on her head and ran all the way to the store.

The employees in the store were shocked to see Chang Zhi in such a mess.

Xiao Dong spoke first: "Sister Chang, you...didn't bring an umbrella?"

Chang Zhi wiped the water off her bag and answered without raising her head: "Ah, I forgot to bring it. Do you have a towel?"

"Yes, yes, wait a minute and I'll bring it to you."

After taking the towel, Chang Zhi sat in the corner of the milk tea shop and wiped her already wet hair with the towel. This was the second time she was soaked this week. She was so unlucky.

Because of the rain, more and more people came to the milk tea shop to take shelter from the rain. People who came in inevitably bought a cup of milk tea, so the staff started to get busy again, and Chang Zhi went to help.

Just after taking the time to ask the deputy manager about the situation in the store, Chang Zhi looked up at the watch and saw that it was almost six o'clock. The clothes blown by the air conditioner were almost dry. She took an umbrella and a cup of original milk tea from the store. Chang Zhi was about to leave from the front desk when she heard a male voice asking.

"Can you give me a few tissues? Thank you."

"Okay," Chang Zhi paused, took a few tissues and handed them to the source of the voice, and looked up at the same time, so she saw the man who was looking at her at the cashier.

Chang Zhi: "..." This man looks familiar... It seems to be the man who splashed her with water when he drove that day?

The second time she saw Wen Yanxing, completely under the incandescent light, Chang Zhi realized that the man looked good, and she was a little amazed.

Wen Yanxing was also shocked when he saw Chang Zhi's face. He didn't expect to meet Chang Zhi here.

He had just moved in the afternoon. He sat at home for a while, watching videos in the air-conditioner. He always felt that something was missing. He wanted to drink milk tea. He Shengbi told him that there was a good milk tea shop across the street downstairs, so Wen Yanxing came to buy a cup.

It has been too long since he drank milk tea. When Wen Yanxing used a straw to poke the milk tea, he accidentally squeezed too hard and squeezed a little milk tea out of the cup and onto his hands.

He came to the front desk to ask for two tissues. Who knew that he would meet Chang Zhi unexpectedly.

Familiar face, familiar legs.

"Ah, you..." Chang Zhi was also surprised and speechless. Is it such a coincidence?

Wen Yanxing laughed twice: "What a coincidence." The smile was polite but not awkward.

The voice is also very nice, Chang Zhi thought, and at the same time said in line with his words: "...It's a bit of a coincidence."

Emmm... Let's end the topic like this? Chang Zhi left the front desk.

Until, she and the man walked out of the milk tea shop side by side and opened their umbrellas at the same time, walked to the same intersection and waited for the same traffic light, walked in the same direction at the intersection in the middle of the road, and then entered the same building and the same elevator.

This is a bit embarrassing.

Chang Zhi finally felt something was wrong, looked up at the man who was also looking at her, and asked in surprise: "You live here too?"

At this moment, Wen Yanxing's heart was extremely complicated. He would never have thought that he would meet this woman who had met him a few times in his new home, especially... He was not sure that he and Chang Zhi might have a relationship that was more than just a few encounters.

It shouldn't be such a coincidence that they live on the same floor. Wen Yanxing thought.

After a light cough to regain consciousness, Wen Yanxing said, "Well, I just moved in today."

Hearing this, Chang Zhi knew that there seemed to be only one person moving today, and this man was another landlord. Chang Zhi was relieved for some reason: "... No wonder I said I hadn't seen you before, what a coincidence hahaha."

"Well... the elevator is here."

After entering the elevator, before Wen Yanxing pressed the elevator floor button, Chang Zhi, who was closer to the elevator entrance, pressed 7 first.

Wen Yanxing: "..."

He seemed to remember which floor he lived on correctly, right?

It's the seventh floor, right? Right? There are only two residents on the seventh floor. He didn't hear any movement from the opposite door all afternoon today. It turns out that Chang Zhi lives there?

Chang Zhi didn't find it strange that Wen Yanxing didn't press the elevator button. Instead, she was more certain that he was another landlord.

But out of caution, Chang Zhi turned around and asked, "Aren't you going to press it?"

"... I live on the seventh floor too." Wen Yanxing answered a little bitterly.

"Ah, what a coincidence." The identities were settled, "It seems that we have become neighbors."

Yes, it's a coincidence, it's really a coincidence. This is the first time that Chang Zhi has encountered such a coincidence.

"Ding——"

The seventh floor has arrived.

Chang Zhi got out of the elevator first, and Wen Yanxing followed.

After all, they are future neighbors. Chang Zhi rented a house here not long after graduation. This is also the first real neighbor in her life. With the eagerness to get along well, Chang Zhi turned around and looked up at Wen Yanxing in a friendly manner——

"I didn't expect that we would become neighbors. It's also fate. Please give me more advice in the future. My name is Chang Zhi, Chang for Chang, Zhi for Zhou Zhiruo, um, the Zhou Zhiruo in The Heaven Sword and Dragon Saber."

Then he stretched out a little hand full of friendship and enthusiasm.

Wen Yanxing looked down at Chang Zhi's friendly smile and the little hand full of friendship and enthusiasm, and hesitated for a moment before shaking it: "My name is Wen Yanxing, please teach me."

When Wen Yanxing held that hand, he felt as if he could crush it with a little force.

Small, soft, and gentle.

But now in China, are there still people who greet each other in the old-fashioned way of shaking hands?

It's really... quite interesting, huh?

After Chang Zhi entered the house, she heard a thunder outside the house before turning on the light.

She was so scared that she quickly turned on the light and locked the door.

Chang Zhi took a 20-minute bath and washed her hair, changed into pajamas and wrapped her hair with a bath towel. Looking at the time, it was almost 6:30, the time agreed with Jiang Huai, so she turned on the computer and prepared to log in to Penguin to receive the file.

When Chang Zhi poured a glass of water and returned to the computer, she saw that Penguin, which should have successfully logged in, actually showed that the network was disconnected and could not be connected?

Chang Zhi put down the cup and frowned. She tried to open the webpage. After loading for a long time, it showed that it could not connect.

Even the antivirus software reminded her to check the network.

No way? Is there a problem with the network at this time? Chang Zhi took out her mobile phone. The wifi could not connect.

She was a little panicked holding the phone.

Switching to data mode, the file was indeed transferred to JAC on Penguin.

What to do? It's half past six now. I have to post the video at seven o'clock. There seems to be no Internet cafe nearby. There are basically restaurants and shopping malls. At most, there is an arcade.

Chang Zhi looked at the rain outside the balcony getting heavier and heavier.

She thought about it, ran out of the study, grabbed the key and opened the door, then ran straight to the opposite door and pressed the doorbell twice.

Although it's embarrassing to disturb others like this, but... Big brother, open the door, I really have something urgent!

Chang Zhi waited at the door for about two minutes, and heard the sound of slippers rubbing against the floor from inside the door, and then the door lock clicked open.

When Wen Yanxing opened the door, he was shocked to see a woman in a sky blue nightgown and a towel wrapped around her hair.

The woman's nightgown had short sleeves on the upper body and a slightly conservative collar, but the hem of the lower part barely reached her knees, and even though she was wearing a pair of flip-flops, her legs still looked long and straight...

But... what kind of way is this?

Wen Yanxing was wearing a nightgown and looked like he had just taken a shower.

To be honest, he thought it was He Shengbi who knocked on the door!!

The two people in pajamas looked at each other in silence in the corridor for a long time.

In the end, Chang Zhi spoke first, and she was a little nervous and stuttered:

"Ahem, Mr. Wen, sorry to bother you... Although the "give me more advice" just now was a polite remark, but, um, I seem to really need your advice now..."

??????

Ah?

Chapter 5 Chang Zhi

A woman in a nightgown, with wet hair and Minions flip-flops on her feet that totally don't match her style.

Wen Yanxing didn't know why he let Chang Zhi in.

She was dressed so casually...

Does he look like a gentleman?

"Is it okay for me to sit here?"

As he was thinking, he heard the woman's cautious question. Wen Yanxing looked up at Chang Zhi. She was holding her own computer, standing in front of him, looking at him expectantly with her watery eyes.

She was referring to the dining table.

Wen Yanxing's heart skipped a beat, and he said dryly, "... whatever you want."

Chang Zhi sat down happily, with her hands on her knees, her back straight, a bit like the upright sitting posture of an elementary school top student, looking reserved.

"Oh, then which wifi is yours?" Chang Zhi asked again.

Wen Yanxing was silent for a moment, then walked slowly to Chang Zhi's side, bending down slightly and holding the mouse.

Smelling a hint of fragrance, Wen Yanxing forced himself to focus on the computer, typing the password on the keyboard with both hands.

Chang Zhi was a little embarrassed.

She asked which wifi was which, but she didn't expect that a man would come and type it in himself, and he was so close...

Chang Zhi also looked at the computer, but her eyes couldn't help but see Wen Yanxing's profile, because he bent down, and the collar of his nightgown fell down. Chang Zhi wanted to move back, but found that she had already filled the chair and couldn't move back.

Because she was in a hurry, she ran back and didn't have time to change clothes. She wiped her hair a little dry and draped it behind her shoulders. At this moment, she could still feel the water dripping down her back, itching and cold through the clothes.

Chang Zhi's hands on her knees shrank into fists, fidgeting.

When the password was entered, the two of them breathed a sigh of relief at the same time.

Chang Zhi looked up at Wen Yanxing, who had already stood up, and forced a smile: "Thank you."

"...Yeah."

Chang Zhi began to enter the URL to log in, and Wen Yanxing stood by. After thinking for a while, he walked to the water dispenser and took a disposable cup to pour a cup of cold water. Suddenly, he heard a sneeze in his ear.

Wen Yanxing looked sideways and saw Chang Zhi's index finger slightly bent, rubbing the tip of her nose and sniffing.

Looking down at the cold water on his phone, Wen Yanxing poured another warm cup.

Then he took two cups of water, put the warm one next to Chang Zhi's hand, and took the cold one himself.

"Here is the water." Wen Yanxing said.

Chang Zhi was waiting for Jiang Huai's documents to be accepted. She was concentrating on being interrupted by Wen Yanxing. She was startled, and then she realized that it was a good intention, so she looked up and smiled sincerely: "Thank you."

Wen Yanxing took a sip of water and stepped back slightly.

In fact, he didn't know what Chang Zhi was doing by borrowing the Internet. She only said that there was an emergency and she needed the Internet and her home Internet happened to be broken.

Just a sneak peek, so I can verify it...

Wen Yanxing felt a little guilty.

Chang Zhi was completely unaware of the man's thoughts. After receiving the file, she curled her lips happily, and then opened the homepage of B station.

On the homepage, the two words "Tang Zhi" were clearly visible in the upper right corner.

Wen Yanxing was just drinking the water, and when he saw the two words, his mind was distracted and he choked.

He turned his back to Chang Zhi and coughed for a while.

"Are you okay?" Chang Zhi heard the noise and showed concern politely. When she turned back, she saw Wen Yanxing's shaking shoulders.

"Cough, it's okay." Wen Yanxing waved his hand and said this. Chang Zhi saw Wen Yanxing coughing and walking to the sofa and sitting down.

...It seems that he coughed a lot, but if he said it was okay, it was okay, right?

Wen Yanxing was sure that he was not nearsighted. He looked at it twice and it was not wrong.

In fact, he thought it was a coincidence at first. It might just be someone who looked alike, although that leg... cough, anyway, he was half-believing and half-doubting.

Now that he had seen the truth with his own eyes, Wen Yanxing knew what Chang Zhi had come for.

Upload the video.

She would upload it every Saturday.

Wen Yanxing recovered and looked at the woman sitting upright not far away.

...It was really too much of a coincidence, right?

Chang Zhi had already started uploading the video. While waiting, she picked up the glass of warm water. She took a sip and then carefully observed the surroundings.

The decoration was nice. As she looked, Chang Zhi discovered that there was a transparent cage on a rectangular table placed in the corner by the window not far away.

After a closer look, there was a quietly lying... hedgehog inside?

Chang Zhi was surprised and turned around to ask Wen Yanxing: "Do you have a hedgehog at home?"

"Ah, yes."

"Can I go over and take a look?"

"Sure."

Chang Zhi suppressed her happiness at seeing the little animal and walked to the cage.

Wen Yanxing slowly got up and followed behind.

Chang Zhi was overjoyed when she saw the cage and the hedgehog. It was actually a large double-layer cage that almost filled the entire table. The transparent part should be made of plastic.

The first layer was covered with soft sawdust, the hedgehog's bed and drinking water, and the toilet. The little hedgehog was curled up on its bed with its eyes closed and sleeping. The dense thorns on its back looked quite cute.

The second layer was a roller and some toys, which looked very cute in different colors.

There were also some things for the hedgehog on the table.

Chang Zhi looked at the little hedgehog, so small that her heart melted. She lowered her voice: "So cute, what's its name?"

Wen Yanxing looked at the hedgehog sleeping quietly in the cage and said, "Second... Second." The words turned around and he swallowed back the words he was about to say.

But he felt something was wrong when he said it.

He noticed it, but the words had already been said, and it was too late to take them back.

The second one is the second one. Wen Yanxing glanced at the hedgehog who was sleeping in the cage and didn't know that his master had tricked him in front of his sister.

The second one? This name... is a bit subtle. Chang Zhi's ears blushed slightly, and she nodded calmly. In order to ease the embarrassment, she asked: "Is there a big one?"

Wen Yanxing was silent for a while and shook his head, "No."

Chang Zhi: "..." It was even more embarrassing.

Chang Zhi quickly changed the subject and pointed to the cage and said: "Is it asleep now?"

"Yeah, it fell asleep when it was tired of playing."

"It looks so quiet and well-behaved." Chang Zhi sighed.

"It's quiet only when it's sleeping." It's crazy when it's awake.

Chang Zhi reluctantly looked away from the hedgehog. She actually wanted to touch it, but it was asleep and she couldn't bear to disturb it.

Forget it, let's go and see if the video has been uploaded.

When Chang Zhi returned to the table, she found that the video had been uploaded before she sat down.

She breathed a sigh of relief.

After turning off the computer, holding the computer and looking at the man sitting back on the sofa, Chang Zhi said, "I'm done with my work, so I'll... go back first?"

"Well," Wen Yanxing nodded and stood up, "I'll open the door for you."

Chang Zhi looked down at her Minion slippers and followed him.

When she reached the entrance, Chang Zhi just heard the sound of the man unlocking the door, and there was a thunder outside the house, and at the same time, the vision was dark for a moment.

The power went out.

Chang Zhi didn't have time to retract her steps. With a panic, she held the computer in her arms, but her nose hit the man's back.

"Ouch." She screamed.

Wen Yanxing's body stiffened, and his heartbeat accelerated due to the sudden extinguishing of the lights and the soft breath of the woman approaching him.

It seemed that something had just hit him?

Chang Zhi behind her hurriedly took two steps back in the dark, her heartbeat was extremely fast, she freed her hand and rubbed her nose bridge, which was a little painful.

"What's wrong?" Chang Zhi heard Wen Yanxing ask.

Her facial features became particularly sharp in the darkness. Hearing the slight concern in the man's voice, Chang Zhi shook her head and whispered, "I'm fine."

In the darkness, it seemed as if the sound of breathing was clearly audible.

Wen Yanxing was silent, opened the door, and walked out in the dark. The automatic sensor light in the corridor was not on. He turned back and said to Chang Zhi, "There is no electricity in the corridor. The whole building should be out of power, and your house should be too."

"It should be too..." Fortunately, the video was uploaded. Chang Zhi held the wall with one hand and walked to the door in the dark. She could vaguely see the man's face in the corridor. She asked, "Did you bring your phone?"

"In the living room."

"My phone is still at home. Let me borrow your phone's flashlight so I can open the door."

Wen Yanxing walked into the house. When he walked in, because it was too narrow and he couldn't see clearly, his arm accidentally brushed Chang Zhi's exposed arm.

Chang Zhi was startled. She was already nervous because of the power outage, and now she was even more nervous. Goose bumps appeared on her arms.

She followed Wen Yanxing to the living room and watched him squat down to find his phone on the coffee table. The light from the screen was cast on his face, the only light in the darkness. Chang Zhi looked at his face and found that Wen Yanxing had very long eyelashes.

Eyelashes are exquisite. She thought to herself.

Wen Yanxing quickly turned on the flashlight on his phone. The non-glaring light at least illuminated the road. Chang Zhi walked in front, and Wen Yanxing was behind with his phone shining on him. He stopped at the door of his house and leaned against the door frame. Chang Zhi walked through the narrow corridor to the door of her house, took out the key from the pocket of her nightgown, inserted it and twisted it twice, and the door opened.

She held the computer in one hand and pushed the door in the other hand, and tried to turn on the light in the living room. Sure enough, there was a power outage.

Alas.

Chang Zhi put the computer on the shoe cabinet, and looked back to see Wen Yanxing still holding his phone to shine on it.

She was full of gratitude, and she turned back, her body behind the door, and her face was exposed in the crack of the door, looking at Wen Yanxing.

"Thank you," after a pause, Chang Zhi said, "The power is out anyway, you should go to bed early."

"I'll close the door first, you... good night?"

After saying these words quickly, Chang Zhi quickly closed the door without giving Wen Yanxing time to speak.

The door clicked and locked.

Wen Yanxing was still leaning against the door frame, motionless.

The light from the phone just now shone on Chang Zhi's face. Chang Zhi's face was flushed and her tone was soft. He actually felt... a little too beautiful.

Chapter 6 Meng Xi

In the dark, Chang Zhi quickly returned to her room, kicked off her slippers and fell to the ground, and threw her whole body into the soft bedding.

Her cheeks were slightly hot, and Chang Zhi touched her forehead with her backhand. The temperature seemed normal again.

What happened?

She touched her phone from the pillow, opened the lock screen to check the battery level, and found that it was only 60% charged.

I don't know when the electricity will come back at home, otherwise this 60% battery... I will die without my phone.

Turning on the flashlight on her phone, Chang Zhi got out of bed and walked to the shoe cabinet in the entrance to take the laptop that she had not put away just now back to the table in the study. Chang Zhi called an employee of a certain power network and agreed to come to repair the network at noon tomorrow. Chang Zhi sat back on the bed.

Flipping through WeChat, the first thing she saw was the pinned message from Deng Jiadai in the morning.

Chang Zhi hadn't replied to Deng Jiadai yet, and it was obvious that Deng Jiadai was not in a hurry.

Although Deng Jiadai is usually naughty, she is quite serious about serious matters.

I shared a dormitory with Deng Jiadai for four years in college, and we ate and lived together, so we knew each other's affairs quite well.

So Deng Jiadai knew what that person meant to her.

Meng Xi...

Chang Zhi's heart choked as she silently said these two words.

Chang Zhi and Meng Xi met in college. When she was a freshman, Chang Zhi met Meng Xi, a sophomore, through a social gathering. Meng Xi was handsome and gentle, and was considered a celebrity in the school, and was the object of secret love for many girls.

When Chang Zhi first met Meng Xi, he had a girlfriend, so Chang Zhi and Meng Xi were just nodding acquaintances in each other's WeChat friends who would not delete or actively chat. Occasionally, they would like and comment on each other's circle of friends, and there was nothing else.

Chang Zhi had the habit of going to the library when she was in college, usually from 3 to 5 in the afternoon. As long as she didn't have classes, she would go to the library to read books and study. She would bring a bottle of water with her, and spend a quiet and comfortable afternoon.

Chang Zhi had never met Meng Xi before, but a month after she met Meng Xi, Meng Xi broke up with his girlfriend, and Chang Zhi often saw Meng Xi in the library.

It wasn't every day, but every few days. When she was about to forget this person, he appeared in her sight again.

Until they met again, Meng Xi broke her glass when he walked past her table.

After the compensation, he pursued her fiercely. He came to her dormitory downstairs to deliver breakfast from time to time. There were people posting about this matter every day on the entire forum. In the second semester of her freshman year, Chang Zhi agreed to Meng Xi.

Then... Chang Zhi lowered her eyes and stared at the glowing WeChat chat interface for a long time.

[10:23]

[Your Jia]: Meng Xi contacted me.

Chang Zhi sighed and sent a message back to Deng Jiadai.

[20:07]

[Tang Zhi]: Didn't you delete him?

Deng Jiadai replied immediately.

[Your Jia]: He asked someone to add me with his account. I didn't know it at first, but I knew it was him after he added me.

[Tang Zhi]: Why are you still nagging him? Why don't you just block him?

[Your Jia]: I owed him before, and deleting him once was already very unkind. Anyway, asking for him is considered repayment. It doesn't matter what you want to do.

Chang Zhi also knew that Deng Jiadai had been indebted to Meng Xi before. In fact, the matter between her and Meng Xi should not involve Deng Jiadai.

After a short hesitation, Chang Zhi still asked.

[Tang Zhi]: ...What did he want to do with you?

[Your Jia]: He asked me for your contact information and said he wanted to meet you.

Seeing this, Chang Zhi was instantly a little furious.

Still want to see her? What the hell, we have already broken off the relationship and I don't even want to hear his name in this life.

�Tang Zhi�: Not giving it to you, not seeing you, you wishful thinking.

�Your Jia�: ... So heartless?

�Tang Zhi�: Or am I stupid?

�Tang Zhi�: I told you not to give it to him, you know what kind of person I am.

�Tang Zhi�: I would be fooled again if I were stupid.

�Your Jia�: Oh, even if you don't say it, I will definitely not give it to him randomly/grievance

�Your Jia�: Actually...Okay, then I'll tell him.

�Tang Zhi�: Talk to him nicely, make it clear, be cool and dignified, understand?

�Tang Zhi�: Then I'll go to bed first, there's a power outage at home, good night.

�Your Jia�: gn/heart

After exiting WeChat, Chang Zhi didn't go to bed immediately. She stood the pillow upright against the head of the bed, leaning her back on the pillow, feeling uneasy.

She looked out the window quietly. There was no moon tonight. The raindrops fell on the windowsill, which did not comfort her but made her more irritable.

When she thought of the word Meng Xi, everything she didn't want to recall instantly came out from the depths of her mind. Chang Zhi turned over and covered her head with the pillow.

Really mmp, does Meng Xi hate her? Is he so powerful now that he is famous?

After thinking angrily for a long time, Chang Zhi opened the pillow and got into the quilt to sleep.

It rained all night last night. When she woke up, the sunlight outside the window had already poured into the bedroom through the windowsill. The bedroom light was on, and Chang Zhi couldn't open her eyes for a while.

She turned over with the quilt in her arms, thinking vaguely, there was a call...

After lingering in bed for a long time, Chang Zhi slowly got up.

She went to bed early last night, and her complexion was particularly good today. Chang Zhi looked up at the clock, it was nine o'clock.

After putting her hair up, Chang Zhi grabbed her mobile phone and went into the milk tea room.

Here I have to say that Chang Zhi rented a three-bedroom apartment. One room was used as a bedroom, and one room was used as a study and guest room. Although it was called a guest room, it actually only had a single bed. As for the other room, Chang Zhi did not like to mix her usual food with drinks such as milk tea, and she did not want to mess around in the store, so she used a room at home to tinker with new drinks.

Now is the season for cherry production, and Chang Zhi had this idea a long time ago, to produce a seasonal limited drink and dessert.

Cherries taste sweet and sour, are small and cute, and are red in color, which looks particularly beautiful. If they are made into drinks, they will definitely be very beautiful, and the number of people who come here should increase a lot.

After all, holding a cup of good-looking and delicious drinks, and a good-looking dessert, sitting in a well-decorated milk tea shop, taking pictures and posting them on WeChat Moments is a current trend.

It can be said that many young people nowadays do not necessarily want to eat food and drinks with high appearance, but more or less want to post them on WeChat Moments.

And when it comes to cost, the highest price of cherries has passed now, and the price has slowly dropped. If it is wholesale, it should be cheaper.

But now Chang Zhi wants to experiment first.

Chang Zhi went downstairs to the nearby supermarket and bought two kilograms of cherries and two cans of cherry jam. After returning home, she washed each one carefully, then took the amount she thought was about right and removed the pits.

First add tea soup, then add an appropriate amount of jam, throw in the pitted cherries, and then stir and squeeze the juice——

Chang Zhi was busy walking around in the milk tea room, stealing one or two cherries from time to time.

Sweet and sour.

The basic steps are completed, and finally put in the milk cap. The red that has become soft after dilution and the pure white milk cap look very beautiful.

Of course, you have to try the new product you made yourself. Chang Zhi took a sip and thought it was okay.

But it was useless for her to say so. Chang Zhi thought about it and searched the cabinet for the medium-sized milk tea cup used in the store. Chang Zhi packaged the drink into the shape of her milk tea shop and prepared to let her employees taste it in the store. She was afraid that it would not be enough, so she made more according to the dosage just now.

So, there were six employees in the store, and the amount made was nine cups, three more cups, Chang Zhi simply put them all in the bag.

Whoever likes to drink it can take it by themselves.

She also added ice, which not only relieved the employees from the heat but also got comments. Not bad, not bad, the best of both worlds.

Carrying this big bag downstairs, Chang Zhi entered the store under the midday sun.

It might be lunch time. There were not as many customers at noon as in the afternoon, but it was almost full.

When the employees in the store saw the boss Chang Zhi carrying such a bag, the employees who had nothing to do for the time being looked at her curiously.

Xiao Dong, who is usually the most outgoing, asked first: "Sister Chang, what did you bring?"

"Drinks," Chang Zhi smiled, "Do you want some?"

"Oh, employee benefits?" Qiao smiled, "Sister Chang is so nice in summer?"

"Isn't our store a milk tea shop... What did you bring to drink?" Xiao Dong came over curiously to see.

Chang Zhi put the bag on the table and took out cups one by one. The beautiful appearance immediately attracted Xiao Dong,

"Sister Chang, it's pretty. Where did you buy it, strawberry juice?"

"I figured out the seasonal limit myself," Chang Zhi shook her head, "It's not strawberry juice, it's cherry juice with milk cap, and it hasn't been named yet. Do you want to try it?"

Xiao Dong listened to Chang Zhi and looked carefully: "I was wondering where to buy it. Isn't this the packaging in our store? Cherry... Drink, drink, drink, you must drink it. I'm craving this recently."

"This is not a free drink. You have to tell me how you feel after drinking it." Chang Zhi reminded.

"Okay, okay." Xiao Dong agreed readily, saying that anything was fine as long as there was something to drink and a break.

The other employees were busy making milk tea, and Chang Zhi also helped them, asking them to try it after they were done, so that they could take a break.

So, the three extra cups left on the counter were left there alone.

Chang Zhi was helping to take orders and collect money at the cashier. Just as she was helping a customer with the change, she heard a slightly familiar voice in her ears -

"Ayan, what do you want to drink? I'll treat you?"

...Isn't this the voice of her landlord He?

Chapter 7 He Sheng

The playlist of the "try" milk tea shop is generally lyrical and gentle.

Although people come and go in the milk tea shop, the shop assistants are also busy, which is completely inconsistent with the atmosphere of the music.

At this moment, Chang Zhi stared blankly at the two people standing in front of the cash register.

Why did Wen Yanxing come to her shop again?

He Shengbi moved his eyes away from the high-hanging drink menu screen and looked at the cash register in front of him, only to find that the person standing there was Chang Zhi.

He was a little surprised, then grinned: "Is Chang Zhi free to come to the store to help today?"

"Yeah," Chang Zhi came back to her senses and responded, "After all, it's my own store, I can't just be a hands-off boss."

After a pause, Chang Zhi said, "It's also good to be the guest cashier and count the money."

He Shengbi was happy, then turned around and introduced to Wen Yanxing: "This is your first meeting, this is your neighbor, the girl who lives opposite you, she is the manager of this store, her name is Chang Zhi."

Then he pointed at Wen Yanxing and said to Chang Zhi: "His name is Wen Yanxing, my friend. I brought him to the neighborhood today and came to your place first. How is it? Is he handsome?" He Shengbi raised his eyebrows at Chang Zhi.

The two who already knew each other looked at each other, and Wen Yanxing looked a little helpless.

Chang Zhi smiled politely.

"What would you like to drink?" Chang Zhi lowered her head and asked to change the subject.

"Oh, by the way," He Shengbi also remembered that they were here for milk tea, "Ayan, I'm asking you, what do you want to drink?"

Wen Yanxing looked at Chang Zhi who was looking down, and put his phone back into his pocket, "Whatever, any recommendations?"

He bought it on his way home yesterday and had already tasted it. In fact, he personally thinks that the milk tea in this store is really delicious.

It was Chang Zhi whom he met yesterday. At first, Wen Yanxing thought she was just an employee, but he didn't expect that this store was actually opened by Chang Zhi.

It was particularly unexpected.

Chang Zhi looked at the drink menu and said with a smile: "Actually, I think everything in our store is delicious. Do you want to try the signature drink?"

He Shengbi shook his head: "No, I've had it several times. I'm not kidding. I come here to buy milk tea every time I get off work. Three or four times a week, I've basically had it all."

Chang Zhi: "Are you taking care of my business so much?"

"Then I'll take care of it only if it tastes good," He Shengbi said with a grin, "Are there any new products coming out recently?"

New products...

Chang Zhi's eyes moved to the cherry milk cap she had just made.

After thinking about it, I can't just let the clerk try this thing. If it works, it will be put online sooner or later, otherwise...

Chang Zhi thought about it, looked up and said to He Shengbi and Wen Yanxing: "New product, I just made a few cups today, but I don't know if it suits your taste."

He Shengbi was curious and asked: "Did you make it newly? Isn't it on the list?"

"Yeah." Chang Zhi smiled and joked, "It's not priced yet. If you don't mind, it's limited today and free."

Hearing this, He Shengbi nudged Wen Yanxing's arm with his elbow and asked: "Do you want to drink it?"

"...I don't care."

"I just like you who are so straightforward today," He Shengbi said to Wen Yanxing, paused, and then said to Chang Zhi, "Okay, then you have two cups first, and A Yan and I will go sit down first."

"Okay."

Asking Xiao Dong to help with the cash register, Chang Zhi carried three drinks and took the store's signature chocolate toasted buns to find the seat where Wen Yanxing and the others were sitting.

They were sitting on a sofa for four people. Chang Zhi shared the cherry milk cap and toasted buns with them. He Shengbi was a little surprised: "Please have some bread?"

Chang Zhi held a cup of cherry milk cap and stood by and smiled: "After all, I still want to hear your feelings after drinking... Do you mind if I sit here?"

Wen Yanxing looked up at her and said nothing.

He Shengbi certainly didn't mind, and hurriedly said: "The whole store is yours, what do you mind or not, sit down, sit down."

He likes to be lively, and Chang Zhi is a beautiful woman, and she seems to be single... Well, Wen Yanxing is also single.

Oh, thinking of this, He Shengbi secretly glanced at Wen Yanxing.

Look at the face... quite a match, huh? He Shengbi saw that Wen Yanxing hadn't been in a relationship for so long, and he was a dead otaku addicted to the Internet, and he was really worried that he couldn't find a girlfriend.

He Shengbi decided to observe first.

At 1:30 pm, more people started to come to the milk tea shop. The three people at Chang Zhi's table were better-looking than average, so they naturally attracted many passers-by to look at them frequently.

There was also a girl who took a photo of Chang Zhi on purpose.

However, the three people did not notice.

Chang Zhi bit the straw and looked at the two people who had just taken two sips with her big eyes.

"What do you feel?" Chang Zhi asked with some trepidation.

He Shengbi liked this very much and was very supportive: "It's quite comfortable to drink this in summer, not too greasy. When will it be released?"

"It hasn't even been named yet," Chang Zhi smiled, half-hearted, "Maybe it will be released this month."

"Then I'll wait."

Chang Zhi moved her eyes to Wen Yanxing's face again.

He was wearing a black T-shirt and casual pants today, a simple basic style, and he looked clean and tidy like the popular young handsome guy nowadays.

I don't know how old Wen Yanxing is.

Including today, Chang Zhi and Wen Yanxing have actually met for the third time, all in the past few days, and Chang Zhi also feels that they are destined to be together.

Moreover, during the simple interactions of the first two times, Chang Zhi felt that Wen Yanxing was a very polite person, seemingly distant but actually very enthusiastic and careful.

He agreed to her sudden request last night, and even poured her a glass of water. Well, he was very enthusiastic and she was very grateful.

Speaking of which, the way Wen Yanxing...drank milk tea was quite pleasing to the eye.

Wen Yanxing leaned against the back of the sofa, his palm holding the entire circle of the milk tea cup. He was originally looking elsewhere quietly, but when he noticed Chang Zhi's gaze, his eyes met hers, and he found that Chang Zhi's eyes were full of expectations.

For a moment, he was not used to having a girl looking at him so eagerly, so Wen Yanxing pretended to be calm and put the cup in his hand on the table.

He Shengbi looked at the two of them, knowing that they were not familiar with each other because it was their first meeting. He wanted to help them get familiar with each other. He said, "Ayan, I'm done. It's your turn to talk about your experience."

Chang Zhi looked at Wen Yanxing more eagerly.

Wen Yanxing looked at the colorful drink, then at Chang Zhi, and said, "It's a bit too sweet. You will get sick of it after drinking it for a long time. You... put less sugar."

"Is that so? I will improve it. Thank you." Chang Zhi nodded. In fact, she also felt that it was a little sweet. She was preparing to try to put less sugar next time.

Wen Yanxing nodded slightly.

The atmosphere froze. He Shengbi wanted to help the two neighbors get to know each other better, so he smiled and found some random topics to praise Chang Zhi again: "Ayan, you don't know how great Chang Zhi is. She moved here for three years, and this store has been open for three years. The business is good every day. The store next door is jealous. Even I want to quit my job and open a store."

"... Miss Chang is very powerful." Wen Yanxing nodded, glanced at He Shengbi again, and did not hesitate to undermine his friend, "You quit? The company is yours, who dares to ask you to quit."

"I'm not just making a metaphor, no, exaggerating," He Shengbi argued, "I want to quit, I'm tired, you see, I've been busy this month and I've only had two days off, and I helped you move one day and took you for a walk the other day, you say I'm good to you?"

"Didn't you come down and knock on my door today and say you want to go on strike and have fun?"

"Well, the case is done today, and it's good for your health to relax a little..." He Shengbi explained.

Chang Zhi watched the two bickering and smiled, and said a little embarrassedly: "In fact, it is not easy to run a milk tea shop. Business in winter is not as good as in summer. In summer, it is too busy. Some people don't want to queue up and leave."

Modest tone.

He Shengbi continued: "It's okay. In fact, there is so much competition in milk tea shops. There are not many people who do as good business as you. Besides, the off-season of milk tea shops is not long. It's enough to make more money in the peak season."

"Yeah..."

The three people gradually chatted. After a while, Chang Zhi's phone rang. After answering, it was said that the network repairman came.

Chang Zhi stood up and raised her mobile phone to Wen Yanxing and He Shengbi who were still sitting: "The network was broken yesterday. The network repairman came today. I'll go back first. You can chat first."

Wen Yanxing and He Shengbi were sitting opposite each other. Chang Zhi smiled at Wen Yanxing and thanked him silently in her heart.

Wen Yanxing was stunned by Chang Zhi's brilliant smile.

He touched his face unconsciously. Is there something on his face that makes her smile so happily?

He Shengbi didn't see Wen Yanxing's little action. He waved to Chang Zhi: "Then you go first. Let's go and chat. Thank you, Boss Chang, for the drinks today."

Chang Zhi smiled embarrassedly: "It's not really an invitation. I wanted to do a survey or something."

After saying goodbye, Chang Zhi went home and led the network repair staff into the house. After checking, they found that the router was broken. They paid more than 100 yuan to replace the router. Finally, the family had a network again.

After having the network, Chang Zhi's first reaction was to see the reaction of the video sent yesterday.

After all, it has been half a day. Every time Chang Zhi posted a new video, she would feel a little uneasy, afraid that the reaction would be bad or disliked. Although this is her hobby, she actually posted it more eager to get others' affirmation.

Chang Zhi thinks that every up master who posts original videos on station B thinks so.

After all, every comment and coin from the audience is a huge support and motivation. Chang Zhi has experienced it, so she understands it better.

Chang Zhi first clicked into her personal homepage. There were dozens of unread private messages. Out of a slight obsessive-compulsive disorder, Chang Zhi clicked in, but unexpectedly found that Yan Zhi had replied to her.

Actually... really replied?

After so many days, Chang Zhi was obsessed with other things and almost forgot about being made into a ghost animal, but now the instigator actually replied to her?

With mixed feelings, Chang Zhi clicked in to see what Yan Zhi replied to her.

After taking a look, she was silent and didn't know what to say.

The message was replied this morning.

At eight o'clock, I got up very early and worked very hard, just half an hour later than the average student party was late for school.

The reply was particularly simple, clear and concise.

It was particularly personal, and I could feel a unique temperament across the screen.

And the most sassy thing is that there is no Chinese letters, pinyin, or English letters in the reply.

Chang Zhi sincerely felt that Yan Zhi was concise, because he didn't type a few more words to emphasize his words like most people do.

Because,

He only replied with a question mark.

When Chang Zhi looked down at WeChat, she found that Anan, a fellow up master in the dance area of WeChat, asked her if she wanted to collaborate on a dance together.

Anan started dancing at home, and has been dancing for two years. She has many fans and good dancing skills.

[Anan]: Do you want to practice dancing together next week? I like this song very much recently.

[Tang Zhi]: ...What song?

[Anan]: It was a dance performed by four people, a Korean dance, a 4-wall dance. I think the dance is very beautiful, and the details are very challenging. Watching the video... I want to wear beautiful bell-bottom pants to show off my slender waist, wear 10-centimeter high heels, and pretend to be a celebrity with perfect lip syncing.

[Tang Zhi]: 10 centimeters? You are very brave, kid.

[Anan]: If I really want to dance with you, you are 168 cm tall and I am 158 cm tall, and your legs are so long, how can I dance with you without wearing high heels. .

[Tang Zhi]: Silly kid, if I also wear 10-centimeter high heels, then you are wearing them in vain?

[Anan]: ...

[Anan]: I actually think what you said makes sense... Wow, you are so excessive, why don't you just not wear them? I don't bother to pay attention to you.../Cold

Chang Zhi chuckled and changed the subject.

[Tang Zhi]: I remember that this song is performed by four people, right? Dancing a two-person version? Whose part will you dance?

[Anan]: Did you agree? I want to dance the part of Luna, it's so beautiful, what about you?

[Tang Zhi]: I don't care.

[A Nan]: I'm planning to find two more people, does Atang have any recommendations? People from the same city, okay?

[Tang Zhi]: You know my circle is small, how about you ask Sister Qiao?

[A Nan]: Got it, okay, I'll take care of what I suggested, and I'll definitely arrange it for you before next Tuesday, I'll go to Taobao to find some clothes first.

[Tang Zhi]: OK~/heart

[A Nan]: I'll set up a FG first, and I want to jump out of a cover jump with a degree of restoration close to full marks, a full mark of uniformity, a full mark of strength, and standard movements

[Tang Zhi]: Just set these with me, dare to say no to others?

[A Nan]: qaq Atang I love you.

After turning off the phone, Chang Zhi breathed a sigh of relief. She was still thinking about it and had a headache, but she didn't expect to solve the problem of what to cover next week so happily.

Or it came to her own door.

Throughout Chang Zhi's career of covering dances, she actually didn't have many opportunities to cooperate with other up-masters. The main reason was that the up-masters were distributed in different cities, and it was unrealistic for them to come here just for a cover dance. Chang Zhi was in a first-tier city, and happened to be from the same city as An Nan and Sister Qiao, so she had the rare cooperation with them.

Chang Zhi was also very fortunate to know these people who were from the same city and got along well with each other.

Unexpectedly, she talked with An Nan for half an hour. When Chang Zhi returned to her computer, she was surprised to find that Yan Zhi actually replied to her.

Or just now.

[Yan Zhi]: Yes.

[Yan Zhi]: I just came back.

[Tang Zhi]: It's so hard to have a serious conversation

Chang Zhi was complaining sincerely. After all, it had been two days since she sent the message, and now she could really say a word.

Busy person.

[Yan Zhi]: ...

[Yan Zhi]: What's the matter?

[Tang Zhi]: Emmmm... It's that video. .

Chang Zhi said this for the first time, and she was a little embarrassed.

[Yan Zhi]: Which one?

Which one? He actually asked which one?

How could he not know that he edited it himself?

Did he have to ask her to name it?

Was he deliberately teasing her?

[Tang Zhi]: Ghost videos.

[Yan Zhi]: ... Well, I edited a lot of videos, but I'm too busy recently to remember them. What do you mean?

[Tang Zhi]: The one about me.

[Yan Zhi]: The one from last week?

Chang Zhi nodded fiercely.

[Tang Zhi]: Yes

[Yan Zhi]: Wait a minute.

[Tang Zhi]: ? ? ? ? ?

...Wait for what?

Chang Zhi stared at the screen, and every minute and every second seemed like a long time.

Five minutes later, Yan Zhi slowly sent a message.

[Yan Zhi]: ... Wait a minute, Penguin*******, I'm going to start a live broadcast.

? ? ? ?

Live broadcast?

Chang Zhi's mind was full of question marks.

She clicked on Penguin in a daze and entered the Penguin ID to apply for adding the Penguin ID. She didn't understand why he suddenly came online and said a few words to her, leaving the Penguin ID and saying that he was going to live broadcast.

What the hell?

Live broadcast what? ? ?

No, this, Yan Zhi is teasing her, right?

She felt fooled in an instant. She stared at the screen for a long time but didn't receive a reply from Yan Zhi Penguin. Chang Zhi was stunned for a while and suddenly angrily clicked on Yan Zhi's homepage and entered the live broadcast room.

She wanted to see what Yan Zhi was broadcasting. Why was he so anxious?

As soon as she entered the live broadcast room, she saw that the interactive interface was replying quickly. The live broadcast interface was the computer desktop, and then there was a low male voice.

"I was delayed today because of something, so the show started a little late... What game do you want to watch? You pick."

This voice... sounds familiar

When Chang Zhi heard Yan Zhi's voice fall, she saw the comments quickly filled with words like "lol", "King of Glory", "Overwatch", "Single Player", "Funny Game", "4399" and so on——

However, Chang Zhi heard Yan Zhi silent for a while, and then said in a puzzled tone.

"Horror game?"

As soon as Yan Zhi finished speaking, someone angrily refuted.

"How could we play horror games?" "I was wondering why it was so easy this time and we had to choose. It was all a routine." "The longest road I've walked is Yan Da's routine..." "I'm afraid if I don't watch it."

"Heh."

Yan Zhi didn't say anything, only the sound of Yan Zhi's quiet breathing came from the headphones.

There was a rhythm, and Chang Zhi's heart also beat along with it.

She opened her fingers, and it was no longer the scene just now.

"Ahem," the screen showed the protagonist's awakening scene, a piece of plane wreckage. Yan Zhi coughed lightly, pretending to be calm, "Ah, it seems that this is the official start. There was a little too much ketchup just now. It was low-quality ketchup at a glance. It's too fake, bad review."

After a pause, Yan Zhi said seriously: "Now I am starting to be serious. Just now, it was just a small warm-up. To be honest, I was not scared at all by such low-level fun."

Puff——Chang Zhi in front of the computer laughed and cried.

The barrage was also full of complaints: "I just watched you pretending to be cool quietly" "I was obviously scared for a while, but you didn't hold on"

On the screen, Yan Zhi began to control the protagonist to start exploring. He led the protagonist around and found himself on the hillside and found a fire under the hillside.

Yan Zhi: "Watch out, my friends. In this kind of game, according to my experience, the surroundings are all dark, but this place is very bright, which means there must be clues below. So now, we have to go over and take a look. Well, first of all, let's jump down—"

Yan Zhi's tone was firm. As he spoke, he controlled the protagonist to jump down.

The wind in the canyon was whistling, and the protagonist was in free fall at a rapid speed.

Two seconds after jumping down, the screen went black.

A scream in the game.

Then the protagonist died.

Back to the game homepage.

Yan Zhi stopped talking.

The barrage was swishing quickly, all of which were gloating "Leap of Faith", "First Blood", "Blowing up is not exciting", "Daily slap in the face", "kkkk, did I tell you to die?" "Is it surprising? Is it amazing? Is it unexpected?"

Chang Zhi laughed in front of the screen unkindly. This person is really funny. He was so sure just now, but now he was slapped in the face.

Is this up-player sure that he is okay with all the tricks in his mind?

"Okay, what I just demonstrated was wrong. If someone jumps down from such a height, he will definitely die. Next, I will demonstrate it to you again." Yan Zhi restarted the game as if nothing had happened.

Yan Zhi live-streamed the game for two and a half hours, then he went off the air and said he was going to eat.

The barrage shouted, "Don't leave."

However, Yan Zhi turned off the live broadcast without hesitation.

Chang Zhi also watched for two hours. Seeing Yan Zhi off the live broadcast, she returned to the private message interface to contact him.

[Tang Zhi]: ... Finished?

[Yan Zhi]: How did you know?

[Tang Zhi]: I'm watching.

[Yan Zhi]: ....

[Yan Zhi]: Excuse me.

[Tang Zhi]: Are you going to eat next?

[Yan Zhi]: ? ?

[Tang Zhi]: What I mean is, do you want to tell me after you finish eating, or before you eat?

Chang Zhi stared at the screen with a serious face.

But Yan Zhi suddenly changed the topic.

[Yan Zhi]: Did you add me as a penguin?

[Tang Zhi]: I did, but you didn't accept.

Less than a minute later, Chang Zhi saw the penguin flashing in the lower right corner, and clicked it to see——

[Yan Zhi has accepted your friend request]

Chapter 10 An Appointment

...Agree now?

Chang Zhi was a little confused for a moment.

She quickly flipped through the Penguin friend list and found Yan Zhi, ready to take the initiative to send a message to him.

But Yan Zhi sent it to her first.

[Yan Zhi]: ...There are too many private messages on Bilibili, so it's not convenient to say, so I added Penguin first.

[Yan Zhi]: But I have an appointment with a friend, so I'm going to have dinner first. I'll come back to see you later, okay?

[Tang Zhi]: ...

Chang Zhi stared at the name in front of the computer screen, wondering if they can still be friends? ? ? It's dragging again.

But what can she do.

First of all, she is not full of anger, Chang Zhi is more interested in knowing the reason.

Is it hate or like...

Alas.

Chang Zhi compromised.

[Tang Zhi]: Okay, okay.

Anyway, a meal won't take all night, right?

After turning off the computer, Chang Zhi checked the time and found that they had already arrived at the restaurant.

She opened the refrigerator and found it was empty. She was too busy to go to the supermarket to buy food these days. She decided to go out to eat.

However, it seemed a bit awkward to eat alone in a busy city.

Chang Zhi wanted to find someone to eat with. She looked through her WeChat list and found that there were not many people living nearby. She specially asked someone to come for a meal... Never mind, it was just a meal.

Chang Zhi took the key, unlocked the door and went out.

Before she reached the elevator, Chang Zhi saw Wen Yanxing who was already waiting for the elevator. She walked to him and asked in surprise, "You guys are back from shopping so soon? Are you going out again?"

Wen Yanxing never expected to run into Chang Zhi as soon as he went out.

After all, he was just practicing Tai Chi with the person in front of him on the computer, and she even watched his live broadcast. How could she go out when he went out?

Wen Yanxing frowned, then said nonchalantly: "I came back because there was nothing interesting. I have an appointment with someone for dinner tonight, so I'll go there now."

"Is that so," Chang Zhi nodded in understanding. The elevator happened to arrive, so she pointed and reminded him, "Elevator."

The two walked into the elevator one after the other.

Chang Zhi stood behind Wen Yanxing and watched him press the first floor button, but she didn't go up to press it.

But why didn't he press the basement floor button? If she remembered correctly, Wen Yanxing had a car.

Chang Zhi stared at Wen Yanxing's back and couldn't help asking, "Aren't you going by car?"

"Driving?" Wen Yanxing asked back. After a moment, he understood what Chang Zhi meant. His eyes deepened and the corners of his lips curved. "It's nearby. No need to drive."

He changed the subject and asked Chang Zhi, "What are you going to do?"

Chang Zhi smiled, "Just like you, eating. I'm afraid I'll run into you then."

Wen Yanxing asked, "Did you make an appointment with someone?"

Chang Zhi shook her head, "No, I'm alone."

Wen Yanxing smiled silently.

The elevator went to the first floor. For some reason, Chang Zhi was really afraid of bumping into Wen Yanxing in the same restaurant, but this feeling didn't mean she hated him.

So Chang Zhi took two quick steps out of the elevator, then turned around and waved, "Then I'll go first. Bye."

"Well, bye."

Quickening her pace and walking out of the residential building, Chang Zhi crossed the road and walked forward from the road of her own store.

After all, it is a downtown area. There are two large shopping malls and a cinema not far away. There are clothes and milk tea shops on the street, as well as various restaurants. There are all kinds of fast food such as Pizza Hut, McDonald's, KFC, Burger King, and there are also formal meals such as tea restaurants.

The night view of first-tier cities is still very beautiful, with neatly built roads and orderly arranged street lights. Today is the weekend, and there are still many people at night. It is bustling and busy.

Chang Zhi lowered her head and looked at her mobile phone, browsing a certain review software.

Although she has lived here for a long time, there are many new restaurants recently, and she doesn't know which one is better.

Sichuan cuisine, Cantonese cuisine, fast food-after browsing three pages, Chang Zhi still didn't show any interest.

There is a hot pot restaurant on the fourth page. Chang Zhi clicked in to read the comments and saw that people who have eaten there posted pictures.

"User 2548744: I came to eat hot pot alone, and the store also put a Pikachu sitting opposite me. Hahaha, it's so cute and I don't feel lonely at all. The food is also very good. I will come next time."

Chang Zhi's eyes lit up and her interest was aroused. She was also alone - Chang Zhi looked at the address and it was not far away.

When she arrived at the hot pot restaurant, there were actually two people queuing in front of her. After waiting for about ten minutes, Chang Zhi was led in by the waiter.

She sat in a double seat. Sure enough, after the waiter knew that she was alone, he held a Kumamon bear and placed it opposite her.

It was perfect.

Chang Zhi ordered her usual hot pot essentials such as enoki mushrooms, beef, potatoes, lettuce, shrimp, etc., and waited slowly for the dishes to be served.

She lowered her head to play a single-player game, and suddenly heard a familiar voice in her ears.

"You want to sit here?" The man's voice was low and gentle, "Okay."

Chang Zhi couldn't help but look back and glanced at the source of the voice.

Two tables away from her, very close, there was a couple, the girl was wearing a skirt, and even with her hair down, she couldn't hide her childish face, the man had his back to her, he was slender, wearing a black T-shirt and casual pants, his slender and beautiful hands were pulling out a chair for the girl next to him.

He turned sideways inadvertently, and his profile was seen by Chang Zhi, which scared Chang Zhi.

...Wen Yanxing? ? ?

Chang Zhi was so scared that the phone in her hand fell on the table, making a "click" sound. Chang Zhi came back to her senses and picked up the phone in a hurry, her heart pounding.

So he said he had an appointment, with a girl?

Chang Zhi poked the bowl with chopsticks, feeling a little weird.

Wen Yanxing hadn't seen Chang Zhi yet.

The summer in S City was hot, and the temperature had soared to 30°C. Wen Yanxing had a little sweat on his back when he walked here from home.

But the younger sister wanted to eat hot pot. After entering the restaurant, she refused to sit near the air conditioner and insisted on sitting by the window. The space was narrow, so Wen Yanxing had to accommodate her.

Wen Luying didn't know her brother's accommodation. She was used to sitting by the window. There were many people in this restaurant. When she saw a window seat, she naturally took it immediately.

After sitting down and ordering dishes, Wen Luying began to talk about the information she had learned at home in the past few days.

"Brother, you don't know that my parents had a quarrel the day after you moved out of home," Wen Luying said this with some sadness.

Wen Yanxing neatly arranged the dishes served by the waiter, and only looked up and smiled nonchalantly after hearing the words, "Really?"

"Let them quarrel, they are a united front when facing me." When thinking of that quarrel, Wen Yanxing's eyebrows turned cold.

Wen Luying pursed her lips and advised: "Brother, don't think like that. My parents don't understand. After all, you graduated from graduate school and came back to work. You don't want to do videos and live broadcasts. They are not the kind of people who follow the trend. It's normal for them not to understand. Well, I mean, I support you anyway..."

Wen Yanxing picked up a bowl of food and poured it into the hot pot. The coldness subsided a little: "I know, don't get involved, otherwise they will stare at you so hard that you can't even write novels."

Wen Luying blinked at him: "I'm still in school. They don't know. It's not too late to tell them when I become famous and make a fortune. Besides, even if they don't let me work full-time, I can work harder and write secretly while working, and they can't control it..."

Wen Luying muttered: "Anyway, I think you are too impatient. Otherwise, you can explain it clearly."

"I don't know why you and your father are like gunpowder barrels that explode at any time, while I am at best a firework stick..."

Wen Luying began to teach her brother the secret of survival at home: "Hey, do you know why? Because I gave in, my parents have no choice but to save face. I think you should give in sometimes, otherwise you won't do that, right-"

"Okay, okay, you are the only one who is smart and willing to give in," Wen Yanxing was overwhelmed by what he heard, and he put a few pieces of beef into Wen Luying's bowl, "Hey, is it enough to fill your mouth?"

Wen Luying complained: "How can you not take enough..."

Wen Yanxing immediately took back his chopsticks: "Then don't eat it, you don't have hands? You are disgusted when I give you food, who spoiled you?"

Wen Luying waved her hands hurriedly: "No, no, not enough, enough... Thank you, brother, brother is the best, muah! Love you!"

On the other side, Chang Zhi couldn't help but secretly look at the table while eating.

Wen Yanxing sat with his back to her, as if he didn't see her. Chang Zhi clearly saw the girl sitting opposite him, with bright eyes and white teeth, and naughty and cute when she occasionally smiled... Is this his girlfriend?

Chang Zhi held a mouthful of green vegetables in her mouth and thought curiously.

But she felt a little weird.

So... a guy like Wen Yanxing likes this type of little girl?

Chapter 11 Girlfriend

Chang Zhi saw Wen Yanxing adding more dishes to the girl, curled her lips, and poked the hot beef in the bowl with chopsticks. Forget it, eat first, and talk about other things later.

Anyway, it has nothing to do with her. They are just neighbors. She thinks too much because of the normal curiosity of gossip between neighbors.

After finishing the meal quickly, Chang Zhi did not say hello to Wen Yanxing. She went around to pay the bill and left. She walked slowly on the road to digest the food. When she arrived at her own milk tea shop, she went in and sat down.

Chang Zhi decided to go home because she thought she would not meet Wen Yanxing by chance.

But she didn't expect that Wen Yanxing would come to buy milk tea with the girl just when she was about to leave.

Chang Zhi sat back quickly, lowered her head and looked up, and observed secretly.

The girl pulled the corner of Wen Yanxing's clothes, pointed at the drink menu and said something, and Wen Yanxing's face was faintly helpless.

They quickly finished their shopping and took the items away. After Chang Zhi stretched her neck to confirm that Wen Yanxing and the girl had left, she ran to the cashier, put her arm on the counter, and asked Xiao Dong, who had just collected the money, furtively.

"Xiao Dong, do you still remember the man and woman just now?"

Xiao Dong was startled by her own store manager, "Sister Chang, who are you talking about?"

"The man in the black T-shirt and the woman who looks so good in the skirt."

"...What's wrong?"

Chang Zhi coughed lightly: "Did you hear what they said?"

Xiao Dong looked puzzled: "Just, order something... What's wrong???"

"No more?" Chang Zhi raised her eyebrows and asked.

"No, what else can I say..." Xiao Dong paused, his eyes suddenly changed, lowered his voice, and said gossipingly, "Sister Chang, I know that guy. He has come to our store three times. He is so handsome. I saw him when Da He was making milk tea the day before yesterday. He also told me that he likes this kind of guy. Could it be that you..." Xiao Dong laughed.

"Bah, nonsense," Chang Zhi glared at Xiao Dong, "It's not what you think. I just know him. I'm just curious. Who doesn't have curiosity? Do you dare to say you don't have it? Don't you?"

"I'm just asking, so fierce," Xiao Dong said aggrievedly, and suddenly his eyes lit up, "Hey, Sister Chang, I remember that the girl just acted coquettishly with the boy. Is it a clue?"

Acting coquettishly?

So sweet? ?

Chang Zhi felt a little irritated.

After leaving the milk tea shop, Chang Zhi waited for the green light to come and quickly crossed the road, but saw Wen Yanxing waving goodbye to the girl under the residential building.

Under the moonlight, the scene of a handsome man and a beautiful woman saying goodbye in front of a residential building is very similar to some TV dramas...

Tsk tsk, couples are so sticky, and single dogs are tortured with goose bumps.

Chang Zhi touched her arm.

Wen Yanxing originally planned to drive Wen Luying home himself, but Wen Luying said that in order to avoid him and his parents quarreling again, he would take the bus home at night, and it would be safer with more people.

The bus stop was not far away, not far away, Wen Yanxing hurried home to feed his ancestors at home, and waved goodbye to Wen Luying.

Turning around and planning to go home, he caught a glimpse of Chang Zhi standing next to the traffic light pole, holding a milk tea and staring at him.

...Hmm?

Chang Zhi coughed lightly to suppress the strangeness in her heart, drank a sip of milk tea as if to cover it up, and when she walked to Wen Yanxing, she smiled and said, "Was that your girlfriend just now? She's pretty."

After saying this, Chang Zhi wanted to take Doraemon's time machine back to one minute ago, shut her mouth and pretend not to see it, and take back that sentence.

Is she crazy to ask this?

Girlfriend?

Wen Yanxing raised his eyebrows, a little surprised, looked at her head lowered because she went to drink milk tea again, and shook his head to deny: "It's my sister."

Eh... sister?

The light shone on Chang Zhi's face. Chang Zhi looked surprised and looked like this plot was wrong, which made Wen Yanxing feel funny and relaxed a little.

Chang Zhi blinked, a little unbelieving: "You don't look very similar..."

"She looks more like my mother." Wen Yanxing said.

Then... Wen Yanxing looks like his father?

"Oh," Chang Zhi nodded, "then your mother should be very beautiful." Dad should be too.

After saying this, Chang Zhi added in her heart.

"Is that right?" Wen Yanxing replied casually.

Chang Zhi added: "It seems that you love your sister very much."

Wen Yanxing: "After all, I only have one sister, there is nothing I can do." Sometimes the sudden appearance of the Father's heart is nowhere to be placed.

Chang Zhi laughed dryly: "To be honest, I almost thought your sister was your girlfriend when I saw her just now."

After a pause, she pretended to be curious and asked: "Have you ever thought of finding a girlfriend?"

Hmm? Find a girlfriend? Inquistin?

Wen Yanxing thought for a moment and said, "Let's talk about it when we meet someone suitable."

"That's right." Chang Zhi nodded in agreement.

The two of them were silent at the same time after this topic. Chang Zhi stood under the street light, looking down at her feet in flip-flops.

Going home? So leave now? Or not? Should she leave first? Or should he leave first?

In the end, Wen Jinzhao spoke first to break the silence: "It's quite late, let's go home."

Oh... Let's go together.

What's the point of going together? It's just on the way.

Chang Zhi walked behind Wen Yanxing and hit her face with her fist.

Annoying, pure neighborhood relationship, what the hell is she thinking about.

The two of them got into the elevator and went up to the seventh floor.

After saying goodbye at the door in a friendly manner, Chang Zhi hurriedly said "good night" and ran out of the house quickly.

Push the door, get in, close the door, all in one go.

Wen Yanxing was caught off guard, and felt that Chang Zhi had run away very quickly every time they met in the past two times.

Was she bold when asking questions?

Wen Yanxing touched his face, somewhat confused.

Did he look scary? Or did he do something to scare Chang Zhi?

No... right?

Then why was she hiding so hastily?

Chang Zhi, who had locked herself behind the door, stroked her chest, and felt that it was really exciting after gossiping.

Recalling her night, she first accidentally ran into Wen Yanxing dating a girl, and then ran into Wen Yanxing buying milk tea with a girl in her own milk tea shop, and even shamelessly asked her own clerk what he heard, and finally... even asked the person himself.

What was she doing? Was she crazy?

So curiosity killed the cat.

Chang Zhi leaned against the door, clenched her fists against her cheeks, and rubbed her face with regret. After rubbing for a long time, her palms opened and turned to cover her face.

No, no, he's just a little handsome and polite, and he helped him twice. Isn't it too much for her to gossip about him? No, I must not interfere with his private life in the future.

Sitting on the sofa and blowing the air conditioner in the living room for a while, Chang Zhi remembered the formality after dinner.

She just took out her mobile phone, but saw Yan Zhi actually sent her a message first.

...Huh?

So proactive?

It's rare to keep a promise...

[Yan Zhi]: I've finished eating, sorry, it's late.

[Tang Zhi]: ...What a coincidence, me too.

[Yan Zhi]: What do you want to ask?

Chang Zhi was a little nervous.

[Tang Zhi]: Actually, it's nothing. Let me make it clear that I'm not angry or anything. I just felt a little overwhelmed when I saw it strange. I want to know whether you cut me in to discredit me or...

Chang Zhi hesitated.

Are you discrediting her or liking her, or like what Youzi, who managed the group before, said, treating her as... an idol?

Chang Zhi held her face and stared at the screen.

[Yan Zhi]: Black? ?

[Yan Zhi]: Girl, if I were black

...Hmm? If you were black...? ? ?

[Yan Zhi]: I don't even bother to pay attention to you.

[Tang Zhi]: ...

Chapter 12 Double Kill

Sometimes you can't prevent the chain reaction brought by some things, and even the parties involved can't predict it.

The ghost animal area of B station has the habit of following the trend. To explain specifically, when a great god finds a new ghost animal material and uses it properly, people who use this material will pop up like mushrooms after rain.

Even...

Chang Zhi's management group and fan group exploded again.

That afternoon, Chang Zhi saw these few messages.

[Yuzi]: Sister Tang, you are popular in the ghost animal area again...

[Hardworking and simple Tang Zhi]:! ? ? ? ? ?

Popular in the ghost animal area again...? Chang Zhi was shocked. The last time she was on it was only that time.

...No, it can't be?

Come again?

[Fu Da Miao]: Several ups followed the trend and made videos. The themes are different, but you are a guest star in them... It's like they picked some more brainwashing dance clips and repeated them.

[Hardworking and simple Tang Zhi]: ... Is this thing something that can be followed?

[Yuzi]: Of course... Yan Da's last video should be considered a small training. Others will follow suit after seeing that it is possible. Sister Tang, you should go and have a look first.

Chang Zhi looked at the ranking list of the ghost animal area of B station. The first place is still the video of Yan Zhi before, followed by the one posted last night - [Zhuge Situ & Tang Zhi] Let's dance.

The third place is a video of a well-known blogger Biba Jun.

OK - Chang Zhi held his forehead.

Chang Zhi clicked in to watch her own video first. The up master slightly modified the classic scenes of Zhuge Liang and Wang Situ, and occasionally inserted clips of her. If you look carefully, there are scenes in each scene. At the end of the film, the screen goes black, which is the up master's message.

——"I recommend the young lady Tang Zhi in the film. She is beautiful, has long legs, dances well, and is friendly and not irritable. I am a true fan 2333"

Chang Zhi: ...

? ? ? ? ?

All fake ones are fake, right? Chang Zhi suddenly realized that she didn't quite understand the meaning of 'true fans'.

Chang Zhi couldn't help but reply in the comments on impulse.

[Tang Zhi]: ...Thank this fan for the ghost video?

There was a question mark at the end. Chang Zhi felt that she was very intriguing, and her politeness was accompanied by a hint of stubbornness.

After commenting, Chang Zhi first went to see the third girl who was ghosted like herself.

After watching, Chang Zhi felt very fortunate.

She only made body movements, but Biba Jun's expression and voice were ghosted.

Convinced.

Chang Zhi went to see her Weibo, and she seemed to be happily forwarding the ghost video without any blame.

She is also a girl... that's all. As long as it's not too excessive, Chang Zhi doesn't want to cause trouble, so she decided to turn a blind eye.

In fact, there are limited themes for ghost videos of her, and she should be forgotten in the world after a long time.

After replying in the management group that as long as the comments were not too extreme, they could be ignored, Chang Zhi opened a MOBA mobile game for routine sign-in.

She didn't play this game very often. She only played it because Deng Jiadai pulled her in. She would occasionally open it to play a few games with others when she was really bored. Even her rank was only Gold III.

Signing in was a habit. After all, even if you don't play often, you can spend a minute to sign in, right?

Who knew that an invitation would pop up as soon as she clicked the sign-in interface.

[Yan Zhi] Invite you to participate in a 5v5 match. Agree or refuse?

Yan Zhi... Who is this? Chang Zhi tried to click on the Agree button, and after entering, she looked at the friends on the right and found out... This is Yan Zhi?

Supreme Black Yao I.

Why would he pull her in? Chang Zhi quickly typed in the team -

[Chang Tangzi: ? ? ? ?]

On the other hand, Yan Zhi, who was broadcasting live, was broadcasting a MOBA game for two hours today.

A new hero Kai was released these two days, and he was going to play two matches to show the audience how to play this new hero.

When he was thinking about whether to play solo or duo, a friend on the right who was originally unavailable lit up, with the ID Chang Tangzi, and the QQ note in the brackets.

It was Tang Zhi.

The note he gave her was Tang.

This ID is really unique and unpretentious, Chang Zhi Tang Zhi...

Yan Zhi casually clicked on the invitation to form a team, but he didn't expect that she actually agreed.

The barrage instantly filled with "Who is this?" "Chang Tang? Is that the girl's name?" "Why did you bring him here when you are only in Gold III?"

Yan Zhi in front of the screen curled his lips.

Less than a minute later, he saw Tang Zhi typing a bunch of question marks on the public screen, and he raised his hand to type a reply.

[Yan Zhi: Live broadcast]

Then he immediately started the game.

Chang Zhi was shocked to see Yan Zhi reply that she was live broadcasting.

Without waiting for her reply, he actually started the game in seconds.

She cautiously didn't click on the confirmation button to enter the game.

Chang Zhi swore that this was the fastest speed she had ever opened a live broadcast.

When the interface was loaded with 100% progress, Chang Zhi quickly found Yan Zhi in the list and clicked into the live broadcast room.

Sure enough, the barrage in the live broadcast room was all brushing——

[Who is this girl? ��Big Brother Yan took the girl to lie down 666��I'm afraid it's going to fail��Tang? If it's a girl, everyone, I have a bold idea...��In front, what if it's a man�

[Don't worry, Yan Zhi has never played games with girls, so it should be a man. ◈

Chang Zhi put down her phone and covered her face with one hand.

Don't do this, don't guess, don't discuss. She has nothing to do with Yan Zhi.

Because she didn't click on the confirmation button among the ten people, she returned to the team formation interface.

Chang Zhi looked up at the computer, and a bunch of people were typing [Why don't you confirm] [Oh my god, a famous up master invited a friend to play games but was rejected——]

Chang Zhi lowered her head again and typed a sentence in the team chat interface.

[Chang Tang zl]: Why did you pull me? ? ?

After Chang Zhi finished sending, she looked up at the computer.

She watched Yan Zhi on the interface click reply to call out the nine-square input method, and then quickly replied to her.

[Yan Zhi]: Friends, live broadcast, give me face.

The barrage was full of [2333333] [666 is a big face] [Yan Zhi's subtext: Friends, don't reject me, I will live broadcast with you, understand?] [Didn't you notice that Yan Da was very silent today and didn't say much] [Because I was rejected, it's embarrassing, hahaha]

[Chang Tang zl]: ....

[Yan Zhi]: It's open.

You...

This time, Chang Zhi had no choice but to enter the game.

In the hero selection phase, Yan Zhi immediately chose Kai, while Chang Zhi chose Li Yuanfang with punishment.

[Yan Zhi]: ...You play jungle?

[Chang Tang zl]: What's wrong?

Chang Zhi heard Yan Zhi muttering in the speaker

"This lineup has a shooter jungler, Daji in the middle, Zhuang Zhou and Arthur in the top... No problem, I'll place an order, take the lie."

The barrage was full of [666666][The big guy is online][It's reasonable to play jungle Li Yuanfang.]

Chang Zhi looked up at Yan Zhi's interface, with 150 inscriptions and 1 Supreme Black Obsidian. Okay, she hasn't played this kind of game yet.

So the game started, and the enemy and our lineups were clearly visible in the loading interface.

Our side: Arthur (Black), Li Yuanfang (Gold), Daji (Gold), Zhuang Zhou (Diamond), Kai (Black)

Enemy side: Da Qiao, Gan Jiang, Moye, Marco Polo, Zhang Fei, Zhao Yun

Yan Zhi muttered and analyzed: "The opponent must be Zhang Fei against me, Da Qiao in the top lane assists Mark, Gan Jiang in the middle lane... I feel that this blank Daji will be very uncomfortable, her hands are not as long as Gan Jiang... What are you asking me? I will definitely have no problem placing an order."

The game started, and five heroes appeared in the crystal. Chang Zhi hadn't played for a week, and she was eager to try. She looked at it and saw that the Tyrant was in the bottom lane, so she would start with the jungle blue, and then directly squat in the bottom lane after clearing the bottom jungle area to start the Tyrant.

Nice, perfect.

Chang Zhi cleared the upper jungle area at 50 seconds and quickly reached the lower jungle area. The long displacement burn of the second skill plus the explosive output of four small darts of the first skill quickly took down the pig, bird and red dad and reached level 4, but unexpectedly found that the opponent's Da Qiao and Marco Polo were actually on the top lane (that is, our bottom lane)

Kai was very uncomfortable being suppressed. Chang Zhi heard Yan Zhi kept complaining——

"This Mark is a bit fierce."

"Is Da Qiao so tough?"

"You are so reckless. It will be embarrassing to give up the first blood later. I will run away first. No, it is a strategic retreat."

"... Yuan Fang wants to stay? Wait, I will take medicine and my state is a bit..."

Chang Zhi hid in the bushes, watching Marco Polo and Da Qiao push deeper and deeper and almost reach our bottom tower. Hearing Yan Zhi's voice, she laughed in her heart twice, it's okay.

At this point, they have gone far in this game.

The big dart of the ultimate skill was thrown on the road they had to take to return to the tower. Yuan Fang moved to face Marco Polo and Da Qiao. Kai took the opportunity to meet him after taking the treatment. Yuan Fang quickly threw the first skill and hit Da Qiao four times, killing Da Qiao, who had half of her health consumed by his ultimate skill. Then, when Mark turned back from Kai to attack him, he rushed to Mark, and used the red daddy and the burning effect of the second skill to kill Mark.

The operation was smooth and natural, as fierce as a tiger.

"First blood!"

"Double kill!"

Everything happened in just half a minute.

And Kai only threw his small dart and endured a few hits from Mark...

[All-Our Daji-Qian Qiao Xiangnuan]: 666666666666 My Yuan Fang is awesome

The barrage went crazy in an instant——

[Place an order, with a lie? ��It's so embarrassing, I was just slacking off and watching him fight 1 vs 2, got first blood and double kill��I have a feeling Yan Zhi will be carried down by the gold brother 23333�

�This is a small account, with this skill, I feel that the big account should be around diamond��Mark Da Qiao should be bronze, silver or gold�

�I bet 50 cents that Yan Da was carried down hahahahahahahahahaha��No wonder he let people give him face, probably a small account, the little brother is right 23333�

Yan Zhi: � � � � � �

Yan Zhi: I'm lying down.

Yan Zhi: I'm lying down in the bushes.

Chapter 13: Black Game

I am most afraid of the sudden silence in the air.

A minute of silence is like a century. Chang Zhi looked up at the live broadcast room. On the screen, Yan Zhi returned to the original place, blue light flashed, Kai's body swayed gently, and there were two corpses beside him, which looked like a master.

Yan Zhi: "I got two assists, not bad, a nice start."

"I'm level 4, watch me, next I'm going to fight two, Yuan Fang... brother, don't come to the bottom lane."

[fg stood up high, waiting to be slapped in the face][Yuan Fang: OK, OK, if you say you won't come, then don't come/ pampering][Yan Da, Da Qiao is also level 4, she will call people, big brother][Did you call her Sister Qiao for nothing?]

Yan Zhi saw this barrage and snorted: "Da Qiao? She dares to call people, that's perfect, one against five, kill one by one, kill one by one, until the other side is wiped out."

His voice was slightly low, with a kind of confident determination.

Chang Zhi was refreshed.

The voice sounded like someone, but... impossible.

The neighbor next door is not the kind of person who talks a lot, is arrogant and confident, and also guest-stars as an up who specializes in editing ghost videos... a dead otaku in the game.

[666666][My brother Yan in society is ruthless and doesn't talk much][Arrogant][As Luna's brother, I must have the heart to fight five people at once hahahahahaha][Inquisting——]

Chang Zhi raised her eyebrows and typed on the public screen in the game.

[Team-Li Yuanfang-Chang Tangzl]: Come on.

[2333 Come on][One-on-five reservation][Yuanfang: Please start your performance]

After getting a double kill, Chang Zhi ignored Yan Zhi and quickly went to the Tyrant. The ultimate skill combined with the first skill flat attack and the second skill burning effect quickly took down the Tyrant.

The whole team reached level 4 and got a bonus buff of the Tyrant.

After clearing the refreshed jungle area again, when Chang Zhi reached the blue daddy, she suddenly heard Yan Zhi say——

"This pineapple bun and Da Qiao are very arrogant. I will wait and see in the bushes. When they move forward a little bit, use skills to collect troops. OK."

Chang Zhi looked up.

As soon as Yan Zhi finished speaking, he saw him throw out his first skill to slow down Marco Polo who was walking behind Da Qiao. He quickly activated his ultimate skill and rushed over with his second skill. He kept attacking Marco and beat Da Qiao to half health. At this time, Da Qiao had already used her ultimate skill to call for help, and our Daji and Zhuang Zhou had already arrived at the bottom lane.

And Kai calmly handed over the summoner skill to kill (immediately causing 14% of the real damage to the enemies in a large range around him).

A red light flashed, Da Qiao cried out and fell to the ground.

When Da Qiao called for help, only one Zhao Yun appeared. Daji's second skill stuns Zhao Yun after Zhao Yun enlarges, and cooperates with Kai and Zhuang Zhou, the three of them fight together.

"Double kill!"

"Triple kill——"

In an instant, he got a triple kill, and the head score was 0:5.

The blue crab on the riverside witnessed the war in the bottom lane with snake-like movement. The wind gently passed through the grass, and there was silence in the Canyon of Kings.

With a triple kill, Kai's economy instantly jumped to second place in the whole game, second only to Li Yuanfang, who was diligent in clearing the jungle.

Yan Zhi: "Very nice, one against two, a fake triple kill."

Yan Zhi: "Don't stop me, I'm going to fight five next."

[I'm so proud of myself][I've never seen such a shameless person][We're not playing the same Kai, right?]

[Yan Da, did you take Tian.mei's money and want to trick me into playing Kai...][66666666]

On the other side, Chang Zhi, after clearing the jungle area of Blue Dad, squatted on Zhang Fei in the top lane but failed.

The reason is... Chang Zhi really didn't know that Zhang Fei could be so tanky?

It was basically impossible to defeat him. After fighting for a long time, she only managed to kill half of him until he returned to the tower.

Chang Zhi decided to give up catching the top laner and go to the middle lane to catch Gan Jiang and Moye.

Who knew that she would run into Zhao Yun in the bushes of the river in the middle lane. Brother Zilong rushed over with a spear and was stunned by Daji. Chang Zhi threw a big block on the road and consumed 1/3 of his blood. Zhao Yun saw that the situation was not good and ran to his own red father's wild area with his big move. Chang Zhi followed behind and attacked, and finally threw the first skill on Zhao Yun and didn't linger.

Yan Zhi seemed to be watching her fight, because Chang Zhi heard Yan Zhi say: "This Zhao Yun is dead, there is no way to avoid it."

Sure enough, Zhao Yun thought he had escaped in the bushes, but the next second, the dart of the first skill exploded and Zhao Yun died directly.

[All-Zhao Yun-National Server Zilong]:... Yuan Fang's dart was poisoned.

[Hahahahahahahahahahahahahahahahaha] [This brother Zilong is so cute] [Why does Yan Da always peek at Yuan Fang fighting]

As soon as this barrage came out, Yan Zhi replied nonchalantly: "I peek? No, I want to learn from others..."

Next, several small team battles broke out. The second and third tyrants were taken down by Chang Zhi alone. The first moment the Lord refreshed, Chang Zhi's Li Yuan Fang passively saw the enemy's three top laners and one mid and bottom lanes, and cooperated with Daji to successfully steal the Lord.

The situation was very good.

Our five people gathered in the middle lane, Chang Zhi was singled out by Zhao Yun, and used the second skill to quickly roll through the wall to the blue father to escape, and ran into Marco Polo head-on.

Marco Polo was at level 12 with full health, and she was at level 14.

Chang Zhi looked at her own health, two bars short of full, she hesitated.

Chang Zhi didn't intend to fight Marco Polo because she was not in good condition. Who knew that he would rush up directly with his ultimate? Chang Zhi simply didn't hide. She used her second skill to roll straight into the bush and zoomed in to intercept. She kept using her first skill plus four flat attacks to trigger the explosion effect of her first skill. When the health was low, she flashed upwards and used her first skill again to kill Marco Polo directly.

At the same time, Kai's triple kill followed the news that Li Yuanfang killed Marco Polo alone.

The team battle that broke out in the middle ended with the death of our Daji, Arthur and the enemy's Gan Jiang Moye, Zhao Yun, Marco Polo, and Da Qiao.

At this time, the master had arrived.

[The little drama in the bottom lane...][Yuanfang and Mark fought really fiercely][One wave, one wave, win, win][Three kills, three kills][Zhang Fei is really good at playing tanks]

The highland tower was broken, and a wave was directly killed.

In the settlement interface, Kai 8-1-8, the highest output, and the second highest score.

Li Yuanfang was 9-0-6, second in output, first in rating, and pushed the most towers, becoming the MVP of this game.

It was almost a crushing game.

The rhythm was very good, the support was also very coordinated, and the teamfight was very neat.

After playing this game, Chang Zhi logged off immediately, fearing that Yan Zhi would drag her to play another game.

Chang Zhi glanced at the number of people in the live broadcast room. It might be because she was broadcasting King of Glory today. The number of viewers was 130,000 and continued to soar. Playing King of Glory under the gaze of 130,000 people...

Chang Zhi didn't know how she survived.

She only knew that she performed exceptionally well in this game. She usually played diamond games with Deng Jiadai, and her gold rank was inherited from the platinum rank last season.

Chang Zhi continued to watch Yan Zhi's live broadcast. Seeing that Yan Zhi was quiet for a long time, there was no movement on the interface, and the barrage in the live broadcast room asked again—

[Where is the up person?] [Did you go to the toilet? ? ��No sound or movement, what's going on��If Yan Da doesn't come back, everyone will leave and 10,000 people will be lost...��Who is that Chang Tang just now, that zl seems to be pinyin��Hey, now that you mention it, the homonym of "Liu Bu" in front is like... Tang Zhi? ? ? �

No way? Chang Zhi's heart skipped a beat, afraid that she would really be exposed, so she decided to buy a name change card and change her name to pray for safety.

But where is Yan Zhi...?

Chang Zhi's phone vibrated, there was a new message.

Whose? Chang Zhi clicked it and saw that it was Yan Zhi who disappeared in the live broadcast room.

[Yan Zhi]: You played well.

[Yan Zhi]: Let's play together if there is a chance^-^

[Tang Zhi]: Well, if it's not a live broadcast, I can consider it.

[Tang Zhi]: But... what about your one-on-five?

The author has something to say: Time for subtext—

Yanzhi: As a part-time live game streaming host, I like and admire girls who are good at playing games.

However, the reality is—

If you tell a girl that you have a chance to play together.

You will be alone forever.

If you tell a boy that you have a chance to play together.

Then you will also...

Don't ask me why...

Chapter 14 Weibo

[Yanzhi]:........................

Yanzhi sent a long string of dots, and Changzhi couldn't help laughing.

It was said that the one-on-five was not completed, embarrassed, right?

[Yanzhi]: Did you watch my live broadcast?

[Tangzhi]: If you pull me, I will immediately turn on the computer and play while listening.

[Yanzhi]:......

Wen Yanxing didn't expect Changzhi to be like this, he was a little embarrassed.

[Yanzhi]: One-on-five, mainly. Still no chance.

[Yanzhi]: But,

[Yanzhi]: Can a double kill plus a triple kill be considered one-on-five?

Changzhi was stunned for a moment.

Then she remembered that Yanzhi said that the bottom lane was barely one-on-three at the beginning and the wave she caught alone in the top lane.

After all, she had the live broadcast on her computer and was listening to Yanzhi's words.

He explained it so seriously...

[Tangzhi]: Well, count it.

[Tang Zhi]: Well-reasoned and convincing.

"Okay, you asked where I was just now? Well, you know, I'm back now, let's continue the live broadcast..."

Yan Zhi hadn't replied to her on the mobile phone Penguin. Chang Zhi looked up and the screen of the live broadcast room had started to move.

Chang Zhi smiled. It was obviously looking for her, and the reason made up in the live broadcast room was really convincing.

Before she finished laughing, someone asked on the barrage.

[Yan Da, was that Chang Zhi just now?] [1 Ask] [It feels like the homophony is quite similar.] [1 1 After all, Yan Da has ghosted Chang Zhi] [Is the goddess so good at playing games? ?]

Seeing this, Chang Zhi's smile froze at the corner of her mouth.

On the screen, Yan Zhi started a ranked match and said, "Chang Zhi? No, no, no, that was a friend of mine, you're overthinking it."

"But now that you mention it, I think she might be a fan of Chang Zhi."

"Add friend? She refused to add me."

Indeed, Chang Zhi immediately set a friend rejection after quitting the match. After listening to Yan Zhi's words, she immediately recharged nine yuan to buy a name change card and changed it to a blank name to ensure safety. At the same time, after confirming that Yan Zhi's match record was invisible to others, she breathed a sigh of relief.

In fact, most of the fans of ghost video up masters and game anchors are male fans. However, for some reason, it may be because of Yan Zhi's voice and wit, he also has a lot of female fans.

Chang Zhi had just glanced at his Weibo before, and there were a lot of people calling him a male god...

Chang Zhi was shamefully scared.

She knew that sometimes, women would criticize women without mercy.

But just now Yan Zhi... called her her own fan.

Men are really full of nonsense.

In the evening, after Chang Zhi finished her meal, Anan, who had arranged to rehearse with her, sent her a message.

[Anan]: [Picture] How about this dress?

Chang Zhi clicked on the big picture and took a look. The black and red V-neck waist-baring top and pure black bell-bottom pants looked particularly good on the model.

Although Anan was not tall, she was also very sexy, and her collarbone was particularly beautiful.

[Tang Zhi]: It looks good and suits you very well.

[Anan]: Hey, I picked this [Picture] for you. Sister Qiao said she would dance the small A position so she would not wear bell-bottom pants.

[Tang Zhi]: OK, OK... Have you found the person?

[Anan]: I was just about to tell you, I looked around yesterday. . No.

[Anan]: There are some things I am afraid I can't keep up with the time, so I think that I, you, and Sister Qiao should discuss who will dance an extra part and find a post-production to help put it in.

[Tang Zhi]: Sure, then you can create a group and we can talk about it.

Anan was very quick and added three people to the group at once.

[Anan]: @Tang Zhi @Qiao Jie, can we do the movements by ourselves tonight?

[Qiao Jie]: Yes.

[Qiao Jie]: But I have to go to work during the day, so I may only do the part of Xiao A. You two can do the rest.

[Anan]: Okay, okay, it's okay, @Tang Zhi, do you want to dance or do I?

Anan's question made Chang Zhi think about it seriously.

She is not very busy these two days, so she doesn't care. The key is to watch Anan.

[Tang Zhi]: Do you have time?

[Anan]: Ah, actually, Tangtang, I don't really want to dance with two people. I am afraid that I, who started late, can't remember and make mistakes.

[Anan]: But Tangtang, if you don't have time, I will do it.

[Tang Zhi]: Okay, then I will do it.

[Anan]: Okay, send me the size of the clothes, I will place the order and pay for SF Express, come on, see you at Sister Qiao's house the day after tomorrow @Sister Qiao

Sister Qiao's house is quite big, she specially decorated a dance studio, Chang Zhi has been there before, the decoration is very exquisite, her girlish heart is about to fly.

Sister Qiao is very straightforward, it seems that Anan told her in advance.

[Sister Qiao]: Okay, do you still remember my home address?

[Tang Zhi]: Remember, my memory is not that bad.

[Anan]: /ok

[Anan]: Remember to copy the moves these two days, strive for perfection, perfection, perfection~ Raise your hands and tell me you can do it! ? ?

[Tang Zhi]: I won't talk to you for now.

[Anan]: Hey, wait, wait, wait——

Anan seemed to suddenly remember something, and hurriedly chatted with Chang Zhi.

[Anan]: Tang Tang.

[Tang Zhi]: ? ? ? What? ? ?

Chang Zhi was a little puzzled. Why did he privately chat with her to knock her down?

[Anan]: Promise me not to wear 10cm high heels. Just give me this hard work. Promise me.

[Tang Zhi]: ....

Chang Zhi didn't know whether to laugh or cry.

Did he knock her down just to talk about this?

[Tang Zhi]: Do you still remember the high heels?

[Anan]: Of course, /smile, I have a big goal this time. I am so short, standing with you, in line, for the sake of beauty, 10cm high heels belong to me. If I don't die, who will die? Don't compete with me.

Chang Zhi thought about dancing in 10cm high heels. Not only do you have to wrap them tightly with several layers of transparent tape, but you will also fall easily if you move too much...

[Tang Zhi]: I was just kidding before. You should take it easy. It's not good to wear such high heels.

After kindly admonishing An Nan, Tang Zhi logged into Weibo and posted a message about his delayed update this week.

She was afraid that if he followed the original schedule, he would not have enough time and would be too late.

[It is Tang Zhi, not Tangzhi v]: This week's update will be postponed to Sunday night, because I am working on a video with @Annan and @Qiaomu~ Look forward to me, right?

After posting this Weibo, Chang Zhi checked the hot searches.

The first two were recently released movies and a star, and the third hot search was the latest hot news. After reading the latest hot news, Chang Zhi saw that the comments in the upper right corner increased after a while, and felt that something was wrong, so she decided to take a look first.

But she didn't expect that in addition to fans who posted [looking forward to] and the like, there were other voices in the Weibo comments.

[If you love me, you can rub against me]: [Picture] Are you the one who played with Yan Da? Why did you reject him at the beginning? ? Who gave you such a big face? ? ? That's enough, but you dared to mock Yan Da? A woman should not be so cheap, okay?

? ?

Chapter 15 Storm

When Chang Zhi saw this comment, many things flashed through her mind.

Her first reaction was——

Damn idiot. She wanted to curse back, but it would have a bad impact, so she had to bear it for now.

Her second reaction was——

Wow, how could she mock Yan Zhi? Looking at the overall situation, when she was dragged to play the game at the beginning, she asked the reason cautiously because she was not familiar with Yan Zhi. Is this wrong?

After the game started, she sent a message to Yan Zhi who said "I want to fight five people alone" saying "Come on."

Cheer him up and mock him? ? Damn idiot,

And finally, Chang Zhi, who calmed down, began to think——

What can her screenshot of the King of Glory settlement interface prove? Even if that person is really her, does this girl have a solid evidence to prove that the account is her? Obviously not, first, because she did not add fans, there is no situation of mass fans being exposed.

Second, the people who play King of Glory in Penguin and know that she is Tang Zhi's friend, she only added her three administrators, Youzi Liufang and Da Miao, and then her real-life friends, Deng Jiadai and Jiang Huai, and some former classmates.

Chang Zhi usually only plays with Deng Jiadai, and the others probably can't remember.

But Chang Zhi has changed her ID now, so the others probably don't know either,

So -

Where does this girl get the courage to throw dirty water on her so confidently?

She must have a bad life with such strong resentment.

From being confused to angry to calm, Chang Zhi took a deep breath and exhaled, calmed down and refreshed the Weibo interface. The Weibo that had just been sent out less than 20 minutes ago, from the 300 comments she just saw for the first time, soared to 800 in five minutes.

It almost doubled.

[Wang Xiaoniu]: Who threw dirty water on you so boldly? / Love me, rub me: [Picture] Playing with Yan Da...

[If you are well, I will be cloudy]: qaq Although I also want to know if the one playing with Yan Da is Tang Tang, but you are too much, right? / Love me, rub me: [Picture] Playing with Yan Da...

[Meow meow meow meow]: Are you crazy? Yan Zhi replied to the barrage and said it was not Tang Zhi, but he still came to criticize. Brainless fans are really scary / Love me, rub me: [Picture] Playing with Yan Da...

[Wang Xiaomin's shit shoveling officer]: The person who just watched the live broadcast said that although Yan Zhi denied it personally, I still doubt that ID. However, the person who teamed up with Yan Zhi did not mock Yan Zhi, the two of them took their teammates to lie down together, how can you see the mockery? ? / Love me, rub me: [Picture] With...

[Tang Tang Tang Tang is super cute]: Even if it is Tang Tang, what does it have to do with you? Brainless fan keyboard warrior. /If you love me, you can rub against me: [Picture] Playing with Yan Da...

Chang Zhi read about a hundred comments and felt touched for some reason.

Her fans were helping her to criticize others...

The reason why Chang Zhi didn't criticize back was because she was a fan of 500,000 fans after all. She had her own position and couldn't criticize back in person. Although it might not be right to watch fans criticize others, she was not a saint. She would not say things like "everyone shut up, she didn't mean it, she just loves idols too much" and so on, which would make fans feel disappointed.

Chang Zhi could only not personally lead the trend. She could only do so little, but she had actually remembered what the fans did for her today, and would give them better feedback more seriously in the future.

Every cute fan who cared about her deserved her gentle treatment.

If you treat me well, I will treat you well. If you treat me badly, I will not even bother to pay attention to you.

Chang Zhi saw that the comments were increasing, so she climbed onto Penguin to the fan group that she had blocked but would occasionally visit.

Sure enough, all three groups were talking about this.

Chang Zhi then ran to the management group and prepared to explain some things.

But she didn't expect that she was flooded with a lot of messages before she could say anything.

[Yuzi]: Sister Tang, did you really add Yan Da? Please expose the Penguin account! I am a crazy fan...

[Fu Da Miao]: Tang Tang, did you... hehehehe?

[Jia Jia Jia Jia Jia Jia Jia Er Ah]: Wow, you actually played games with other men besides me? Why? Who brought you to Platinum, who taught you to play Li Yuanfang? ? ? ? You actually used the Li Yuanfang I taught you to bring other men to lie down! Tell the truth! !

[Jia Jia Jia Jia Jia Jia Jia Er Ah]: Tell me clearly in private chat, remember, I will poke you.

[Just a post-production-Jiang Huai]: Yan Zhi's video was edited very well... I know he ghosted you but why did you add him and play games with him? ?

[Liufang]: Sister Tang is quite charming... Yan Da seems to have only played with boys, you are the first girl I have seen...

Chang Zhi: ...

She doesn't know which one to reply to first with so many messages, just like a barrage of messages that she can't read at a glance.

And their focus is completely different from her normal fans... What's going on?

[Simple and hardworking Tang Zhi]: ... Have you read my Weibo?

[Yuzi]: Yes. The fan group is going crazy.

Chang Zhi looked at Yuzi's tone, which seemed to be completely unhurried... So calm?

Yuzi seemed to understand what she was thinking.

[Yuzi]: This is the difference between knowing the truth and not knowing the truth. I was so excited to see you guys playing together. Hehehe, that's not as important as this, but I scolded you back for you, praise me.

[Simple and hardworking Tang Zhi]: ... ...

Is there such a thing? ?

Chang Zhi held her forehead, suddenly feeling a little frustrated with this group of people.

[Simple and hardworking Tang Zhi]: @Yuzi @Liu Fang @Fu Da Miao, please help me communicate in the group and control the situation. I am afraid that some people will overreact and both sides will start to curse each other, and then everything will be wrong.

Chang Zhi's worry is not unreasonable. Many times, the fans of two groups cursed each other to death because some brainless fans became the fuse, but the fact is that the two sides actually had nothing in common.

[Yuzi]: Well, I know... But Tangtang, does Yan Da know that his fans cursed him?

Chang Zhi was stunned.

Yan Zhi... should still be live streaming.

[Simple and hardworking Tang Zhi]: How do I know.

[Yuzi]: Hey, didn't you add him? We were just playing together, are you... hehehehe.

[Simple and hardworking Tang Zhi]: Stop it. If you don't know the guy Yan Zhi and I are playing with, it has nothing to do with you or Tang Zhi, understand?

[Yuzi]: ...Okay, okay, I understand.

[Fu Da Miao]: Yan Zhi knows, right? He just posted a Weibo post. Sister Tang, go check it out. Wow, he's so handsome. I'm going to become his fan.

! ? ? ?

Chapter 16 Temporary closure

[Simple and hardworking Tang Zhi]: What did he post? ? ? ? ?

Before Da Miao could take a screenshot for her, Chang Zhi happened to log into the Weibo interface that had just been opened. She clicked on it and searched for Yan Zhi. She clicked on the first search result with the most followers.

The Weibo post five minutes ago.

Long Weibo picture.

[Yan Zhi v]: First of all, I don't know why some people would doubt what I said clearly in the live broadcast, and even directly found irrelevant people and did some not-so-good things.

To explain this matter, the person who teamed up with me was not Tang Zhi but a friend of mine. First of all, I took the initiative to invite him because he had never played with me before. When he refused the invitation for the first time, many people watching in the live broadcast room knew that it was my friend who refused because he didn't know the truth. It was normal. After asking clearly, he opened the second time. Then, to be honest, I don't really understand how to tell ridicule. He didn't ridicule me. I personally felt that after a game, the whole game was very pleasant. He had a good rhythm and made me lie down in a very comfortable game. I was really relieved.

To be honest, after this incident, I suddenly had a deep feeling. Everyone should investigate the truth of the matter before speaking. Everyone should be responsible for what they say and do, including me. This sentence is the same whether it is on the Internet or in life.

I am not a great person. As an up master and anchor, I should bring you laughter and joy. I don't want you to hurt others because of me, nor do I want you to be troubled by someone with ulterior motives. But this matter has been caused by me, and it has also caused some bad effects, so here, I would like to solemnly apologize to Miss Tang Zhi for the trouble caused by this matter.

The above.

——Yan Zhi, stay. �

Yan Zhi's Weibo was posted for five minutes, and there were already many comments.

�lxdss: I feel sorry for Yan Da. Oh, we Yan Da will bear the blame with tears. �

�Xiaowangshu: I read that comment and the words used are really weird. Tang Zhi's originally clean Weibo was messed up like this, but it has nothing to do with Yan Da and Tang Zhi. I can only feel sorry for both sides�

�Hello, goodbye, goodnight: So the idols should take the blame for what the fans did! Girls, calm down! Stop arguing! �

�Tangtang is beautiful as a painting: As a fan of Tangtang, I was half angry after reading this Weibo. In fact, I don't really understand the girl's psychology. The irritation is illogical and stupid. After thinking for a long time, I felt that it's not Yan Zhi's fault. Maybe she is just jealous of our Tangtang? �

This Weibo is very long. Chang Zhi read it carefully word by word. After reading it, she felt mixed emotions.

She sat in front of the computer silently, the fan was whirring, the curtains were moving, and the sun was setting outside the window, and it was about to fall at night.

Like every storm, it will eventually return to calm.

Chang Zhi's mood was a bit complicated, especially when she saw "People should be responsible for what they say, including me." Here, her heart was even more shocked.

In fact, she and Yan Zhi knew each other that this was a statement that was half true and half false.

The fact is that the person was indeed her, but she couldn't say it.

Chang Zhi herself didn't want to cause trouble, but Yan Zhi... wanted to protect her.

It can be seen from the barrage of answers that specifically picked out doubts during the live broadcast.

He knew about cyber violence, he knew his influence, and he also knew that what he said couldn't be inconsistent.

As he said, people should be responsible for what they say, but in this matter, he was in a dilemma. He invited first, he defended her first, and he said it in front of hundreds of thousands of viewers to cover up for her. If he said it was not, then it could only be not, and Mom could only say one sentence to the end.

Otherwise, it would be a crisis of trust.

What's more, if Yan Zhi told the truth and slapped himself in the face, Tang Zhi would be the one who suffered more.

Brainless fans are the most deadly.

There is no way.

So the lie must be made up, until everyone forgets it.

He may also want to be frank, but he knows that the consequences of being frank are actually more serious.

This world is very complicated, and what we see is limited. There are so many statements in the world, and behind the public relations, the truth of the matter may not be fully revealed.

Complex, bitter, and at a loss - three emotions mixed together, Chang Zhi silently clicked on Yan Zhi's attention.

She didn't know what she should do. She stared at the computer for a long time. After she came to her senses, it took a long time before Chang Zhi finally posted a Weibo.

[It's Tang Zhi, not Tangzhi v]: I love you

I love you and you.

Thank you, and I'm sorry.

After posting the Weibo, Chang Zhi clicked on the chat interface of people who knew her game ID one by one.

Youzi, Liufang, Da Miao, Jiang Huai.

She flipped through the list and confirmed it repeatedly.

In the circle, Anan and Sister Qiao only added WeChat, so it doesn't matter.

She started to send messages, her fingers tapping the keyboard, her voice anxious and sincere.

Real insiders should be sensible.

Keep your mouth shut.

Chang Zhi can only cooperate with Yan Zhi in this way.

After getting a positive reply from Youzi and the others, Chang Zhi was actually not used to trusting people 100%, but at the moment, although she was worried, she had to be relieved.

After explaining it, Chang Zhi breathed a sigh of relief. She didn't check her Weibo, but instead re-read Yan Zhi's historical messages.

Although she didn't want to admit it in her heart, Chang Zhi did find that she was curious about Yan Zhi.

A lot.

She really wanted to know what kind of person he was.

Unlike before, when she just flipped through it hastily, Chang Zhi looked at it one by one, from life, to videos, to live broadcasts.

The more she flipped through the comments, the fewer reposts and likes there were. It was obvious that there was room for gradual improvement.

Yan Zhi rarely posts about his daily life, but Chang Zhi still discovered that Yan Zhi used to be a jet lag party, and his age should be around 25 to 30 years old. He also raised a hedgehog?

Chang Zhi suddenly thought of the hedgehog she saw at Wen Yanxing's house not long ago.

Coincidence, right?

Chang Zhi looked at the Weibo post, which was posted last year. The hedgehog lay docilely on the man's palm, with its eyes closed and its nose turned up, looking small and cute.

The man's palm was broad and his fingers were slender. Judging from the proportion of his hands, he should be a tall man.

The accompanying words were - "The new member of the family, originally wanted to name it Qiuqiu, but it escaped from the sofa while I was away. It took a long time to find it, so it was renamed Erqiu."

Chang Zhi felt relieved because of the different names.

Coincidence, coincidence.

But it seems that Yan Zhi's avatar is that hedgehog. When she first saw it, she thought it was a picture she searched online.

It turned out that he took the photo himself. Looking at the professional photo, Chang Zhi thought, it seems that he should add another skill label to Yan Zhi, photography.

The cute penguin in the lower right corner flashed, and when he put the mouse on it, it showed Yan Zhi's message before he clicked it.

Chang Zhi didn't feel surprised, maybe it was because of what happened just now.

[Yan Zhi]: I just saw that comment after the live broadcast.

[Yan Zhi]: Sorry, I didn't expect things to develop like this.

[Yan Zhi]: What she said was very unpleasant.

[Yan Zhi]: ...Are you okay?

To say that I'm okay... Actually, I'm not okay. When I was scolded, I felt inexplicably wronged and wronged. I can't forget that feeling.

Chang Zhi's fingers pressed on the keyboard, thinking seriously about how to reply to him so that he would feel more relaxed.

I can't burden him, right?

[Simple and hardworking Tang Zhi]: Actually, I'm fine. I'm fine now. I saw your Weibo post as well.

[Simple and hardworking Tang Zhi]: Emmmm, so serious. I didn't realize you were such a serious person.

[Yan Zhi]: ....

[Yan Zhi]: I... don't look like a serious person?

Chang Zhi raised her eyebrows slightly and pursed her lips to suppress the corners of her lips that were about to rise.

[Simple and hardworking Tang Zhi]: A little bit, it seems a little different from when I watched you live~

[Simple and hardworking Tang Zhi]: You talk a lot during live broadcasts, and you make so many witty jokes one after another. I don't know where the jokes come from.

[Yan Zhi]: It's different during live broadcasts... Maybe it's because I'm naturally funny.

[Yan Zhi]: I'm still very serious when I need to be serious, like just now.

[Simple and hardworking Tang Zhi]: What about now? I see that you seem a little reserved when chatting with me now.

[Yanzhi]: No,

[Yanzhi]: To be honest, I am trying to talk to you in a humorous way.

[Simple and hardworking Tangzhi]: Why? ? ? ? ?

[Yanzhi]: Nervous, I have never teased a girl.

[Yanzhi]: But now I want to try to make you happy.

Chapter 17 Love Song

When Chang Zhi saw those two lines of small words, her heartbeat quickened.

She felt her ears begin to feel hot, and then her cheeks.

Even the fan at the highest setting could not relieve the heat.

... Yan Zhi, is it really okay to talk to her like this?

[Simple and hardworking Tang Zhi]: ... Why?

Yan Zhi... What does this mean?

Why do you want to make her happy?

Chang Zhi suddenly felt a little nervous, and her heartbeat became a little faster, as if it was about to jump out of her chest.

[Yan Zhi]: I'm afraid you're still unhappy.

[Yan Zhi]: I feel like you just comforted me with a forced smile, "It's nothing", and my conscience hurts a little.

[Simple and hardworking Tang Zhi]: No way, I'm just telling the truth.

Ah... That's what he meant. I thought too much.

I felt a little disappointed for some reason, and the temperature of my cheeks slowly cooled down. The moment I was teased a minute ago, I was at a loss, but now it seemed awkward.

She was the one who had the wrong idea.

But this awkward misunderstanding made her feel a little bit comfortable and warm in her heart.

Chang Zhi supported her forehead with one hand, thinking like this.

[Yan Zhi]: What programs do you want to watch?

[Simple and hardworking Tang Zhi]: What are you going to do...eh?

[Simple and hardworking Tang Zhi]: Wait, will you do it if I tell you? What the hell?

[Yan Zhi]: Well, it's a necessary process to please you.

[Simple and hardworking Tang Zhi]: Then how can you let me say it myself? It's too casual.

[Yan Zhi]: Then this is my personal gift, a single live broadcast, free ordering, exclusive customization, and you can return it if you are not satisfied?

[Simple and hardworking Tang Zhi]: Haha...

Chang Zhi in front of the computer was a little amused.

[Simple and hardworking Tang Zhi]: So serious, then wait a minute, let me think about it.

Chang Zhi held her chin up in front of the computer, feeling troubled.

It can't be too difficult, so... sing a song.

[Simple and hardworking Tang Zhi]: A song, seventh on the hot search list of xx software, no less than 2 minutes, how about it?

Chang Zhi didn't open the music software, she just said it casually.

Otherwise, it would be boring to just pick a song at random.

Three minutes later, Yan Zhi sent a screenshot,

[Yan Zhi]: [Picture] This song?

Chang Zhi took a closer look, it was "Little Lucky" by a singer named Tian

She had listened to it once before and thought it was okay, so she added it to her collection

[Yan Zhi]: ... I rarely listen to songs recently, I haven't heard this song yet, I'll listen to it twice first.

[Yan Zhi]: Some of the lyrics of this song are okay, um.

[Yan Zhi]: However, my singing is average, if you really can't stand it, just turn off the recording, don't save face for me, delete it.

[Simple and hardworking Tang Zhi]: Well, I didn't mean to save face or anything. I cherish my ears very much. I turned them off without your reminder.

That being said, Chang Zhi felt that people who dared to sing should not be too bad.

At least they wouldn't be tone-deaf or rush the beat.

She could still sing a few lines, but whether it sounded good or not was another matter.

[Yan Zhi]: I thought my face was worth a lot.

[Simple and hardworking Tang Zhi]: Can you rely on your face to eat?

[Yan Zhi]: ....

Six periods, Chang Zhi vaguely saw Yan Zhi's depression after being humiliated.

So Chang Zhi comforted him——

[Simple and hardworking Tang Zhi]: But I don't think I've seen your face. It's okay. Whether face is worth money depends on who you are facing.

...It seems better not to say it.

Sure enough, Yan Zhi changed the subject directly.

[Yan Zhi]: Wait for me for ten minutes.

After ten minutes, Chang Zhi washed her face and poured a glass of water. She sat back in front of the computer and found that Yan Zhi had already sent a recording file.

It was five minutes in total, and the file name was - [Special Program].

Tsk, special program.

Chang Zhi repeated it in her mind and clicked to confirm the reception. The transmission was completed in less than a minute.

Originally, she was going to listen to it with the speaker. After thinking about it, Chang Zhi found the headphones from the bottom layer of the bedside table, put on the headphones, and then clicked on the audio.

The prelude was melodious and the melody was brisk. Chang Zhi tilted her head and stared at Yan Zhi's head on the screen. She couldn't imagine what he would sing this song like.

This is a very gentle song.

But soon, she knew what Yan Zhi's singing was like.

The prelude was not long, about ten seconds.

"I hear the raindrops falling on the green grass, I hear the bell ringing in the distance—" A slightly low male voice slowly entered her ears, the tail tone naturally stretched out, gentle and delicate.

Chang Zhi fell in love with Yan Zhi in the first sentence he said.

Really fell in love with him.

This is different from his somewhat sloppy tone during the live broadcast. Yan Zhi's voice is indeed low. Chang Zhi thought that maybe the live broadcast is for the atmosphere, and the voice is deliberately made to sound more positive.

Chang Zhi subconsciously slowed down her breathing.

This is like a surprise, a different feeling. You didn't have many expectations at first, and you didn't expect it in advance, but suddenly, the moment his voice sounded in your ears, it filled all your expectations of him.

From 60% to 100% seriousness.

She is not a pure voice control, but she can't help but indulge in it.

He is so serious, not just saying the lyrics, but gently knocking on the heart with every word.

The whole person seems to calm down because of this gentle song and this gentle voice, and the heart with a joke is also quiet because of this.

Chang Zhi lowered her eyes, her eyelashes fluttered slightly, and she remembered the maintenance not long ago.

Who knows... maybe he is a very gentle person.

The next day, Chang Zhi was awakened by the doorbell.

Last night, she watched the computer video and learned the dance moves of 4 walls until one o'clock in the morning. She practiced in the living room for two or three hours, and the moves were probably connected.

Chang Zhi closed her eyes and reached out to the bed to find her phone. She couldn't find it after a long time. She was still half asleep and half awake, and she was startled. She thought the phone fell to the ground. She sat up suddenly and looked back. The pure white phone was lying quietly in the place where she had just lain.

Chang Zhi rubbed her eyes and breathed a sigh of relief.

It turned out that she was pressed.

The doorbell was still ringing. Chang Zhi jumped out of bed, went into the bathroom and quickly washed her face. She quickly straightened her messy hair and tied it up into a bun. She looked at the toothbrush and hesitated.

There should be nothing to do so early, right?

The person who rang the doorbell seemed to be in a hurry... Never mind, let's go see what's going on first.

Chang Zhi didn't even change her pajamas and ran to the door.

Who is it so early in the morning? Chang Zhi was puzzled.

When she arrived at the door, Chang Zhi carefully opened a crack and saw a beautiful hand first.

After opening the door completely, she was shocked to find that Wen Yanxing was standing in front of the door.

Chang Zhi: "???"

Wen Yanxing: "..."

The cold air from the door hit him. Wen Yanxing looked down at the water droplets at the connection between Chang Zhi's chin and neck, and the blue nightgown he had seen before. He could tell at a glance that she had just gotten up.

Looking down again, Chang Zhi's toes in flip-flops moved uneasily.

Chang Zhi wanted to die.

She hadn't brushed her teeth yet... Why did Wen Yanxing knock on her door so early? ?

She... She shouldn't be breathing, right?

What if she talked later... No, the picture would be too beautiful.

Chang Zhi quietly moved a little further behind the door, half of her face was buried behind it.

Chang Zhi coughed a few times to clear her throat, and looked up at Wen Yanxing: "So early... what are you doing?"

Wen Yanxing saw Chang Zhi's clothes and her hair tied up perfunctorily, and couldn't help asking: "Ten o'clock, it's not early... did you just get up?"

Speaking of just getting up, Chang Zhi thought of the fact that she hadn't had time to brush her teeth. She hid the lower half of her face behind the door and nodded gently: "Yeah, I slept late last night."

How late was it to sleep until ten o'clock in the morning... Wen Yanxing, who had a regular schedule, thought of his sister who was out at night and hid during the day. Chang Zhi was the same as his sister?

Chang Zhi saw that Wen Yanxing was silent, and thought about going back to brush her teeth quickly, "You haven't said anything yet."

Wen Yanxing remembered the business and coughed lightly: "... collecting rent."

Huh?

Collecting rent?

Chang Zhi's brain short-circuited for a moment, and then she remembered what He Shengbi had said before.

Yes, Wen Yanxing is also her landlord.

Chang Zhi blinked, looked up and said, "Is Alipay OK?"

Wen Yanxing thought for a moment and said, "WeChat."

"Well, then come in and sit down first. Wait for me for five minutes. I'll go get my phone."

Chang Zhi opened the door for Wen Yanxing, then quickened her pace and ran back to the room.

Closing the door, Chang Zhi covered her face with both hands.

Oh my god, I talked to someone without brushing my teeth, and it was my neighbor. Fortunately, there was a door.

Rushed into the bathroom in the bedroom, brushed her teeth quickly, and then opened the closet and took a set of clothes to change.

The speed was so fast that it exploded. The whole process took no more than five minutes. It was comparable to the speed she rushed to catch up with the morning reading in her senior year of high school.

After packing up, Chang Zhi took her phone and opened the door. Wen Yanxing was sitting quietly in the living room. When he heard the noise, he looked up at her.

Wen Yanxing really thought that Chang Zhi was going to get her phone, but he didn't expect that when he saw Chang Zhi again, she had actually changed out of her nightgown.

Her hair was obviously combed.

Wen Yanxing: "..." This action was too fast, he thought it would take a girl more than half an hour to get ready.

Chang Zhi didn't know what Wen Yanxing was thinking. She waved her hand with her phone, walked over and said, "I don't think I've added you on WeChat. Should I add you first?"

Wen Yanxing: "Okay."

Chang Zhi sat in the other corner of the sofa: "Shall I scan you?"

Wen Yanxing nodded and opened the WeChat QR code.

When Chang Zhi went over to scan the code, she thought to herself that it was fortunate that she was smart enough to run back to brush her teeth while taking the phone.

Wen Yanxing's WeChat avatar was pure black, and he looked straight at first glance. His ID was a bunch of incomprehensible letters and numbers, ynzwyx7.

She raised her hand and typed a polite note in WeChat - "Mr. Wen".

Wen Yanxing used the corner of his eye to easily see the note that Chang Zhi had filled in for him, thanks to his height advantage.

Wen Yanxing: "..." Mr. Wen, this note is really nice, both polite and unfamiliar.

He secretly raised his phone with one hand and also made a note - "Miss Chang".

Chang Zhi sat next to Wen Yanxing and clicked on the private chat to transfer money.

Four digits were transferred, and suddenly she had the illusion of supporting someone.

She quietly raised her eyes to look at Wen Jinzhao's profile, ahem, she thought too much.

He owns half a building in the commercial center, who knows which rich second generation.

After confirming the payment, Wen Yanxing stood up and didn't want to stay any longer.

He nodded slightly and whispered, "Then I'll leave first."

Chang Zhi sent Wen Yanxing to the door and watched Wen Yanxing walk out without going to the opposite door but towards the stairs.

She couldn't help but ask, "Are you going out?"

Wen Yanxing said, "Go downstairs to collect rent."

Chang Zhi: "...Okay, I thought you were going out."

The rent collector... is also very hard, and has to go downstairs one floor at a time.

After sighing, Chang Zhi closed the door and leaned against it, simply staying still, looking down at her phone.

I just added Wen Yanxing, and there are updates from my friends in the circle of friends, and...

A friend message suddenly popped up in the WeChat address book.

[[05xm25] Request to add you as a friend.]

Chapter 18 Adding Friends

This is...

Her WeChat does not have the function of adding friends nearby, so there should be no possibility of strange people adding her.

So who is this person?

Chang Zhi stared at the messy ID, totally clueless. She clicked on the business card to see that the Moments were set to be invisible to non-friends, and the way to add was through search.

Chang Zhi did not rush to approve, but slowly walked to the sofa and sat down, sinking into the soft sofa. She casually pulled over a pillow.

I don't know why, maybe it was a woman's intuition, but she felt very strange.

She clicked on approval.

[Tang Zhi]: I approved your friend verification request, and now we can start chatting.

[Tang Zhi]: Who are you? ? ?

After sending the message, while waiting for a reply, Chang Zhi clicked on his Moments.

It was visible for three days, and there was only one post quietly lying there.

It was a picture of the gate of S University.

S University is Chang Zhi's alma mater, located in the neighboring city of G, a three or four hour drive from here.

Chang Zhi went back with Deng Jiadai once last year, after all, they had been in and out of there for more than three years.

It seems that this person is from the same school as her, so... who is he? Almost all the classmates she knows have added him as a friend?

[05xm25]: [Picture] Alma mater. The past cannot be changed, but the future can still be pursued.

There were actually five or six likes, and Chang Zhi was shocked.

Looking carefully, many of them were from her college classmates, and two of them were two girls from the photography department that she knew before.

There were also two comments.

[Huang Jiayi]: How can you still have time to go back to school when you are so busy?

[Liu Yiyi]: Haha, senior's new play is so popular~ It's been flooded with comments.

Know someone from the photography department...

Filming.

Chang Zhi's heart tightened, and an incredible idea appeared in her mind, which was what she didn't want to believe the most.

[05xm25]: Tangtang.

...Chang Zhi, Tang Zhi, fans usually call her Tangtang or Tang Jie, only a few girls think that calling her Tangtang is cute.

But Tangtang is also her nickname.

There is only one male who calls her that, and that is...

Meng Xi.

Chang Zhi grabbed the pillow in her arms, and her five green fingers made a shallow dent in the pillow because of the force.

Happy and sad, troubled and complicated feelings rose along with the feeling of her heart being squeezed, and Chang Zhi took a deep breath.

After a while, the chat interface jumped, and another row of words appeared in an instant.

[05xm25]: Tangtang... I am Meng Xi.

Ah, yes, Meng Xi.

xm, mx Meng Xi, 0525, the day of debut.

What label should she give him? Handsome guy? Big star? Husband that countless fans are shouting for? Male god? The photography department of the s world? Or... the ex?

[Tang Zhi]: Where did you get the WeChat? I didn't ask Deng Jiadai to give it to you, did I?

[05xm25]: She didn't give it to me... I can't tell you.

[05xm25]: I was too busy some time ago, and I'm only free now.

Chang Zhi held her phone, squatted beside the sofa, and let out a long breath, feeling annoyed.

[Tang Zhi]: What does it have to do with me whether you are busy or not? What do you mean you come to me when you are free? What do you think of me?

Her words were full of hostility, like a cat whose tail was stepped on, fiercely showing its sharp claws.

That's right, Meng Xi didn't think of her as anything, and didn't care about her feelings at all.

[05xm25]: I didn't...

[05xm25]: Tangtang, I can explain the previous incident, I really... have my reasons.

[05xm25]: It's hard to explain here, I want to see you.

Chang Zhi's heart moved, but she frowned again.

[Tang Zhi]: What the hell, do you think I'm stupid? You think you can fool me once, can you fool me a second time?

[Tang Zhi]: You disappeared before without any explanation, and now you come back to say, oh, I had my reasons, brother, look, it's been a few years now,

[Tang Zhi]: I had so many opportunities to explain before, but you didn't show up once, now, I'm not interested in listening.

[Tang Zhi]: You just be a big star, you go your way and I go mine, I'm an ordinary person and don't want to have anything to do with you, ok?

Chang Zhi put up all her defenses, not wanting to show any hypocrisy to Meng Xi.

[05xm25]: ...Tangtang, calm down, I admit that I chased you because of a bet with others at the beginning, but later, I was really sincere.

[Tang Zhi]: ...Do you think it makes sense to say this?

[Tang Zhi]: Live your life well.

After sending this message, Chang Zhi clicked on the business card without hesitation and blocked Meng Xi.

The avatar and chat interface disappeared along with this person, and Chang Zhi was a little dazed.

Ah, it's gone.

Just like that, it's gone again.

To be honest, as long as they are not cheating and coming out, no one can be calm when facing their ex. Most of those who say they have no feelings are pretending to be calm and self-hypnotizing. As they talked, it became a complicated mood.

It has nothing to do with love or resentment. I just feel that in the past, this person has accompanied you in laughter and joy, and accompanied you in sadness and sadness, but in the end they were separated, and I can only sigh.

And Meng Xi is Chang Zhi's first love, and it is also the past she wants to forget.

Chang Zhi was with Meng Xi in her sophomore year. As her first love, Meng Xi almost satisfied all her vanity as a girl.

He is handsome, has a good personality, has a little money at home, is smart and good at studying, and has a lot of life skills.

Chang Zhi was low-key and almost transparent in college. She often stayed with Deng Jiadai, who knew everything about her.

Many girls around Chang Zhi liked Meng Xi, but Meng Xi only pursued her, which surprised many people.

When she was pursued and when they were together, he would bring her breakfast downstairs at 7:30 every morning, and then they would go for a morning run together. There were some small surprises and romances from time to time. They left their footprints in S University, G City, and so many places.

From the initial affection to the fall, it was actually very simple, just because of this meticulous care.

Meng Xi was a veteran in the love field, and Chang Zhi, who had never been in love before adulthood, was simply powerless.

Sometimes Chang Zhi wondered, if she hadn't heard what Meng Xi's friends said, what would she be like now?

Chang Zhi had great endurance. She could endure almost anything and had survived many things. However, she could not endure the deception of the person she loved, the fact that the perfect relationship she thought she was in was actually planned, the fact that it was a gamble, and the fact that she became the object of the boys' bragging to their friends.

How did she bother them? What was so good about her that she deserved others' calculations?

And all this happened just when she was in the most pain.

Her only close relative also passed away. After knowing the whole story of how he cheated on her, he left without saying goodbye under her crazy bombardment, and she was finally alone in the world.

She was busy with her aunt's funeral, the first seven days, the burial, all hosted by her alone.

But he didn't show up like this. How could a living person disappear out of thin air?

Chang Zhi finally sent a message to Meng Xi to break up and never see each other again, but he didn't reply to her.

Chang Zhi blocked him, moved out of school, and changed her WeChat number.

It was not a peaceful breakup, but a unilateral breakup on her part.

But why? If she left, she left. If she became famous, she became famous. If she didn't explain, she would disappear. Isn't that a default? Why did she start to want to see her and contact her again? She couldn't find the person in the world at first, but now she was looking for her all over the world.

You see, as soon as he appeared, her most painful memories were forcibly pulled out from the deepest drawer of her memory, bit by bit, poking her heart.

Chang Zhi's hand holding the phone loosened weakly, and the phone rolled from the sofa to the carpet along the pillow, making a soft sound.

Chang Zhi raised her head and leaned on the back of the sofa. The midday sun shone into the living room from the window, dazzling. She raised her hand to cover her eyes with the back of her hand.

She had seen the evil darkness in the world with cold eyes, watched the adults tear their faces and red eyes for the sake of interests, and she didn't know how to cherish it. She was rescued but complained about the world, went hysterical and crazy, and was finally defeated and faced the reality helplessly. In the end, the warmth she finally poked her head out of her shell and touched was also fake.

Chang Zhi cherishes the time like this too much.

Stable, regular, guarding a milk tea shop, dancing the dance she has loved for so many years. She doesn't want anyone to destroy such a life.

No one can do it.

Wednesday is the day Chang Zhi agreed with Anan and Sister Qiao for rehearsal.

A new day, Chang Zhi put on her makeup, and took the car to Sister Qiao's house.

In the morning, there were not many people on the road. It was a weekday, and Chang Zhi had a smooth journey after going to work.

Anan asked her where she was on WeChat, and Chang Zhi asked her to wait for her at the current station and go together.

Chang Zhi got off the car and saw Anan at a glance.

There was no way, Anan was too conspicuous. She was 158 cm tall, with a baseball cap turned upside down, and a lot of bags around her. She squatted next to the bus stop and lowered her head to play with her mobile phone.

Small but cute, she looks tender and cute, like a little doll.

Chang Zhi's mischievous heart followed, she quietly went around the back of the bus stop, stood behind Anan for a while, saw her serious and focused look, smiled and patted her on the back.

"Fuck!" The originally soft and tender voice suddenly screamed out and became sharp. Anan turned around and saw Chang Zhi standing beside her, smiling maliciously.

"Are you childish?" Anan stood up and patted her clothes, with an accusing look on her face, "You scared me to death."

Chang Zhi laughed and pointed at the black travel bag and asked, "What did you bring? It's such a big bag, people who don't know would think you're going on a trip."

Anan picked up the bag from the ground: "The camera and your clothes arrived yesterday. SF Express is really awesome."

"Oh, and my makeup bag," Anan looked up and pointed at her face, "I got up late today, I'm afraid of being late, so I'm going out without makeup. Wait for you to help me put on a domineering queen makeup. Don't refuse. I know you have good skills. I've seen you post videos before."

"... Queen makeup?" Chang Zhi stared at Anan's face, which still had a little baby fat, and said in a weird tone, "You don't usually go this way, do you?"

Anan put the bag on her back and said, "That's usually the case. Today, I'm the domineering me with ten-centimeter high heels."

Chang Zhi: "Did you really bring it?"

Anan: "Otherwise, I'm not kidding. Hehehe, I worked very hard to make the formation highly harmonious."

Chang Zhi couldn't help but raise her hand to touch Anan's head, and had the illusion that her daughter had grown up: "Thank you for your hard work."

Anan hugged her head and dodged: "...Ahhh, I've told you so many times not to touch my head. I'm an adult!"

The two of them went to Sister Qiao's house. Sister Qiao opened the security door downstairs for them. It was the eighth floor. There were only stairs in the old residential building. Chang Zhi saw that Anan was about to die after climbing two floors with the bag on her back. After all, Anan had carried it all the way. Chang Zhi took the backpack on her own initiative. As soon as she took it over, she almost couldn't hold it with one hand, and her arm fell down.

Heavy, this bag is really heavy.

Chang Zhi looked at Anan's small arms and legs. How did she have the courage to carry such a heavy backpack on the road? ? ?

Anan, who had thrown off her backpack, looked relieved and said to her with a smile: "Come on, Tangtang, there's still six floors to go, it'll be quick."

"Oh, by the way, don't fall, there's a new SLR camera I bought with all my hard work inside, love you."

Chang Zhi: "................."

Finally, they 'dragged' the backpack to the eighth floor. The two of them pressed the doorbell and stood there panting. Sister Qiao heard the doorbell and opened the door immediately.

"Sister, your house is really too high." Anan's eyes were filled with tears when she saw Sister Qiao.

Chang Zhi didn't say anything, took the bag in, and was too tired to talk.

I was full of fighting spirit and lost half of my energy just by climbing the stairs. It was so painful.

Sister Qiao is 26 years old this year, her id is Qiao Huan, and she is one year older than Chang Zhi, so Chang Zhi and Anan call her "sister"

Sister Qiao's house is well decorated, with a log style and exquisite furniture, which is almost Chang Zhi's dream home.

"Come, come and try on the clothes. It's very sunny today. I washed them yesterday and touched them on the balcony this morning. They are dry." Anan sat on the sofa unceremoniously, holding her backpack, unzipped it, and took out four pieces of clothes.

Sister Qiao sat next to Anan, touched the clothes, and said, "The quality is quite good."

Anan looked proud: "That's right, after all, I have been shopping on Taobao for many years, and I can tell which store is cheap at a glance."

Chang Zhi: "I will just watch you perform quietly, please start."

Chang Zhi took her two sets of clothes into a room to change, but she was a little nervous when she came out.

Chang Zhi stood in front of Anan and Sister Qiao, pulled the hem of the clothes, and asked hesitantly: "... Anan, is this dress you bought... too short?"

The top is red, white and black, with beautiful bell sleeves. Chang Zhi can imagine how beautiful it will be when she touches it, but this waist.

...It's too exposed, the breasts are almost exposed.

A-nan stood up and looked Chang Zhi up and down, shaking her head: "No, it suits you very well, your breasts and legs are long and curvy, and your waist is perfect."

Sister Qiao covered her mouth and laughed: "I don't like to wear clothes that expose my waist, but fortunately this set of pants and T-shirt covers it tightly."

Chang Zhi: "......................."

A-nan glared at Sister Qiao: "So your good figure is wasted. To be honest, in order to wear this set of clothes, you may not believe it, I stuffed two breast pads into my bra today." A-nan pointed at her clothes and said.

After a pause, she added: "But I don't know if it's because of the size of the underwear that I feel crowded..."

Chang Zhi: "..."

Sister Qiao: "..."

I am really convinced.

A-nan set up the camera position, then turned back and said to the two: "First, line up the formation, according to the four people, and Tangtang will dance the more parts alone later, and then find someone to cut it in and it will be perfect."

Chang Zhi was a little confused:"What's the method?"

Anan: "Anyway, this is what I think. You two in different positions will dance with us, and then dance separately. At the end, we will edit and find someone with good skills to cut out your separate parts and copy them into the video."

Sister Qiao nodded: "I think it's okay... I'll play the song first?"

Anan squatted down to put on her high heels, waving one hand: "Wait, get me some tape, I need to stick my 10-centimeter pillar tightly, otherwise, if my foot twists, what should I do if it breaks."

"...Take it easy." Chang Zhi reminded, "Wrap a few more layers... Oh, what are you doing, like this."

Chang Zhi squatted down, took the film to help Anan stick the heels and shoes together again, stood up and stepped back a few steps, nodded: "It's not very obvious."

Sister Qiao watched from the side, and then said: "Can we start now?"

Anan made a heart shape to Sister Qiao coquettishly.

The music started, 4 walls has a somewhat dreamy style, with soft and capable movements, and many small details on the hands.

It was the first rehearsal for the three of them. After all, their tacit understanding was average. They changed formations several times and couldn't keep up, so they had to start over.

Repeating the dance is actually quite boring, no matter how much you like it... Have you ever danced radio gymnastics for a whole day?

Chang Zhi was under a lot of pressure because she had to remember two kinds of movements.

This busyness lasted the whole afternoon until it got dark.

The three of them watched the video together, and then saw that it was getting dark, so they discussed going out to eat something together, and having a spicy hot pot in the evening. Anan finally handed the recorded video to Chang Zhi.

Anan had a serious face, as if she was entrusted with an important task: "Your post-production is much better than our own editing."

Chang Zhi was under a lot of pressure: "Okay, I'll send it to him in the next two days."

Anan stretched her arms and lazily, and sighed: "Ah, it's easy and efficient to work with you guys. It was done in a short time. Tangtang, let's cooperate often in the future."

She agreed casually, and Chang Zhi said goodbye to the two at the intersection and went home.

When Deng Jiadai came back from a two-week business trip, Chang Zhi went to the airport to pick her up.

As soon as Deng Jiadai saw Chang Zhi, she hugged her and even let go of her suitcase. Chang Zhi staggered in her hug and felt helpless.

Looking at Deng Jiadai who looked happy, Chang Zhi helped her pull the suitcase and said, "You don't want your boyfriend to pick you up, but I want you to pick you up. What's wrong with you?"

"Because I love you more," Deng Jiadai said cheerfully, "So the first thing I want to do when I get home is to see you."

Chang Zhi sneered at Deng Jiadai's words, and she snorted, "Forget it, the first person you see when you get home is your dear boyfriend, and I am at best the first acquaintance you see when you get off the plane. I don't know who you are, but when you value love over friendship, you are absolutely... love! Countless absolutelys are omitted here!"

After listening, Deng Jiadai suddenly looked into the distance and said with a complicated expression, "If you had three legs, I could also..."

"Shut up," Chang Zhi said, "Why are there so many dramas? The Central Academy of Drama finally gave you an admission letter?"

Deng Jiadai laughed obscenely: "No, no, no, no, I graduated from a driver's college. An experienced driver feels uncomfortable if he doesn't drive for a day. Today is not the right time. I will take you to the bottom of Akina Mountain to taste the freshness first, and then take you to the top of the mountain to see all the mountains."

"I'm bothering you, go away." Chang Zhi looked disgusted.

Deng Jiadai didn't care and took Chang Zhi's hand: "Okay, no more jokes, let's not talk about anything else, I have a lot of questions to ask you?"

"What do you want to ask me?" Chang Zhi glanced at her.

Deng Jiadai smiled and pulled Chang Zhi into the car: "Let's find a place to sit and talk."

Deng Jiadai took Chang Zhi to her own milk tea shop, and Chang Zhi was speechless.

Chang Zhi: "I thought you were going to take me to some new and interesting place, but you ended up taking me to your own store?"

Deng Jiadai dragged her luggage and found a seat in the corner, and said with a smile: "Boss Chang, please treat me."

"Shame on you," Chang Zhi said, "What do you want to drink?"

Deng Jiadai: "The most expensive thing... fruit tea?"

"Okay, okay."

When she came back, she brought two cups of milk tea and handed the fruit tea to Deng Jiadai, and Chang Zhi sat down opposite Deng Jiadai.

Deng Jiadai took a sip, moistened her throat, and began to ask: "What's going on between you and Yanzhi?"

"Yanzhi?" Chang Zhi inserted the straw into the cup. "What's going on?"

Deng Jiadai sat up straight: "Tsk, don't play dumb. Last time, I was a ghost and played games with you. You actually used the Li Yuanfang I taught you to lead other men..."

"I saw your Weibo. The latest one was a heart. Why did you put a comma after it? Tsk, tsk, tsk..." Deng Jiadai shook her head. "You may not believe it, but I smell the sour smell of love."

The sour smell of love... Chang Zhi's heart skipped a beat.

She stirred the milk tea with a straw, "Then you may have smelled it wrong. Have you been quite idle recently?"

Deng Jiadai: "Why?"

Chang Zhi: "Gossiping is a disease. You need to take time to treat it. By the way, there is something wrong with your nose. There is only the smell of milk tea in the air. Where does the sour smell come from?"

Deng Jiadai: "..."

Chang Zhi: "There is nothing between Yanzhi and me. We are just friends."

Deng Jiadai was a little disappointed: "Oh, okay, Yanzhi has a nice voice and sounds like he won't be bad... I... thought you finally got it. But online dating is not good either. It's too unreal." Seeing Chang Zhi avoiding the topic, Deng Jiadai stopped talking about it and changed the subject.

"Liu Yunyun's wedding is next Saturday. She is short of a bridesmaid. Are you going?"

Liu Yunyun? Chang Zhi was stunned for a moment, and her brain searched, and she remembered that this was a classmate.

Deng Jiadai has a pretty good relationship with her, while Chang Zhi and Liu Yunyun are just good friends, but not particularly good friends.

Chang Zhi knew that Liu Yunyun was going to hold a wedding. She posted her marriage certificate and invitations a month ago.

Chang Zhi said, "Why are you asking me? She hasn't told me yet."

"She just told me last night. It's still a suggestion, but you must attend the wedding, right?" Deng Jiadai said.

Chang Zhi glanced at Deng Jiadai and asked, "Do you want to be a bridesmaid?"

"Yes." Deng Jiadai nodded, "Do you want to think about it?"

"Is it too hasty..." Chang Zhi asked.

"Wait a minute, I'll ask her," Deng Jiadai looked up after a while, "It's not too hasty, it's mainly because of Liu Yunyun's personality, you know, she's a bit arrogant and proud."

"...Then why did you agree?" Chang Zhi asked Deng Jiadai.

"Ahem," Deng Jiadai coughed lightly, a little embarrassed, "She married the boss of a film and television company... you know."

Chang Zhi: "................."

Well, she knew that this guy... what should she say.

"Hey, come on, let's go together." Deng Jiadai simply encouraged Chang Zhi in her ear, "I guess there will be stars coming, it would be great to ask for an autograph or something."

"I don't chase stars."

Chang Zhi didn't bother to pay attention to her, she lowered her head and chatted with Liu Yunyun.

Liu Yunyun was very enthusiastic and seemed to be sincere. Chang Zhi thought that she would just be a bridesmaid for once, that was all.

Finally, she agreed to Liu Yunyun. When she looked up, she heard Deng Jiadai say, "Speaking of bridesmaids, I remember what we said before. When we get married, we should be bridesmaids for each other."

Chang Zhi thought of the previous agreement: "Yeah."

"Tangtang, you should find someone as soon as possible," Deng Jiadai finished the last sip of fruit tea, "You are only in love at the age of 25 this year. I think you are losing out."

Chang Zhi said evasively: "It's not that I want to lose out. I have to... wait for it."

Deng Jiadai was disappointed: "Then you have to go and look for it."

Chang Zhi shook her head: "...Who should I find?"

Deng Jiadai thought for a while and said, "How about I introduce you to a partner?"

...Ah? ? ?

After seeing Deng Jiadai off and returning home, Chang Zhi thought of the dance video. It was still early, only five in the afternoon, so Chang Zhi simply called Jiang Huai in private chat.

[Simple and hardworking Tang Zhi]: Are you free today? Can you help me edit a few videos?

[Jiang Huai]: ... I forgot to tell you that I'm on a business trip for the past two weeks and won't be back until next weekend. Are you in a hurry?

Jiang Huai is on a business trip? Then she... Chang Zhi has a headache.

[Simple and hardworking Tang Zhi]: The video will be posted this Sunday. If you're not free, I'll think about it and see if there's anyone else.

Chang Zhi supported her chin with one hand and scrolled through her friend list one by one.

One by one, either I'm not familiar with them or I can't do it.

Scrolling to the bottom group, she clicked on it, and Yan Zhi's avatar was lit.

Chang Zhi's mouse stopped, put her hand down, sat up straight and thought seriously.

Yan Zhi...

Is Yan Zhi a ghost animal video maker?

The ghost video was edited, right?

Is it possible... Chang Zhi's hand hovered over the keyboard, hesitated for a moment, and then pressed the key.

[Simple and hardworking Tang Zhi]: Are you there?

[Yan Zhi]: What's the matter? ?

[Simple and hardworking Tang Zhi]: Well, I... I just want to ask a question,

[Yan Zhi]: You said,

[Simple and hardworking Tang Zhi]: Are you free recently... Help me edit a video, okay?

Chang Zhi sent a few screenshots and explained.

[Simple and hardworking Tang Zhi]: Well, it's like this, my family is on a business trip, so I'm not free for the time being, but this is still a bit urgent, you know...

[Simple and hardworking Tang Zhi]: I basically don't know anyone who can do post-production, editing, you, if you don't want to...

Chang Zhi held a faint expectation, but the words she typed became more and more timid.

[Yan Zhi]: ...Okay, send the file.

So much so that Chang Zhi didn't react after Yan Zhi agreed.

Eh... agreed? So easily? ?

In the other part, Wen Yanxing sat at the computer and agreed, thinking that he was also possessed by a ghost.

Recently, he also planned to release a new video. He had cut half of the video and was making the audio. Moreover, he planned to change the live broadcast platform recently and was in contact with the platform... With a lot of things on hand, he actually agreed to help.

Wen Yanxing touched his face and thought about the song he sang the day before yesterday. He felt really strange.

Chang Zhi on the other side sent him a "thank you" and then sent the file. He clicked to receive the file. The network speed was very fast. In less than five minutes, all four files were received.

Wen Yanxing opened a video file casually and took a few glances.

There were three girls in the video, and he saw Tang Zhi at a glance.

Tang Zhi had her hair down, her skin was fair, her waist was slender, and when she turned around, the curve of her back was beautiful. She stood in a horse stance, twisted her waist, and spun around, smiling sweetly...

Wen Yanxing forcibly turned off the video.

He also turned off the chat interface and QQ with Chang Zhi.

He almost turned off the computer.

He rubbed his forehead and rested his elbows on the computer desk.

Crazy, he was actually... obsessed with watching dance videos? ?

Is it addictive?

Next to the keyboard, Hedgehog Erqiu rubbed his empty cup, moved his body and stood up to climb into the cup.

With a slight sound, Wen Yanxing looked at the teacup next to him and saw Erqiu with his two feet in the cup. Erqiu quickly fell down, and his hands climbed on the edge of the cup and looked at him innocently, as if saying -

What are you looking at? I'm just climbing a cup and I didn't do anything bad.

Wen Yanxing: "..."

Wen Yanxing felt that Erqiu even glared at him: What are you looking at? Haven't you seen a hedgehog that likes to climb a cup?

"I haven't done anything bad yet, so I don't need to use a cup to drink water?" Wen Yanxing picked up Erqiu from the teacup, stared at it and said, "You are also a worry."

Erqiu still looked innocent, but he kicked his legs and moved around to express his dissatisfaction with Wen Yanxing's casual grabbing it out of the cup.

It climbed for a long time! So aggrieved! Want to bite people!

After being convinced by this little guy, Wen Yanxing casually threw Erqiu back into the cup and made up his mind to buy a new cup. He was too lazy to watch Erqiu's satisfied look after entering the cup. Wen Yanxing sat in front of the computer, fidgeting, and couldn't help but open... that video again.

He moved the mouse to drag the progress bar to the place he just saw.

The music switched, and it just happened to be pulled, Chang Zhi turned around neatly and smiled at the camera.

Soft waist, slender legs

She danced really well, not as gentle as usual, but with a confident and shining look.

He only saw her among the three people.

When she changed her moves, she looked at the video and took the opportunity to make a heart shape with her hands.

Crossing her thumb and index finger, she seemed to be looking at him and smiling on the screen, with curved eyebrows and eyes.

Wen Yanxing was stunned for a moment, and pursed his thin lips.

The music was playing loudly, and Erqiu was still struggling in the cup.

In twenty minutes, Wen Yanxing had watched all four videos unknowingly, and even wanted to watch all the videos that Chang Zhi had posted before.

...? ? ? ? !

He turned off the video, leaned on the computer chair, looked up at the ceiling, and felt incredible.

He felt like he was possessed by a demon.

How long had he known Tang Zhi?

Even if he happened to know Chang Zhi in real life, but...

Although he might watch the video more than a dozen times in order to edit it, he would not want to... watch all the previous ones, right?

His mind was empty until the two balls rolled themselves into a ball and rolled onto his palm, making his palm itch.

At one o'clock in the middle of the night, Chang Zhi woke up from a dream, thinking it was daybreak. She habitually touched her phone first. In the dark, the phone screen glowed.

One o'clock in the morning.

Chang Zhi half-closed her eyes, opened WeChat first and then Weibo, and suddenly found a reminder that someone she followed had updated Weibo.

Who posted on Weibo so late...

[Yanzhi v]: Received a file, it's poisonous, sleepy, confused.

[One minute ago] From Web Weibo.

Chang Zhi: "........................???" Received what file?

Wait, wait, it can't be...

Chang Zhi woke up all of a sudden, scared.

Author has What I want to say: Big! Thick! Long!

No rebuttals allowed! I won't listen to any rebuttals! Anyway, I am thick and long today!

I will irresponsibly translate Mr. Wen's Weibo-

"I received a file, it's poisonous. I'm so sleepy, addicted to it."

Chapter 19 I saw it wrong

Chang Zhi sat up and rubbed her eyes, fearing that she had seen it wrong... In the darkness, the dim light of the screen illuminated her face. After waking up, Chang Zhi found...

This is true.

It was really sent not long ago, she was not wrong.

Not long ago... Didn't she send four files to Yan Zhi this afternoon? Could it be that she was talking about her?

Chang Zhi thought uneasily: Could it be that Yan Zhi started editing her video so quickly, and the result was that she was frustrated? Oh my God, is her dance very frustrating? No way!

Thinking of this, Chang Zhi immediately clicked on to find the group that Yan Zhi was in. At 1:30 in the middle of the night, Yan Zhi's bright colorful avatar was particularly conspicuous among the gray avatars.

Chang Zhi's first reaction was-he was online as expected.

[Simple and hardworking Tang Zhi]:! You haven't slept so late?

[Yan Zhi]: ....

[Yan Zhi]: Why haven't you slept? ? ?

[Simple and hardworking Tang Zhi]: I went to bed at ten o'clock, and I woke up after having a dream... Are you busy?

[Yan Zhi]: Hmm... count it?

[Simple and hardworking Tang Zhi]: Busy until so late...

[Yan Zhi]: Not really busy, hard to say.

[Simple and hardworking Tang Zhi]: Then I ask you to help with the editing, will you be very tired?

Sitting up straight was too tiring, Chang Zhi leaned back, and her back hit the headboard, making a heavy sound in the night. Chang Zhi felt pain, rubbed her back, sat up again, and completely got rid of the sleepiness.

[Yan Zhi]: No, it's okay.

[Simple and hardworking Tang Zhi]: Oh, then... then did you watch the video I posted in the evening?

[Yan Zhi]: . . . .

A string of capitalized periods, Chang Zhi was devastated. Are you really talking about her? Forget it!

[Yan Zhi]: I saw it, all four of them saw it.

[Simple and hardworking Tang Zhi]: Am I...dancing in a way that is unbearable to watch?

[Simple and hardworking Tang Zhi]: You can comment on me! But you can't say anything about my friend, it feels weird. .

[Yan Zhi]: ...Where did I say that your dancing was unbearable to watch?

...Huh? Chang Zhi hooked up the pillow beside the bed with her toes, kicked it into her arms, and then stuffed it behind her back to lean against it, feeling comfortable, her body immediately relaxed, but her heart was startled by Yan Zhi's words.

[Simple and hardworking Tang Zhi]: Weibo, wait a minute, I'll take a screenshot...

[Simple and hardworking Tang Zhi]: [Picture] This, it's poisonous... Could it be that you are talking about the video I posted?

Wen Yanxing: ...

In front of the computer screen, Wen Yanxing looked at the video that was shrunk into a small window with a complicated look.

On the desktop was the post-production editing software, and he paused the several videos that were opened separately.

In the multi-window taskbar on the desktop, there were 'Tang Zhi's submission' and 'Tang Zhi's video'...

Erqiu didn't know why he was so excited in the middle of the night. He forced it into the cage, but it refused. It climbed up and down on the table and almost fell off the table several times.

Suddenly it was quiet, but it lay on the keyboard and pressed a string of garbled codes in the chat window, staring at the screen and squatting there.

Wen Yanxing forcibly picked it up and put it next to the keyboard. Seeing that it still wanted to climb, he pulled out the keyboard and put it on his knees. Anyway, the USB cable was very long, so he deleted the garbled codes on the chat interface one by one.

Erqiu looked aggrieved, squatting in front of the computer and looking up at the screen, leaning over and tapping the screen with his little hands, while looking back at him.

Wen Yanxing looked at Erqiu's little thorn with its back to him, and felt strange in his heart - was it looking at Chang Zhi?

It was late at night, and Wen Yanxing almost had an illusion, thinking that Erqiu wanted him to continue playing the video... After all, it had been quiet for a long time when he was watching just now.

Wen Yanxing stretched out his index finger to scratch its thorn and said, "... Do you want to see this young lady dance?"

Erqiu turned around and hugged Wen Yanxing's fingers with her short hands, her white and tender belly facing him, looking up at him eagerly, as if she was saying "yes" in a coquettish way.

Wen Yanxing chuckled and scratched Erqiu's belly with his other hand.

Erqiu twisted his body, called twice, looked up at him eagerly, and he couldn't help laughing at this pitiful little look.

But the next moment, Wen Yanxing put away his smile and said seriously: "I won't give it to you."

Erqiu: "..........."? ? ? ?

Erqiu seemed to understand, and instantly retracted his short hands, climbed down and pointed his butt at Wen Yanxing, completely ignoring him.

Forget it! Trashy shit shoveler.

On the other side, Chang Zhi saw that Yan Zhi hadn't replied to her for a long time, she whispered "Oh", threw the phone away, and huddled in the quilt just to be quiet.

Is she sick? She cares so much about Yan Zhi's comments? No no no no, she doesn't even care about the negative comments from black fans.

But Chang Zhi couldn't help but stick her head out to touch the phone to see if Yan Zhi had replied to her.

...He actually replied! Chang Zhi stared at the three message prompts, feeling nervous, she swallowed her saliva, and finally clicked in.

Panic.

[Yan Zhi]: Very good dance.

[Yan Zhi]: Very good, great, very... fairy.

[Yan Zhi]: The best among the three.

Chang Zhi didn't know why, but the corners of her lips couldn't help but want to rise. She pulled the corners of her mouth down with her index finger, but she couldn't control it... Forget it!

She rolled around with the quilt in her arms, and then she realized what was happening and let go of her hands and covered her face.

Chang Zhi let go of her hands for a long time, looking at the dark sky, thinking: What is she doing? It's not like she hasn't been praised before. So what?

In fact, Chang Zhi knew how she danced.

But when Yan Zhi praised her, she didn't know why she wanted to laugh.

She found an emoticon from the emoji library on her phone and sent it over.

[Simple and hardworking Tang Zhi]: (//▽//)

[Yan Zhi]: Is this shy?

Chang Zhi replied slowly,

[Simple and hardworking Tang Zhi]: Yes...

[Yan Zhi]: (≧▽≦)/

Chang Zhi in front of the screen said "Oh!" and stared at the screen, at a loss for a moment.

What kind of style and operation is this?

[Simple and hardworking Tang Zhi]: Learn from me, it's shameful to act cute!

[Yan Zhi]: It's not cute, it's expressing joy, just like you.

Chang Zhi threw her phone away and pulled the pillow to cover her face.

This person, this person...!

A lot of dirty talk...

There's nothing wrong with this, but for some reason, Chang Zhi just felt something was wrong.

She rubbed her face and typed again to change the subject.

[Simple and hardworking Tang Zhi]: It's almost two o'clock, aren't you going to sleep?

Wen Yanxing looked at the half-edited video at hand, and then looked at Erqiu who was drowsy because Wen Yanxing didn't click to play.

[Yan Zhi]: Sleep.

[Yan Zhi]: Go to bed early, good night.

[It is the simple and hardworking Tang Zhi]: You too, good night~

Wen Yanxing put the sleeping Erqiu back into its nest, drank a glass of water, and then sat back in front of the computer.

At four in the morning, he finished editing the video.

By the way, he uploaded several recent live broadcasts, then opened the chat window with Chang Zhi and sent the video.

Chang Zhi put her phone on the bedside table, arranged her pillow, and squatted in the quilt again.

She rubbed her face hard with the quilt. She obviously wanted to sleep, but for some reason her mood calmed down, but her mind was blank.

She tossed and turned several times, and finally fell asleep hugging the quilt.

In the early morning, she opened her eyes hazily and subconsciously touched her phone.

[Yanzhi sent you a file, do you want to receive it?]

What... Chang Zhi looked carefully, it was four in the morning.

What happened to the two o'clock we agreed to go to bed? Chang Zhi rubbed her eyes and flipped through the chat history in disbelief.

Well, Yan Zhi just said he would sleep, but didn't say when he would sleep

But staying up late to help her edit the video, Chang Zhi bit her lower lip.

[Simple and hardworking Tang Zhi]: Thank you, you didn't sleep so late... There's no need to work so hard. . .

Yan Zhi didn't reply to her, Chang Zhi thought he should be catching up on sleep, right?

After washing up, Chang Zhi received the file on the computer.

Clicking it to see, Yan Zhi edited her alone and her dancing together, and the timing of the mix-in was not at all inconsistent.

She shared the file with Anan and Sister Qiao, and Anan typed a row of '6666' on the screen

[Anan]: Give me your post-production, I want to hook up, the guy who edited the video so well, so handsome, I want to flirt

Hook up... hook up? Want to flirt?

[Tang Zhi]: This is not edited by my post-production, I found someone else

[Anan]: It's okay, it doesn't affect me, hahahaha

Chang Zhi thought, if I give you Yan Zhi's account, she will be finished.

[Tang Zhi]: I found it on Taobao.

[Anan]: ...

[Anan]: Master, I kneel to you, Taobao still has this? Post-production? It's expensive, right? It's a waste of money.

[Tang Zhi]: It's okay.

[Anan]: Here's a link.

Chang Zhi immediately opened Taobao, searched for a store that does post-production videos and sent it to An Nan.

They agreed on a time to post the video together, and Chang Zhi privately chatted with the deputy manager of the milk tea shop to deal with the market for seasonal drinks.

It took more than a week to plan, seasonal, as soon as possible.

The purchase contact was made, and the formula was also improved.

The next step is promotion.

Chang Zhi's "try" milk tea also has its own public account, but it is for old customers. For new customers who have never been, she usually starts with WeChat and Weibo.

In the Internet age, marketing is very important... Of course, this does not mean that her shop was hyped up. It was mainly a little publicity, plus word of mouth. After a long time, the location was in the downtown area, people came and went, and there were more and more repeat customers. Then it became completely stable.

It is not about stability that never changes, but stability in development.

Chang Zhi has always wanted to make a breakthrough. There are more and more Internet celebrity milk tea shops now, and she also wants to experience the feeling of having so much business in her shop that customers have to queue for an hour or two to drink.

The public account that Chang Zhi cooperates with most often is "One Day Multiple Meals". As far as Chang Zhi knows, the operator of this public account is a girl. She manages three public accounts, one for emotions, one for chicken soup, and one for food. She has many fans and a considerable income.

Why did Chang Zhi find her first? Mainly because she writes good reviews.

And they have also met.

Chang Zhi changed her small account to a special work account for milk tea shops.

[Atang]: Come to my store the day after tomorrow. New products are on the market. Let's promote them.

[Lin Xi]: What time?

[Atang]: Come whenever you are free.

Lin Xi agreed, and Chang Zhi went to find another girl with good writing skills.

Write soft articles.

Chang Zhi has known this girl for half a year. She wrote all the articles she posted on the official account.

[Atang]: My store has new products coming out. Can you write a soft article for me when you are free? The price is negotiable.

The other party replied immediately,

[Lu Zhiyao]: When do you want it? Is it still illustrated like before? =v=

[Atang]: Yes, illustrated. I will send you a few pictures this afternoon. Please write it for me before the day after tomorrow.

[Lu Zhiyao]: Okay, I will prepare it well~

[Atang]: Do me another favor and think of a name. Cherry fruit tea. I have been thinking for a long time but I don't know what to call it.

[Lu Zhiyao]: OK~ Remember to send me the pictures, so I can get inspiration after seeing them

[Atang]: OK, I'll pack up and go to the store, I'll send it to you in an hour.

In the afternoon, Wen Luying received Chang Zhi's pictures and a simple description, and spent more than an hour to write a beautiful soft article, but the name...

Cherry tea, cherry tea, peach tea are all overused, and it's easy to confuse them with drinks with cherry blossoms and peaches.

Wen Luying was almost crazy, she almost got stuck thinking about it.

At nine o'clock in the evening, she privately chatted with her brother.

[Lu Zhiyao]: Brother, you read more books than me, can you help me think of a name?

[ynzwyx7]: ...?

Chapter 20 I can't afford to support myself

[Lu Zhiyao]: The name of the milk tea, a customer, well, you know I can't support myself by writing articles! !

[ynzwyx7]: Since you want to support yourself, you should think about it yourself, instead of asking me for help.

[Lu Zhiyao]: I used to think about it myself, and I still have to write a soft article with pictures and texts of one or two thousand words. Today, oh, brother, please help me, help me think about it. Dear brother! !

[ynzwyx7]: ...Then you tell me.

[Lu Zhiyao]: Fruit tea, well, anyway, it's cherry juice with something added.

Cherry...?

Wen Yanxing was slightly stunned, and suddenly remembered the cup he drank in Changzhi's store some time ago.

Before he could think about whether there was any connection, he heard a snap, the sound of porcelain falling to the ground. Wen Yanxing frowned and looked over. Erqiu stood on the edge of the table and curled up into a ball.

On the ground, the white cup broke into pieces, and the residue flew to his feet.

Wen Yanxing: "..."

He directly grabbed Erqiu, who curled up into a ball because he knew he had made a mistake. His palms itched and pricked, and he carried Erqiu to the corner.

Erqiu stuck his head out against the wall.

Wen Yanxing said righteously: "Erqiu, you made a mistake, stand here as punishment."

Erqiu retracted his head and didn't want to listen.

Wen Yanxing: "Didn't I tell you last night? I just bought a cup..."

Erqiu turned his back aggrievedly and buried his head in the corner.

Wen Yanxing glanced at it, took a broom to sweep up the pieces, and the sound of the pieces falling into the trash can made him think about the possibility of buying another cup.

After packing up, Wen Yanxing sat back on the sofa and took out his phone to reply to Wen Luying.

[ynzwyx7]: I'll tell you after lunch.

[Lu Zhiyao]: You still have an hour.

[ynzwyx7]: After lunch, it's not the time to eat. I really doubt whether you will be deceived in the future.

[Lu Zhiyao]: ...Are you sure you are my brother? ?

[ynzwyx7]: I don't know, if your parents didn't take you by mistake.

[ynzwyx7]: But our intelligence is indeed different.

[Lu Zhiyao]: qaq you, goodbye!

At three o'clock in the afternoon, Lin Xi came to the store.

Lin Xi is her online name. When we first met, she said her real name was Ning Nanxi.

Ning Nanxi in person is a very petite girl with long straight black hair, a white and clean face, and a pair of large-framed glasses. She sits there quietly, like an SD doll.

She sat in the corner of the store holding her iPad, and Chang Zhi personally made a cup of cherry fruit tea whose name had not yet been decided.

After the finished product was made, she also took the new cherry cakes that the store had released in the past two days.

Ning Nanxi's voice was gentle, and it floated into her heart like spring breeze and drizzle. Seeing Chang Zhi holding the plate and putting the food in front of her, she looked up at Chang Zhi and said, "Thank you."

Chang Zhi sat down opposite her, watched Ning Nanxi open the lid, and tilted her head slightly to take a sip.

"How is it?" Chang Zhi asked.

Ning Nanxi looked up, recalled the taste, and said: "Sweet, not too greasy, it's okay."

Chang Zhi smiled: "Do you think it will sell well?"

Ning Nanxi thought about it, reached out and stroked her glasses, and seriously suggested: "Cherries are small and cute, and taste sweet and sour. Girls should like it very much. If you put a whole cherry on the milk cap inside, people who are loyal to appearance will also buy it.

"Well," Chang Zhi nodded, pointed to the dessert and said, "So we also launched cherry cakes at the same time as the afternoon tea series, with discounts in the early stage to attract customers."

"That's good," Ning Nanxi smiled, then lowered her head, put the iPad aside, clicked on a note and started typing.

Chang Zhi sat opposite her, lowered her head to look at her phone, and received the name sent by Lu Zhiyao.

—— Full Cup of Lizi.

Chang Zhi stared at these four words, thinking seriously but to no avail, so she asked Ning Nanxi: "What do you think of the name Full Cup of Lizi? "

Ning Nanxi listened to the movement of her fingers, raised her head and tilted it, saying: "Cherry? Cherry? Cherry is cherry, a full cup... From a marketing perspective, it gives people a feeling of being very generous, much better than cherry tea or something like that. ”

Chang Zhi thought, yes, it is better than those simple and crude names.

And this way. Some people who don't understand it may feel curious and ask, or just buy it directly.

Ning Nanxi stayed in the store until five o'clock. After Chang Zhi sent her away, she thought that there was no food at home, so she simply ordered a nearby spicy hot pot takeaway with the store clerk Xiao Dong, and she would treat them.

After eating, it was already seven o'clock. Chang Zhi left the store. It was already dark, and the street lights were on. Chang Zhi originally wanted to go home directly, but she didn't want to.

She stood at the door of the store and thought for a while, and decided to turn a corner to the supermarket.

Buy vegetables for tomorrow's lunch, and by the way... sanitary napkins.

There is no way. I counted on my fingers that the day is coming. Girls have to go to the supermarket to replenish their stocks every month to prevent the embarrassment of not being able to leave the door when it suddenly comes——

It's not that you can't buy it online, but Chang Zhi bought it online last time... Chang Zhi didn't know if it was a psychological effect or something, she always felt something was wrong after using it, and then she threw it away and ran to the supermarket to buy it again.

The supermarket is quite close to here. On weekdays, there are not many people at night. Chang Zhi went down to the underground supermarket on the first floor of the mall.

Daily necessities such as sanitary napkins, toothpaste, shower gel, and shampoo are available as soon as you enter the door. Chang Zhi pushed the small blue cart, passed the shampoo and shower gel area, and went straight to the sanitary napkin area.

After picking a certain brand of 420 giant long and daily necessities, Chang Zhi pushed the cart and walked to the toothpaste area.

In front of the shelf in the toothpaste area, Wen Yanxing, wearing a white T-shirt, casual pants and flip-flops, stood there, looking up and down, and the supermarket employee next to him was constantly recommending-

"Sir, we have an event now. Buy a white toothpaste and get a slightly smaller one..."

"Or you can take a look at this, Zhuxian, a new product of green tea, it sells very well..."

"Ailuge is also OK, it's also an old brand..."

This is what Chang Zhi saw when she pushed the cart to this point.

The tall man was annoyed by the chattering of the mall attendant, and his eyes wandered on the shelves, hesitating.

Is this... Wen Yanxing?

Chang Zhi paused.

Wen Yanxing lowered his head and politely asked the saleswoman: "Auntie, which ones did you recommend just now?"

The auntie reacted and immediately took them down one by one, pointing and saying: "This is Bai Ren, this is Zhu Xian, oh... and Ai Lu Jie."

"I want all three. "Wen Yanxing said.

The aunt was stunned for a moment, as if she couldn't believe it, and then nodded: "Okay, Alujie is giving away cups at an event now, I'll get you one..."

Wen Yanxing didn't expect to get a cup for buying toothpaste, so he thought he didn't need to buy a cup.

Chang Zhi saw the aunt take a few steps and bring back a Hallo Kitty cup, which was pink and very girly.

Wen Yanxing: "..........."

The aunt smiled awkwardly: "I'm sorry, the more yang cups have been given away, and this is the only one left... Oh, the cup can also be used. If it doesn't work, you can go back and give it to your girlfriend or something. It's a waste not to take it, right?"

What the aunt said makes sense...

Wen Yanxing took the cup and put it in the shopping cart. He looked up and saw Chang Zhi coming from the other side with a shopping cart.

Wen Yanxing was stunned and said: "What a coincidence, you are also in the supermarket. "

Chang Zhi didn't dare to disturb him just now, and now she came to say hello. She smiled: "Yes, there is no food at home... Are you here to buy toothpaste?" Her eyes were on his shopping cart, "Why did you buy so many toothpastes?"

Wen Yanxing coughed lightly and explained: "I studied abroad before, and I didn't know what toothpaste to use when I came back, so I tried all of them."

So that's how it is, no wonder you bought so much.

Chang Zhi made a cold joke: "I almost thought you were eating toothpaste."

Wen Yanxing: "..." This girl's cold jokes are not ordinary.

Wen Yanxing's eyes swept to the Hallo Kitty cup that the saleswoman had just given him, and took it out and suggested: "Do you like Hallo Kitty?"

"Halle Kitty?" Chang Zhi was stunned, and saw the cup in Wen Yanxing's hand, and said, "It's okay."

"I'll give this to you, anyway I don't need it. "Wen Yanxing said, "It will only gather dust if I keep it, so I might as well give it to you and make the best use of it."

Chang Zhi was at a loss and said "ah" blankly.

Wen Yanxing really thought so. He was about to hand it to Chang Zhi, but when he looked down, he saw Chang Zhi's shopping cart.

There was still a lot of space in the shopping cart, and only four things were placed in it. Wen Yanxing could see everything at a glance.

... Four packs of sanitary napkins.

Wen Yanxing's ears instantly turned red.

Chapter 21 Ears turn red

Why do some people's ears turn red?

It's nothing more than embarrassment, nervousness, and shyness.

Wen Yanxing felt his ears were hot, but he couldn't tell why.

He had lived for so many years, and had seen Chinese beauties, foreign girls, natural and additive-free products, and artificial products made according to molds... but he had never felt this strange.

On the other side, Chang Zhi fell into deep thought.

If you run into someone you know in the supermarket, do you go shopping with him separately, or choose to go shopping together?

One more thing... If that person is your next-door neighbor, what if you two go home together?

One last thing... He got a promotional item, but he doesn't need it himself, and he enthusiastically wants to give it to you. Your state is in the middle of wanting and not wanting... Should I take this cup or not?

Chang Zhi was caught up in this complicated question, and there was a struggle in her mind.

Reject, or agree?

Wen Yanxing glanced at Chang Zhi and added, "I'm here to buy a cup, too," Wen Yanxing said, "The cup was broken by my pet. I don't have a good aesthetic sense... Can you help me pick a nice one?"

Pet? Chang Zhi immediately thought of the hedgehog with a strange name.

For some reason, Chang Zhi said, "Okay then."

Wen Yanxing put the cup in Chang Zhi's shopping cart, carefully trying to avoid touching it, but the back of his hand still rubbed against a pack.

Wen Yanxing: "..."

Chang Zhi: "..."

Chang Zhi now wanted to go back to the past in a time machine.

It was so embarrassing. They were just neighbors next door. Although they were handsome, they didn't have any special relationship. They were of the opposite sex. Although they had a good impression of each other, it was not a special impression. But they were bumped into buying sanitary napkins.

Chang Zhi felt that it was useless for her to forcefully change the subject.

The two of them ignored the matter in tacit understanding. Wen Yanxing looked straight ahead, pretending not to see it, but in his heart he was thinking, there is a sister and a mother at home, two women, he has seen the packaging bags before, and he knows that women can bleed for seven days a month without dying, but the person he met was Chang Zhi...

He turned his head slightly, his eyes met the shelf with exquisite small boxes.

She glanced at Wen Yanxing secretly, and there was no expression on Wen Yanxing's face.

She looked at the shelf next to him again-

Her expression became like this: =�=! ?

Here I want to explain that the shelves in the daily toiletries area are arranged in an mn shape, and the toothpaste shelf is at the left corner of the m. Chang Zhi met Wen Yanxing here, so she went forward and saw the shelves with men's facial cleansers and electric toothbrushes, as well as-

Colorful small boxes.

Condoms.

They are actually placed in the daily toiletries area! Are condoms included in this range? When did this supermarket change its layout again? !

Six points crossed Chang Zhi's mind.

Her eyesight was 5.2, and she could see several famous brands at a glance.

Chang Zhi quickened her pace and walked forward, wanting to get out of here. Wen Yanxing behind her didn't know if he was particularly popular with passers-by and was liked by the sales aunt. First, he was recommended by the aunt selling toothpaste and bought three toothpastes, and then he was stopped by the aunt selling family planning products?

"You are so handsome, young man, do you have a girlfriend? There is an event here now, and it is rare for family planning products to have an event. I know that you young people don't like to get married too early, so you have to be careful. Be careful not to get pregnant-"

Wen Yanxing was stopped by the aunt with a sharp eye after just one look, and Chang Zhi, who agreed to Wen Yanxing's action, was also stopped.

When the aunt saw Chang Zhi who stopped with Wen Yanxing, she suddenly understood something: "Are you two boyfriend and girlfriend?"

Chang Zhi opened her mouth to deny it.

"Oh, look at this pretty little face. If it were me, I couldn't help it either," the aunt pointed to a famous brand on the shelf, "Young man, treat the girl well. This Durax is a new model that has been released recently. It's super thin and is really discounted at only..."

Wen Yanxing interrupted her with a cough: "Auntie, we don't need it..."

The aunt stopped, looked at them up and down, smiled for a while, and said:

"Okay, then I wish you... a baby soon?"

Chang Zhi fled the scene in a panic, and Wen Yanxing followed closely.

In the long aisle, the shelves on both sides were arranged in an orderly manner. There were not many people in the supermarket at night. The speakers played the latest popular singles. The sales aunties and ladies in work clothes were bored waiting for the next customer to stop.

Chang Zhi and Wen Yanxing pushed the small blue cart one after the other, passing by toilet paper, hangers and other sundries, and went to the place where thermos cups, bowls and cups were sold.

Chang Zhi pointed at that and turned to Wen Yanxing and said, "Do you want to go and see it?"

Wen Yanxing looked in the direction of her finger and nodded, "Yes."

The two walked in together, passed the area with thermos cups and lunch boxes, and stopped in front of the shelf with various cups.

"What kind do you like?" Chang Zhi looked up at Wen Yanxing who was staring at the shelf.

Black and white printed ones - these daily necessities now have a variety of styles. Thinking of the hedgehog at home who wants to do something as soon as he is released, Wen Yanxing said: "... resistant to falling?"

Chang Zhi saw the one with Doraemon printed on it in front of her at a glance, and Doraemon has always been her favorite. Chang Zhi couldn't help but reach out and take it down, raised it to Wen Yanxing, tilted her head slightly and looked at his face and said: "Is it a plastic cup? Like this?"

Wen Yanxing looked at the size that was obviously for children in Chang Zhi's hand and nodded: "Yes, a plastic cup, but... it should be a little bigger than this."

Chang Zhi then realized that the cup in her hand was for children. She felt embarrassed and quickly put it back, and asked: "What color do you like?"

"Anything is fine," Wen Yanxing glanced at the green cup at the bottom of the shelf and added, "Just don't be green."

Chang Zhi raised an eyebrow and asked: "Are you afraid of green? Do you have a girlfriend?"

"No," Wen Yanxing shook his head, thinking of the song "Forgiveness" he saw recently on Station B, with a full screen of green, "I just don't like green recently."

He reached out and took a pure black cup on the shelf and asked, "How about this one?"

"The black one is not good," Chang Zhi leaned over to look at the bottom of the cup and shook her head, saying, "You can't see if it's dirty inside, and it can't be washed clean."

"This one," she just finished speaking, relying on her height of 168 cm, she reached out and easily touched the top layer of the shelf. She held the transparent thickened plastic cup in her hand and said seriously, "This one is clearer to see, easy to wash, and looks good like a glass cup."

Wen Yanxing lowered his head slightly, watching her chattering seriously and carefully, and suddenly remembered his loving parents at home.

He seemed to hear the sound of his heart beating briskly in his chest, and suddenly felt that such a life, which he had never thought of before, was also pretty good.

Simple food, firewood, rice, oil and salt.

"What's wrong," Chang Zhi saw that Wen Yanxing did not respond, and looked at him in confusion.

"It's okay," Wen Yanxing came back to his senses, "Are you selling cups? You know so much."

"Are you praising me or criticizing me?" Chang Zhi asked.

"Praising you," Wen Yanxing took the plastic cup from her hand, bent down slightly and put it in the shopping cart, "I think you are very good, you know how to live, and you are doing well in your career, um, great."

Yeah, very good.

On the day when the full cup of cherries was launched, the official account soft article was also released at the same time.

With the help of the official account, a 7 yuan discount was organized for customers who came to the store with this article. Chang Zhi finally went from being a hands-off boss to having to join in and help.

Too busy.

Ning Nanxi's official account has many fans. It is a public account that recommends food in the same city. As long as the vast majority of people who follow Ning Nanxi will choose to try her recommendations first.

Every issue is guaranteed, and it is all achieved through busy days. If you want a good reputation, you must have something yourself.

Chang Zhi helped with the cash register, and was busy all over, WeChat, Alipay, cash, ordering, urging——

Fortunately, the dance cover was filmed and was waiting to be uploaded tomorrow, otherwise Chang Zhi would really go crazy.

The self-cultivation of a shop assistant is to treat customers with a smile——As the store manager and boss, Chang Zhi is friendly with a smile and thoughtful service.

The business of "Try Milk Tea" has always been good. It's not that no one has contacted Chang Zhi, wanting to work with her to promote the brand and become a milk tea shop with chain stores everywhere, but Chang Zhi refused. Her original intention... Chang Zhi herself was not sure whether the product quality would be reduced for profit because of more stores in the future, so how could she dare to cooperate with others?

However, she only wanted to open one or two branches, which were within her ability.

Unfortunately, the funds were insufficient and the risks were too great, so she was not qualified to gamble.

Chang Zhi took the time to look at the team. Looking at the team that was barely outside the store, she felt busy, and at the same time, she felt that it seemed that the day of opening branches like the Internet celebrity store with a daily income of one million was just around the corner.

Just like that sentence -

People always have to have some dreams, what if they come true?

Qin Huai likes the "Try Milk Tea" shop very much.

She likes it so much that she is the first to try every new product, likes it so much that she has tried all the products in the store, and likes it so much that she wants to drink it every day.

Qin Huai lives one stop away from here. Since the "Try" shop opened, she came here for shopping and was attracted by the buy one get one free promotion. She dragged her friends to try it once, and then she couldn't stop.

Try it, try it, you will never forget it once you try it.

This shop is not like other milk tea chain stores that simply add creamer to it. In fact, customers can tell whether the milk tea is good or not by drinking it. The price of "Try" is only three or four yuan higher than that of chain milk tea shops. It is really the real stuff... Qin Huai buys it two or three times a week, sometimes ordering takeout, sometimes sitting in the store, playing with her phone and using the air conditioning. In short, she is really a die-hard fan.

Qin Huai never knew who the manager of "Try" was, but she always admired such a conscientious manager. Until that afternoon when she saw a beautiful young lady come in, Qin Huai heard Xiao Dong, whom she often dealt with, call her "Sister Chang".

Later, this "Sister Chang" helped in the busy days of the store. After that, a new employee came, and Qin Huai didn't come to the milk tea shop because of something, so she didn't see her.

Until not long ago, on Sunday, she came to the store and saw that "Sister Chang" appeared again.

She entered the store with a bun and greeted the employees familiarly. She sat close to the cashier and heard someone talking about "employee benefits?" and someone calling "boss".

She also saw "Sister Chang" helping at the cashier, and later sat with two boys with two drinks she had never drunk.

Qin Huai knew that this young lady was the manager.

Fair skin, beautiful face, long legs, big breasts, young and promising...

White, rich and beautiful.

She sat not far away and watched "Sister Chang" smile gently. A series of compliments appeared in Qin Huai's mind, and "Sister Chang" instantly became her idol.

Inspirational.

Qin Huai saw the new products released by the "Try Milk Tea" public account last night. On Saturday, in order to try it as soon as possible, she came this morning, but she didn't expect so many people to line up.

It's like a delicious cake that you have hidden for a long time. Although more and more people want to share it with you, it is a gradual increase, not a sudden increase like now.

Qin Huai was a little sad, but she thought that "Sister Chang" should be very happy to see such a prosperous business.

Qin Huai also wanted "Sister Chang" to take the business further, prosperous and thriving.

She also has a few fans, although not as many as big V, but most of them are from the same city, so she is going to recommend it on Weibo.

Qin Huai took out his mobile phone, and he had thought of the first draft in his mind, ready to strongly recommend it, and with pictures and texts.

Chapter 22 A Bad Thing

Sometimes, you don't know if your good intentions will turn out to be a bad thing.

Because you never know what will happen in the next second, you never know which ones are marketing, which ones are real, which ones are out of goodwill, and which ones are out of malice behind those hot searches on Weibo.

You also never know, in the comments, behind those popular accounts, are there people who sit in front of their computers and open software to brush comments and make a living, or are the indignant netizens who typed that line of words and sent it out.

After all, things are unpredictable, and accidents sometimes happen.

Qin Huai took a picture of this store, took a picture of Chang Zhi at the cash register, and posted it on Weibo.

[Xiao Huai'er]: I recommend a store, "Try Milk Tea", located at xxx, 99% of people who often visit this street have drunk it, the store manager is a young lady and super beautiful! Milk tea conscience ~ [Picture] [Picture]

The comments were a row of people from the same city: "I've tried this shop and it's OK" "... The manager is so young??" "Wow, this girl is so pretty" "Baifumei, I always go to this shop when I go to x street to drink milk tea, I thought the manager should be a middle-aged uncle" "I haven't tried it, but this manager looks familiar..."

Chang Zhi has never been in the dance cover area. She said on Weibo that she opened a milk tea shop. Her work and entertainment are clearly divided, and she even has two accounts.

I don't know who found out that Chang Zhi is the dance cover [Tang Zhi] on station B, and a hot topic called #The most beautiful store manager dance# was quickly pushed up.

The first marketing account forwarded it, and the second marketing account forwarded it——

In the afternoon, Chang Zhi obviously found that more people were looking at her, and some even took pictures. She frowned and stopped to ask the girl why she was taking pictures of her.

There was a faint fresh fragrance in the milk tea shop. The shop was full of people, some were laughing, and some were talking seriously. Behind her was the sound of the machine shaking the milk tea, the sound of ice cubes being shoveled, the sound of employees complaining because of the space and the busyness, and all kinds of sounds intersected together, but Chang Zhi clearly heard the words of the little girl in front of her.

The little girl was still wearing a school uniform. When she heard Chang Zhi ask her, she was surprised and said: "Aren't you the manager of this store? Don't you know why we are taking pictures of you? You are about to be a celebrity on the top ten hot searches..."

Chang Zhi was stunned. Xiao Dong, who was packing milk tea next to her, heard this and stopped moving. He turned his head and looked at Chang Zhi and the little girl who answered the question differently.

The people in line behind her heard the girl's words and interrupted: "Excuse me, are you unaware of this?"

Chang Zhi didn't know what happened, but her heart skipped a beat when she heard about the hot search. She instinctively felt panic. She shook her head stiffly, and then she heard the passers-by lower their voices and say to each other-

"It doesn't seem to be hype."

"Maybe they are pretending. Anyway, if they come here to take a photo and post it on Weibo later, there will definitely be a lot of likes and comments."

"Is this store really opened by her? Oh my god, she must be a rich second-generation?"

"Oh, I tell you it's not necessarily the case. She looks so beautiful..."

Do you think she can't hear it?

With a bad feeling growing in her heart, Chang Zhi helped the girl place the order, then pushed the cash box of the cash register in, took off her apron, stuffed it in the corner of the drawer, and said to Xiao Dong, who was originally the cashier and now the packer in the store:

"Xiao Dong, please help me watch it, I'll go back and take a look."

Xiao Dong heard the conversation and was confused. She nodded: "Okay, Sister Chang, you go quickly."

On the other side, the busy employees didn't know what happened, they just knew that the afternoon was unusually busy.

Chang Zhi walked out of the queue and said "Excuse me" several times. There were customers around her who didn't know what was going on and the educated youth were whispering, but she didn't care.

As she walked, she opened her phone and found that her Weibo was stuck for a long time. She logged out and logged in again. The comments, private messages, and mentions on Weibo were much more terrible than the last time she experienced. She casually clicked on the comments and found that it was not bad under her own Weibo-

[Tangtang is as beautiful as a painting]: Tangtang actually opened a shop. Oh my god, she is really a white, rich and beautiful girl. I have felt that before...

[Don't give me your love]: Sister Tang is awesome. She never said that she opened a milk tea shop. It is also located in the commercial street of a first-tier city. She is really white, rich and beautiful. Chang Zhitang only seems to be a hahahahaha. I decided to call her Ah Zhi to show her affection...

[Laughing and Forgetting Book]: #The most beautiful store manager dance# My Tang is really going to be famous...

Chang Zhi saw the hot search brought by this comment and immediately clicked in.

The popularity was actually pushed to the ninth place!

Above the topic of Chang Zhi are the latest hit dramas and popular stars, as well as the hot news happening today, and the national topic...

Chang Zhi, who has never been on the hot search, feels panic and uneasy.

She quickly returned home, without changing her shoes, and ran directly into the room to sit in front of the computer.

The Weibo with the topic at the top is a marketing account.

[Third Master v]: Former tofu beauty, pork beauty, Wuhan University campus beauty... Later, there is the most beautiful milk tea store manager Chang Zhi. Chang Zhi graduated from S University. After graduation, she started her own business. After opening the store for two years, the business is booming. She also dances on a famous barrage video website and has hundreds of thousands of fans. Such a versatile girl really makes Lao San admire her...

[Comment]

[You'd better not love me]: Where did you get the money to start a business at such a young age? Rich second generation? [335 likes]

[Ah Hello Goodbye]: Chang Zhi and I went to the same junior high school. She was pretty but introverted. Her grades were average. But as for dancing, as far as I know, she started learning dancing in the first year of junior high school. It's not surprising that she did a flip dance. I heard that something happened in her family in the third year of junior high school, so she dropped out. I don't know what happened after that. Did she repeat the year? She was admitted to a first-class university? ? [1035 likes]

[Flying Dragon in the Sky]: MMP, another woman who relies on her face and sells her body. The hot searches on Weibo are all useless. [250 likes]

[The Most Beautiful School Flower in the World]: Buying hot searches? Stirring up popularity? Want to be famous? Forget about being pretty, but you did plastic surgery. I don't know where a college student gets the money? [444 likes]

[Hehe]: I really can't stand these people who spend money to get themselves on the hot searches. Can't they just open a store? Do they want to enter the entertainment industry by buying hot searches? ?

[Men Don't Cry]: I went to see it in the same city. She's quite tall, with long legs and big breasts. I really envy her godfather.

It's getting more and more outrageous.

Chang Zhi flipped through the topics and saw a "junior high school classmate" who revealed her real name, a straight male who spoke too much, and some who thought she bought this trending search to get more attention...

To be honest, when Chang Zhi saw the classmate who revealed her junior high school life, her heartbeat suddenly accelerated and an unknown panic spread in her heart.

She was very anxious, for a long time, she hadn't been so anxious for a long time.

Chang Zhi stopped scrolling down the web page with her mouse hand, and the middle finger pressing the mouse wheel was motionless.

She stared at the dim screen of the computer, as if her soul had left her body.

No one can feel no pressure when seeing themselves on the trending search.

In particular, the two words "most beautiful" on the trending search negated all her efforts.

She was even questioned about hype, the source of money, the authenticity of her face, etc.

With sarcastic and disdainful words, based on their own malicious thoughts and guesses, they regarded her as a despicable person who wanted to be famous, so they had sufficient reasons to trample all her efforts underfoot with peace of mind.

She seemed to have become a clown for people to laugh at, and the malice surged like a tide, drowning her and making her feel difficult to breathe. It was like a green vine that emerged from the ground and entangled her, making her unable to move.

Chang Zhi casually pressed F5, the interface refreshed, and the latest Weibo post appeared.

[A person who loves to tell the truth]: Chang Zhi, graduated from S University, ID Tangzhi on B station, has been doing cover dance for two years, bought fans to brush up her image, and became a new star in the dance area of B station (I don't know why, maybe it's for vanity?), her face, legs and breasts are all real, she once studied in a public high school in S city (it seems that her high school entrance examination results were too bad, so she paid to get in), extremely rebellious, openly contradicted the teacher in class, abused classmates, ranked last in the grade, and was reported six times in two years (it's strange that she was not expelled)............

[A person who loves to tell the truth]: I'll show you another picture. Have you seen Chang Zhi in Shamatte? [Picture]

Chang Zhi threw away the mouse, her body seemed to have no strength, leaning on the back of the chair, she took a deep breath, raised her head, and felt terrible soreness in her eyes.

Why, after she settled down, he wanted to tease her again.

When people live a comfortable life, they will gradually forget the past, but this does not mean that the past has disappeared. It has always existed in the minds of everyone who has experienced it.

You see, it's just like now, at this moment.

All those pasts she didn't want to mention, even if she became better now, worked harder, was more sunny, more positive, encouraged herself, and finally dared to try to show her love in front of everyone, she could not escape the day when that layer of skin was peeled off, and all of her, in the way she least wanted, was nakedly displayed in front of everyone -

Accept criticism.

The author has something to say: I don't know if Tangtang will lose a lot of fans after this chapter is published (or I will lose fans...)

The last Weibo is true and false.

The setting was what I thought of from the beginning. This is the only sad point in the whole article, which is what the little sister experienced in her school days. I didn't know if you saw it before I laid the groundwork for several places... (Actually, it's not sad. The little sister has to go through these things anyway to truly face the past, live calmly, and give her heart to our Yanzhi 2333)

There will be sweetness after bitterness.

I will explain the reasons for the content of that Weibo post later.

I just want to say that in real life, most of the people you see who are glamorous or lively and outgoing may really be like this, but there will always be some people who have experienced things you can't imagine.

And most of them never mention those things, pretending that they never happened. Days pass by, and those sad days become memories. When they become comfortable, they think they have forgotten them. In fact, how can they forget something that doesn't exist?

Life is like a play, this word is true.

Chapter 23 Remember Forever

Chang Zhi will always remember that afternoon.

When Chang Zhi was in the third grade of junior high school, something happened at home.

That afternoon, the weather was fine, the sun was bright and dazzling, and the sound of chalk rubbing against the blackboard... Chang Zhi was sitting in a math class, immersed in a big question, but the head teacher suddenly walked to the back door with a serious look and called her out in front of the whole class.

At that time, Chang Zhi thought that she had made some mistakes and the head teacher wanted to teach her. The eyes of the class were all on her. She walked out of the back door nervously, but who knew that the head teacher handed her a note and told Chang Zhi that her parents had a car accident and were being rescued in the hospital, and her second uncle who lived near their home was waiting for her outside the school.

Chang Zhi took the note in confusion, but when she heard that her parents were in the hospital, her tender hands clenched the note, and her mind went blank instantly.

Math problems, teachers, leave notes, all the sounds and other things left her in an instant, and she was left with overwhelming panic.

Will her parents be in trouble?

Will she become a child without parents?

She ran all the way from the fifth floor to the school gate. The school bell rang and her uncle was standing at the door.

But it was too late.

She stood outside the operating room door, watching the lights in the operating room dim and the hospital corridors become terribly silent.

Behind her, her mother's parents had passed away two years ago, and her mother's relatives, her second uncle and her eldest uncle, were discussing her where she would belong.

The eldest uncle is a weak character. He grew up with his aunt and uncle's wife, but his aunt is strong. Before knowing the amount of compensation, he yelled at Chang Zhi in front of him: "Husband, you can't act on impulse. We have three children, and Xiaoxiao is going to elementary school. How stressful..."

The eldest uncle looked at Chang Zhi who was lowering her head, pulled his aunt and uncle aside, and said: "But... we can't just leave Tangtang alone, right? She is my nephew..."

"No, our child will be successful in the future. Living in the city is stressful enough. With your salary, will you raise another one and make us three mothers starve?"

The second uncle is usually cunning, and he doesn't know how much the compensation is. But when he saw the man who hit and killed his sister and her husband, he was dressed in a suit and drove a car that he couldn't afford in his lifetime, so he started to think about it. He whispered to his wife: "Why don't we raise him? We only have one son, so the pressure is not too great. It's two lives. I estimate that the other party will have to pay tens of thousands..."

The uncle-in-law looked at Chang Zhi, who was already quite tall, and added: "It's only a few years anyway. She will take the high school entrance examination this year, right? If she passes, let her study. If she doesn't pass, she can go out to work, which is also good..."

They thought she couldn't hear them at all if they lowered their voices, but she heard a few words, and her already angry heart was even more painful.

Because it was an accidental car accident, the other party was also injured, but even so, he was the main person responsible, and he seemed to be a rich second-generation or an official second-generation. The death compensation, funeral expenses, and support... a total of a considerable amount of money was paid.

However, the eldest uncle-in-law and the second uncle also contributed a lot. Chang Zhi saw the corners of their mouths with her own eyes and stood there wanting to laugh sarcastically.

They began to argue. Whoever supported her would find a way to swallow the money in the future.

That was a considerable amount of money. At their current level, they might not be able to save it even if they worked hard for two or three lifetimes.

Even the relatives on her father's side, who were not sure how distantly related, came to join in the fun, saying that Chang Zhi was a member of their Chang family and should belong to them...

She was snatched up like a precious commodity among a group of adults.

She didn't want to follow anyone, and she didn't want to do anything.

She just felt sad.

Her home was gone, her happiness was gone, and her blood relatives were not sincere.

Chang Zhi's aunt rushed back to China three days later, and saw Chang Zhi, who was in a daze all day long, like a walking corpse.

My aunt married a wealthy businessman in her early years, and later divorced for two years because she couldn't have children. The wealthy businessman was a man of friendship, and he divided nearly half of the family property with my aunt. After that, my aunt went abroad to travel alone.

She was also a strong woman when she was young, and she took Chang Zhi away with an unquestionable attitude.

Some people will become stronger after suffering a blow, but some people may become depressed.

Chang Zhi admitted that her psychological quality was not up to standard at all.

She is introverted, cowardly, and likes to escape when encountering problems.

In the high school entrance examination, Chang Zhi did poorly, and was ten points away from the worst public school. She didn't want to study anymore, and she didn't have the mood to study. But her aunt insisted that she go to high school, and she squeezed her into the worst class by paying 10,000 yuan for one point.

This class basically paid money to get in, and some even spent more than 100,000 yuan. This classroom was newly renovated, and there was not even time to install surveillance.

During that time, she seemed to be possessed, and she had no intention of studying at all. Her mind was full of resentment towards the world and fate. She was disgusted with the world, she disdained many things and even felt hypocritical. She refused to accept any information, and she wanted to sleep in class every day.

Chang Zhi became an alternative.

She deliberately concealed it, and her classmates didn't know what she had experienced.

I don't know if being alternative will attract attention, and I don't know who started the rumor that a handsome guy in the rocket class liked her. More and more people talked about her behind her back. She occasionally heard it, but she ignored it all.

That day, someone put a gift box on her desk. In the gift box, there were a bunch of snacks and a letter that was obviously written by a boy, but the handwriting was neat.

She stood by the desk, feeling that all eyes were on her, and suddenly she felt like laughing.

Is she sick?

Chang Zhi didn't open the letter, but put the gift box under the chair. It is undeniable that her mood was a little bright.

But she knew nothing would happen.

The next day, she was late for morning reading again. She stood at the back of the classroom for morning reading. After the teacher left, she returned to her seat and wanted to take the draft paper from the drawer, but pressed something soft.

Her fingers subconsciously retracted, one hand borrowed the edge of the table, the chair moved back, and she bent down slightly to look at the drawer.

Motionless, soft, gray fur, long and thin tail, is...

Chang Zhi had goose bumps all over her body. She suppressed the scream that was about to come out of her mouth, her hands began to tremble, and her cheeks began to numb.

Chang Zhi seemed to hear a gloating laugh in a corner.

She rushed into the bathroom to wash her hands again and again, and went home to use shower gel, soap, disinfectant, and even shampoo and laundry detergent... She rubbed her hands over and over again, her hands were shaking, and she felt sick and wanted to vomit. She opened her mouth and suppressed the nausea.

Her aunt asked her what was wrong, she shook her head and said it was nothing. At night, she hid in the quilt and cried bitterly facing the seemingly endless darkness.

She didn't sleep well that night.

The next day, she got up at five o'clock for the first time, arrived at school at six o'clock, opened the door of the next class in advance, put paper towels on other people's desks, climbed on the desk to look at the window, and stared at the corridor.

The school has morning reading at 7:20. At 6:00, even the boarding students in a trash class like theirs haven't gotten up yet.

There are few people passing by in the corridor, and no one looks familiar.

The class she hid in was at the bottom of the class like them. She waited for a long time and almost thought that the students in this class were coming. Finally, she saw a girl with a small box and her hair down at the stairs.

She is a classmate of theirs. Her grades are in the upper reaches of their class, but her grade is in the middle and lower reaches.

Chang Zhi watched her go in, jumped off the desk, and waited for two minutes to enter the classroom. The girl had already walked to her desk and stuffed the box in.

Chang Zhi's seat was by the window, and there was a residential area outside. Chang Zhi blocked the female classmate in her seat and asked, "What are you doing? What do you want to put in my drawer again?"

The female classmate's eyes were erratic. Chang Zhi took out the box from the drawer. It didn't weigh much, but she felt that something was moving inside.

The nausea from her fingers came back. Thinking of the dead mouse yesterday, she put the box on the table with a bang: "Are you sick? I offended you before, so you have to do this to me?"

The girl grabbed the box that Chang Zhi had put on the table and threw it out the window.

Chang Zhi pulled the hand that was still stretched out of the window and shouted angrily: "What are you doing? I told the teacher?"

The girl giggled and said maliciously: "Are you happy with the gift yesterday? I told you to accept gifts randomly again. You can't accept gifts from everyone. You still want to tell the teacher? Go ahead, there is no surveillance and no evidence. Do you think he will believe me or you? You are the last in the grade, hahaha..."

Chang Zhi couldn't bear it anymore. She was so hot-blooded that she slapped the girl in the face. The crisp sound echoed in the classroom where only the two of them were, but it scared the students who were about to come in from the door.

After beating the person, Chang Zhi looked at her hand in disbelief.

She hit someone, she actually hit someone...

"Bitch, you fucking dare to hit me..."

Chang Zhi breathed quickly, her eyes were sore, and she said angrily: "I fucking hit you!"

The voice that should have been gentle became unusually sharp, like the thorns of a hedgehog that hurt people.

She was notified and her parents were called, but the teacher didn't believe her. In addition, the slap mark on the face of the female classmate made her think that Chang Zhi had a bad character and asked her to take a week off from school.

The aunt apologized and took her home. Looking at Chang Zhi standing at the door, she wanted to scold her, but couldn't.

She felt distressed. A good child has become like this. Chang Zhi used to be so well-behaved. Other parents forced their children to take interest classes, but she took the initiative to ask to practice dancing. At such an old age, she practiced hard. Her studies were not bad, not the best but also in the upper middle. The original confident posture has now turned into this gloomy look.

The aunt said a few words to her earnestly, and Chang Zhi stood at the door and couldn't say anything.

Very disappointed, her parents must be very disappointed... She also hated herself like this.

She shut herself up in her room and kept silent. A week later, she packed her schoolbag and arrived at school at six in the morning.

Memorizing.

She pinched her thigh when she was sleepy, and her thigh was bruised. She hit her forehead to stay awake when she was tired. She seemed to have tried her best, but someone couldn't bear to see her do well.

The head teacher called her to the office. There was only her and the head teacher in the office. The head teacher asked her if she had a premature love affair.

Chang Zhi said: "I didn't!"

"You still say no? All the classmates in the class saw you walking with that guy from Class 2."

"The head teacher came to me in person."

"What do you mean no? Didn't he give you something? I saw the box the other day and thought it was something else. Chang Zhi, forget about your poor grades, but don't drag him down, okay? You are a hopeless case, but he is in a key class and he has to take the entrance exam to a key university..."

The more Chang Zhi listened, the more ridiculous it became. She shook her head: "Teacher, I really didn't have a premature love affair. I don't even know that person..."

The head teacher saw that she refused to admit it, and he got angry. He took out two letters from the drawer and slapped them on the table: "Still quibbling? Could it be that my classmates would lie to me? The evidence is in front of you. You either take the initiative to break up with him or drop out of school!"

Chang Zhi's tone was also a bit aggressive: "Teacher, I didn't do it, I really don't know who that person is..."

The head teacher said that she not only had a premature love affair, but also talked back to the teacher and was morally corrupt.

This time she was almost expelled. Her aunt begged for a long time and gave her money. The school agreed to keep her for half a year. If her grades were still so bad, she would leave.

She was reported twice.

Chang Zhi worked hard day and night to study for the balance. Facing the contempt of the teacher who had heard of her deeds, she endured and held her breath.

When the final class results came out, she entered the key class of liberal arts and met Deng Jiadai.

Chang Zhi ignored the rumors outside and ignored the isolation of those "good students" in the same class.

Later... she was admitted to S University, which surprised all her former classmates.

Chapter 24 Great Strength

Chang Zhi used great strength to dare to continue reading.

This Weibo post was quickly pushed to the top. Time passed slowly. It was almost evening. The dark room gradually became darker. The weather was terribly hot and humid. Chang Zhi felt a dense sweat on her forehead, which slowly flowed down her side face.

Chang Zhi closed her eyes, took a deep breath, and returned to her Weibo post with a trembling hand.

"I saw that Weibo post, is it true?" "No way, Tang Tang used to..." "After seeing the Weibo post, I feel like turning from a fan to a passerby..."

"That photo looks fake, I feel like the hair color was photoshopped, damn, it looks black..." "It's photoshopped, my friend who made the pictures saw it, the hair should be black in the original photo..."

"Tang Tang, please explain!" "Tang Jie used to be so pretty and young, although she looked a bit like a cold beauty..." "Wait for an explanation..."

"I told you that Tang Zhi was so popular before, she was so good at buying fans, what's so good about buying them?" "Who said buying fans is an idiot?" "No matter what, talking back to the teacher and scolding classmates are all black spots..."

She knew it.

This is how the world is, once someone gets into trouble, many irrelevant people will come around and throw stones at them.

She covered her eyes with one hand, propped her elbows on the computer desk, closed her eyes and couldn't think of anything.

There was a knock and a doorbell outside. When Chang Zhi stood up, she felt black in front of her eyes. She supported herself on the table to slow down. She slowly moved her steps and dragged her tired and heavy body towards the door.

She opened the door and saw Deng Jiadai standing outside.

She looked worried: "Tangtang, are you okay? I saw the trending search and came to find you immediately. How are you?"

Chang Zhi leaned against the door frame and looked at her for a long time. She blinked to hold back her tears. She grabbed Deng Jiadai's hand on her arm and said calmly: "I'm a little tired."

Deng Jiadai looked at Chang Zhi with a calm face and suddenly panicked.

She knew all those things. She accompanied Chang Zhi through them. She watched Chang Zhi study hard with books day by day, open her heart to her day by day, and watch her get better and better day by day.

Even after the incident between Meng Xi and her aunt, Chang Zhi only lost contact for one day. The next day, she hugged her and handled all the funeral affairs calmly.

In the early days of the store, Chang Zhi was worried about the turnover every day. She was also cheated by the raw material supplier. She slept only four hours a day that week.

Deng Jiadai watched Chang Zhi walk step by step to where she is today. Who knew that someone would bring up the past again, open her scab-healed wound in the most cruel way, and even stab it with a sharp knife tip, making her feel miserable.

Deng Jiadai saw the person in front of her soften. She staggered back a step because of the sudden weight, but still caught it.

"Tangtang?" Deng Jiadai exclaimed, helping her squat down. Chang Zhi closed her eyes and let her do whatever she wanted unconsciously.

Deng Jiadai was so scared that she checked Chang Zhi's breathing. Fortunately, she was still breathing. She reached out and touched Chang Zhi's forehead. She felt sweaty. She was shocked and called 120. For the first time in her life, she felt at a loss.

Wen Yanxing was sitting in front of the computer. Since the afternoon, he had been looking for materials, writing lyrics, and preparing for the next ghost video.

Suddenly, the door was knocked hard, and the sound made people's hearts tremble. Wen Yanxing stopped what he was doing and frowned.

He walked to Xuanhuan and heard a strange female voice shouting: "Excuse me, is there anyone at home? Someone has fainted here..."

Wen Yanxing paused, and his thoughts paused for a moment. Then he quickened his pace and opened the door, and saw a strange woman squatting beside Chang Zhi, who was lying flat on the ground with her eyes closed. Chang Zhi's door was the door, and the living room inside could be seen.

His heart was shocked and he opened his mouth to speak.

Deng Jiadai was shocked to see that it was a man who appeared. She had no time to care about what kind of person Wen Yanxing was. She thought it would be better if it was a man.

"Sir, my friend fainted. I just called an ambulance. It should be here soon. Can you help me carry her down..." Deng Jiadai's nose was sour and her hands were shaking. She was about to cry.

Wen Yanxing squatted down without saying anything. He passed his hands under Chang Zhi's back and knees, and lifted Chang Zhi up with a little effort.

The weight was not heavy at all, but surprisingly light. She was obviously tall, why...

Wen Yanxing lowered his head slightly and looked at Chang Zhi's closed eyes. Suddenly, he felt panic and uneasiness from nowhere.

Deng Jiadai followed and helped Chang Zhi. Her voice was crying: "Thank you... Thank you..."

They soon arrived downstairs. What they heard was the whispers of passers-by. Wen Yanxing ignored the people who looked at him in surprise and the crowd watching him. He put Chang Zhi on the stretcher with a stern face. The medical staff looked at him in surprise.

Deng Jiadai could only say thank you, but she didn't expect Wen Yanxing to look at her and ask expressionlessly-

"Can I go with you?"

She was shocked.

After the examination, the doctor said that Chang Zhi was under too much pressure and had too many emotional fluctuations in a short period of time. Deng Jiadai went to pay the bill and asked Wen Yanxing to look after Chang Zhi. Wen Yanxing watched Chang Zhi in a ward with three beds squeezed out of the hospital.

The smell of disinfectant filled the hospital, which made people feel uncomfortable. There were two other patients in the ward. One was registered and fell asleep with his eyes closed. The other leaned on the pillow and coughed from time to time while hanging water. The cough was so severe that it seemed that he would cough out his lungs and die.

Chang Zhi was also hung with water, and Wen Yanxing stared at her.

She lay there with her eyes closed, motionless like a sleeping beauty.

Wen Yanxing frowned, thinking that she would not have a fever or something... He carefully reached out and touched Chang Zhi's forehead.

It was a hot day, but the touch felt icy and cold, chilling his heart. His heartbeat suddenly started pounding, and the temperature of his whole body was soaring.

Wen Yanxing hurriedly withdrew his hand, but when he withdrew his hand, he noticed that a few strands of her hair were stuck to her cheeks because of sweat. He hesitated for a moment, then reached out to gently help her peel off the strands of hair, and then gently straightened her hair.

The man in the bed next to him coughed even louder. Wen Yanxing frowned and looked back, wanting to say something, but seeing the man's slightly vicissitudes of life, his face was red from coughing, and he swallowed his words again.

Is the air conditioning in this broken ward really turned on? How could it be so hot? Wen Yanxing couldn't help but unbutton a button on his collar.

He put his eyes back on Chang Zhi on the bed, thinking it was really stuffy here. Seeing that Chang Zhi seemed to be sweating, he reached out to help her pull the quilt down.

Looking down again, Wen Yanxing saw Chang Zhi's hand sticking out of the quilt.

Slender and green, white and soft, like flawless white jade.

Chang Zhi didn't wake up or react, and he boldly stretched out his fingers to touch her.

When he touched her, it felt like the temperature of her forehead he had just touched, like ice cubes just taken out of the refrigerator, so cold that he wanted to withdraw his hand, but he didn't know where the idea came from-

He wanted to hold this hand and warm the coldness with his temperature.

Chang Zhi suddenly snorted, and her eyebrows gradually wrinkled into a river.

Wen Yanxing quickly pulled his hand away, like a child who had done something bad, and put his hands behind his back, his mind was blank

Woke up... now?

Chang Zhi felt as if a long time had passed, and as if no time had passed.

She opened her eyes, and the first thing she smelled was the smell of disinfectant, and then a lemon fragrance mixed in it.

...It was like lemon-scented soap.

She thought dazedly, why was she lying there?

Chang Zhi shook her head and stared at the white ceiling for a while before her eyes focused. She couldn't help rubbing her eyes with her hands half open. She turned her head and saw the chair, the legs in black pants, and a hand on the legs.

A slender hand with faint blue veins on it, the fingers slightly bent, and the joints looked distinct.

Chang Zhi opened her eyes wide and looked up along the hand. The owner of the hand was also looking at her quietly.

She met his eyes unexpectedly. His eyes were as black as round obsidian. She vaguely saw her surprised and pale face.

"..." Chang Zhi opened her mouth in surprise and wanted to say something, but she couldn't make a sound.

Wen Yanxing slowly took back the hand that had just been behind his back when Chang Zhi suddenly woke up. He looked at her surprised look, thought for a long time and choked out a sentence: "...Are you awake?"

Yes, yes, you are awake? ... So fast.

In response, Chang Zhi coughed twice, as if clearing her throat.

Wen Yanxing: "............"

Chang Zhi wanted to sit up, but Wen Yanxing stopped her: “Just lie down and talk.”

“Well... did I faint?” Chang Zhi’s voice was a little hoarse, “Where’s my friend?” She was asking Deng Jiadai.

“Your friend went downstairs to pay the bill, and should be back soon.” Wen Yanxing said.

Chang Zhi nodded silently, and asked after a while: “...Why are you here? Did you...bring me to the hospital?” Wen Yanxing appeared here, and she could only think that he sent her here, otherwise he would not be here.

Wen Yanxing looked at the IV bottle hanging on the shelf, and his voice sounded calm: "...your friend knocked on my door, and I saw you lying on the ground when I opened the door."

"I'm so sorry..." Chang Zhi curled her lips and said apologetically, "No one should do this in front of you...Is it scary?"

"...It's okay," Wen Yanxing pretended to be calm, and he stood up, "The IV bottle is finished, I'll call the nurse, you lie down for a while, I'll be back soon."

Chang Zhi then found that her other hand was pierced with a needle, and the needle hole was covered with white transparent medical tape for fixation.

She watched the man stand up, walk around the two beds to the door, look around and stop a nurse.

Chang Zhi retracted her gaze and saw the two patients in the next bed.

One was asleep, and the other was coughing.

The man who had been coughing started coughing again. Wen Yanxing called the nurse over, but the nurse was stopped by the man.

"Hey, miss, cough cough... I'm still coughing after hanging the drip. What should I do? This... is useless." The man coughed and his face turned red, and he said while coughing.

The nurse was originally called to change the drip bottle, but was suddenly stopped. She didn't understand this knowledge very well. She looked at Wen Yanxing and said with embarrassment: "This... how about you drink some water?"

The man looked around and saw the water dispenser next to the door: "I'm here... alone."

Wen Yanxing stood by and walked over to help him pour a glass of warm water.

Slightly bending down to hand over the water, the man looked at him and said thank you gratefully.

Chang Zhi looked at Wen Yanxing's movements, pursed her lips, and her heart softened.

The nurse came over to help her change another drip bottle. Wen Yanxing stood by and looked at Chang Zhi with a bitter face, comforting her and said: "It's okay, it will be soon, there is still one bottle, don't worry."

Chang Zhi: "..."

Chapter 25 The Second Bottle of Water

Deng Jiadai came up after paying the fee, and Chang Zhi just started to drink the second to last bottle of water.

When she came in, she saw Chang Zhi leaning on the pillow, and Wen Yanxing sitting by the bed looking at her.

A strange atmosphere.

Deng Jiadai paused, coughed lightly, and then quickly walked to the bedside and pulled a chair to sit next to Chang Zhi.

Chang Zhi breathed a sigh of relief when she saw Deng Jiadai coming.

God knows she felt weird when Wen Yanxing looked at her from time to time. Chang Zhi winked at Deng Jiadai, meaning why did he follow her?

Deng Jiadai was also desperate, she didn't know anything. So she shook her head slightly.

Wen Yanxing naturally noticed this eye contact and guessed what Chang Zhi wanted to ask, but he probably didn't know the answer.

He stared at the bottle, hoping that time would pass faster.

Chang Zhi finished the injection at nearly ten o'clock in the evening. There were not many people in the hospital, and she insisted on going home.

At night, the corridor of the hospital was a little scary. Chang Zhi got out of bed and walked slowly. Even though there was a man and a woman next to her, she was still a little scared.

Chang Zhi looked back at the road she had walked, and suddenly she felt a little dazed. The last time she stayed in the hospital was this late, several years ago.

She seemed to see her little self leaning against the wall, with messy hair, lowering her head, and clutching the corner of her school uniform.

...Yes, it was in the past.

She followed Wen Yanxing and Deng Jiadai to the stairs.

It's not that there is no elevator, but Chang Zhi felt that it was scary to take the elevator in the hospital at night. She always felt that there would be a sudden power outage.

And maybe because she had just woken up from a faint not long ago, her legs and feet were a little weak, and she felt much better after walking.

This floor was the fourth floor. Chang Zhi walked down slowly. When she was on the stairs to the second floor, her foot slipped and a strong arm caught her, saving her from a tragic fall.

It was Wen Yanxing.

There was almost no sound in the hospital. The only sound in the stairwell was the slight echo of her slippers rubbing against the stairs.

Wen Yanxing held the stair railing with one hand and held Chang Zhi's abdomen with the other arm. She couldn't help but grab his clothes and finally stabilized her body.

The scalding temperature for her transmitted warmth through the clothes. Chang Zhi's heart seemed to stop for a moment. She paused there and looked at him. Wen Yanxing looked back quietly, with her in his eyes.

Chang Zhi felt that her perception and vision seemed to be wrong. She actually saw a faint concern in his eyes.

Wen Yanxing waited until she stood firm before slowly withdrawing his hand.

Chang Zhi looked down at the flip-flops on her feet that she should wear at home. The slipper prints were visible between her toes. One of the eyes of the Minion was staring at her, as if peeping into her heart and asking her what she was thinking.

The little man in her heart covered his face in panic, and her fingers curled slightly.

At 10 o'clock in the evening, the last bus back to Chang Zhi's home had passed. The three of them stood at the bus stop, blowing the cold wind, waiting for a taxi.

When Deng Jiadai just left the hospital, she told Chang Zhi that she would stay at her house tonight. Chang Zhi knew what Deng Jiadai was thinking. As a friend for so many years, there was no need to consider it. She could stay at her house without thinking.

She would take him in even if he was old.

Wen Yanxing stood behind them like a backdrop, but he blocked the direction of the wind without leaving a trace.

He stared at the road seriously. A red taxi... had someone, a green taxi, had someone... the second taxi had someone, the third taxi... had no one. Wen Yanxing stepped forward and waved to stop them.

The taxi stopped steadily in front of the three people.

Deng Jiadai and Chang Zhi sat in the back, and Wen Yanxing sat in the front passenger seat.

Chang Zhi leaned on Deng Jiadai's shoulder and felt a heavy sleepiness coming up in her head.

Deng Jiadai gently touched her hair to comfort her.

Wen Yanxing sat in the front and took out his mobile phone after a while.

He hadn't been online for the whole day. He wanted to update the preview at night, but he didn't expect to encounter Chang Zhi's incident.

He opened the Weibo on his mobile phone skillfully, and the first thing he saw was the keyword in the search bar -

[Everyone is searching: Chang Zhi]

Wen Yanxing: "..." He turned around and looked at Chang Zhi, who closed her eyes and seemed to be asleep.

He quickly clicked on the search, and Wen Yanxing was startled by the popularity.

There were thousands of replies, such as "little gangster girl", "social sister", "godfather and goddaughter"...

Wen Yanxing kept scrolling down, reading ten lines at a glance. The more he read, the darker his face became, and the more he held the phone, the stronger he seemed to be, as if he was going to crush it.

He looked up, and saw Chang Zhi's sleeping face reflected in the mirror, frowning and looking very uneasy.

He felt a nameless anger in his heart, raised his hand and impulsively sent a Weibo, and then put the phone back into his pants.

When they got home, Deng Jiadai woke Chang Zhi up.

After saying goodbye to Wen Yanxing at the door, Deng Jiadai and Chang Zhi entered the house.

Deng Jiadai casually threw her bag on the sofa: "I feel like I have a strange smell of hospital."

Chang Zhi smiled helplessly and said: "I scared you today."

Deng Jiadai pretended to be calm: "Yes, a little bit, a big living person suddenly fell in front of me, I almost thought you couldn't bear it and died."

"It's not good if I die," Chang Zhi said indifferently, "Many people want me to disappear."

"Don't," Deng Jiadai said in a panic, "I will be very sad, can you bear to make me sad?"

Chang Zhi looked at her for a long time, then walked over and sat next to Deng Jiadai and hugged her.

Deng Jiadai was stunned, then raised her hand and patted her back.

The light of the white flag lamp was straightforward and dazzling, and the embrace was really warm-

Warm enough to make her want to cry.

"Okay, okay, stop hugging me," Deng Jiadai was so tight in Chang Zhi's arms that she felt uncomfortable all over. "We are both covered in hospital germs. Can we take a shower?"

After Deng Jiadai, Chang Zhi felt much better.

"Well, I'll get you some clothes." Chang Zhi couldn't help laughing. "You came at the right time. I just washed a pair of new underwear yesterday."

Deng Jiadai: "...What color?"

Chang Zhi: "Red, sexy and passionate, unrestrained and natural."

Deng Jiadai: "..................I like this. Bring it up to me."

Chang Zhi: "Okay, Your Majesty."

Deng Jiadai stared at her face. Chang Zhi thought she was going to say something, but Deng Jiadai said, "You're so bold. Call me Queen."

Chang Zhi couldn't help it anymore. She laughed and scolded, "Forget it. Don't push it."

Deng Jiadai smiled at Chang Zhi and looked like she deserved a beating.

...This female 'lunatic'.

I know she is only serious for half a day.

Perhaps it is rare to have such a friend, no need to say much, no need to do much. She will always find you, comfort you, and hug you when you need her. She uses her not-so-broad shoulders to temporarily block the wind and rain for you, like a piece of driftwood floating towards a drowning person, a lotus leaf that appears in a storm and is enough to block the rain.

No need for too many words, she knows you well, witnesses your past, and understands your heart.

Both of them took a comfortable hot bath, Deng Jiadai had to sleep in the guest room, and had to sleep in the same bed with Chang Zhi.

Chang Zhi let her go, it didn't matter anyway, the bed was big enough, more than enough for two people

The small table lamp was turned on in the bedroom, and the dim light was warm. Chang Zhi was lying, Deng Jiadai leaned on the pillow, and was replying to her boyfriend's message intently. After replying the message, she looked down at Chang Zhi who was half-opened and asked, "Do you dare to check Weibo now?"

Chang Zhi half-closed her eyes and handed her phone over without saying a word: "Not yet, if you want to check it, check it out. I'll take a nap first, and I'll check it out tomorrow when I'm full of energy again."

Deng Jiadai took her phone. Chang Zhi's phone had her fingerprint saved, so she unlocked it and opened Weibo.

The discussion in the middle of the night was still very intense. These netizens seemed to have no idea how to sleep. There were a lot of people who spread rumors at ordinary times, but when it was their turn to refute the rumors, there were only a few people who forwarded them.

Tsk, Deng Jiadai shook her head and sighed.

Deng Jiadai saw a new Weibo notification of a person Chang Zhi was following. How could she know... She had an impression of this name. It was Chang Zhi who used Li Yuanfang, whom she taught her, to lead the man who was lying down.

She glanced at it quickly, then suddenly stopped and woke up Chang Zhi who was sleeping: "Tangtang, this Yanzhi... is it talking about you?"

Chang Zhi was a little impatient when she was woken up from her dream, until she heard the word Yanzhi. Chang Zhi, who still had her eyes closed, was stunned, opened her eyes suddenly, and snatched the phone from Deng Jiadai's hand.

Under the dim light, the white light of the screen shone on Chang Zhi's face.

On the screen, Songti, regular script, and small black characters were clearly visible -

[Yanzhi v]: Anyone who exposes other people's privacy for improper purposes, forgive me for being blunt, is garbage.

Chapter 26 The phone murmurs

"Are you talking about... me?" Chang Zhi murmured to the phone.

In the seventh hour when she was on the hot search, forced to recall the old things, and her shoulders were almost crushed by public opinion-

Yan Zhi, her online "friend",

They may not have chatted for even a day. He was just a man who played a game with her and experienced a small storm with her.

She didn't know his last name or first name, and didn't know how he behaved.

But he waded into this muddy water with sharp words in front of his 2.6 million fans, except for some of her die-hard fans who defended him, while the rest were either black or watching.

Yan Zhi didn't even know the truth of the matter.

But he used the most reliable language and the most ostentatious way to silently comfort her.

Chang Zhi stared at the screen of her phone, and courage surged from nowhere.

[Simple and hardworking Tang Zhi]: If I'm not being sentimental... Thank you.

[Simple and hardworking Tang Zhi]: Thank you for...posting on Weibo.

[Simple and hardworking Tang Zhi]: Actually, I don't know if we are friends. To be honest, we are not very familiar with each other.

You can just ignore it. Just chat privately like them and don't mention it. Just comfort her...

Like An Nan, like Sister Qiao.

Don't mention whether it is true or not, and don't ask "is it true or not" like the journalists. First of all, comfort her, because they know her and trust her enough.

The mobile phone input method is a nine-square grid. As soon as Chang Zhi typed "I", Yan Zhi replied.

It was twelve o'clock in the middle of the night.

[Yan Zhi]: We will get familiar with each other in the future.

[Yan Zhi]: Because... there is a long way to go.

At six o'clock in the morning, Chang Zhi woke up.

She got out of bed quietly without waking up Deng Jiadai who was still dreaming. Chang Zhi sat at the computer desk and turned on the computer.

Taking out the editing software from her computer that she hadn't used for a long time since she got Jiang Huai, Chang Zhi clicked on the finished version of the "4 wall" jump video that Yan Zhi sent her that day and prepared to edit it.

She searched for a simple teaching material on the Internet and added 20 seconds of subtitles at the end of the video.

Black background with white text, the early morning light shines through the curtains, and a ray of sunlight shines on Chang Zhi's face. Chang Zhi looks serious, sits upright, and puts both hands on the keyboard, as if she is doing something very serious.

She carefully typed out the notice word by word on the keyboard.

Drag the font to the middle of the black screen, adjust the ultimate move, save, and browse it.

Even if something like this happens, the video still has to be posted.

This is to fulfill her promise to fans, and... to insert a small advertisement for her own selfishness.

Chang Zhi is back on Weibo. Today, she is no longer in the top ten hot searches, but the discussion is still very hot.

Various elementary school classmates, junior high school classmates, and high school classmates, who came out of nowhere, "real name" revealed her evil deeds.

After a day and a night of baptism, Chang Zhi's mentality was much better. She casually read a few Weibo posts from so-called "old classmates".

Some of them made Chang Zhi laugh and cry. The school was right, but it was not her who made up the story, which was too outrageous.

For example, one post was from a girl who claimed to be her "kindergarten" classmate -

[Coder: I used to be a kindergarten classmate of Chang Zhi, a senior class. I vaguely remember that she was very cute when she was young and many boys liked her. Then she always ordered those boys to help her do things. To be honest, I was quite jealous at that time, but now it seems that you can tell a person's future by looking at him when he is three years old.]

Chang Zhi casually clicked on this girl's Weibo, scrolled down two posts, and saw a Weibo post from early July

[Coder: Hahaha, summer vacation is finally here~]

...Summer vacation?

Chang Zhi has graduated from university for many years, and she has long forgotten what summer vacation is. Is this girl really from the same generation as her?

This is nothing.

For example, Chang Zhi was involved in a love triangle in junior high school. She loved him and he loved her, but she didn't love him but loved him, and he actually loved her... and so on.

Below this Weibo comment is a row of 66 and ridicule, and there is also a sentence... "Society, I am Chang Jie, beautiful and have many spare tires"?

Chang Zhi sneered, and couldn't help but want to reply, "Then I wouldn't be single now."

But she held back and didn't reply.

Chang Zhi thought rather self-deprecatingly that if she replied like this, there might be a new black spot "Chang Zhi claims to be single, is it a personality or real?"

I agreed with An Nan and Sister Qiao to post the video in advance, at 11 o'clock in the morning, but only her version was extended.

After Chang Zhi finished these things, Deng Jiadai had already woken up, sitting on the bed hugging the quilt, looking at her sleepily.

Deng Jiadai said, "Tangtang, you got up so early."

Chang Zhi: "I'm going to do a live broadcast tomorrow to clarify what happened in the past few days. Tell me, should I start from the beginning or pick out a few things?"

Deng Jiadai thought for a while and said, "Let's explain the most serious Weibo post. I saw that one. It's really crazy to exaggerate. But you did hit that Liu... This is quite troublesome. I don't know if she saw it. Will she add insult to injury?"

Chang Zhi sneered, "If she saw it, I think it's entirely possible."

Deng Jiadai touched her nose and said, "Suddenly, I have a terrible guess. Could she have posted that Weibo post?"

"I don't know," Chang Zhi shook her head, "someone who knows me, hates me, or is jealous of me."

"Anyway, it's not someone who likes me," Chang Zhi added.

"Anyway, you don't have to tell everything clearly, and you don't want to tell your ancestors about it," Deng Jiadai lifted the quilt and sat on the bed. "It's really sad, so just say it in one sentence."

Deng Jiadai looked at Chang Zhi and said, "Anyway, just one sentence, you have to remember that I always support you."

Chang Zhi ate the loving breakfast made by Deng Jiadai, and while waiting for eleven o'clock in front of the computer, she replied to several people in the fan management group - thanking, explaining and notifying the news of tomorrow's live broadcast

Around ten thirty, the penguin in the lower right corner flashed, and it turned out to be Yan Zhi's message.

[Yan Zhi]: [Picture] [Picture] [Picture]

[Yan Zhi]: Zombie account, water army.

Chang Zhi was stunned, and clicked on the first picture, which turned out to be several Weibo accounts posted by Yan Zhi.

This is...

The picture showed that the registration time of four accounts was the same day of the previous year, and the time of posting Weibo was roughly the same. There was also chicken soup with the same content, and the followers and fans were all 5-15 characters in the name, which was also a big chicken soup user.

These are all typical characteristics of zombie accounts, and... Yan Zhi took screenshots, and they replied to her topic many times.

Picture 2 is a Weibo account named "Speed Fire", and the chat records between Yan Zhi and him are about how to make people famous or discredit them, and the chat records end at the price the seller said to buy the software and the price of hype.

Picture 3 is a screenshot of a software. Chang Zhi looked carefully and realized that this is... a software dedicated to Weibo water army? ?

There are many buttons in the software, keywords, designated users, designated Weibo, small account grouping...

Yan Zhi... bought this software? ? Chang Zhi's eyes widened slightly.

She looked at the screenshots, although she didn't know how to use this software, but she understood what Yan Zhi meant, Yan Zhi meant...

[Yan Zhi]: I found something wrong when I looked at Weibo last night, and I checked it out and found that someone bought water army to brush you, enemy?

[Simple and hardworking Tang Zhi]: I don't know... how did you find this kind of thing. .

[Yanzhi]: Check carefully and you will find the traces. Follow the zombie account and I have found the seller.

[Yanzhi]: If you don't know who wants to hack you... wait for me.

[Simple and hardworking Tang Zhi]: ? ? ?

[Yanzhi]: Wait for me obediently and chat back.

[Simple and hardworking Tang Zhi]: ....What are you doing? ?

Yanzhi... Chang Zhi waited for a long time, but he didn't reply to her.

She vaguely knew what he was going to do, but she didn't understand why he wanted to...

Why? On the other side, Wen Yanxing himself was also... puzzled.

At 11 o'clock in the morning, Chang Zhi posted the video on time.

[Reprint: 4wall-f(x) Qiao Jie, Tang Zhi, An Nan. Up: Tang Zhi]

Half an hour after the upload was successful, Chang Zhi opened the video and saw the most important message at the beginning of the video, except for those messages mocking her for "daring to post videos".

[Airdrop coordinates, 3:50 main film.] [I just want to say one thing, Tangtang's fans please watch the video patiently...]

Chang Zhi dragged the progress bar to that position, she stared at the full barrage without blinking, and the subtitles she enlarged and bolded in the middle of the video——

[This video was released on time, which is my promise to fans.]

[I know that what happened in the past two days has made you who have always loved me very uneasy and sad. I am also very sorry for this. It happened suddenly and I was also confused at the time.]

[Thank you for your trust before I even opened my mouth. Heart, I love you so much.]

[So, tomorrow at 15:00, I will start a live broadcast. It is the first time to start a live broadcast. I hope to give you who support me the best explanation.]

Chapter 27 Video

On the evening of the day the video was sent, Chang Zhi received a message from Yan Zhi.

He sent two pictures in silence. His style was as concise and capable as before.

Chang Zhi looked at the message on the computer screen. Because Yan Zhi sent a long picture, the content font was forced to shrink and compress, so it was not clear. Chang Zhi hesitated for a moment and did not choose to enlarge and click it.

[Simple and hardworking Tang Zhi]: You... spent the whole afternoon on this?

[Yan Zhi]: No, it took a little effort to find clues at the beginning, but it was pretty fast.

[Simple and hardworking Tang Zhi]: Thank you... I don't know what to say except this, I... always feel a little strange.

[Yan Zhi]: Why do you feel strange?

[Simple and hardworking Tang Zhi]: No, it's just... you helped me a few times. . Why?

Few people are so willing to help someone they don't know, and it takes energy and time, and it may not be pleasing.

Yan Zhi took about a minute to reply to her——

[Yan Zhi]: I don't know, maybe because... I saw injustice and drew my sword to help?

[Simple and hardworking Tang Zhi]: Then shouldn't I pledge my love to you?

Chang Zhi looked at the "typing" displayed on the screen.

She wanted to withdraw the message by right-clicking the second after sending it, but she didn't know why she withdrew her hand.

After a long time, "typing" disappeared from Yan Zhi's name.

[Yan Zhi]: ...That's OK.

Chang Zhi stared at the words, her fingers curled into a ball.

She blinked, and after a long while she raised her head and touched her nose, feeling that she suddenly lost the ability to speak.

[Simple and hardworking Tang Zhi]: You answered so smoothly... If other girls asked you this, you would answer like this.

[Simple and hardworking Tang Zhi]: Boys should be single-minded, don't be too fickle, otherwise girls won't like you.

After sending these two paragraphs, Chang Zhi almost wanted to turn off the computer - she didn't know what was going on in her mind, a strange feeling, similar to hoping that the other party would only say this to her, but she didn't want that kind of feeling...

She was wandering in it, looking back at that paragraph, she felt that her position was too strange.

[Yan Zhi]: ....

Looking at the "typing" that appeared after Yan Zhiming's name, Chang Zhi hurriedly typed a paragraph and sent it out to get back to the topic.

[Simple and hardworking Tang Zhi]: So, someone really hired a water army to black me?

[Yan Zhi]: ... Well, she paid 60,000 to buy you to be on the hot search for the twelfth hour, but... I guess she didn't expect that you would be pushed to the third place by netizens and the popularity would last so long.

[Simple and hardworking Tang Zhi]: She? A woman? ... Shouldn't she be happier to be the third place? She deliberately blackened me, did I touch her interests?

After typing this paragraph, Chang Zhi flipped the record up and clicked on the picture.

Dance

The person who hired the Internet army to discredit her is a beautiful, rich girl who has recently emerged in the home dance circle - Yueya.

Chang Zhi had seen recommendations for her to cover dance before, and because she happened to cover the dance of that song recently, she clicked in to watch it.

Chang Zhi had a deep memory because Yueya was really similar to her in some aspects. Apart from being a girl living in a big city, covering dances in her villa at home, and wearing branded clothes, her hairstyle, style, and clothing matching were also similar. Chang Zhi clicked in to check her submissions, and found that the dances she covered were almost the same, and the release time was basically the same as the time when Chang Zhi released the video...

But to be honest, Yueya's dance was just average, not to the extent of being eye-catching.

Chang Zhi looked at the name and was puzzled.

[Yan Zhi]: Not really, people in the same circle as you think it's a red eye disease. I saw that the source of this topic at the beginning was to recommend your store. I don't know why it became so distorted. It should be her operation.

[Yan Zhi]: ...But I found out one more thing. She seems to be from the same high school as you, one year younger than you.

The same high school? Chang Zhi stared at the four words and fell into thought.

[Simple and hardworking Tang Zhi]: So... Thank you.

Chang Zhi didn't know how Yan Zhi found out, but the pictures and texts posted were well-reasoned... Let's put it this way, in her eyes, Yan Zhi now feels that there is nothing that Yan Zhi can't do. She doesn't know when she started to have a blind trust in him.

[Yan Zhi]: You're welcome.

When Chang Zhi saw this, she wanted to end the conversation and close the dialog box, but after thinking about it, she felt it was not a good idea. She was going to find an emoticon to send over and end the conversation with her message.

Who knew that she had just opened the emoticon library, and Yan Zhi sent another message.

[Yan Zhi]: And... Supplement: No.

...No? Chang Zhi didn't understand what he meant. What was no? She flipped up the chat records between her and Yan Zhi, but she couldn't match them up.

Until she turned to the part where she hurriedly changed the subject, she was stunned for a moment, and her cheeks suddenly flushed.

[Yan Zhi]: I am not fickle.

Chang Zhi's feet trembled when she saw these four words, and she kicked the wire of the host. The screen went black, but Chang Zhi breathed a sigh of relief, as if she was alive.

But after a while, she despairingly found that her mind was full of two words-

Yan, Zhi.

During dinner, bathing, and before going to bed, Chang Zhi did not dare to turn on Penguin, but she kept thinking about this matter in her mind.

Yan Zhi meant that he was confessing to her?

But why, she is now under a lot of black material, just like a lot of debts are not a burden, Chang Zhi now feels a little broken... But... what is there about her that is worthy of Yan Zhi's love?

Chang Zhi crossed her legs, pursed her lips, her eyes were dull, and her mind was empty.

Speaking of affection, she has a little affection for Yan Zhi. He helped her a few times, and they had a pleasant chat every time.

However, it cannot be said that they are in love with each other. It can be regarded as a degree of friendship.

Also... Yan Zhi has a nice voice, but he also makes ghost videos and live broadcasts, and he looks like a dead otaku... And Chang Zhi remembered a law she heard from somewhere - "People with nice voices are usually ugly."

So Yan Zhi... wouldn't be the kind of person who is fat all over and has acne all over his face because of staying up late?

Chang Zhi hugged the pillow to cover her face. Why did she think about these things?

But speaking of voice... Chang Zhi thought of someone for no reason -

Wen Yanxing.

When she first heard Yan Zhi's voice, she thought that their voices were similar, but when Yan Zhi was live broadcasting, she found that their tones of speech were different.

She thought Wen Yanxing had a nice voice, was handsome, and had money, so he broke the law.

Thinking of Wen Yanxing, Chang Zhi's heart beat faster for some reason.

Chang Zhi thought of the last night in the hospital, when Wen Yanxing supported her, she clearly felt her nervousness, and... she felt that this emotion was very familiar.

Chang Zhi collapsed and fell back, staring at the ceiling and felt that she was going crazy.

Forget it, forget it, there is still a lot to do tomorrow, and Ren Yanzhi didn't say anything... Why did she think so much?

Chang Zhi lifted the quilt and crawled in, covering her ears and forcing herself to sleep.

The next day, at 15:00 in the afternoon, Chang Zhi prepared before, and then started the live broadcast in front of the computer on time.

She sat in front of the computer, and on the computer desk was the camera and microphone that she had bought last year and had not used.

The number of people in the live broadcast room gradually increased, from a few thousand to tens of thousands, and there were more than a dozen bullet comments such as "waiting for explanation" and "support".

There were also mocking comments such as "Please start your performance" and "Such a rubbish dare to start a live broadcast..."

Chang Zhi cleared her throat and spoke.

"Well, it's my first live broadcast... I didn't expect it to be for such a reason."

"First of all, I want to apologize to my fans. I'm sorry to make you sad and worried, because this happened really suddenly."

As the bullet screen passed by, her fans brushed [It's okay]. Chang Zhi curled her lips and felt warm.

"First, let me explain the matter about the manager of the milk tea shop," Chang Zhi paused, surprised to find that the live broadcast room had suddenly increased by 30,000 people. She saw someone brushing the bullet screen:

[Yanzhi shared the live broadcast] [Support Tangzhi, although I'm not a fan, I hope I won't be slapped in the face] [It's amazing that you dare to open a live broadcast to clarify after being scolded like this...] [Am I the only one who cares about the relationship between Yanzhi and Tangzhi? They already follow each other. And... . . .]

Seeing the two words Yanzhi, Chang Zhi's mind was shaken. Restraining the urge to open Weibo, Chang Zhi pretended to be calm and said, "First of all, I know that some people on the Internet said that I wanted to become famous by opening a shop with my godfather. This is completely slander. If I remember correctly, I can sue, right?" Chang Zhi looked very serious.

[Suing, what a shame][Where did the money come from?][The money just appeared out of thin air? Forget it]

Chang Zhi saw these comments and sneered. Regardless of the impact, she directly responded: "Isn't this my right as a citizen? Did I remember it wrong? Defamation and defamation are not crimes and should not be sentenced or punished?"

"Ignore these people. Let's get back to the point. I don't know why those so-called classmates, who have revealed so much, didn't just reveal that my parents died in an accident in the third year of junior high school, and then I received compensation and inherited the estate, and used the money to start my own business when I grew up?"

Chang Zhi paused and looked at the camera with a smile: "Every penny I spend now is earned by myself, so what qualifications do some people have to point fingers at me and make random rumors?"

The comments were boiling instantly, but Chang Zhi felt sad.

She never thought that one day she would be forced to explain the source of the money, forced to tell the truth, and say that her parents died unexpectedly.

Never thought about it.

Chapter 28 Damn

[Oh my god, I feel so bad...][Fuck those who said godfather exploded on the spot, are they sick][Tangtang, hug you, we didn't know about it.]

[I feel bad for Tangtang, no one would want this to happen][Suddenly, I feel so inspired...][I'm starting to believe that someone has red eyes...]

Chang Zhi looked at the screen, blinked her eyelashes, and manipulated the mouse with her hand, saying: "Okay, I've explained this question, let's look at another Weibo."

Chang Zhi took a deep breath and clicked on the Weibo page that was opened before, the one with the most vicious black Weibo.

The live broadcast room showed a computer screen with half of the screen and half of the face. Chang Zhi used the mouse to count the words on it, explaining: "First of all... I won't mention the name. I did graduate from S University. As for buying fans, I can tell you for sure that I didn't do it."

"First of all, I don't make money from fans. My fans should all know that I never said that I opened a milk tea shop, and I never participated in paid activities, or opened a Taobao store or other derivatives. Secondly, it's unnecessary. To be honest, buying fans can't change anything. If I buy fans, then do I have to spend money to buy a wave of popularity for my previous videos that were quite popular? I can't make a penny. Am I stupid or stupid or stupid?" Chang Zhi tilted her head slightly and asked, "If it were you, would you do this?"

[666666][Definitely not. I'm not stupid...]

[I used to believe that Weibo post, but suddenly I feel it's full of loopholes][You make so much sense that I can't refute it...]

After a pause, Chang Zhi continued to read: "Well, the face, chest and legs are real, of course they are real, I am afraid of pain, I have never been to the hospital or had surgery, and I am quite satisfied with my appearance. I won't talk about the chest because it's too embarrassing, anyway, there is nothing stuffed... Legs, can your legs be fake? Am I disabled and need a prosthesis or something?"

[This operation is good][qwq So I am a fan of Tangtang because she is so real...]

[I said that, you believe it? ◈◈Artificial Limb 66666◈

"My high school entrance exam results, I admit that I was not in the mood to study because of family matters. My grades plummeted. I was a student who chose to go to that high school... I was rebellious. I didn't fall in love early, I didn't take drugs, I didn't go to bars, I didn't go out to socialize. I did degenerate a little in the first semester of high school, but..."

Chang Zhi's hand holding the mouse stopped, and she said slowly, "After that, because of a conflict with a classmate, maybe I left an impression of a bad kid who didn't study in the teacher's mind before, the teacher chose to believe the classmate who had better grades than me instead of me. I don't know if you know that feeling of being unable to defend yourself. After that, I was notified, and I felt so cowardly that I let my parents and aunt down, so I worked hard to study, and was divided into the key class of liberal arts and science..."

Chang Zhi still remembers that feeling.

The feeling of being isolated and helpless, and the whole world doesn't believe you.

◈Wow, I hate teachers being so partial...◈◈I have had such an experience, hug...◈◈............Did I wrong you? ◈◈...I'm sorry◈

Several long comments suddenly appeared in the barrage, and they passed by one by one. The rest of the comments were silently reduced, as if they had become the narration of the owner of that comment, and Chang Zhi noticed it at a glance——

�Chang Zhi, I'm sorry that I was watching and didn't say anything before. I was Chang Zhi's former classmate in high school. I came early that morning, so I should be the only witness. The reason was that l put a dead mouse in Chang Zhi's desk the day before. The classmates in our class knew about it, but because l was more dominant and Chang Zhi didn't play with us much, no one reminded her�

�Chang Zhi should have wanted to see who did it the next day. Anyway, she came very early. I heard l say the day before that she was going to put a box of live cockroaches and caterpillars. Why did I see it? Because it was English morning reading that day, I came early to recite the text. As a result, I saw l scolding Chang Zhi at the door. The scolding was very ugly. I didn't dare to go in. Then Chang Zhi and l had an argument...]

[After that, it was just like Chang Zhi said. It was l who complained first. L was also a relative of the head of the grade... I didn't dare to say it before because I was afraid that someone would scold me, but... Chang Zhi, I'm sorry, I didn't expect it to turn out like this. I regretted it before. I should have said it earlier, not only now but also in high school. .]

[This is the belated truth. I really feel sorry for you...]

Chang Zhi watched the end of the barrage pass by, and then the screen was filled again, and the discussion was all about the dozens of long barrages just now.

[Screenshot][Is this school bullying][Oh my god, dead rats, living cockroaches and caterpillars, goose bumps all over my body][How can a girl be so vicious...][I can't imagine how Tang Zhi got through it, I feel bad...][You should have said it earlier if you knew, then who is the l?]

Chang Zhi looked at the comments, lowered her eyes and stared at the keyboard for a long time without speaking.

She knew who was talking, her surname was Yang, she couldn't remember her name, but after she typed l, she ran out and bumped into her.

She knew that classmate Yang must have seen it, but later the teacher asked her parents to come. When she told the teacher about the prank, the teacher scolded her for having a rich imagination, and no one in the class testified for her.

At that time, she looked at classmate Yang, who lowered his head, very low.

Chang Zhi instantly felt as if she was dead.

Chang Zhi was silent for a long time, so long that the barrage of comments asked her why she didn't speak. Chang Zhi sniffed, looked up at the camera and said: "I seem to know who you are. I can understand you. After all, I used to be a little lonely and "weird". Helping me means being isolated. I also understand your choice. But thank you for coming out to help me clear my name now... Thank you."

Chang Zhi's voice was a little hoarse, and she blinked hard: "Cheers, let's continue to look at Weibo. The last in the grade, that was also in the first semester of the first year of high school. There were six reports. If you say too much, it's just two... I got into S University based on my ability. The college entrance examination is the most rigorous exam. There should be no objection to this, right?

The live broadcast ended at five o'clock.

In two hours, she had explained everything she wanted to explain.

The reason why Chang Zhi wanted to start the live broadcast was not to explain to strangers and haters. Her original purpose was to explain to fans.

It was just to give an explanation to fans.

After all, it's not that she hasn't experienced being wronged and unable to refute before.

Chang Zhi hoped that no matter what, she would at least be a positive and inspiring image in front of them, and didn't want to make them sad because of this incident.

Chang Zhi understood the uncomfortable feeling of having the person she loved shattered in an instant.

It was too sad, and her heart ached faintly, as if someone was pulling it apart.

Chang Zhi sat on the sofa, rubbed her eyes, and saw several bags of garbage that had not been thrown away for three days by the door.

Find something to do, go downstairs to throw away the garbage far away, and then walk home slowly.

Chang Zhi walked over and picked up three bags of garbage, two in one hand and one in the other, and stuffed her mobile phone in her pocket. The garbage bags were full and heavy.

Chang Zhi stood in front of the door with the garbage and realized that she had no hands to open the door. She put down a bag and opened the door. Chang Zhi pushed the door and took the garbage out. When she turned around to lock the door, she heard the "click" sound of the door lock behind her. She turned around with the garbage and met Wen Yanxing who had just opened the door and leaned halfway.

At Wen Yanxing's house, the bathroom is designed near the entrance. After watching the live broadcast and washing his hands, he heard the sound of a door opening and closing outside. He knew that Chang Zhi was going out, so he quickly shook his hands and opened the door.

He happened to meet a woman with red eyes and a red nose, who looked decadent. Chang Zhi was wearing casual shorts and a loose white T-shirt, casual at home.

Wen Yanxing paused when he opened the door. Although she was not dressed up, it looked good on Chang Zhi, making her long legs look even longer, and her slender body looked even more fragile.

... I feel like I will fall down if the wind blows. He thought to himself.

Wen Yanxing saw Chang Zhi holding three bags of garbage in her hands, pretending to be nonchalant and picking up the garbage bags that he had just poured out of the trash can by his door yesterday, and naturally chatted with her: "Hey, what a coincidence, are you going to take out the garbage too?"

Chang Zhi was a little confused, and she said in a hoarse voice: "Well... you too? "

"Well," Wen Yanxing closed the door, raised the garbage bag in his hand, looked at her and asked, "Together?"

Chang Zhi was stunned. She didn't know why her reaction after the live broadcast was always slow. She asked slowly after half a minute: "...Are you inviting me to throw away the garbage with you?" So there is such an operation?

Wen Yanxing asked back: "Yes, is it not possible?"

Chang Zhi sniffed, lowered her eyes and looked at the flip-flops she was wearing casually on her feet. Her tone was slow and there was no ripples: "It's not impossible, but I may go a little further to throw away the garbage. If you want to go together, then go together."

After Chang Zhi said this, she struggled to pick up the garbage and walked towards the elevator. Her back looked like a paper man, as if she would fall at any time.

Chang Zhi had just taken two steps when she was stopped by Wen Yanxing. Wen Yanxing said: "Wait a minute, I will help you get two bags? "

Chang Zhi stopped and felt that the bags of garbage were heavier. She said, "No, I'll carry them myself."

"Don't... these bags look heavy. I'm afraid your shoulders will collapse from carrying them," Wen Yanxing recalled Chang Zhi who almost fell down the stairs that day. "You said that neighbors should help each other... Give it to me. "

Chang Zhi stood there, thinking quickly in her heart, is he talking about her going to the hospital yesterday? Or is he concerned about her?

Wen Yanxing bent down and took over Chang Zhi's two bags of garbage before she could refuse.

He wanted to take them all, but was afraid that Chang Zhi would be embarrassed.

Chang Zhi lowered her head and stared at her other empty hand, then looked up at Wen Yanxing who had walked in front of her first.

The nervous mood came back again.

She pursed her lips, said nothing, and followed into the elevator.

There is actually a garbage room nearby, but it is too close. Chang Zhi wants to go to a nearby community, which also has a garbage room. There is also an open park when she walks out.

Chang Zhi originally wanted to relax, alone, at night, quietly, and don't think about anything.

Unexpectedly, after she threw away the garbage, Chang Zhi thought Wen Yanxing would go back first, but he still followed her, and... walked into the park at night shoulder to shoulder with her.

Chang Zhi: "...You, don't you want to go back? ? "

Chapter 29 Finally I couldn't help it

It was getting dark, and it was time for dinner. The number of people in the park gradually decreased.

Chang Zhi saw Wen Yanxing following her into the entrance of the park. She finally couldn't help asking Wen Yanxing why he didn't go back.

Wen Yanxing paused, lowered his head and looked at her with his back to the light: "Walking."

Chang Zhi said: "... I thought you were just taking out the trash with me."

"I also thought you were just taking out the trash with me," Wen Yanxing repeated her words, "so it's such a coincidence that my next trip is also a night tour of the park."

Chang Zhi was choked, she stopped talking, and couldn't help thinking in her heart, what does Wen Yanxing mean by this?

The further you walk into the park, the denser the trees are. The setting sun shines on the stone path. A gust of evening breeze blows, and the fallen leaves flutter, spinning in the air before reluctantly falling to the ground.

Chang Zhi felt something touching her head. She shrank her neck in shock, and when she turned around, she saw Wen Yanxing's hand awkwardly suspended in the air.

Chang Zhi realized that it was Wen Yanxing's hand that touched her just now. She was nervous and asked loudly in panic, "What are you doing?"

"Ahem," Wen Yanxing awkwardly withdrew his hand, pointed at her hair and then at the ground, "A leaf fell on your head. I didn't have time to get rid of it, and you shook it off yourself."

...What leaf? Chang Zhi looked down, but saw a pile of fallen leaves. She turned her head away and lowered her voice: "Oh, so that's it."

"When are you going back?" Chang Zhi asked again.

Wen Yanxing asked back: "When do you want to go back?"

"I," Chang Zhi thought for a while, "You must be tired, so I'll go back if my legs hurt."

"Yeah," Wen Yanxing nodded, "Call me if you're tired."

Chang Zhi: "..."

Chang Zhi paused for a long time before tilting her head and asking him, "Do you really want to walk with me?"

"Yeah," Wen Yanxing couldn't deny it, but he walked to Chang Zhi's side unconsciously and walked shoulder to shoulder with her.

"I saw the Weibo." After a while, Wen Yanxing suddenly said.

Weibo? Chang Zhi was stunned, and then understood.

Is it about her being on the hot search? It's inevitable, after all, the other party revealed her name, and the neighbors around her, as long as they are online, will know it's her.

But for some reason, Chang Zhi didn't want Wen Yanxing to see these. But the fact is that he still saw it...

Instantly thinking of those bad things again, Chang Zhi stared at the ground, not knowing what to say, and silently asked: "Then what?"

"Just want to say," Wen Yanxing looked at her little head that was only left to him because she lowered her head, "There's no need to care too much about other people's eyes, you have done very well."

He hesitated for a moment, and finally raised his hand and tentatively placed his hand on Chang Zhi's head.

Chang Zhi was stunned, motionless, time seemed to stop at this moment, the wind stopped, the leaves stopped falling, the sunset went slower, and her heart, beating fast, was completely opposite to their appearance.

Then, she felt a warm hand gently caressing her head, and the tingling sensation spread from the top of her head to her heart.

Wen Yanxing's low voice also came from above her head, the voice was very light, and the tone was unexpectedly tinged with a hint of tenderness——

"Don't think that you are the only one fighting alone, there are many people accompanying you. Besides, if your uncle and aunt see how good you are now, they will be very happy."

Chang Zhi looked up at him, and he just took his hand away, and her shadow was imprinted in his ink-colored eyes.

She nodded gently, feeling much more relaxed, and she replied: "Well... thank you."

Wen Yanxing asked: "Have you eaten?"

After Chang Zhi finished the live broadcast, she went out in the evening and didn't even think about eating.

She shook her head: "No."

"Me neither," Wen Yanxing said with a soft look in his eyes, "then let's have a meal together."

...Ah?

He invited her...to eat?

Chang Zhi stood there, and along with the sound of her heartbeat, she heard herself agreeing in a mysterious way: "Okay."

Hearing Chang Zhi's response, Wen Yanxing's lips curled slightly.

There is a Sichuan restaurant near the park. Chang Zhi chose this restaurant after asking Wen Yanxing if he could eat spicy food. She had been here before and knew that this restaurant was opened by a Sichuan couple and the taste was very authentic.

At mealtime, the small restaurant was full of people, men and women, all kinds of people, various dialects and Mandarin mixed together, lively and full of life.

There was only one air conditioner and eight pendant fans in the store. Although it was not very cool, it was much better than the temperature outside. Chang Zhi and Wen Yanxing found a double seat in the corner. The square table was just enough for Chang Zhi to put her arms on it.

The store owner brought a bottle of boiled water and two disposable plastic cups, poured a cup for each of them, took a menu and gave them to them, and let them look at it themselves.

Chang Zhi knew that the Mapo Tofu in this restaurant was delicious, spicy and numbing. She found the location of the dish and looked up to ask Wen Yanxing: "Do you eat tofu?"

"Um... Mapo Tofu?" Wen Yanxing saw the dish that Chang Zhi pointed to, "Order it if you like, I'm not picky."

Chang Zhi looked up at Wen Yanxing: "Really?"

"Really," Wen Yanxing nodded, "I don't care about meat or vegetables, I can eat green onions, ginger, coriander, onions, and garlic... But I'd better not have garlic, the smell is too strong."

"You still eat coriander," Chang Zhi looked at him in surprise, "Don't you think the taste of coriander is weird?"

Chang Zhi can't eat coriander. She can tolerate putting it in hot pot, but if she eats it directly, it's really...

"Is it weird?" Wen Yanxing asked, "The taste of coriander... Compared with ordinary dishes, there's nothing special about it. I don't feel anything special."

"But it seems that some people can eat it, and some people can't," Wen Yanxing added.

"Well, then I am the type that cannot eat it," Chang Zhi said, pointing to the menu, and then said, "Since you don't have any taboos...then I will take care of it? If you order something you haven't eaten before, don't blame me if it doesn't taste good."

"Okay."

The young girl next to her held up a small notebook, listening to the conversation between the two, and decided to silently write down the mapo tofu that the two had just talked about.

Considering that there were only two people, Chang Zhi ordered two more meat dishes and did not ask for the restaurant's soup.

She didn't like to drink soup in the summer very much. She was afraid of heat, and soup tasted better when it was hot... Although she knew that some soups could clear heat and reduce fire, she understood the reason, but she couldn't do it.

The girl who took the order took the order to the kitchen.

After ordering the dishes, it was time to wait. The fan whirred overhead, and the rotation made bursts of noise. The wooden table was a little greasy. Chang Zhi wiped the place where the bowl was placed in front of the table with a paper towel, but it didn't work, so she finally gave up.

The food in this restaurant is quite good, but there is always a greasy spot on the table that is hard to wipe clean. However, as a small restaurant, there are quite a lot of customers, so it is inevitable to be so busy.

Wen Yanxing watched Chang Zhi busying around with a tissue and taking care of his table, and the corners of his lips rose unconsciously.

Chang Zhi put the tissue on the edge of the table against the wall, and looked up to see Wen Yanxing's smile that he couldn't retract in time.

"What are you laughing at?" Chang Zhi asked.

Wen Yanxing shook his head and commented: "You like cleanliness very much, which is good."

"No," Chang Zhi pointed at the table, "Don't you think so? The tabletop is too oily. If you touch it by accident, it feels weird. If you don't believe me, just touch it."

Wen Yanxing had not noticed it until Chang Zhi said so. He touched the table with his fingers, rubbing his thumb and index finger. It felt greasy and uncomfortable. He took a tissue to wipe it off. He couldn't wipe it clean. He was silent and said: "...Okay...it's pretty bad."

Chang Zhi couldn't help laughing: "Go home and wash it with detergent or soap and it will be clean."

Wen Yanxing nodded.

Chang Zhi took a sip of water, and another customer came in. Because there was no seat, she stood there and looked around. Chang Zhi secretly thanked herself for coming early.

If you come late, you have to stand there and wait for a seat. In the hot summer, people's appetite is inevitably poor. Spicy food stimulates appetite, so this store has such good business.

Chang Zhi looked at the people around her and then returned her gaze to Wen Yanxing.

Wen Yanxing looked down at his phone. From her angle, it looked like a penguin interface.

Chang Zhi supported her chin with one hand, thinking about the incident in the park. She looked at his face and asked, "Do you care about every girl... Oh no, I mean, do you care about people you know when they are in trouble?"

"What kind of care do you mean?" Wen Yanxing asked.

"Just..." Chang Zhi recalled, unable to describe it, so she had to say, "Just now, the kind of care you cared about me?"

Chang Zhi looked at her fingers and continued, "I'm just curious. Don't you have a sister? You wouldn't think of me as a girl like your sister, so..." You touched my head, right?

Wen Yanxing looked at her quietly, and the air suddenly became quiet.

Just when Chang Zhi felt that she shouldn't ask these questions, Wen Yanxing spoke up-

"No." Wen Yanxing looked very frank, "My concern for my sister is the concern of a family member, and my concern for you... I don't know what kind of psychological concern it is."

"Maybe it's a special concern."

Chapter 30 New Topic

After Chang Zhi's live broadcast ended, a new topic quickly emerged on Weibo——

Hot topic on Weibo: #Sorry, for the words I typed on the keyboard#

Introduction: Inspired by the recent incident of the female milk tea store manager, have you ever made a wrong statement because you didn't know the truth? Have you ever added bricks and tiles to the black material that has no real evidence? Take this as a warning, and I hope that we can be cautious in our words and deeds in the future, not to spread rumors or slander...

[Why is he happy]: #Tang Zhi is sorry# I'm sorry that I once criticized you because I didn't know the truth. I watched the live broadcast replay and silently deleted it. It really hurts my face and... I'm sorry.

[Meow and Rabbit]: #Tangzhi I'm sorry# I originally thought it was a story about a social girl who became a rich and beautiful woman, but later I found out that it was a story about an orphan who inspired her to become a rich and beautiful woman. The previous comments have been deleted, hope you can forgive me...

[Voice of the World]: There have been cases where haters caused celebrities to suffer from depression. I was deeply impressed at the time and decided to be careful with my words in the future. I didn't expect that I would be slapped in the face in a few days. I thought what I said was right, but it was all false. . . I'm sorry.

[Loving you is the most important thing]: Am I the only one who wants to know who L is? Liu? Liu?

Chang Zhi saw these messages after she returned home.

She was still dizzy and at a loss when she returned home. When she saw these messages, her rationality returned, but she was neither happy nor sad.

Even if it was the topic of #Tangzhi I'm sorry#, she was indifferent and expressionless after reading it.

The hurt is the hurt. You said sorry, which means that the matter is over, but it does not mean that the hurt has disappeared.

Chang Zhi scrolled down the interface expressionlessly, and a microblog was pushed to the top.

She looked at the microblog, which was very short, and finished it in a flash. After reading it, she felt complicated and mixed emotions.

[biezhao5le]: Please, some of you, please stop disturbing my life. I admit the mistakes I made when I was young and ignorant. I apologize. It has been so many years since the incident. We all have our own lives. You can scold me, but please don't harass my family. [This account has been abandoned]

[Comment]

[Sky Blue]: Netizens are powerful. They can figure out a surname. From the records, it seems that she stepped on Chang Zhi twice. What does she do? :)

[The Daily Life of Li Nanshen]: Haha, what do you mean by being ignorant? You admit it. I was originally skeptical about what Chang Zhi said, but seeing your attitude, I believe it?

[Oh my, what's wrong with you]: People do what they do. The mistakes I made at the beginning were not bad at the time, but they will be bad later. After all, good and evil will be rewarded.

[Incompetent in naming]: It seems that he only said reluctantly for the sake of his family: "Ah, I was wrong, I apologize, I apologize, but don't tell my family..." Wow, it's disgusting, I've never seen such a person before.

The comments were almost all one-sided condemnation. Chang Zhi watched coldly, but the dark side of her heart had to admit... She was secretly happy.

Now you understand, God will take its course, and no one will be spared.

In fact, Chang Zhi didn't say the name during the live broadcast, and always used classmates instead, but the vast number of enthusiastic netizens are always very enthusiastic about promoting justice, and she didn't expect it to turn out like this.

Looking at the ID that has been changed to "Don't look for me", Chang Zhi didn't want to watch it anymore.

It's meaningless. Chang Zhi thought carefully, she is living a very satisfied life now. l No matter what, it has nothing to do with her.

Without looking at this, Chang Zhi went to do her business, but before that she received a message from Yan Zhi.

[Yan Zhi]: The matter is resolved?

[Simple and hardworking Tang Zhi]: Forget it.

[Yan Zhi]: ...That's it? You're not going to talk about the water army thing?

[Simple and hardworking Tang Zhi]: No, I can't waste your kindness, I was just going to talk about it.

[Simple and hardworking Tang Zhi]: I heard that you recommended my live broadcast today?

[Yan Zhi]: Well...no matter what, there are still a lot of people following me, and there are also people who know about this matter but don't know about the live broadcast and are still living in a dream. If you forward it, more people will know that you want to clarify, and it will be easier for you to clear it.

[Simple and hardworking Tang Zhi]: I was stunned when I saw the barrage.

[Yan Zhi]: Are you very touched?

[Simple and hardworking Tang Zhi]: A little bit, I can't repay you.

[Yan Zhi]: Then... promise me your body.

Seeing this line of words, Chang Zhi was slightly stunned.

This is the... second time.

[Simple and hardworking Tang Zhi]: Don't make a fuss. Promise me your body or something, qwq I will take it seriously if you do this again.

[Yanzhi]: ...

[Yanzhi]: Have you always thought this was fake?

[Simple and hardworking Tang Zhi]: No... What else?

[Yanzhi]: ... But I am serious.

[Simple and hardworking Tang Zhi]: ...

Inexplicably, Chang Zhi saw a sense of grievance in that line of words. She suddenly lay down in front of the computer, her head buried in her arms, her face hot, her mind full of garbled characters, and it took a long time to restart.

Seriously, seriously, seriously... If this is true, then Yanzhi's inexplicable concern and enthusiasm have a reason.

But, but... Wen Yanxing. Chang Zhi sighed in her heart.

Although Chang Zhi herself didn't understand, she knew that she seemed to have a special feeling for him. If she had to describe it, it might be called heartbeat.

But she had a good impression of Yanzhi, after all, Yanzhi was so good to her.

Chang Zhi almost hated herself to death. The balance was tilted to both sides. It was not that she did not like Yan Zhi, but that she did not dare to like him. She just knew that online love basically had no results. Either it was a spiritual love that died in the open, or they were in different places and ended up being mobile phone boyfriends and girlfriends. The last possibility was so small that it was unbelievable - to go to the end.

Chang Zhi had no confidence in herself and did not have the perseverance and courage to achieve the last one.

So her subconscious love was more inclined to Wen Yanxing.

But it was because of this that it was more annoying!

[Simple and hardworking Tang Zhi]: ...... Is this a confession?

[Yan Zhi]: Looking at your expression, I began to think that this was a rape of a commoner.

Rape of a commoner - Chang Zhi could not hold back for a moment.

[Simple and hardworking Tang Zhi]: Then should I cooperate with you to shout for help?

[Yan Zhi]: ... Go ahead and shout until your throat is hoarse and see if anyone will respond to you.

[Simple and hardworking Tang Zhi]: If I really shout, there will definitely be someone.

[Yan Zhi]: I didn't hear it, I didn't see it.

[Simple and hardworking Tang Zhi]: ... ... applause for your performance

[Simple and hardworking Tang Zhi]: Seriously... you don't know where I'm from or what I do, how can you like me?

[Yan Zhi]: I know where you're from, Z City.

[Simple and hardworking Tang Zhi]: ! ! ?

[Yan Zhi]: It's written in your profile, and on Weibo. .

[Simple and hardworking Tang Zhi]: Okay, what about you.

[Yan Zhi]: In the same city.

—— In the same... In the same city!!

Chang Zhi stared at these two words, and the balance in her heart that was about to tilt to one side was straightened out a lot.

Chang Zhi felt like she was standing there swaying, she covered her face and couldn't help shouting in annoyance.

[Yan Zhi]: As for the last question, I'll tell you when you agree to marry me.

[Simple and hardworking Tang Zhi]: Ah, you are just teasing me... Seriously, let me think about it for a whole night.

[Simple and hardworking Tang Zhi]: I will tell you tomorrow morning, I won't disappear.

Chang Zhi doesn't want to lose Yan Zhi as a friend.

After all, they got along well in the few chats they had, and they also have a common big circle on Bilibili...

She doesn't want to tease him, she wants to calm down and think seriously, but she decides to do the business first.

Chang Zhi downloaded a picture-destroying app, took the screenshots Yan Zhi sent her, only left the water army, and then pieced them together into a long picture.

Upload the picture and post on Weibo.

[It's Tang Zhi, not Tangzhi v]: I don't know why someone is willing to spend a lot of money to blackmail a small up like me. But I don't care what you want, anyway, I already know who you are with the evidence in my hand. Two choices: 1. Take the initiative to apologize on Weibo, leave it hanging, and don't delete it in the future. 2. Sue you. [Long picture]

[Comment]

[You are the cutest]: 6666 There is a reversal! ! ?

[A little star in the sky]: WOC, it turns out that Weibo really has such a magical thing as water army software, it costs a lot of money, it's terrible.

[Oh my God]: Didn't you say a few days ago that Chang Zhi self-promoted to become famous, slapped in the face? Does it hurt? Do you want to laugh me to death and inherit my inheritance?

[Little Jasmine]: The sound of slapping in the face rang in the air, hahaha, who would self-promote and blacken himself like this?

[I am willing to do it for you]: Okay, haters, shut your stinky mouths, look at the hammer, does it hurt?

Chapter 31 Fans

Never underestimate fans.

Because you never know what groups your fans are made up of, students, workers, white-collar workers, technology geeks...

There are thousands of people in the world, and there will always be people whose skills are adapted to the current situation.

Everything is possible.

An hour after Chang Zhi posted on Weibo, someone followed the few contents of Chang Zhi's picture and touched Yueya.

Later, some of Chang Zhi's fans found that Yueya had liked several Weibo posts many times, and most of the content was slandering Chang Zhi.

She accidentally followed one of the zombie accounts, and unfortunately, the zombie account had software advertisements.

People with a guilty conscience cannot bear this kind of pressure.

Yueya had just graduated not long ago. She was an art student who was admitted to university, but her academic performance was not good, and the school she was admitted to was still average. After graduation, because her family had some money, she stayed at home for a year.

Last year, "The Pure Land" swept B station, and Chang Zhi also did a cover dance, collaborating with Anan. Yueya saw it and started to watch Chang Zhi's videos crazily.

Then, she started to learn by herself in her room and joined the home dance area.

Once she accidentally heard a senior schoolmate she knew mentioned Chang Zhi, and she was shocked at the time. After seeing the photo, she didn't expect that this "Tang Zhi" was really the Chang Zhi she had heard about in school before.

Later, when Yueya posted a cover dance again, some people said that she was imitating Chang Zhi. She posted whatever Chang Zhi posted... Yueya started to feel unhappy.

Obviously, everyone danced to Chang Zhi, so what's the point of picking her? She just followed the crowd and occasionally had her own works, okay?

It's easy to turn from a fan to a hater. It only takes a moment.

Chang Zhi has been suppressing her for a long time, and Yueya is unwilling to accept it. She has been dancing for more than a year and participated in many exhibitions, but she still can't make a difference.

Later, she pushed the issue herself. Yueya didn't know what was going on. Maybe it was out of resentment, maybe jealousy, or maybe she wanted to see Chang Zhi go from having no black spots to being pushed into the mud and getting stained with stains that couldn't be washed off.

But later she regretted it, and then Yueya saw Chang Zhi's Weibo.

Yueya walked around the room anxiously, and finally sat back in front of the computer and sent a private message.

[Yueya Wanwan]: I'm sorry.

Chang Zhi didn't expect Yueya to be so cowardly that she sent her a private message in less than an hour.

[Tang Zhi]: Do what the Weibo content says.

[Yueya Wanwan]: ....

Half an hour later, almost half of the people in the dance circle of Station B knew what Yueya had done.

A long apology letter, and an announcement of retirement.

Yueya's fans, who were not many to begin with, lost a large number of fans because of this incident.

An Nan, Sister Qiao, and other friends in Chang Zhi's circle forwarded Chang Zhi's Weibo.

Yueya is a player who has never been seen before and will never be seen again in the circle. She hit a wall when she first invested money. Various ups denounced her for corrupting the atmosphere, and Yueya could only retire in disgrace.

The aftermath of the online storm is still there, but life must go on.

Chang Zhi woke up before six o'clock.

Early in the morning, Chang Zhi sat in the quilt, staring at the dark room in a daze.

The brain of the card machine started again, and Chang Zhi remembered what she was going to do this morning - tell Yanzhi her answer.

But she didn't think about the money until she went to bed last night.

I don't know if you have such confusion.

Originally living a regular life, suddenly one day, two different people broke into your life and intersected with you in two completely different ways.

Chang Zhi couldn't tell which feeling came first, but she knew it was not good.

She lay on the bed, opened WeChat, and privately chatted with Deng Jiadai at five in the morning.

[Tang Zhi]: Are you there? Help me, sister.

Although she knew Deng Jiadai should be sleeping at this time, she knew that Deng Jiadai would get up at 7 o'clock at the latest, and she hoped that Deng Jiadai would see her message at first sight.

Who knew that Deng Jiadai actually... replied to her.

[Your Jia]: What are you doing, you got up so early? I'm squatting on the toilet.

[Tang Zhi]: ...Get up so early to open the toilet?

[Your Jia]: I ate too much these two days and got angry. You know, I ate more vegetables and had a stomachache in the middle of the night. If not squatting now, when else?

[Tang Zhi]: ...Suddenly I don't want to ask you.

[Your Jia]: Don't, you aroused my curiosity and you have to answer me.

[Tang Zhi]: I'm afraid you will hold it back when you get excited...

[Your Jia]: Why are you so heavy-mouthed? No, no, hurry up and say it.

[Tang Zhi]: I have feelings for two men at the same time, one I have met and the other I have not met. The former is just so-so in chatting with the latter, the former seems to have feelings for me and the latter confesses clearly... If it were you, which one would you choose?

[Your Jia]: .... I was so scared that I collapsed instantly. .

[Your Jia]: Three years... Damn, your iron tree has bloomed?

[Tang Zhi]: Fuck your iron tree, it's not used like this.

[Tang Zhi]: I am serious about this question, look at me, I am very serious, answer me, what should I do, I am so confused, I set up a fg last night and said this morning that I would not disappear, but I really want to stay at home and not look at anything...

[Your Jia]: Okay, let me see, let's not talk about the first one, the second one... How do you know?

Chang Zhi was scared,

[Tang Zhi]: How do you know?

[Your Jia]: Then the first one is Mr. Wen who sent you to the hospital that day.

�Tang Zhi��..................

�Tang Zhi��Did you install surveillance in my room? Or install something weird on my phone?

�Your Jia��Girl, you have a really big imagination. Don't worry, there is no such thing. How could there be such a thing?

�Your Jia��Actually, even a fool can see that Mr. Wen carried you to the ambulance out of humanitarianism. Why did he follow you to the hospital? Watching the fun? Funny. Besides, Yan Zhi always speaks for you. Just look at it yourself. How long has it been? How many times.

�Your Jia��But speaking of it, I personally like people who can be seen in real life and have actual actions. I prefer your neighbor. By the way, have you met Yan Zhi in person?

�Tang Zhi��No, he said he is from the same city as me. . Yan Zhi also helped me. He was the one who hired the Internet troop...

�Your Jia��It's good to be from the same city. Meet him and decide after meeting him.

[Your Jia]: But I'm afraid of this kind of otaku. It's not my prejudice. If you stay at home for a long time without seeing the sun and day and night, you may get fat and acne. Be prepared before the meeting. By the way, you actually chatted with him... Interesting.

[Tang Zhi]:... Don't say that as if it's exaggerated.

[Tang Zhi]: What should I say? Should I just tell him that we should meet?

[Your Jia]: How do you know he's not an up of B station? You're not an up of B station? I saw it recently. Isn't there a BW event this Friday, Saturday and Sunday? Aren't you going?

[Tang Zhi]: Go, he invited me before, the flight is on Thursday afternoon... I don't know if he will go.

[Your Jia]: Let me give you another bad idea. I came here like this before. Wait, I'll clean my ass first.

[Tang Zhi]: ....

Dislike, dislike, dislike.

About three minutes later, Deng Jiadai slowly replied to her.

[Your Jia]: Lying on the warm bed, I will tell you the method.

[Tang Zhi]: Okay, you tell me.

[Your Jia]: First, take out your wallet, and then find a one-yuan RMB.

[Tang Zhi]: You want me to toss a coin? Are you okay? Tossing a coin for this kind of thing...

[Your Jia]: I told you it's a bad idea, just ignore it and do it as I say.

[Your Jia]: How can I know the number, Mr. Wen with flowery face, tell me after you toss it.

So, at five o'clock in the morning, Chang Zhi got out of bed, found her wallet, took out a one-yuan coin from it, and fell into a daze.

The index finger was slightly bent, the coin was placed on it, and with a little force, the coin was thrown up, and it made a few points in the air, and was caught by Chang Zhi with both hands closed.

She maintained the posture of catching the coin, and moved away the hand covering the result in the dim light.

Flowery face, it was Wen Yanxing.

At that moment, an impulse came from nowhere, and Chang Zhi thought, it must be fake, why not throw it again? Throw it?

However, she still took the coin with the flower side facing up and reported to Deng Jiadai.

[Tang Zhi]: ...flower side.

[Your Jia]: Well, do you want to throw it again?

[Tang Zhi]: ....

[Your Jia]: If you want to throw it again, I don't need me to tell you, I think you should already know the answer.

Chang Zhi looked at what Deng Jiadai said, and then looked at the coin in her palm.

The palm of her hand was a little sticky, and she was sweating...

Some of the fog in front of her was suddenly cleared, and Chang Zhi tightened her hand and made up her mind.

[8:30 am]

[Simple and hardworking Tang Zhi]: Friday's bw, are you going? I didn't find your name on the list.

[Simple and hardworking Tang Zhi]: If you go, let's meet.

[Yan Zhi]: ....

[Yan Zhi]: OK.

Chapter 32 Variety Show

On Thursday, Chang Zhi got up very early.

She had watched a variety show last night to calm down, and only packed half of her luggage. She was so sleepy that she fell asleep immediately.

Today, she got up early to pack the remaining half of her luggage.

Her flight was at 2pm, and she originally planned to play for a day on Friday, then attend the show on Saturday, and then travel alone for a few days until Tuesday.

Now she wants to meet Yan Zhi, um... Chang Zhi carefully picked a few sets of ladylike and fresh clothes and skirts.

Most boys will have a good impression of this type of girl, right? Pure... pure?

Shoes... Will high heels make her look more elegant? Taller ones? No, this is in the south, what if Yan Zhi is not tall, wouldn't it be embarrassing?

So Chang Zhi chose low-heeled shoes and sneakers.

After packing her luggage, Chang Zhi looked at the carefully selected clothes, even with small accessories, and covered her face and felt that she was exaggerating.

Hey... I don't know what will happen yet, why is she so attentive?

Chang Zhi kicked the lid of the suitcase down with a kick, then squatted down to zip it up.

She ate something casually at noon, then went out with her luggage.

At the elevator, she ran into Wen Yanxing, who was carrying a black backpack. Chang Zhi paused with mixed feelings.

Wen Yanxing heard the sound of high heels tapping on the ground, and turned around to see Chang Zhi wearing a classic white shirt and A-line skirt, with slightly curly hair obediently draped over her shoulders.

Wen Yanxing's eyes were fixed on her collarbone.

Only one of the three buttons was fastened, and the beautiful collarbone was faintly visible. Looking up, Chang Zhi looked innocent. Wen Yanxing coughed lightly, looked away, and asked knowingly: "Where are you going? Carrying a suitcase."

Chang Zhi looked down at the suitcase, looked up and said: "I have something to do in Shanghai."

"Oh," Wen Yanxing nodded, pretending to ask casually, "What time is the flight?"

"Two o'clock." Chang Zhi said.

Wen Yanxing nodded, fortunately he bought a high-speed rail ticket...

Chang Zhi glanced at the bag he was carrying, which was bulging and looked very heavy.

"Are you going out to play?"

"No," Wen Yanxing shook his head, lying without changing his face, "Go home and stay for two days."

"Oh..." Chang Zhi nodded, and then said nothing.

She thought of the moment of tossing a coin yesterday. Obviously, he didn't do anything to her, and she didn't do anything to him, but she didn't dare to look at Wen Yanxing.

They parted ways downstairs at home, and Chang Zhi went to the airport.

Waiting, boarding, three hours later, the plane arrived in SH city.

The next day, Chang Zhi got up early.

She pondered for a long time over the several sets of clothes she took out of the suitcase.

Pink? Too tender. Blue? I don't think the effect is so good. It looks too soft and so deliberate... Chang Zhi struggled internally, and finally chose a plaid skirt and a T-shirt, casual and natural.

Carefully put on a full set of makeup in front of the mirror, and finally applied the newly bought YSL No. 12 male-killing color. Chang Zhi looked in the mirror, satisfied, perfect.

When she was ready to go out, she took out her mobile phone and Yan Zhi sent her a message.

[Yan Zhi]: Have you woken up?

[Simple and hardworking Tang Zhi]: Of course, look at what time it is now... How can I not wake up at ten o'clock.

[Yan Zhi]: Just asking formally, otherwise how can I find you.

[Simple and hardworking Tang Zhi]: I'm going out... See you at the venue or outside?

Chang Zhi typed this sentence and sent it out, feeling a little nervous.

[Yan Zhi]: Let's go inside the venue, it's too hot outside.

[Yan Zhi]: I'm leaving too. ^�^

Chang Zhi looked at that smiling face and couldn't help curling her lips.

There was a super-large melting TV outside the bw venue, and Chang Zhi stopped to take a picture and sent it to Yan Zhi.

[Simple and hardworking Tang Zhi]: [Picture] The TV vividly shows my current state 2333.

[Yan Zhi]: I'm almost there. It's quite appropriate.

Chang Zhi put on a white hat, lowered the brim of the hat and lined up. To enter the venue, she had to walk through a passage that had no end in sight. The first thing Chang Zhi saw was a sea of people.

Chang Zhi suddenly felt a lot of pressure in her heart... It was too painful to walk such a long way...

The venue was bustling with people and noisy, and she finally entered the venue.

The whole venue was filled with the atmosphere of B station. Chang Zhi saw those bullet screen posters: "Funds are burning", "So boring, I closed it after watching it 300 times", "Stuck in a strange place" and so on.

For people who have feelings for B station, BW is really worth coming, in addition to the large number of people.

After all, there are also a lot of up masters coming! ! ! !

Chang Zhi held down her hat with one hand and held her mobile phone in the other hand as she shuttled through the crowd.

Occasionally, someone saw her back and thought that this girl was really a killer from behind.

[Simple and hardworking Tang Zhi]: Where shall we meet?

After sending this message, Chang Zhi looked up at the dark crowd.

I had never expected that it would be hot outside the venue, but inside the venue... there were so many people and it was so crowded.

[Yan Zhi]: I'm queuing here in the examination room.

...Examination room? ! Chang Zhi was stunned.

I saw it in the promotion before. BW has a special Bilibili exam room this time. The two-dimensional test paper will be taken on the spot. The top ten in each test can collect one of the eight chapters.

[Simple and hardworking Tang Zhi]: ... Are you going to take the exam?

[Yan Zhi]: Collect chapters.

[Simple and hardworking Tang Zhi]: Then you line up first, I'll come to find you.

As soon as Chang Zhi arrived outside the exam room, she saw a long queue.

She held her forehead with one hand and typed on her phone with pressure.

[Simple and hardworking Tang Zhi]: There are too many people. I can't find you. Where are you?

Wen Yanxing looked back and found Chang Zhi standing at the end of the line. He replied-

[Yan Zhi]: I'm in the middle of the line. Wearing a hat, white clothes, black pants, sneakers... I saw you, at the end,

Ah? He saw her?

Chang Zhi was panicking, and hurriedly walked out of the queue, walking towards the middle one by one.

White shirt, black pants, sneakers, hat... in the middle.

Chang Zhi muttered silently.

When she reached the middle of the queue, she saw a familiar figure.

The straight and broad back, even in a loose T-shirt, was particularly stylish. Looking up, the man was wearing a black hat, his head was lowered, holding a mobile phone in his slender hands, and his thumb was pressing something on the screen quickly.

Chang Zhi stopped, and the lock screen of her mobile phone lit up, showing a message on it.

[How to know]: Have you reached it?

Chang Zhi walked over quickly and stopped beside the man.

She felt as if she realized something, and had a guess in her heart that she dared not say out loud. Chang Zhi's heartbeat accelerated, and she walked over quickly and stopped beside Wen Yanxing.

She looked up at him and suddenly said, "What a coincidence, why are you here too?"

Wen Yanxing was startled. He was still waiting for a reply, but Chang Zhi walked up to him quietly and spoke suddenly.

This is not what he thought!

Shouldn't Chang Zhi have walked over without seeing him and then he shouted to stop, and Chang Zhi turned around and saw him so surprised that she couldn't speak?

What the hell?

It's totally different from what he thought! The same! Fall.

Wen Yanxing coughed lightly, a little embarrassed, and his voice was low: "...You're here?"

"I'm here?" Chang Zhi raised one eyebrow and said with a smile, "You've been waiting for a long time, aren't you tired of queuing?"

She looked at the phone in his hand. The screen was unlocked, and there were still chat records with her on it.

Wen Yanxing felt guilty, and he continued with Chang Zhi's words: "It's okay, it won't take long, and there are many people who can get in after one exam."

Chang Zhi nodded, and she felt the same way: "Yeah, there are a lot of people."

"Well, it's normal to have a lot of people. After all, it's the first bw, and the tickets are..." Not expensive,

Before Wen Yanxing finished speaking, Chang Zhi suddenly punched him on the arm with a fist. Wen Yanxing was caught off guard and almost fell backwards after being hit by Chang Zhi's punch. He swayed and barely stood firm. It was the first time he found that a girl could have such great strength?

? ? ? ?

The girl standing behind Wen Yanxing stared at the two of them in amazement, and there were a lot of question marks in her heart - meow meow meow?

Wen Yanxing felt that his worldview had been overturned. Chang Zhi... Shouldn't Chang Zhi be the kind of woman who looks weak but strong inside? How could she be so strong? She almost knocked him down by hitting him, a 70-kilogram man? ?

What is this operation? ? Can it be like this?

After being beaten, Wen Yanxing subconsciously grabbed Chang Zhi's hand that was about to be withdrawn after beating him, because he felt that if he didn't grab it, he would not be able to get forgiveness.

He grabbed the tightly clenched fist with one hand, and it fit perfectly. The cold feeling passed through his skin and entered his internal organs. Wen Yanxing was in a trance for a moment, and then he felt a dull pain in the arm that was beaten.

Sure enough, the next moment, he heard Chang Zhi's angry voice——

"Aren't you going home to stay for a few days? Why are you here?? Do you live in SH City? Your home is in BW???!!"

Chapter 33 Grab Chang Zhi's Hand

Wen Yanxing grabbed Chang Zhi's hand tightly, and Chang Zhi shook it to break free.

The girl behind Wen Yanxing silently said to the people behind her: "Please step back a little..." The people behind her stepped back, and she quickly took a big step back. The mysterious man and woman in the hat in front of her were about to fight for no reason. She was really afraid of being beaten. The girl covered her ears. She couldn't hear anything. Don't let her get hurt!

On the other side, Chang Zhi, who had no idea that passers-by saw her as a terrorist, stared at Wen Yanxing, her face flushed with anger, and she whispered: "Let go!"

Wen Yanxing pulled her, shamelessly pried her fingers apart, and then held her hand. He shook his head and said: "No."

Chang Zhi shook her hand, but couldn't shake it off. Wen Yanxing's nervous palms were sweating, and the warmth was transmitted to her hand.

Chang Zhi looked around, then raised her head and continued to stare at him fiercely, saying to him: "Are you really not going to let go?"

"No." Wen Yanxing said this in a sonorous and powerful voice.

Chang Zhi snorted and let him hold her hand, but she said sarcastically: "Always singing the opposite tune, why are you so childish? How come you are like a primary school student."

Wen Yanxing asked back: "Then are you the girlfriend of the primary school student?"

Chang Zhi's face flushed instantly, she bit her lip and turned her head away from Wen Yanxing, saying: "Did I promise you?"

Wen Yanxing raised his eyebrows slightly: "Then why do you want to see me?"

Chang Zhi refused to admit it, and said stubbornly: "I'm curious, curious about what you look like, and I just want to meet my online friend in person, okay?"

Wen Yanxing smiled and raised his hand that he had just shamelessly grabbed Chang Zhi: "What is this?"

"Then if you insist on grabbing me, what can I do?"

Wen Yanxing grabbed her hand with a little force and gently pulled it to his side. Chang Zhi involuntarily took two steps towards him, with her shoulder against his arm.

"So are you going to deny it?"

Chang Zhi didn't move. She didn't answer, but her heart was beating. She looked into the distance, where people were bustling around, and she was filled with mixed feelings.

She had never thought that these two people would be the same person.

Before she looked for Yan Zhi, she thought about what he looked like.

Yan Zhi might be thin and white because he didn't go out often and often ate instant noodles at home. He might also be fat because he was prone to obesity and sat in front of the computer for a long time. But because he was from the south, he might not be very tall. He might also wear a plaid shirt full of straight male aesthetics and black flip-flops.

Before meeting her, Yan Zhi might have combed his hair meticulously and shaved his beard clean like her.

Chang Zhi never thought that the person she met yesterday was the one she was looking for today. The neighbor next door was the one who had teased her after being a ghost.

Thinking of the entanglement of the past few days, Chang Zhi wondered what she had done.

This world is too mysterious... Chang Zhi wanted to hit Wen Yanxing hard again.

But then again, the current Wen Yanxing is just like the Yanzhi she knew.

Chang Zhi turned her head away from Wen Yanxing and suddenly said, "It's all fake."

Wen Yanxing was puzzled: "What's fake?"

"You were so gentle and polite before," Chang Zhi looked up at him and commented, "It's all fake."

After saying that, Chang Zhi seemed to be still not satisfied, and finally concluded: "Inconsistent, a gentleman scum, a beast in human clothing, a human face..."

Seeing that Chang Zhi was getting more and more excited, Wen Yanxing quickly interrupted and pointed at his arm: "It hurts."

Chang Zhi glanced at him, and then used the other hand that was not caught by him to punch him again below.

Wen Yanxing: "................."

Chang Zhi tilted her head slightly, smiled at Wen Yanxing and said, "Take it, and keep yelling and hitting me."

Wen Yanxing was devastated. This Chang Zhi was different from the kind girl he usually saw. Where did the girl who didn't hit people or say bad words go? ? ——But he still liked her.

There is no cure.

Seeing Wen Yanxing, who was 1.8 meters tall, lower his head and was hit by her twice, looking aggrieved, Chang Zhi, who saw such a scene for the first time, almost couldn't hold it. She paused to recover her emotions, and immediately said with a stern face: "I said, have you pulled enough? Let go."

"I said I won't let go." Wen Yanxing shook his head, "Are you angry?"

Chang Zhi glanced at him up and down, and said disdainfully: "What do you think? Let go, your hands are full of sweat."

Wen Yanxing, who was disdained: "................." sad.

Wen Yanxing asked slowly: "What if I let go and you leave?"

Chang Zhi took a deep breath and said sincerely: "...It's true, my hands are sticky and uncomfortable, let go, I won't leave."

"Really?"

"Really."

Wen Yanxing slowly let go of his hand, and Chang Zhi pulled her hand back at lightning speed, lowered her hat, turned around and left!

Wen Yanxing: "!!!!"

In fact, Wen Yanxing had already lined up to the front, and now that Chang Zhi had left, he didn't line up anymore, and took long strides to chase after her, barely grabbing Chang Zhi's wrist.

"...You don't keep your word." Wen Yanxing said, "You said you wouldn't leave."

Chang Zhi glanced at him: "Aren't you still lying to me?"

"...I was wrong." Wen Yanxing apologized very sincerely.

Chang Zhi smiled: "When you were wearing a vest, did you feel secretly happy?"

"No," Wen Yanxing shook his head, "After I found out that I liked you, I kept thinking about how to speak."

"I thought of many ways. At first, I wanted to pursue you seriously in real life, but there were too few opportunities for us to have intersections. I have never pursued a girl, but I know that if I want to pursue a girl, I have to create opportunities, but I really can't think of any other way except hiding behind the door to listen to when you go out and pretend to meet you by chance-

"After I fell in love with you, I wanted to find a chance to tell you that I was Yan Zhi, but I was afraid that you would have no idea about me at that time, and would stay away from me after knowing it."

"If things become like this, I want to pursue you," Wen Yanxing looked at her, very frankly, "it will be very difficult. "

As soon as the words fell, his hand slid down and held Chang Zhi's hand again, and shamelessly passed through her fingers, interlocking their fingers.

"You can forgive me, give me a chance, a chance to please you," he said in a gentle tone, his dark eyes staring at her quietly, she vaguely saw her and the pedestrians passing behind him in his pupils, but all his focus was on her.

Gentle, full of affection.

Eyes can't lie.

Chang Zhi raised her eyebrows slightly, looked aside, and didn't know what she was thinking.

After a long time, she raised her head slightly, opened her red lips slightly, and sighed imperceptibly, her tone slightly raised: "Then I, see how you perform?"

Lost to you.

Wen Yanxing held her hand slightly after hearing this, he looked at her, and after a while, he responded softly and carefully-

"Okay, you see how I perform. "

Because of this incident, Wen Yanxing had to line up for dozens of minutes and he had to go back to the end.

Who knew that when they walked over, the girl who had just stood behind them looked at them and suddenly asked them to stand back.

Wen Yanxing and Chang Zhi looked at each other.

The passerby girl looked at the black and white hats, which looked like the black and white devils, as if they had just finished arguing... She said sincerely: "It doesn't matter, anyway, you were in front of me just now..."

She didn't seem to know Chang Zhi.

Chang Zhi hesitated, but Wen Yanxing nodded slightly, smiled, and thanked her first: "Thank you, but let's line up again. "

There is only so much time in a day. If you queue up a little longer, you can spend more time communicating with each other instead of waiting in such a boring way. Only a fool would cut in.

When Wen Yanxing pulled Chang Zhi to the end of the line, Chang Zhi realized that Wen Yanxing was still holding her hand. She pouted and waited until they stood at the end of the line before she moved her hand and said, "Stop pulling. Are you being annoying? I asked you to show off. How can it be considered taking advantage of me?"

Wen Yanxing almost choked on his saliva when he heard this - where is the old Chang Zhi? Where did she go?

In fact, if you think about it carefully, there were clues before. For example, when chatting with him online, Chang Zhi never accepted it. She would occasionally directly fight back what he said, so...

Wen Yanxing looked at him forcibly holding Chang Zhi's hand, and chose to chat calmly: "You may not believe it, but this is actually one of my performances. This is a physical communication in emotional communication. Physical communication is conducive to promoting the relationship between men and women. It is not taking advantage..."

Chang Zhi smiled: "Are you serious? "

"Well, seriously..." Before Wen Yanxing finished speaking, Chang Zhi suddenly stood on tiptoe, her pretty face close to his, her eyes staring at him, her warm breath seemed to sprinkle on his face -

Wen Yanxing's brain was blank, and he felt that he could not hear any other sound except her. He could only see Chang Zhi's lips opening and closing, and heard her say very seriously:

"According to what you said, the eyes are the windows of the soul, and we are communicating with our hearts," after a pause, Chang Zhi looked into his eyes and continued, "Well, so now, I see you lying with your eyes open from the window of your soul. "

Chapter 34 Do you really want to take the exam?

When it was Chang Zhi and Wen Yanxing's turn in line, Chang Zhi repeatedly confirmed with Wen Yanxing: "Do you really want to take the exam? What if I don't know? It's embarrassing to be last."

Wen Yanxing shook her hand, raised his eyebrows slightly: "Sit behind me, copy my answers, I guarantee you'll be in the top ten."

Entering the examination room, the first thing you see is the blackboard with the words "bilibili big examination room" written on it, as well as the words "Study hard and make progress every day" and the five-star red flag on the blackboard.

Chang Zhi couldn't help but laugh. Looking at the layout of this examination room, it really looks like the classroom where I went to school before.

Chang Zhi sat in the seat behind Wen Yanxing, facing the blackboard, and saw the warm reminder on the blackboard - "Please don't run away with the examination pen."

When the test paper and answer sheet were handed out, Chang Zhi was confused by the first question.

"What are the names of Ryougi Shiki's eyes in "Kara no Kyoukai"?"

"a. Mystic Eyes of Death B. Death...c. Death...d. Mystic Eyes of Death Immediately."

Chang Zhi was confused. She had never seen this show before. Thinking of Wen Yanxing's words that he would copy the answers for her, Chang Zhi rolled her eyes, pulled her chair closer to the table, and then moved her butt to the edge of the chair, raised her leg and gently kicked Wen Yanxing's chair.

Wen Yanxing didn't seem to feel anything. He buried his head and filled in the card carefully, and there was no movement.

Chang Zhi kicked again with more force.

Wen Yanxing still didn't move.

Chang Zhi was annoyed and poked Wen Yanxing with a pen. Wen Yanxing had been lowering his head, but he sat up straight in an instant after being poked.

He tilted his head slightly, and Chang Zhi tilted her head, holding the pen against her chin and looking at him. She stretched out an index finger with her beautiful hand and said silently—

"What do you choose for the first question?"

Wen Yanxing looked back and also made a sneaky gesture, stretching out four fingers, and Chang Zhi made an "ok" gesture

Then she smiled secretly and lowered her head to fill it in.

This feeling really resembled the exams in the past. She had an exam in high school and was assigned to the front and back desks in the same exam room as Deng Jiadai. When checking the answers, they were so sneaky.

At that time, they just put the answer sheet on the edge of the table, and then she looked over.

It was okay for Chang Zhi to answer other questions, but she would be a poor student if she answered these questions-Wen Yanxing quickly finished a test paper, then put the answer sheet on the edge of the table and tapped the table with a pen.

Chang Zhi stretched her neck, silently memorized the position of the blackened part of the answer sheet, and then filled in her own answer in the same way.

Finally, the results came out. Wen Yanxing scored 90, the first in this exam room. Chang Zhi seemed to have copied a few questions wrong, and scored 80, the fourth in the exam room.

Chang Zhi looked at the results, leaned on Wen Yanxing's arm and laughed, "I didn't expect you to be a top student?"

Wen Yanxing raised his eyebrows: "Sea turtle, you can't help but admit it."

Chang Zhi stood up and looked at him: "Hey, you graduated from abroad, showing off your academic qualifications to me?"

Wen Yanxing smiled: "No, I just want to show that I am also a high-quality stock, and I am selling it to you. How about you buy me first? You will definitely not lose money, it will only go up and not down."

Chang Zhi asked back: "You said you would buy it, have you ever thought about what if I can't afford it?"

Wen Yanxing said calmly: "Then I'll give it to you, free of charge."

Chang Zhi smiled: "Why don't I know how you are so slick?"

"To please you." Wen Yanxing said very seriously.

Chang Zhi couldn't help but smile more brightly.

When Chang Zhi had finished laughing, Wen Yanxing looked at her with a smile on her face. He told the truth, looking a little helpless: "Well, someone drew the answer on my paper and copied it directly."

"Wow," Chang Zhi was dissatisfied, "Are you so lucky?"

"Yeah," Wen Yanxing agreed, "I think maybe I am the emperor of luck."

Chang Zhi suddenly grabbed the corner of Wen Yanxing's clothes, with a cunning look in her eyes: "Absorb the luck, okay, you are done, your luck has been sucked away by me."

Wen Yanxing raised his hand to take off Chang Zhi's hat, and then raised his hand high.

Chang Zhi was startled and stood on tiptoe to grab it, but Wen Yanxing was as steady as a mountain and stretched his hand higher.

Chang Zhi blushed, pursed her lips and said angrily: "You took my hat after taking in the European energy, too much, give it back to me!"

Wen Yanxing raised his eyebrows, looked up at the white baseball cap in his hand, then pointed at his black baseball cap with his other hand, and suddenly said: "Do they look like couple hats?"

Chang Zhi paused, looked at both sides, and her face became even redder.

Yes... they look alike.

"Don't change the subject," Chang Zhi covered her forehead with a blush on her face, "No, give me back the hat quickly, I think I'm quite popular, what if I'm recognized by fans!"

Wen Yanxing smiled and deliberately said: "I stole the hat by my own ability, you have to exchange it with me if you take something."

Chang Zhi looked up at him slightly: "It was originally my hat, what should I exchange it for."

Wen Yanxing raised the other arm that was not holding the hat, and tentatively said: "Holding it?"

Chang Zhi was stunned.

After a while, she mumbled, "Are you sick of me? Give it back to me first."

"Not cheating?" Wen Yanxing confirmed again and again. There was no way, Chang Zhi had a criminal record.

Chang Zhi said coquettishly, "Oh, give it to me first."

Just because of Chang Zhi's sudden cuteness, Wen Yanxing couldn't stand it. He gave in, giving in to the attack of the girl he liked so much.

Chang Zhi only felt a weight on her head, and saw Wen Yanxing put the hat back on her head, and helped her to fix it intimately. He used his index finger to help her tidy up her naughty hair, with a focused expression. Chang Zhi felt a tingling sensation where he touched her.

The surroundings seemed to be suddenly quiet. Chang Zhi lowered her eyes and didn't dare to look up at Wen Yanxing. The blush on her face was so hot that even the air conditioner couldn't lower it.

Oh, why is it so hot here?

After finishing, Wen Yanxing raised his arm, looking ready: "Come on."

Chang Zhi held her hand with shame and helplessness.

Obviously different from a girl, Chang Zhi took Wen Yanxing's hand and felt his muscles almost immediately. They went from meeting in person to holding hands to holding hands within one day...

Chang Zhi held her forehead with one hand.

Heaven and earth are conscientious. She was forced to do it, and she didn't expect it to be so fast! It's all Wen Yanxing's fault. He looks quite serious and behaved quite seriously before. Once he was exposed, he was simply shameless and his face was as thick as a wall!

The two of them grabbed the stamped "passport" and walked all the way to a game place called "Sea at the End of the World".

The rule of this game is to find the small square printed with B station in the ocean square. Ten people form a group. Wen Yanxing and Chang Zhi started a seemingly endless queue again.

BW is indeed crowded.

The sound in the hall was mixed and noisy. Chang Zhi was wearing new shoes today. Although they were not the kind of high heels, the shoes still had a three-centimeter heel. After standing for a long time, she was very tired.

Chang Zhi was initially forced to hold Wen Yanxing's arm as promised. Now, she almost completely leans on Wen Yanxing and feels like a useless person.

Wen Yanxing didn't mind, and let Chang Zhi lean on him with half of her body weight. He just sighed when it was almost their turn -

"Sweet burden."

Chang Zhi: "............" stood up straight immediately, and took the hand that was holding Wen Yanxing's arm.

Wen Yanxing: ".................. I didn't say you were heavy, why are you walking?"

He used his right hand to hold his left arm, and said generously: "Lean on me."

As soon as Wen Yanxing finished speaking, it was their turn in the queue.

Chang Zhi glanced at him, saw Wen Yanxing's strange expression, and smiled with her hands covering her mouth.

The two entered the "sea of cubes". With so many cubes piled together, it was difficult to walk. Countless people fell, not to mention finding the cube with the small TV logo. Chang Zhi moved slowly without falling. Seeing others find one after another, she was anxious.

No matter how good her eyesight is, she can't stand the poor ability to find things.

She looked back at Wen Yanxing who was following her. Well, he found one.

She couldn't help but ask: "How did you find it so quickly?"

Wen Yanxing raised his head and answered: "Good eyesight."

"...But my eyesight is also good?"

"...That may be a matter of luck."

"You will lose me like this."

Wen Yanxing looked at Chang Zhi who was walking in front of him, changed his words, and said sincerely: "I know, you walked in front of me and pretended not to see it and picked it up for me. Thank you."

Chang Zhi: "............"

Chang Zhi gave up communicating with Wen. Ou Huang. Yan Zhi. Yan Xing.

She looked back again and searched around, finally finding one not far away. Chang Zhi's eyes lit up, she stretched out her hand, took a big step forward, but she fell forward without keeping her balance.

Wen Yanxing, who was following closely behind Chang Zhi, saw this and reached out to grab it, but it was too difficult to keep his balance here. He lost his balance and fell forward with her.

There were boos from outside the game field-

Chang Zhi covered her face with one hand, feeling ashamed, and quickly thought of "Fuck", "Ahhh, he's on me", "Why do you want to play this game", "Shame..." "So heavy..." "...Ah...chest..."

Wen Yanxing: "............"

Under him was the girl's soft body, and a burst of fragrance passed through his nose. The only thing left in Wen Yanxing's mind was the word "leave"-

Was the thing pressing on his chest too soft...

It seemed that he wanted to "save the beauty" at the beginning.

Chapter 35 The spectators

For the spectators, it all happened very quickly. But for the parties involved, everything turned into slow motion.

Wen Yanxing came back to his senses when Chang Zhi covered her face with one hand and used her fingers to open a small space between her eyes to look at him and push him.

He got up in a panic, and one hand sank into the sea of cubes and almost fell back. When he stood up, he did not forget to pull Chang Zhi up.

When he pulled Chang Zhi, he couldn't help looking at her legs.

... He didn't look away after looking at her.

Chang Zhi was wearing a mid-length skirt with leggings inside. Fortunately, she didn't show her underwear when she fell... But when Wen Yanxing pulled Chang Zhi, she exerted force on her legs, and the lines of her muscles were smooth. When Chang Zhi stood up straight, Wen Yanxing's mind emerged that night when he edited the clip of Chang Zhi dancing.

... He lost consciousness several times, and kept thinking in his heart that the first leg was well-deserved.

Wen Yanxing

Chang Zhi covered her face, which was so hot that she couldn't stand it. She held her hat down with her other hand, feeling extremely angry and grief-stricken.

After the game, Wen Yanxing looked open-minded and met everyone's gaze, while Chang Zhi kept her head down, afraid that people would see her face. She almost ran away and pulled Wen Yanxing to a corner.

Wen Yanxing was pulled by Chang Zhi to walk quickly, with a smile on the corner of his lips, and even had the mind to tease: "Why are you in a hurry? Walk slowly and be careful not to fall again."

Chang Zhi pulled his wrist, and turned back to glare at him after hearing this, with a blush of anger on her face: "You still want to fall on me? You think you are not heavy enough to crush me to death!"

"Ahem..." Wen Yanxing thought about his height and weight, and defended, "My weight is reasonable. Although I don't go out often, I also exercise. My body shape and weight... are both qualified."

Body shape?

Hearing Chang Zhi looking back at him, from top to bottom, broad shoulders, narrow waist, long arms and legs, indeed, a real clothes hanger.

Wen Yanxing met Chang Zhi's gaze, and he suddenly lowered his voice and muttered: "Actually, weight... you have to get used to it in the future anyway."

He almost said this to himself, Chang Zhi didn't hear it clearly, only heard one or two words, she looked back at him: "What did you just say actually?"

"No," Wen Yanxing shook his head, covering up the fact, "I just quietly praised you."

Chang Zhi looked at him suspiciously.

"... What are you praising me for? Why don't I believe it so much."

How to praise the girl you like naturally and unconventionally?

Wen Yanxing's brain was working fast, and he finally came up with a sentence temporarily-

He held Chang Zhi's hand with his backhand: "I praise you so much that it's hard for me not to like you."

Chang Zhi stopped, turned around and looked at him face to face, the corners of her lips raised quietly, but she pretended to be unbelieving: "Fake."

"Real," Wen Yanxing said, "I really can't think of a reason not to like you."

Chang Zhi thought, did Wen Yanxing suddenly light up his skills?

Thinking about the time she watched "Yanzhi" live broadcast before, he was also talking nonsense, and his mind was very fast when he spoke, so she felt it was reasonable.

In fact, it is true, how can a broadcaster not talk nonsense? Wen Yanxing doesn't show his face, has good skills and doesn't talk nonsense, and there are very few who are very popular.

This is the real him.

A handsome otaku who can talk about live games:)

Chang Zhi felt that people like herself who don't communicate with people every day may not be able to talk to Wen Yanxing in the future.

At five o'clock in the afternoon, Wen Yanxing and Chang Zhi came out of the BW venue and had a meal nearby. At eight o'clock, Wen Yanxing took Chang Zhi back to the hotel.

Chang Zhi found a chain hotel nearby. Coincidentally, the hotel Wen Yanxing stayed in was also in this area, but not the same one, two streets away.

When sending Chang Zhi back, it was already dark.

While walking on the road, Wen Yanxing sighed: "I really want to go back and check out and move here."

Chang Zhi glanced at him: "You're only staying for a few days, isn't it... just across the street?"

"That's right," Wen Yanxing nodded, and then seemed to remember something, "When are you going back?"

Chang Zhi thought about the schedule for the next few days and said: "Next Tuesday. I want to play for a few days, and I have to participate in BW tomorrow."

Wen Yanxing unconsciously held Chang Zhi's hand again, and Chang Zhi was too lazy to resist his behavior.

Although there was also a reason for comfort because of the love in her heart.

Wen Yanxing squeezed her soft little hand, and then said: "Well, let's go back together next Tuesday?"

Chang Zhi asked in surprise: "Are you okay over there?"

Wen Yanxing: "...Freelance, free to arrange."

"What about live streaming?" Chang Zhi asked again. She remembered that Wen Yanxing was going to live stream. "Haven't you been live streaming every day recently? Are you not going to live stream?"

Wen Yanxing slowed down and followed Chang Zhi's steps slowly, saying: "I brought my computer and headset. I won't show my face, and it's the same for live streaming in the hotel."

After a pause, Wen Yanxing said: "...In fact, I've only been live streaming on Bilibili for the past two weeks. Last week, I signed a one-year contract with Feiyun Live. I will change the platform next week and start live streaming there."

Change live streaming platform? ? ...What does it mean?

Chang Zhi didn't react for a while, and after a long time she said: "...Do you mean to leave B Station?"

"No," Wen Yanxing shook his head and explained, "The ghost videos are still updated at the same frequency as before, and the live broadcast recordings will also be submitted to B Station, but the live broadcast location has changed."

Chang Zhi breathed a sigh of relief, thinking that Wen Yanxing would not do these things anymore.

"And..." Wen Yanxing stretched out his tone and added, "If I change to this platform, my income will be more stable, and you won't think that my freelance job is unreliable." At this point, Wen Yanxing seemed to remember something and smiled helplessly.

Chang Zhi was stunned.

Then she heard Wen Yanxing say in a very calm and natural way: "In fact, I don't know how many fans I can bring by changing the live broadcast platform. Maybe this is a new beginning. In short, I want to work hard, at least let you feel that I can rely on you and support you, well... not only can I support you, but I have to live better than now."

His attitude was sincere, and his eyes were full of sincerity when he looked at her.

...Is this for her?

Chang Zhi blinked, and her heart was suddenly filled with inexplicable emotions.

The street lights were bright, and there were not many people on this street, even a little quiet. Only the words he just said echoed in her ears.

She lowered her head, and the mottled traces on the concrete ground crisscrossed. This was a road that thousands of people had walked on, and now she and he were standing here.

It seemed to be the first time that someone stood by her, holding her hand, and put her into the future, not the kind of illusory future that could not see the end, but the actual future that could be seen not far away.

The long and empty emotions were suddenly filled with warmth. It took Chang Zhi a long time to find her voice. Her voice was muffled: "I don't want you to support me. I have my own store and I am very rich."

Wen Yanxing was just telling his plan very realistically, but he didn't expect Chang Zhi's reaction to surprise him.

He looked at the girl who lowered her head and spoke in a low voice, and began to panic. He bent down slightly to see Chang Zhi's face, and Chang Zhi immediately covered her face and lowered her head even lower.

Wen Yanxing felt a little unwell. He stretched out a hand to touch the back of Chang Zhi's hand covering her face. He felt that Chang Zhi's face was really small, and he couldn't see her expression because of this.

Could it be... crying?

Chang Zhi's nose was sore when Wen Yanxing touched her with concern, and she felt that she was very useless.

She cried through his palm, and her voice was soft and like a spoiled child: "Don't touch me!"

Wen Yanxing: "................."? ?

Damn it!

What should I do if I make a girl cry for no reason? I'm waiting online and it's urgent? !

Wen Yanxing pulled Chang Zhi, who was at a loss. Chang Zhi kept covering her face and didn't move. Wen Yanxing's little man was already anxious.

Then his eyes suddenly lit up, and he thought of something, and let go of Chang Zhi's hand.

Chang Zhi noticed that Wen Yanxing had loosened his grip on her hand and almost put it down, but then she felt that her makeup must have been ruined, so she decided not to... Before she could finish her thought, she felt a hand on her shoulder from behind, and with a little force, she was pulled into his warm and broad chest.

Chang Zhi's face was pressed against his clothes, and through the clothes she could hear his strong heartbeat in his chest, thumping in her ears, and she bit her lip and passively endured it.

A hand gently patted her back, and the voice was helpless and doting: "...What's there to cry about?"

Chang Zhi put down her hands, and without hesitation put her hands through his waist and tightly hugged him. She mumbled in a hoarse voice: "...Who told you to say you would support me? I didn't look down on you, I didn't think you were unreliable... Oh, it's all your fault for talking nonsense... Anyway, I'm really rich and don't need you..." Chang Zhi reached out and hit Wen Yanxing twice, and her words were incoherent.

It's all Wen Yanxing's fault, he had to say something touching, poking her tears, poking her so hard that she couldn't help but fantasize about the future.

The next moment, she heard him say again-

"...Who made me like you." His chin rested on the top of her head, "Seeing the grievances you suffered in the past, I couldn't help but want to give you everything."

Chapter 36 Red Eyes

Wen Yanxing spent a lot of effort to coax Chang Zhi from sobbing to leaving his arms with red eyes.

Chang Zhi's nose was red, she sniffed and lowered her head.

Wen Yanxing stared at her for a long time, sighed helplessly, stretched out his hand to gently lift her face, and wiped the corners of her eyes with his fingertips.

Chang Zhi raised her head and let his warm hands wipe her face.

Wen Yanxing suddenly laughed in a low voice: "Do you think others will think I am bullying you if I hold your hand and walk out like this?"

Chang Zhi tilted her head and thought for a while: "It's possible, then you want to go separately from me? Pretend that we don't know each other."

"No," Wen Yanxing said this firmly, holding Chang Zhi's hand, "Let's go out together."

Chang Zhi raised her eyebrows slightly and looked at him.

The next moment, Wen Yanxing took off her hat which she had worn backwards since leaving the club with his other hand and put it on her right way. Chang Zhi stared with her eyes wide open, a little confused. The brim of her hat was pushed down by the man's hand. Wen Yanxing's smiling voice came from above her head: "Silly girl, if you go out like this, people will only say that we are wearing couple hats and loving each other."

Chang Zhi: "............Wearing black and white hats means we are a couple?"

Wen Yanxing shook his hand holding Chang Zhi and said calmly: "No, this is it."

Wen Yanxing sent Chang Zhi to the hotel. He originally wanted to go in and sit down and chat about life. Well, it was an absolutely normal chat and exchange of feelings.

But Chang Zhi quickly swiped her card to enter the door and blocked him outside the door. Like a wolf guard, she smiled at him with half of her face exposed through the crack of the door, and then quickly closed the door.

Wen Yanxing, who was turned away: "............"

He leaned against the door, smiled helplessly, took out his mobile phone and started a private chat with Chang Zhi.

[Yan Zhi]: Why did you close the door so quickly? It's like you're guarding against wolves.

[Simple and hardworking Tang Zhi]: I just don't want you to come in.

[Yan Zhi]:? ?

[Simple and hardworking Tang Zhi]: Chaos.

[Simple and hardworking Tang Zhi]: Also, it's okay if you don't let me think about it. Now I get angry when I see the two words Yan Zhi.

[Yan Zhi]: ....

Wen Yanxing understood immediately, and he replied very tactfully——

[Yan Zhi]: Change WeChat next time, or change my name? You are so generous, please forgive me.

[Simple and hardworking Tang Zhi]: Deposit.

[Yan Zhi]:? ? ?

[Simple and hardworking Tang Zhi]: Will you lie to me again in the future?

[Yan Zhi]: I won't lie to you, I swear to heaven.

[Simple and hardworking Tang Zhi]: It's useless to swear to the sky, you have to write it down in black and white, ah, wait a minute.

...Waiting for what?

Wen Yanxing leaned against the door, his ear against the door panel, and faintly heard the sound of slippers rubbing against the floor in the room?

What is Chang Zhi doing?

The sound of slippers stomping on the floor came in from the door, and Wen Yanxing felt that someone inside knocked on the door. He turned his back away from the door, thinking that Chang Zhi would open the door, but he didn't expect to stuff a piece of paper and a pen from the crack under the door.

She also stretched out her index and middle fingers and made a "V" sign

Wen Yanxing: "............" What can't you say with the door open?

Wen Yanxing laughed.

He put his phone back into his pocket, looked around to make sure there was no one around, then squatted down to pick up the paper and squatted by the wall to read it.

"Party A: Chang Zhi/Party B: Wen Yanxing.

Party B shall not conceal or deceive Party A in the future, and Party A shall do the same.

If you violate this, you will never talk to the other party again!

Party A's signature: Chang Zhi, Party B's signature: ——"

Chang Zhi's handwriting is quite delicate, written neatly on the paper, but the exclamation mark was deliberately written in red pen... After reading it, Wen Yanxing couldn't help but knock on the door.

Chang Zhi's voice came from inside: "...Go ahead."

"You really won't let me in?" Wen Yanxing asked, "Shouldn't contracts be discussed face to face?"

Chang Zhi suppressed her laughter and asked through the door: "Do you have any questions?"

"Of course," Wen Yanxing said seriously, "Open the door first, and I'll tell you slowly."

Chang Zhi said with caution: "...I can hear it here too, my room is really messy and not cleaned up."

"...I don't mind," Wen Yanxing sighed after saying this, and said, "I suddenly remembered that you came to my house before, and you ran like this after the power outage. At that time, I didn't know you, so I could forgive you for doing this. Now we are like this, and you still block me outside the door..."

Chang Zhi tried to recall, and said uncertainly: "...But at that time I was going back to my own home, and I didn't ask you to come."

Seeing that this was not going to work, Wen Yanxing changed the subject: "...someone just passed by and looked at me. If you don't let me in to talk, I might be kicked out by the security guards, and you won't be able to sign the contract."

"Then...my room is really messy, and I haven't packed my luggage yet," Chang Zhi said hesitantly, "you left after signing?"

Wen Yanxing nodded: "Otherwise, what else can I do?"

"Okay then."

Wen Yanxing stood up.

There was a sound of the door handle being pressed down. As soon as Chang Zhi opened the door, Wen Yanxing squeezed in, still holding the paper and the pen she had stuffed out.

He raised his hand to rub her head. Chang Zhi hugged her head and stepped back. Wen Yanxing said: "What do you mean by being so careful about me?"

"I'm afraid you won't leave." Chang Zhi said casually.

Wen Yanxing said with a straight face: "I'm not that kind of person, okay?"

Chang Zhi looked at him and curled her lips: "But I think you're pretty thick-skinned today."

Wen Yanxing clenched his fists, put them to his mouth and coughed lightly, and raised the paper with his other hand: "This is obviously an unequal treaty. You know that if you lie to me, I can't ignore you."

Chang Zhi raised her eyebrows and asked him: "Then you won't sign it?"

"Sign, of course," Wen Yanxing nodded, "but if I make a surprise in the future and hide it from you, you won't suddenly ignore me, right? Then I won't be at a big loss."

Chang Zhi thought about it and took the paper and pen from him, stuck them on the wall, and added a line of words-

"Except for making surprises:)"

After writing, Chang Zhi stuffed the pen and paper into Wen Yanxing's arms, with a cunning look in her eyes. She nodded in self-approval and said: "Perfect."

Wen Yanxing signed his name on the paper. Chang Zhi folded the paper and put it in her pocket. She tilted her head and asked him, "Are you going back?"

Wen Yanxing accused, "I just signed an unequal treaty with you, and you chased me away. This is..."

Chang Zhi: "I'm not chasing you away. It's so late. I just asked because I care about you. I'm afraid it's unsafe for you to walk at night."

Wen Yanxing: "...I heard that this is called crossing the river and destroying the bridge."

Chang Zhi: "Then what do you want to do?"

Wen Yanxing: "Well..." Wen Yanxing looked around Chang Zhi's face and finally fixed on her slightly open lips.

Since he held her hand today, he has been thinking about this for a long time...

Wen Yanxing stood at the door and bowed his head slightly: "I'll leave if you give me a reward."

Chang Zhi: "...What reward?"

Wen Yanxing raised his hand and pointed his index finger at his face. The meaning was self-evident.

Chang Zhi: "..........."

Chang Zhi's face was slightly red. She blinked and hesitated for a moment before she mustered up the courage to stand on tiptoe and kiss Wen Yanxing on the face.

But Wen Yanxing turned his head away, whether intentionally or unintentionally, so Chang Zhi's lips just touched -

Their eyes met.

Chang Zhi quickly stood up, lowering her head and the blush on her face had spread behind her ears.

He actually...

Wen Yanxing was kicked out.

The door was locked, but Wen Yanxing was not angry at all. He stood at the door and touched his lips as if he was savoring something.

- This might be a man's instinct?

When you see a girl you like, especially when you are alone, looking at her lips slightly opened when she talks, you can't help but wonder if it's really as soft and sweet as imagined.

Facts have proved that -

I haven't tasted the sweetness yet, but it's soft... It's really soft and makes people want to try it again.

Chapter 37: Being a Thief

The next day, Chang Zhi arrived at BW early.

When he separated from Wen Yanxing at the door, Wen Yanxing looked around and saw that there was no one around, so he lowered his head and kissed Chang Zhi on the face like a thief.

Touch and leave.

Chang Zhi was caught off guard and looked a little dazed after being attacked.

Wen Yanxing couldn't help but wave.

But Wen Yanxing found a reasonable reason for himself and said seriously: "This is to repay you for yesterday."

"What share?"

"Kiss my share, one kiss for one kiss, win-win."

...What the hell win-win!

Chang Zhi touched her face, thinking about whether she should go to touch up her makeup later, and said: "What's there to repay... Is the powder delicious?"

Wen Yanxing raised his hand and touched his lips.

"I don't know, but you smell good." He looked very straightforward.

Chang Zhi blinked: "... I won't talk to you anymore. Didn't you not have breakfast? Go ahead. I'll go in first."

Wen Yanxing nodded: "Waiting to see you."

Chang Zhi met Anan and Sister Qiao in the venue. They were all dressed up seriously today. Anan looked at Chang Zhi and suddenly couldn't help pinching her face.

It was the expected soft touch. Anan sighed.

Chang Zhi: "???" What are you doing? ? She was confused.

Anan looked her up and down, and without waiting for Chang Zhi to ask, she suddenly said in a deep voice: "I don't know why, but I suddenly feel that you exude a sweet aura today."

Chang Zhi tilted her head and said: "Let's not talk about what aura first... Is this the reason why you suddenly touched my face like a strange aunt?"

Anan shook her head and denied: "No, I just felt that your face was so red, red like an apple and felt very soft, I couldn't help it, I wanted to touch it."

Chang Zhi was silent, and suddenly thought that it was Wen Yanxing who suddenly knocked on her door and sent her to give her a little surprise today. Before leaving, he flirted with her and kissed her on the cheek...

Chang Zhi said with a guilty conscience: "Actually, the blushing is because of the hot weather. The temperature is quite high today."

Anan scratched her hair and felt that she had a strange intuition. She said: "Maybe... the weather is hot."

Sister Qiao has been playing with her mobile phone next to her, saying nothing, very low-key.

After several people changed their clothes, Chang Zhi took a photo with Anan and Sister Qiao. Anan stared at herself in the photo and muttered beside her: "Why is my face so big in this photo? Tangtang, are you going to post it on Weibo?"

Chang Zhi nodded: "Yes... I have a photo of a beautiful picture, do you want to Photoshop it?"

Anan raised her hand and made an Erkang gesture: "Wait, give me the phone and I'll do it myself."

Chang Zhi reluctantly clicked on the homepage of the phone and opened the photo software, then handed the phone to Anan.

Anan lowered her head, her expression focused, her fingers quickly slid across the screen, and she looked like she was familiar with it - whitening, local skin smoothing, face reduction, and she said angrily from time to time: "Oh, my hands are shaking again, and I accidentally Photoshopped your face, Chang Zhi... I was wrong, forgive me..."

Hearing that she was Photoshopped, Chang Zhi leaned over to see that Anan Photoshopped her face crooked when she Photoshopped herself.

Chang Zhi: "... With your skills, I almost thought I didn't know when I sleepwalked to get plastic surgery and turned into an alien."

So she undid it and started over.

Chang Zhi looked at Anan who was waiting for her to Photoshop her face, but after a while, Anan touched her arm. She lowered her head to look. Anan pointed at the pop-up message on the screen and said in a strange tone: "This, Tangtang, your message... um, 'Private exclusive has an owner', who is it?"

"Huh?" Chang Zhi was startled and quickly snatched the phone and opened QQ.

[Private exclusive has an owner]: I heard that you get annoyed when you see my previous ID, so I changed my ID. Are you satisfied?

[Private exclusive has an owner]: Private is you.

After seeing this line of words and the chat history, Chang Zhi knew who this person was.

Anan was curious and wanted to come over to see it. Even Sister Qiao, who was concentrating on her phone, looked up and asked "Who is it?" Chang Zhi put the phone in her arms like she was holding a treasure and walked ten meters away from the two people.

A Nan and Sister Qiao: "..."

Sister Qiao suddenly said: "You are so wary of us, men? Private, tsk tsk... There are men in the golden house?"

Chang Zhi ignored them and replied with her head down.

[Simple and hardworking Tang Zhi]: You scared me to death, the phone was just in someone else's hand.

[Simple and hardworking Tang Zhi]: Your name... is so stupid.

[Private has an owner]:... I swear sovereignty for you.

[Simple and hardworking Tang Zhi]: Who do you swear to?

[Private has an owner]: Everyone in the world.

[Private has an owner]: Because I feel that changing it directly to "Tang Zhi's boyfriend" or "Chang Zhi's boyfriend" is too direct, I thought about it for a long time before I thought of this.

[Simple and hardworking Tang Zhi]: Then you are probably a bad namer...

[Simple and hardworking Tang Zhi]: Change it back, and when we chat on WeChat in the future, we won't be angry when facing your weird garbled characters.

[How do you know it's already taken]: That's not garbled text, it's the abbreviation of my name.

Chang Zhi looked at the name on the screen and was silent. Does it make any difference? ?

But speaking of WeChat... Chang Zhi immediately exited and looked at the WeChat ID of Wen Yanxing - [ynzwyx7]

As for the abbreviation, Chang Zhi silently matched the numbers one by one in her heart.

[Simple and hardworking Tang Zhi]: How do you know, Wen Yanxing, 7th floor? What is n?

[How do you know it's already taken]: I typed it randomly. I don't know why, but I thought something bad would happen if I didn't add this n.

[Simple and hardworking Tang Zhi]: ....

[Simple and hardworking Tang Zhi]: If you didn't add n, maybe I would have figured it out, but I didn't care after I added you on WeChat.

After talking a lot with Wen Yanxing, when Chang Zhi looked up, Sister Qiao and Anan were pointing fingers at her.

Chang Zhi was confused: "...What are you doing?"

Anan was amazed: "Look, as soon as he looked up and saw us, the smile disappeared from his face."

Sister Qiao agreed very much and said with deep conviction: "She didn't smile when she looked at us, but she smiled like a fool when she looked at her phone. Oh, it's unfair treatment."

Chang Zhi touched her face and asked: "...What are you talking about? How did I treat you unfairly?"

Chang Zhi took the initiative to bring this up, and Anan pouted and accused: "I smell the scent of love. You betrayed our FF group, didn't you? I just saw your ID on my phone, so jealous. When did you have a boyfriend? You were still single when you were with us last time?"

Sister Qiao added: "No wonder you blushed this morning. He sent you here, right? What does the man look like? Is he handsome? Is he tall? Is he rich?"

Chang Zhi said she was frightened. She asked curiously: "...I haven't said anything. Why do you feel that you know so much?"

A Nan put one hand on her shoulder and laughed: "It seems that my intuition this morning was right. Tell me the truth."

Chang Zhi put her phone in her pocket and didn't dare to say too much. She just said vaguely: "It's... my neighbor."

"Neighbor, the one you posted on Weibo before, just moved in? Oh, so fast?" A Nan exclaimed, "There are photos."

Chang Zhi remembered this after A Nan's reminder.

She shook her head: "... No."

Sister Qiao was not worried at all and told her: "It's okay. Show us when you have it and I'll check it for you."

Chang Zhi: "... Thank you very much."

When the club was open, people greeted Chang Zhi from time to time while she was waiting.

A Nan took her hand, and Chang Zhi waved to her fans. Suddenly, she saw a familiar outfit in the crowd.

It was someone who sent her here this morning and kissed her secretly.

He stood in the crowd, and his height made him stand out, so she saw him at a glance. Wen Yanxing was also looking at her at this moment, smiling at her tenderly.

Chang Zhi paused while waving her hand, and felt inexplicably at ease, and curled her lips in a good mood.

The performance was very fast, and Wen Yanxing saw Chang Zhi's figure occasionally appearing on the big screen. The director seemed to be poisoned and loved to shoot at her legs.

He was stunned at first, but then he thought of so many people... and suddenly became unhappy.

After Chang Zhi's show ended, Wen Yanxing wanted to find her, but he was blocked outside by a group of people surrounding Chang Zhi.

Wen Yanxing: "..."

Chang Zhi was too busy.

This was her first time to publicly participate in such a show, and she met many fan girls.

The girls and some guys surrounded her, chattering: "Sister Tang, you look so good in person..."

"Sister Chang, please sign for me, on my clothes, come on, rough men are fearless."

"Tangtang is great, it's the first time I see her in person... Tangtang, please keep working hard in the future!"

A girl complained: "Sister Tang, the director just now was so toxic, I want to see your face, but I don't know why the camera always scans your legs..."

Another girl poked this girl and explained in a low voice: "Actually, I think it's because Sister Tang's legs are too long..."

Chang Zhi was signing for the man who asked her to sign his clothes. When she heard this, she looked up and teased: "Hey, I heard it, I know, you are secretly praising me behind my back again."

The fans laughed immediately, fans and "idols", all laughed and talked.

Wen Yanxing, who couldn't squeeze in, said: "..........." The excitement has nothing to do with me, I feel very depressed.

Wen Yanxing didn't succeed in meeting Chang Zhi face to face until the end of the evening.

It was too difficult - Wen Yanxing realized for the first time that the girl he liked was really popular.

Chang Zhi took off her makeup, tied her hair into a ponytail again, put on a baseball cap, and met Wen Yanxing at the door of the milk tea shop outside - because she showed up at the venue today, and many people knew her, so it was like this.

When Wen Yanxing saw Chang Zhi like this, her face was white and clean without makeup, two words popped up in his mind.

Pure.

After that, it was aggrieved.

Wen Yanxing said aggrievedly: "There are too many people who like you. Did you see me this afternoon? I couldn't squeeze in outside."

Chang Zhi remembered the scene she saw today and nodded: "I saw you, but I was helpless. There were too many people. I couldn't rush out to catch you. I don't know if you don't show your face during the live broadcast. I'm afraid that if you show your face in the future, I won't even be able to see you when you participate in some program."

Wen Yanxing: "...Why?"

Chang Zhi said: "Wow, your fans are several times more than mine, okay? There are so many people, I will be squeezed to the outside, at most behind the road you walked."

"And," Chang Zhi added, "When there are so many beauties surrounding you..."

"No," Wen Yanxing shook his head, "I am pure in body and mind, clean and self-disciplined, and will only belong to you, don't worry."

He promised seriously.

Chapter 38 Like a painting

At night, Chang Zhi posted a Weibo saying bw, and a group of fans on Weibo were so excited——

[Hahahaha, Sister Tang is also super beautiful in person][My Tang is as beautiful as a painting, her legs are really thin and long and white][By the way, I was the only one who discovered something, I met Tang Tang twice, and both times I saw a handsome guy in a black hat standing near Sister Tang playing with his phone?][+1 in front][Senior fan 2333][Hey, I saw it too, I saw the side profile of the black hat guy when I was about to leave for the autograph, so handsome]

Chang Zhi saw this comment and held out her phone to Wen Yanxing——

"Look, your fans are just for looks," Chang Zhi smiled slyly, "You're still talking about me? You can attract people's attention just by standing there."

"Cough," Wen Yanxing clenched his fist and pretended to cough to cover up his embarrassment, "Why don't I send them a message saying I'm your boyfriend?"

Chang Zhi originally wanted to tease Wen Yanxing, but now Wen Yanxing has turned the tables on her.

Chang Zhi... Anyway, she had an inexplicable feeling, and felt inexplicably guilty about the fact that she kidnapped "Yan Zhi".

There was always a feeling that she would be dissed again.

Wen Yanxing saw that Chang Zhi did not react, smiled, and did not care.

Chang Zhi spent the three days after Saturday with Wen Yanxing.

Wen Yanxing seemed to treat her hotel room as his own home, and even moved directly to this hotel on Sunday night, but he was not on the same floor with Chang Zhi.

Wen Yanxing knocked on her room door on time at 8 o'clock every morning, and she must have finished washing and dressed neatly. Then he held a computer cat and watched her busy in the room on the small sofa in her room, walking around, tidying up this and that.

While browsing Weibo and browsing Bilibili, he looked up from time to time at Chang Zhi who was sitting in front of the dressing table.

Chang Zhi faced the mirror, and her cosmetics were spread out on the table, neatly arranged.

She held a bean paste-colored lipstick and a coral-red lipstick in her hands, drew two strokes on the back of her hand, and then ran to the armrest of the small sofa where Wen Yanxing sat, stretched out her white and tender hand to show him, and asked the lipstick color number question that defeated countless otakus-

"Do you think I look better in coral red or bean paste?"

At that time, Wen Yanxing was watching a new ghost video recently released by an up called British Black Rat. Suddenly, a soft and fragrant girl sat next to him, stretched out her beautiful hand in front of him and showed him the back of her hand. Wen Yanxing pressed pause and looked at the two similar colors on Chang Zhi's hand. He didn't hear the question clearly.

"What did you ask just now? I didn't hear it clearly." Wen Yanxing asked, "What looks good with what?"

Chang Zhi looked at him and repeated, "Coral red and bean paste color."

Wen Yanxing was silent, holding her hand, looking at the two reddish marks on her hand for a while, and asked: "Which one is bean paste color? Which one is coral red?"

Chang Zhi: "...Coral on the left, bean paste on the right."

"Is there a difference?" Wen Yanxing came closer with curiosity and looked at them carefully. "They are both red, it seems, both are good-looking."

"No, no, no," Chang Zhi shook her head and denied, "The bean paste color is not as red as the coral red. I think both colors are pretty. It's a bit difficult to choose."

Wen Yanxing: "...Why don't you apply it and show me?"

Chang Zhi thought about it and nodded in agreement.

Chang Zhi stood up like a diligent little bird and applied each color once to show Wen Yanxing. Wen Yanxing really couldn't tell the difference, so he said the coral red she applied last: "...This one."

You were hesitant just now, and now you answer so quickly? Chang Zhi raised her eyebrows and asked, "Then tell me, what color is this on my lips?"

Wen Yanxing was silent for three seconds. Fortunately, Chang Zhi had said not long ago that the first time she painted her lips was bean paste color. He remembered this and responded wittily, "Coral red, in fact, it is easy to recognize when it is painted on the lips. It is not ostentatious, it makes you look white and tender, and you look particularly beautiful today."

He praised Chang Zhi's face without changing his expression and sincerely.

Which girl doesn't like to be praised? And it was a compliment that looked very serious.

Chang Zhi was so satisfied with such a fierce praise, "It just happened that I have already painted it... But do I look good today?"

Wen Yanxing glanced at the video that he had not finished watching, and held down his hand that wanted to press the start button. He chose the safest answer, "Every day you are more beautiful than yesterday."

Chang Zhi was very satisfied, so she went to pack her bag and prepared to go out with Wen Yanxing.

Tissues, wet wipes, power banks... a lot of things.

Wen Yanxing let out a long sigh, as if relieved of a heavy burden. While Chang Zhi was packing her bag, he continued to watch the video.

Wen Yanxing always sent Chang Zhi back to her room after dinner, but Chang Zhi would never stay with Wen Yanxing for even a second. After saying goodbye at the door, she would send him away directly. Wen Yanxing wanted to do something, such as kissing or other basic contact... However.

Chang Zhi was really defensive.

It was easy to grab a little hand, but it was a little difficult to kiss the face. Kissing the mouth could only be done by sneak attack, but Chang Zhi would not be angry. If she wanted a more advanced kiss, it seemed that she had to think about it for a long time.

They bought the tickets the afternoon before they went back. Chang Zhi wanted to go back early, so she chose the plane ticket. In the afternoon, Wen Yanxing sat by Chang Zhi's bed holding a computer. Chang Zhi sat on the bed with her chin on Wen Yanxing's shoulder, watching him choose the ticket.

"What time do you want to go back tomorrow?" Wen Yanxing respected Chang Zhi's opinion. Anyway, the two of them, one is a freelancer and the other is a hands-off shopkeeper, are really not in a hurry these days.

Chang Zhi thought for a moment and said, "We'll pack tonight and get up at 8 a.m. It takes time to dawdle and it takes time to go to the airport... Let's do it at 10 a.m., so we can arrive in the afternoon."

Wen Yanxing fully respected Chang Zhi's opinion.

Chang Zhi had always wanted to see the night view of SH City. In the past two days, she was busy eating and drinking with Wen Yanxing in various places, or the weather was bad at night, so she didn't see it.

But today was different. It was the day before leaving SH City, and the weather was so good. How could she not see it?

The two experienced the "undersea tunnel" to reach their destination, and then bought tickets to go up to the sightseeing floor.

The floor was partially transparent, and there was a sense of insecurity when she walked up. Chang Zhi held Wen Yanxing tightly, a little weak: "...Are you afraid of heights?"

Wen Yanxing glanced at her, then lowered his head and stomped on the glass under his feet.

Chang Zhi, who let go of her hand in horror and was stunned, said: "................."

Wen Yanxing comforted her: "It's quite solid. Look at so many people standing there. It's okay."

"... It's crazy." Chang Zhi commented.

Chang Zhi walked carefully on the steel part where the floor and the glass meet, bending over, and Wen Yanxing laughed.

"Do you still want to see the night view outside?"

Chang Zhi looked up, her eyes looked at Wen Yanxing, and she could vaguely see some scenes.

She reached out and grabbed Wen Yanxing's sleeve, feeling weak: "Then you have to hold me."

Wen Yanxing smiled and let Chang Zhi hold his arm tightly.

However, when his arm was close to an obviously soft area, Wen Yanxing's body stiffened.

... Cough.

He touched his hair.

The two of them came to the railing, which was a large piece of glass with only a small gap at the top. Wen Yanxing raised his hand, put his hand in, and then took it out to encourage Chang Zhi——

"Come, feel the wind hundreds of meters above the ground."

Chang Zhi looked up at him: "Are you childish?" While complaining, she raised her hand and put it in. The cool wind blew on her hand, and Chang Zhi retracted her hand.

Outside the glass, the night view of SH City was in full view, with a calm river surface, flashing neon lights, slowly flowing river water, and the reflections of the roadside looming in it...

Chang Zhi turned around and put her mobile phone in Wen Yanxing's hand, "Take a few photos for me?"

Wen Yanxing pointed to the glass below with a malicious intention and asked: "Are you sure you want to take pictures here? Do you dare?"

Chang Zhi looked down and then looked up, looking at the ceiling and looking away.

After more than ten seconds, she looked at the other people sitting on the glass floor taking pictures. There were adults and children, making V signs and shouting "cheese", it was very lively.

It was really difficult to choose between taking a rare photo and being afraid of heights...

But she was actually half a person living in the photo.

Chang Zhi was torn between herself and herself. After a long while, she seemed to have made up her mind and said, "I'm standing here. Come on, take a picture."

Wen Yanxing shook the phone she had stuffed into his hand: "Password."

Chang Zhi pressed her hand on it and unlocked it with her fingerprint. Wen Yanxing said, "Should you consider adding a fingerprint for me?"

Chang Zhi lowered her head and clicked on the camera. She replied with ease, "What about you? You didn't add one for me on your phone either."

"My phone doesn't have a password," Wen Yanxing said sincerely, "Didn't I just sign an unfair clause with you a few days ago? I immediately cancelled the password when I got back."

Chang Zhi was in a hurry to finish the photo shoot and returned the phone to Wen Yanxing: "I'm sitting on the ground. You take a picture for me."

After saying that, she looked down at the ground.

Wen Yanxing looked at her, thought about it, stepped forward, lowered his head and switched the phone from rear to front, and said to Chang Zhi in a coaxing tone.

"Tangtang, look up and look at this."

Chang Zhi looked up without any defense, and then her lips felt hot.

Then she saw Wen Yanxing holding his phone with a satisfied look on his face.

Chang Zhi was suddenly kissed, and was confused: "...Huh?"

...What happened?

Chapter 39 Suddenly Understand

Chang Zhi looked at Wen Yanxing's phone, which was locked instantly, and suddenly understood something.

She rushed over and reached out to grab it, but Wen Yanxing caught her and moved his hand away cleverly.

Chang Zhi looked up at him: "Did you just take a sneak shot of me?"

Wen Yanxing blinked and said: "You are so beautiful... I can't help it."

"Don't," Chang Zhi shook her hand, but couldn't reach it, "Give me the phone, let me see what you took a picture of."

Wen Yanxing raised his hand stubbornly, and Chang Zhi couldn't reach it even if she threw herself into his arms.

Chang Zhi was a little flustered, but suddenly she remembered something, pouted her lips, and stood up straight, with her white and tender palms spread out in front of Wen Yanxing.

"You don't have the password anyway, I can still see it when I get back." She smiled cheerfully, "It doesn't matter whether you give it to me now or later, I'm not in a hurry."

Wen Yanxing: "................."

He looked at his phone, and then at Chang Zhi, who was smiling cunningly like a little fox.

Wen Yanxing chose to back off: "You are not allowed to delete it after you have read it."

Chang Zhi always had a bad premonition in her heart, and after thinking for a while, she said cautiously: "I'll think about it after I read it."

Wen Yanxing put the phone in her hand.

Chang Zhi quickly held it firmly, turned around and turned her back to Wen Yanxing, unlocked the album with fingerprints, and clicked on the latest picture——

The scene displayed on the screen made Chang Zhi stunned.

Wen Yanxing held her face with one hand, his lips pressed against hers, and her hair was a little messy because of Wen Yanxing's actions, her cheeks were slightly red, her eyes were wide open, and she looked stunned.

Behind her was half of the sky and the neon lights of the city.

Wen Yanxing leaned over at some point and looked at her eagerly.

Chang Zhi's hands rubbed the edge of the phone.

"Don't delete it," Wen Yanxing held Chang Zhi's wrist, "The first photo together is of great significance."

Chang Zhi lowered her eyes and said in a deep tone: "... In the first photo together, you took me so ugly?"

...Huh?

Wen Yanxing's brain was stuck for a moment.

After half a minute, he asked hesitantly: "... Don't you blame me?"

Chang Zhi thought about it carefully, and actually felt a little strange when she saw it at first.

Shy.

The first time she saw herself being kissed in a photo, although it was not that kind of... well, in short, a strange feeling of shyness followed.

It's not because she was kissed and photographed that she was shy, but because the photo was too ugly.

"...What's so strange about this," Chang Zhi still moved her finger away from the delete key and locked the phone screen, "But it's too ugly, don't look at it, don't look at it anymore."

Wen Yanxing: "It's not ugly, no... Why can't I look at it if I took it?"

Since it concerns herself, Chang Zhi decided to be unreasonable for once: "You took a photo of me, and I won't show it to you if I say I won't."

Wen Yanxing was aggrieved: "...There's me in the photo too, so send it to me."

Chang Zhi glared at him: "What are you going to do with it?"

Wen Yanxing: "...Look at it yourself."

Chang Zhi: "The protagonist in the photo, you can see it every day when you open the door, why look at the photo."

Wen Yanxing: "..................." What he said seems to make sense, but it seems to be wrong.

A good husband...doesn't fight with his wife.

...However, after returning home that night, Chang Zhi, like a thief, quietly grouped the photos and gave them a rather obscure name: Useless Photos. Then she set a digital password and finally breathed a sigh of relief.

I definitely couldn't bear to delete them, so I had to keep them.

The next day, Chang Zhi went to the airport with Wen Yanxing.

After boarding the plane, Chang Zhi felt a little sleepy sitting next to Wen Yanxing.

I don't know why, I went to bed very early last night, but every time I take a long trip, take a vehicle, a plane, a train, etc., I feel sleepy as soon as I sit down.

And the phone was not allowed to be turned on... Chang Zhi poked Wen Yanxing with her finger, who was reading a magazine she didn't know what it was, and looked up and said in a soft voice: "I want to sleep."

Wen Yanxing lowered his head slightly and saw Chang Zhi covering her mouth with her hand and yawning. Water beads overflowed from the corners of her eyes because of sleepiness. He closed the magazine and asked her: "Do you want to cover yourself with a blanket?"

Chang Zhi was stunned: "Ah...?" Where did the blanket come from on the plane?

Wen Yanxing picked up his black travel bag, took out a black piece of clothing from it, shook it and unfolded it, and put an oversized coat in front of her, saying: "This."

Chang Zhi: "...Isn't this a coat?"

Wen Yanxing glanced at the clothes that almost covered her thighs: "To you, is this clothes?"

Chang Zhi: "..."

The air conditioning on the plane was actually a little high, but the mid-length pants she wore today were fine, but because of the short-sleeved top, she still had goose bumps. The coat came just in time, Chang Zhi put her hands into the oversized sleeves, and since the sleeves were too long, she simply didn't care, she put the coat on backwards, and then leaned her head on Wen Yanxing's arm.

Suddenly, there was a lot of weight leaning on him. Wen Yanxing looked down and saw Chang Zhi raising her hand, smelling the sleeves, then looking up and asking him: "This smell is so comfortable, what laundry detergent do you use?"

"Why ask this? It smells like lavender." Wen Yanxing asked again, "What's wrong?"

"It doesn't look like it," Chang Zhi sniffed again, but couldn't smell it. Then she thought of something, and suddenly covered her face with her sleeves for a long time before she said hesitantly: "Well... okay, I think this may be your smell."

After a pause, she added: "... It smells pretty good."

Then she stretched out a hand to hug his arm, rubbing him and closing his eyes quickly.

Wen Yanxing, who was caught off guard, was stunned for a long time, watching him close his eyes against him, his breathing gradually calmed down, and the hand that was half covering his face slowly slid down. His heartbeat also went from fast to slow.

He dared not move, lowered his head and looked at her closed eyes, long eyelashes, rosy face from sleep, and slightly pursed mouth. A feeling of softness that he had never felt before surged into his heart.

His arm was leaning on him and was a little stiff and tired. He carefully raised his other hand and gently touched Chang Zhi's hair.

Soft, smooth, and slippery.

Wen Yanxing's eyes were soft, and the corners of his lips were slightly raised.

He really wanted her to lean on him like this until the end of time.

- Whether she was leaning on him to sleep or to rely on him.

Chapter 40 Liu Yunyun's Wedding

Saturday, Liu Yunyun's wedding.

Chang Zhi and Deng Jiadai came to stay at the hotel the night before, and got up at five o'clock the next day with the bride to put on makeup and change clothes.

Speaking of Liu Yunyun, Chang Zhi lived in a dormitory with six people in college, including Liu Yunyun. Because of the past, Chang Zhi found it difficult to open up to others. At first, she was inseparable from Deng Jiadai, and later she only became friends with the other four roommates in the dormitory.

Liu Yunyun is an only child, from a well-off family. She was spoiled and raised since she was a child. She has a strong personality and is the type who likes and dislikes clearly. In the dormitory, she only plays well with Deng Jiadai and another girl named He Xiaomi. This time, He Xiaomi is also one of the bridesmaids.

Chang Zhi remembered that Liu Yunyun liked to chase stars, read novels, and play games when she was in college, but she didn't expect that she would marry the young CEO of Tianyu who is only in his early thirties.

In fact, this news still made a little splash in the entertainment circle.

After all, Liu Yunyun is unknown and not an insider. She graduated from college only a few years ago. When she suddenly appeared in the public eye, she became the wife of the CEO of Tianyu, a company that has trained many stars.

Liu Yunyun is pretty, but the CEO of Tianyu is just an ordinary person. She is a money worshiper, but Liu Yunyun is not short of money to spend, and she still spends money lavishly after graduation.

After the wedding news was made public, many people said on the Internet that Liu Yunyun is a money worshiper.

Thinking of this, Chang Zhi glanced at Liu Yunyun who was putting on makeup, and her eyes and eyebrows were smiling - the happiness and joy of marriage.

Chang Zhi thought about it, and she was overthinking just now. Liu Yunyun has a distinct personality and personality. She has known her for so many years. Although she doesn't know her well, she is in the same dormitory after all. How could she be the kind of person that is spread on the Internet?

Chang Zhi secretly said to herself that she couldn't just follow the crowd.

Liu Yunyun sat in the middle, Chang Zhi and Deng Jiadai sat on both sides. Liu Yunyun's makeup was done quickly. She pursed her lips in front of the mirror, then stood up and looked at Chang Zhi who was tilting her head to let the makeup artist toss her. She smiled and said gently: "You are really going to have a hard time today. You got up at five o'clock like me. Are you sleepy?"

Deng Jiadai half-opened one eye and said: "I went to bed early last night, it was okay. I saw you posting on WeChat Moments in the early morning this morning. What's wrong? Can't you sleep because of excitement?"

Liu Yunyun nodded: "Of course, who wouldn't be excited for the first marriage? I only slept for three hours. I really have insomnia. I am very afraid that the wedding will suddenly cause some strange situation."

Chang Zhi comforted Liu Yunyun: "Don't worry, don't think too much, the wedding will go smoothly."

Liu Yunyun nodded, paused and said: "I really trouble you this time. I was just worried about missing someone, and I didn't expect you to agree to be my bridesmaid."

Chang Zhi smiled and said, "We are all former classmates and roommates. It's okay."

Liu Yunyun nodded.

While waiting for the groom's flower car, He Xiaomi helped Liu Yunyun with her hair, and Chang Zhi and Deng Jiadai started chatting.

The bridesmaids' dress was a white mid-length dress with bare shoulders. Chang Zhi wore high heels. Deng Jiadai glanced at Chang Zhi, whose collarbone was exposed, and then looked down at herself. She put her elbow on Chang Zhi's shoulder and sighed, "I feel a little awkward standing next to you."

Chang Zhi: "...what's wrong?"

Deng Jiadai raised her hand and pinched Chang Zhi's little face without hesitation, saying jealously, "You are taller than me, your legs are longer than mine, your skin is whiter than mine, and your shoulders and collarbones are so beautiful. Look at me, my arm fat...I want to cry."

Chang Zhi dodged Deng Jiadai's hand to avoid her from biting her. Chang Zhi suggested seriously, "If you move more, you will lose weight."

"I understand the logic, but I'm just too lazy to move," Deng Jiadai said with a sad face. After a moment of frustration, she suddenly said energetically, "Fortunately, I had the foresight to trick the man, otherwise I would be really tired... By the way, how about Mr. Wen and Yan Zhi last time?"

Deng Jiadai suddenly looked gossipy, and Chang Zhi blinked, not quite understanding Deng Jiadai's jumping thoughts.

"What's up?" Chang Zhi put away the smile on her lips and pretended to be innocent, "What's wrong?"

"Hey," Deng Jiadai nudged Chang Zhi's waist with her elbow, and Chang Zhi covered her waist to avoid it. Deng Jiadai said, "Don't play dumb, didn't you say we'd meet last time? How is it, isn't Yan Zhi handsome?"

"Well... well..." Chang Zhi stretched out her tone, and Wen Yanxing's appearance flashed through her mind.

Wen Yanxing sent her here last night, and was reluctant to leave before leaving, saying that he would pick her up this afternoon.

Deng Jíadai was just asking casually, but Chang Zhi's ambiguous attitude whetted her appetite. She lowered her voice and asked curiously, "Tell me quickly, is he handsome? Did you succeed?"

Chang Zhi knew that Deng Jiadai was quite curious, and she cleared her throat, "How should I put it, I did meet him, but I just felt that it was a little unrealistic."

"What's unrealistic?" Deng Jiadai asked, her face suddenly dimmed, and she hissed, "Did you die in public, did you break up?"

Then Deng Jiadai began to comfort her-"I told you... It's actually quite easy to die in public on the Internet, don't be sad, there are many good men, isn't there Mr. Wen? Although this is not good for him, he likes you, you can also try it..."

Chang Zhi felt something was wrong the more she listened, and interrupted quickly, "Don't, what nonsense, who told you that it was broken? Bah, it wasn't."

Deng Jiadai groaned and widened her eyes: "Then why are you so hesitant? You didn't brag? Is this true or not?"

"...I think it's too dramatic, I'm just organizing my words," Chang Zhi said seriously, "This matter is a bit complicated, I'll keep it simple, let me tell you this, I was still entangled before, but when I went there, I found out that Yan Zhi and Wen Yanxing are the same person."

Deng Jiadai: "................."

Deng Jiadai was silent for a long time, so long that when Chang Zhi thought she was going to do something, Deng Jiadai suddenly asked her again: "Tangtang, do you mean that the person who helped you online lives opposite you in real life and still likes you?"

Chang Zhi was a little puzzled: "I guess so."

Deng Jiadai raised her hand and touched Chang Zhi's forehead with the back of her hand, with a look of disbelief: "You are not sick, are you? Are you hallucinating because you are so sad that you die in the spotlight?"

Chang Zhi was embarrassed and angry, and slapped Deng Jiadai's hand away: "...What hallucination, you don't believe me? Is it so fake that I tell the truth?"

"Isn't it such a coincidence?" Deng Jiadai looked into Chang Zhi's eyes and found that Chang Zhi's eyes were full of seriousness. She covered her face, "Oh my God, you are so beautiful, it's a match made in heaven. No matter who you choose, you will end up happily. Sure enough, the iron tree blooms differently."

Chang Zhi: "............"

"What are you talking about so happily?" Liu Yunyun had done her hair, came over to look at them, and asked, "What time is it now?"

Chang Zhi picked up the phone on the table and looked at it: "Seven o'clock."

"It's time," Liu Yunyun said, she looked somewhere else and suddenly sighed, "What should I do, I'm so nervous."

Deng Jiadai patted Liu Yunyun on the shoulder to ease her nervousness, "You should think about your husband, who may be more nervous than you now."

Liu Yunyun thought so too.

At 7:30, the boss of Tianyu led his three groomsmen to knock on the door.

Deng Jiadai obviously knew how to play a trick on people. She opened the door a crack and stretched out her hand, not afraid of strangers at all: "If you want to pick up the bride, take the red envelope first."

"Okay," the boss is the boss, generous, "Wait a minute."

The first person Deng Jiadai saw was the Tianyu boss standing in front of her. Then her eyes looked behind him dishonestly, and she was surprised to find that the person standing next to him was the powerful actor Gu He. Next to Gu He was someone Deng Jiadai didn't know. Judging from the face of the passerby, he should be a friend, classmate, or brother. Looking to the side, it was actually...

After getting the red envelope, Deng Jiadai quickly closed the door. Holding the red envelope, she felt terrible and didn't even mention the second level she had prepared.

Seeing this, He Xiaomi asked, "What's wrong?"

Deng Jiadai glanced at Chang Zhi, waved to He Xiaomi and said, "It's okay, I'm afraid they will break in, let's continue."

Turning around, Deng Jiadai wiped the sweat from her forehead. Thinking of the face of the man she just saw, she couldn't help but feel regretful.

If I had known... I wouldn't have mentioned this to Chang Zhi.

What should I do next? Deng Jiadai looked back at Chang Zhi, who knew nothing.

Next, before opening the door for the groom, Deng Jiadai kept intentionally or unintentionally preventing Chang Zhi from going to the door to see the groomsmen. Chang Zhi was confused and at a loss.

But the time that should come will come. The groom's group went through five levels and cut six generals. Chang Zhi finally saw the appearance of the third person when she opened the door.

There were more people in the room, and it became lively. The groom was asked to carry the bride on his back to do exercises to succeed. The voices were noisy and full of laughter.

Chang Zhi never thought that she would meet him again in this situation.

Her smile froze in an instant, and then gradually disappeared from her face.

The man wore a straight suit and his hair was neatly combed. His eyebrows were clear and handsome, and his fairer skin compared to ordinary men made him look gentle and refined.

The moment he raised his eyes to look at her, Chang Zhi happened to see him.

Their eyes met in the air through the two people in the middle.

Chang Zhi couldn't help but grab her skirt.

...Meng Xi.

Chapter 41 Appearing Here

Chang Zhi didn't expect Meng Xi to appear here.

Really, she couldn't have imagined it in her dreams.

She watched Meng Xi's slightly frowned brows gradually soften, and watched him open his mouth to call her name——

Chang Zhi turned her head away, grabbed Deng Jiadai's arm, opened her mouth silently, and leaned over to pretend to whisper to her.

Meng Xi lowered his eyes and closed his mouth.

The group got in the car and headed for the reserved location. Several wedding cars drove in an orderly manner.

The wedding was outdoors, a Western-style wedding.

Balloons, flower baskets, white railings and pink flowers, pink and tender, full of girlish hearts and joy.

Liu Yunyun got out of the car carefully in her wedding dress, followed by Chang Zhi, Deng Jiadai and others.

The sky was clear, the white clouds were leisurely, the temperature was just right, and the atmosphere on the scene was just right.

After getting off the car, Chang Zhi saw Meng Xi, she lowered her eyes and pretended not to know him.

Deng Jiadai touched her arm and whispered, "Tangtang, I really didn't know he was coming. No, I didn't think about it at all."

Chang Zhi raised her eyelids and said, "Me too... Is he so free?"

Deng Jiadai looked around: "Didn't you tell me before that he found you himself? Didn't he know in advance and come to be the best man?"

"I don't know," Chang Zhi shook her head and said, "I don't know why he is always obsessed with seeing me? To explain? What's there to explain? Wasn't it an explanation that he just disappeared before?"

After saying this, Chang Zhi looked at Meng Xi again.

Meng Xi was chatting with Gu He, and he didn't know what interesting things he was talking about with a faint smile. In fact, Meng Xi really has a very deceptive and harmless appearance. Although Chang Zhi didn't pay special attention to it, she also knew that he was very popular in the entertainment industry, so advertisers and crews liked him very much.

His gentle and jade-like appearance is also suitable for costume dramas. Chang Zhi heard that Meng Xi has acted in many costume dramas.

Being kind and handsome is the advantage.

Deng Jiadai looked at her and suddenly said, "... He doesn't want to rekindle the old love with you, does he?"

Chang Zhi was stunned for a moment, then sneered, "Forget it, there are so many beauties in the entertainment industry. If he doesn't come earlier or later, I won't like him."

"That's right," Deng Jiadai nodded and teased, "You have your Mr. Wen now. Of course, you don't like him."

When Wen Yanxing was mentioned, Chang Zhi retorted, "Even if I'm still single, I won't like Meng Xi again, okay? You picked up the tissue that fell on the ground and wiped your mouth. Isn't it disgusting?"

"Pfft," Deng Jiadai nodded, "That's right."

The two helped to receive the guests together. While they were busy, Chang Zhi looked down at her phone.

Wen Yanxing sent her a text message. That's right, it was not WeChat but a text message on the phone.

Chang Zhi clicked it while muttering that this man was poisonous.

[Wen Yanxing]: One hundred free text messages per month.

[Wen Yanxing]: I missed you the first night and morning after you left.

[Chang Zhi]: .... It seems like we didn't live like this before.

After sending this message, Chang Zhi suddenly realized that her tone was a little too familiar.

But text messages are not like WeChat, they cannot be withdrawn.

So Chang Zhi watched the small circle disappear in the middle of sending - sent successfully.

[Wen Yanxing]: That's different. We were not familiar with each other before, but now we are very familiar with each other. How can the treatment be the same?

[Chang Zhi]: Who is very familiar with you?

[Wen Yanxing]: Well, not very, then, very familiar?

Chang Zhi understood the latter sentence, but the former one...! ? It can't be what she thought it was weird, right?

Chang Zhi stared at this sentence for a long time.

[Chang Zhi]: If I remember correctly, we are still in the same city, it's not that exaggerated, I will finish at 5 o'clock this afternoon and leave, go back.

[Wen Yanxing]: It feels like a long time since we last met. I'll pick you up? When is the right time to leave?

[Chang Zhi]: You can come earlier, it's okay.

[Wen Yanxing]: I want to come now.

[Chang Zhi]: ....

Chang Zhi was at a loss for a moment. Deng Jiadai came over and took a look, and said, "Oh, I want to come now... Let him come, he can eat for free, and he doesn't have to pay. It's a good deal for two people to eat."

Chang Zhi said, "Can you be more normal?"

"Okay, okay," Deng Jiadai nodded vigorously, helping to collect red envelopes with her hands, "But I think this is feasible."

"Then ask your boyfriend to come too," Chang Zhi glanced at Deng Jiadai, "I think this is feasible too."

After saying this, Chang Zhi handed the pen to the guest.

She looked up inadvertently, but saw a beautiful face.

Chang Zhi, the most popular and most disparate CP on Weibo in the first half of this year, was stunned.

Yuan Ke held Wen Jinzhao's hand, bowed his head and said thank you softly, took the pen with one hand and bent down to write. Deng Jiadai didn't expect to meet last year's new movie emperor and his internet celebrity girlfriend. She couldn't help but pull Chang Zhi's skirt, her hands trembling with excitement.

Chang Zhi didn't understand this matter, just glanced at Deng Jiadai and found that her eyes were already shining.

Star chasers are really terrible - she sighed in her heart.

After writing her own and Wen Jinzhao's names, Yuan Ke put down the pen and looked up to see Chang Zhi standing in front of him clearly.

It was the first time for Yuan Ke to see such a beautiful person outside the entertainment industry, and his eyebrows raised slightly.

Chang Zhi thought they were going to go in, but Yuan Ke smiled, his eyebrows curved, and left a compliment with a flying look: "You are pretty."

Chang Zhi didn't react for a while, pointed at herself, and was confused, but Yuan Ke and Wen Jinzhao had already turned around and went in.

Deng Jiadai jumped over and hugged her hand, shouting: "Ah, Yuan Ke praised you, my mom seems to have cut this autograph and collected it at home..." Deng Jiadai sighed as she looked at the note with several celebrities' names deleted.

The guests arrived and the wedding began. The wedding march was played by a girl, and Liu Yunyun walked onto the red carpet with her father's hand and a smile on her face.

But gradually, when she walked in front of the CEO of Tianyu, Liu Yunyun's eyes became wet.

Liu Yunyun's father put Liu Yunyun's hand on his son-in-law's hand, patted it, and said nothing more.

Chang Zhi suddenly had an idea, raised her mobile phone to record a short video, and sent it to Wen Yanxing on WeChat.

[Tang Zhi]: [Short video] The wedding has begun.

[wyxynz7]: Not bad, let's all preview it.

[Tang Zhi]: ... ... ah?

[wyxynz7]: It's nothing, you continue, I'm going to go out to your place now.

Chang Zhi was startled, and instantly forgot what happened in the short video.

[Tang Zhi]: No, why are you here so soon? It just started, I left at five in the afternoon.

[wyxynz7]: I wanted to see you earlier. Are you wearing a shoulder-baring dress?

[Tang Zhi]: How did you know?

[wyxynz7]: You took a picture of your friend.

Chang Zhi rolled her eyes, turned on the front camera, took a selfie and sent it over.

[Tang Zhi]: [Take a selfie] How about it, do I look good in this style?

In the photo, she smiled at the camera with her lips pursed, her cheeks flushed, and the lines of her neck and collarbone became clearer under the camera.

[wyxynz7]: ....

Wen Yanxing had never expected that Chang Zhi would send him a selfie. He clicked on it and saw that Chang Zhi looked sweet and lovely, and that off-shoulder skirt... Wen Yanxing clicked on the large picture and zoomed in with two fingers.

He discovered that his girlfriend not only had beautiful legs, but also had beautiful shoulders and collarbones.

She was so beautiful, so beautiful that he wanted to take her home and curl her up to admire her alone.

Wen Yanxing silently pressed Save and set this picture as the screen saver.

After that, he returned to the homepage of his mobile phone and glanced at Erqiu who was sitting on the table in a daze thinking about life. He showed the screen of his mobile phone to Erqiu and boasted: "How is it? Is your master's girlfriend beautiful?"

Erqiu was thinking about the life of a hedgehog, and suddenly a picture of a beautiful sister appeared in front of him. He suddenly came to his senses and thought that this beautiful sister looked familiar. He stretched out his claws to pounce on her, and Wen Yanxing took the phone with evil intentions.

"I just want to show you in advance, recognize people, and forget about moving. I won't give it to you."

After saying that, Wen Yanxing stuffed his phone into his trouser pocket, adjusted his clothes and hair in front of the mirror, and then walked to the entrance.

On the other side, Chang Zhi had no idea what Wen Yanxing was doing.

[wyxynz7]: After seeing the photos... I'm already putting on my shoes.

[wyxynz7]: Wait, I want to see you sooner.

[wyxynz7]: By the way, let's preview how to do a wedding xd

Chapter 42 People have three urgent things

From outside to inside, everyone is here, and the banquet begins.

People have three urgent things.

Chang Zhi was wearing a skirt. Wen Yanxing sent her a message saying that he was on the way. She said hello to Liu Yunyun and then put the phone in Deng Jiadai's hand.

"If there's a call later, help me pick someone up," Chang Zhi said, "I'm going to the bathroom."

Deng Jiadai grabbed the phone and looked at her in confusion: "Pick someone up? Who?"

Chang Zhi smiled, her eyes wandering: "My neighbor."

"Your neighbor, who is your neighbor...ah!" Deng Jiadai realized that Chang Zhi was referring to Wen Yanxing, "Wow, she quietly called someone over and asked me to pick him up, that's too much!"

Chang Zhi raised her hand and touched Deng Jiadai's head: "It's not certain yet, I really have to go to the bathroom, I'll talk about it when I get there."

After saying this, Chang Zhi walked to the bathroom in her high heels.

The bathroom has always been a place for trouble, and it has always been the easiest place to block people.

The lights in the corridor were a little dim, and the signs for the men's and women's bathrooms were clear. Chang Zhi came out of the women's bathroom and saw Meng Xi leaning against the wall with his head down.

She unconsciously slowed down her pace, then stopped, and the sound of her high heels on the ground stopped abruptly.

Meng Xi looked up and looked at her, as if he had known that she would appear here a long time ago, with a hint of confidence and relaxation in his eyebrows after seeing her.

Chang Zhi frowned slightly, then relaxed, she slightly tightened her fingers, trying to walk straight past Meng Xi, ignoring her, but he really stopped her.

Meng Xi walked in front of him in two or three steps, and his handsome face was stained with anxiety, which was forcibly suppressed by him. He took a breath: "Tangtang, let's talk."

Chang Zhi looked up at him, there was no one in the corridor behind him, only her and him here.

She frowned slightly, tilted her head slightly, looked up at him and looked impatient: "Are you free?"

Meng Xi was stunned, and did not expect Chang Zhi to ask him back instead of saying the expected rejection.

In the gap when he didn't answer, Chang Zhi smiled softly: "If you are free, take more dramas and don't always disturb my life. My life is full and I don't have time to tangle with you... Don't block me, let me pass?"

After saying this, Chang Zhi nimbly passed through the space on the right side of Meng Xi, and Meng Xi was obviously angry. He turned around and grabbed her wrist and called her name, "Chang Zhi!"

As soon as Chang Zhi touched his hand, she felt uncomfortable all over. She shook her hand, but couldn't get rid of it. His gradually increasing strength made her raise her eyes and glare. For the first time in so many years, she called out his name: "Meng Xi, you hurt me!"

Meng Xi's hand loosened, but still stubbornly grabbed her: "You have been making trouble with me for so many years, can you give me a chance to explain?"

"I'm making trouble?" Chang Zhi laughed as if she heard a joke, "Meng Xi, are you still asleep? How did I make trouble with you?"

Meng Xi pulled the corner of his mouth: "One-sided breakup, blocking, changing mobile phones, WeChat, changing cities... Isn't this a fight?"

Hearing this, Chang Zhi felt a sense of inexplicable anger and resignation in his heart, and memories flashed through his mind like fragments.

"What do you mean by a fight? Don't you know what you did?" She bit her lower lip and said angrily: "Are you going to let go?"

Meng Xi just looked at her: "I will let go after you listen to me."

The next moment, Chang Zhi stretched out her other hand without hesitation and pinched a small piece of flesh on Meng Xi's hand that was holding her wrist, tricky and strong.

Meng Xi felt pain, his expression wrinkled, he looked at her white jade fingers, using her nails as hard as if to pinch off his flesh, but still stubbornly refused to let go.

He looked at her with a piercing gaze: "Haven't you been giving me a chance to explain all these years?" After a pause, he suddenly sighed, "At least, listen to me."

Her nails felt wet, and Chang Zhi came to her senses. She subconsciously loosened her fingers, and her hands were stained with blood. She was immediately at a loss and pulled her hand back.

Meng Xi looked at the crescent-shaped pinch marks and the blood beads on his wrist. The pain climbed up along the nerve endings and stimulated him. He watched Chang Zhi shrink her fingers, and then finally looked at him straight in the eye.

Chang Zhi took a deep breath, calmed down her emotions, and said seriously: "I really don't know what you have to explain to me.

Is it false that you made a bet with your roommate to pursue me? Is it false that you disappeared without replying to messages and disappeared without a reason? What do you mean by unilaterally breaking up with me? Isn't it false that you disappeared by yourself to dump me unilaterally?"

"The bet is true, but is it false that I like you?" Meng Xi grabbed her hand slightly and said impulsively, "Are you blind? Blind eyes and heart, how have I treated you for several years? Just feed the dog like this?"

"What about disappearing?" Chang Zhi looked back fearlessly, "You said you really like me, but why should I insist on a relationship that has a bad purpose from the beginning?"

"Disappear," Meng Xi took a deep breath, "I went back to my hometown during the summer vacation and told my mother that I would take you to see her. My mother opposed it when she heard that both your parents were dead. I explained to her but she didn't want to pay attention. On the same night, you sent so many messages. Do you think I was not annoyed by so many things at that time? How can I explain to you when you were angry? I can't guarantee what you will do after listening to it."

After a pause, Meng Xi continued, "I wanted to wait until you calmed down before explaining to you, but who knew you would block me so quickly, and even Deng Jiadai. After that, I asked Jiayi for your phone number and WeChat. Day after day, you didn't answer the phone or add WeChat. When I asked them where you went, no one knew. You disappeared completely... What can I say? I even found out which city you were in recently?"

"Wait, Jiayi? Huang Jiayi?" Chang Zhi was stunned, "Did you... contact me at that time?"

Meng Xi looked puzzled, "Didn't you?"

Chang Zhi recalled, "But I changed my phone at that time. No one added me except my former classmates, and the phone was..."

"Don't you know Huang Jiayi too? She is my classmate. She gave me WeChat. Impossible..." Meng Xi's words stopped abruptly, and a joke from his roommate flashed through his mind for no reason-

Huang Jiayi has always had a good relationship with him since they met. She seems to be careless, but she is actually very careful. When he didn't know what gift to give Chang Zhi, she helped him. At that time, his roommate joked-"Look at how enthusiastic Huang Jiayi is towards you. If she wasn't helping you choose a gift for Chang Zhi, I almost thought she liked you."

Meng Xi replied at the time, "Who would be so careless?"

...But even now, he and Huang Jiayi still have intermittent contact.

At first, Chang Zhi didn't reply to him, and it was Huang Jiayi who comforted him.

Huang Jiayi asked him if he wanted to find a girlfriend again, and he said selfishly that he would wait and his career was the most important.

Huang Jiayi always complained to him that she had been single for too long, that she didn't know how to fall in love, and that no one wanted her.

Every time he updated his status, Huang Jiayi always replied to him in Moments or private chats, comforting him or joking with him.

Huang Jiayi often asked him where he was and whether he wanted to get together.

But the last time he successfully added a WeChat account, it was not Huang Jiayi.

It was another former male classmate. He occasionally mentioned it, and the other party quickly sent it to him. He tried to add it, but unlike previous experiences, the message fell on deaf ears. That time, it was accepted in less than half a day.

Meng Xi was silent.

Wen Yanxing arrived at the hotel at three o'clock in the afternoon.

It took a long time for someone to answer the phone. It was not Chang Zhi who answered the phone, but a familiar female voice.

Wen Yanxing was silent, and asked after a long while: "Where is Chang Zhi?"

Deng Jiadai was a little anxious holding Chang Zhi's phone. Chang Zhi went to the toilet for more than ten minutes. Could it be that she turned it on or dropped it in the toilet?

She almost had an urge to go to Chang Zhi.

Then the phone rang, with the note "Mr. Wen."

Deng Jiadai answered the phone, and just after she said "Hello", Wen Yanxing could tell that it was not her and asked her directly where Chang Zhi had gone.

Deng Jiadai covered her mouth and walked to the corner secretly, whispering in a tone full of embarrassment, "I am Chang Zhi's friend, we should have met. Chang Zhi went to the bathroom and hasn't come back for more than ten minutes. I don't know what happened, cough... Where are you? I'll tell you which floor you are on."

On the third floor, a whole floor, Wen Yanxing felt like he was walking in the elevator when he heard that Chang Zhi had gone to the bathroom for more than ten minutes and hadn't come back.

He stood in the elevator and stared at the familiar screen jumping, thinking that Chang Zhi might be... cough.

Doesn't she like to eat vegetables? He thought helplessly in his heart that he would have to urge her later, more than ten minutes... It's not good.

Ding sound, the elevator door opened, Wen Yanxing called Deng Jiadai again to ask if Chang Zhi had come back, and after getting a negative answer, Wen Yanxing thought that Chang Zhi's phone was in someone else's hands again...

He asked for the direction of the bathroom and walked over, ready to wait for Chang Zhi at the bathroom door.

Wen Yanxing was a little helpless. If he had come later, it wouldn't be so embarrassing, right?

But he was anxious. Not seeing each other for a day is like missing each other for three years, and not seeing each other for half a day is the same. Maybe... couples in the passionate love period are always so annoying and sticky, right? Wen Yanxing thought as he walked.

Actually... it can be regarded as a sweet embarrassment.

Wen Yanxing stepped into the corner of the corridor where only the two of them were facing each other.

Chapter 43 Complex Heart

When Chang Zhi heard Meng Xi say this, she felt so complicated that she couldn't speak at all.

Meng Xi had a gloomy face and remained silent, but confusion and contradiction flashed in his eyes from time to time.

In fact, her conversation with Meng Xi lasted only seven or eight minutes.

After a minute, Chang Zhi slowly spoke——

"Even if you say this now, even if there is another hidden story..." Chang Zhi lowered her head and looked at her shoes, "It's been a long time since the incident, and you and I have each developed, and I know very well that no matter who I was in the past or who I am now, I can't forgive the deception and impure motives at the beginning of the relationship..."

Meng Xi tightened his grip on her wrist, and bitterness flashed in his eyes. He said dryly, "So, you mean you won't forgive me?"

Meng Xi's voice was obviously much lower. Chang Zhi looked up at him and looked away in just one second.

She was a little dazed. In fact, she couldn't remember why she agreed to be with him in the first place? Do you like him? But now I have no feeling when I recall it. I only remember the last part when he left. Now I can't even smile with relief after listening to his words.

"I don't know," Chang Zhi shook her head and answered Meng Xi, "... I don't know when I will know."

Meng Xi was silent.

At this moment, footsteps were heard from behind, and both of them were startled. Meng Xi subconsciously withdrew his hand, and Chang Zhi turned around to look at who was coming -

Wen Yanxing was wearing casual clothes, holding two mobile phones, and stopped there to look at him.

Chang Zhi: "..."

Meng Xi: "..."

Wen Yanxing: "..."

The three people looked at each other, and there was a suffocating embarrassment in the air.

Obviously, Wen Yanxing had just seen the scene where Meng Xi grabbed his hand.

Even if Wen Yanxing didn't like watching TV, he had seen Meng Xi's photos on Weibo.

This... seems to be a celebrity.

Wen Yanxing looked at Chang Zhi's hand that was shrunk behind his back.

Chang Zhi felt guilty for no reason. She was going crazy. When did Wen Yanxing come? He came from another district to this district in less than half an hour. Is the traffic condition in S City so good?

My ex and my current boyfriend met. I was caught in the middle and didn't know what to do. I was waiting online. It was very urgent.

However, no matter how Chang Zhi collapsed and shouted, no one answered her.

Meng Xi, who was standing aside, frowned and looked alert when he saw the stranger who suddenly appeared because of his special identity. Seeing that Wen Yanxing was not passing by but stopped there, he looked at Chang Zhi's expression as if he knew this person. He asked Chang Zhi cautiously: "Tangtang... Who is this gentleman?"

Chang Zhi's scalp tingled when she heard the word "Tangtang".

This nickname that only her parents and besties called her and made her miss and love it so much made her want to find a crack to hide on the spot.

She looked at Wen Yanxing quietly, and sure enough, she saw Wen Yanxing's eyebrows raised, looking at her with a smile.

Chang Zhi shrank her neck, but the next second she thought, that's not right, she didn't do anything wrong, why was her mind full of what to do and how to explain?

So she straightened her back and was about to speak when she saw Wen Yanxing striding towards her——

"Boyfriend," Wen Yanxing stopped beside Chang Zhi and said briefly, staring at him with dark eyes, "Excuse me, who are you?"

Meng Xi: "..........."

Chang Zhi covered her forehead, her heart was a little broken, but strangely, a secret feeling of joy crept up from an unknown corner.

Meng Xi's expression changed from fright, shock, disbelief, to frustration after seeing Chang Zhi's lack of argument——

As expected of an actor in the past two years, Chang Zhi couldn't help but sigh at how fast her expression changed.

Meng Xi pointed at Wen Yanxing in disbelief, and then said in a tone full of distrust, "Tangtang, is he your boyfriend?"

When Wen Yanxing heard the sweet nickname Tangtang appear in the mouth of the strange man in front of him for the second time, his eyebrows frowned.

He reached out and grabbed Chang Zhi's hand, and then interlocked his fingers. Meng Xi stared at the two people holding hands sweetly in amazement.

Chang Zhi: "................."

Chang Zhi was very upset and didn't want to struggle or explain at all - but it was good this way, it hit Meng Xi completely.

It seemed a bit unkind.

Feeling Wen Yanxing holding her hand tighter and tighter, Chang Zhi stuttered, "Well, uh... This is my friend, Meng, Meng Xi, the person next to me... um..."

Meng Xi's face was ashen, and his eyes were fixed on Chang Zhi. Chang Zhi turned her head.

It's time to say goodbye.

She thought to herself.

Completely, thoroughly.

Chang Zhi was led back to the banquet by Wen Yanxing.

Because there were many people at the banquet, Chang Zhi was dragged to a corner with few people before she could find Liu Yunyun on the soft red carpet.

Chang Zhi let Wen Yanxing drag her. Even a fool could tell that Wen Yanxing looked very angry.

But they saw a man and a woman walking over as soon as they stopped.

The woman seemed to have no bones and pressed her whole body on the man's half body, and the man supported her effortlessly.

The woman hugged the man, stopped and muttered: "Don't... I finally had a drink, come again."

"Are you making trouble again?" The man lowered his head and looked at the woman's face, his tone full of helplessness, "Why did you drink so much for someone you have nothing to do with? I should have known not to bring you here. I wonder if you will have a headache tomorrow when you wake up?"

The woman hummed twice: "... I haven't drunk for a long time."

The man had a blank expression: "I remember that I met you twice, and you drank and messed up things."

The woman laughed: "So I picked you up."

The man sighed helplessly and looked up to meet the eyes of Chang Zhi and Wen Yanxing.

Chang Zhi x Wen Yanxing: "................."

Chang Zhi looked at the couple in front of her, her mind was full of, aren't these Wen Jinzhao and Yuan Ke who just registered with her? Ah ah ah, Yuan Ke is drunk? Wen Jinzhao's conversation with her is so doting? Envy envy envy............

And Wen Yanxing was silent for a long time.

Then, when Wen Yanxing opened his mouth, Chang Zhi heard Wen Yanxing shout out a name that made her expression "0.0" turn into "=�="-

Wen Yanxing: "... Cousin, you are here too?"

Wen Jinchao looked down at the squinting woman in his arms, and then looked up at Wen Yanxing who was holding Chang Zhi's hand. He suddenly realized that Chang Zhi, the familiar girl, was the girlfriend of his cousin who had not opened his mind for more than 20 years.

Hmm...

Thinking of the complaints his mother told him on the phone two days ago, Wen Jinchao's mind quickly passed through a line of words-big gossip, shocking big gossip.

But as an actor, his professional quality and expression management are quite good. In fact, the surprise on his face before a moment, and then he said very frankly: "The boss of the company invited you. Why are you here too? Do you know people in the entertainment industry?"

Today, the boss of Tianyu invited almost all the artists under their company who are a little famous.

Wen Yanxing shook his head, pointed at Chang Zhi, and said calmly: "Girlfriend, bridesmaid."

Chang Zhi was still immersed in the shock of seeing □□'s private communication with his girlfriend, but was suddenly named by Wen Yanxing, and subconsciously showed a super well-behaved smile.

After coming to her senses, she stuttered and said: "...Hello."

Wen Jinchao smiled harmlessly: "Hello."

Chang Zhi's other hand involuntarily grabbed Wen Yanxing's clothes, and then realized it.

Wen Yanxing... is Wen Jinchao's cousin?

Oh my God! She looked up at Wen Yanxing's profile, then at Wen Jinchao's, and was surprised to find that the two people's eyes can be said to be super similar:)

!!!!!!!!

Wen Yanxing really didn't want to communicate with this cousin anymore, he still had important things to do... Besides, Wen Jinchao didn't seem to be in a good condition either. Wen Yanxing pointed at Yuan Ke who was clinging to Wen Jinchao like a koala: "Brother, are you feeling a little uncomfortable now?"

Wen Jinchao hugged Yuan Ke, "Your sister-in-law is drunk, I'll take her to sit for a while, I won't say much to you, you can go and do your work with your girlfriend."

Wen Yanxing nodded.

After watching the two people leave, Chang Zhi grabbed Wen Yanxing's clothes and said in a very upset tone: "You didn't tell me that Wen Jinchao is your cousin?"

Wen Yanxing smiled: "You didn't ask."

Chang Zhi touched his arm, looked up at Wen Yanxing eagerly: "Let's discuss something... Can you help me get an autograph from your cousin? Although I am not a fan of stars, I have also seen the dramas they acted in. I even commented on their public Weibo..."

Wen Yanxing put his hand on Chang Zhi's head and rubbed it hard, saying in a bad tone, "Is this the time to talk about this? Do you have something to say to me?"

"Don't," Chang Zhi grabbed Wen Yanxing's arm and shook it, "It's not important, do you agree, help me get an autograph?"

Wen Yanxing: "Can I go to my aunt's house to get his high school test paper for you?"

Chang Zhi looked puzzled: "What do I need that for?"

Wen Yanxing pulled the corner of his mouth and smiled sarcastically: "There is also a signature on it."

Hearing this, Chang Zhi really knew that Wen Yanxing was really angry.

Chang Zhi was also very desperate.

She lowered her eyes and took Wen Yanxing's hand, and admitted her mistake: "I was wrong."

But she still didn't explain... because she really didn't know how to explain this kind of thing!

Chang Zhi, who encountered such an embarrassing thing for the first time, was almost crazy.

Wen Yanxing ignored her.

This was the first time that Wen Yanxing ignored her-

Deng Jiadai came to find her, and Chang Zhi told Wen Yanxing that she was going to help, but she was very worried about Wen Yanxing's appearance.

"I..." Chang Zhi raised her eyes and looked at Wen Yanxing, hesitating, "I'll tell you when I get back?"

Wen Yanxing remained silent.

This situation lasted until the end of the wedding. Liu Yunyun gave her a big red envelope, and then Wen Yanxing drove her home, got off the car silently, entered the building silently, took the elevator silently, and... entered the house with her silently.

Wen Yanxing suddenly spoke up when he took the second step into Chang Zhi's house.

"Tell me again, who is that person?"

"..." Chang Zhi was silent, "I thought he was nothing before, but now I think he's barely a friend."

The next second after she said that, Chang Zhi didn't even know what happened at that moment. She was pulled in front of a hot chest, and then the door that she hadn't had time to close was slammed shut with a bang, and her whole body was shocked - her

back was against the door panel, and she could feel a chill through her clothes.

Goose bumps appeared on her back, her brain was blank, and her eyes widened in surprise.

Watery, innocent and hateful.

Then, Chang Zhi felt that the shadow completely enveloped her, she was almost pressed against the corner of the door, hot breath sprinkled on her face, soft lips pressed against her -

Without hesitation, he pried open her lips and tongue with a hint of roughness and eagerness, like a brutal invader, sweeping every inch of her lips.

He even bit her lower lip in dissatisfaction, protected the back of her head with his hands, and then forced her lips and tongue to follow him——

Chang Zhi raised her head and was forced to bear it.

Wen Yanxing was full of irritability, and Chang Zhi quickly came to her senses and hammered her hands on his chest to push him away, but her strength was obviously not as strong as a man...

Wen Yanxing freed one hand to grab her two hands and pressed her tighter. A certain part of her chest was even pressed uncomfortably. Before she felt suffocated, Chang Zhi bit his tongue hard.

Wen Yanxing felt pain and subconsciously let go. The smell of rust spread between her lips and tongue. Chang Zhi successfully pushed Wen Yanxing away.

Chang Zhi's hair was messy, and her hair was loose and hanging down.

Her chest was heaving because of her shortness of breath. She bit her lower lip hard, and her mind was full of the scene just now.

The room was quiet. It was already dark outside the window. It was dim in the entrance and people's faces could not be seen clearly.

No one spoke, so the only sound in the whole space was the quiet breathing of two people.

Wen Yanxing looked at her quietly, with the smell of rust and a faint pain spreading in his mouth, and his eyes were deep.

Chapter 44: The warmth on the lips

The warmth on the lips.

Chang Zhi didn't expect that this embarrassing scene was broken by Wen Yanxing.

A minute after pushing Wen Yanxing away, Wen Yanxing went from expressionless to lowering his head. Although his expression could not be seen clearly, people could feel and imagine how aggrieved he was.

He spoke in a low voice and accused: "You lied."

"What friend? He held your hand," Wen Yanxing looked up at her and repeated again, "He held your hand and you didn't shake it off. I said I was your boyfriend, and you still wanted to deny it. He is your friend, I don't believe it."

Chang Zhi: "..................I..."

These words recounted the incident from beginning to end in simple language.

Chang Zhi found that it was indeed... all her fault.

If Chang Zhi was originally a balloon that was about to burst, now it was completely deflated.

It's all... her fault.

The next moment, Wen Yanxing was obsessed with the question again: "... One last time, who is it?"

She had no confidence at all, and said dryly: "This... How can I tell you..."

"Is there anything you can't tell me... Xiaosan?" Wen Yanxing's face changed when he said these two words.

"Not very likely."

Wen Yanxing frowned slightly, "... Ex?"

Chang Zhi: "..."

Seeing Chang Zhi's silent reaction, Wen Yanxing knew the truth about himself.

Wen Yanxing was silent for a moment: "What are you afraid of about your ex? You're so secretive that I thought he was some weird person." When he said this, his expression was a little strange. "How long ago was this ex? Why are you still entangled with him?"

Chang Zhi confessed honestly: "...Several years."

Wen Yanxing's face was full of disbelief. "Entangled for several years?" After a while, he sighed again, "Actors are actors, thick-skinned."

Chang Zhi: "...It only started in the past few months. There were some things that were not made clear before. He always wanted to tell me. In fact, I didn't want to hear it, but he seemed to not give up until he said it..."

"What, he still wants to revive? Why didn't you tell me earlier?" Wen Yanxing grabbed her arm, looking serious, "I really regret not beating him up today so that he couldn't touch you even if he was hundreds of meters away from you."

Chang Zhi realized that Wen Yanxing was...jealous?

The person in front of him said that he wanted to beat Meng Xi up, Chang Zhi pursed her lips and nodded, "Okay."

Wen Yanxing: "......???" God unfold?

Chang Zhi understood Wen Yanxing's doubts, and she explained: "I don't want to care about him either. You know that people who have been cheated will hate that person very much."

"I won't cheat on you," Wen Yanxing said seriously after Chang Zhi's words.

Chang Zhi asked back: "How do you know what will happen in the future?"

Wen Yanxing smiled, but looked very sure: "Then just watch."

Chang Zhi raised his eyebrows and asked him: "Is there any reward for watching all the time?"

"Reward you my whole life," Wen Yanxing was in an unexpectedly good mood after knowing that Meng Xi was Chang Zhi's ex. He changed the subject and opened his mouth, "You bite it really hurts."

Chang Zhi: "..."

"I almost thought you were going to murder your husband," Wen Yanxing added.

"It's you?" Chang Zhi stared at him and touched her mouth. "You're the one who scared me to death, okay?"

Wen Yanxing stared at her face and said seriously, "I was afraid you'd run away."

His face twisted for a moment after he said this, and he hissed and slowed down his voice, "It hurts so much when you open and close your mouth when you speak."

"I have watermelon frost here," Chang Zhi suggested after all it was her job, "this... will it work for this kind of wound?"

Wen Yanxing shook his head and said, "I don't know, you try it."

She turned on the living room light at the door, and the entrance, which was originally dim because of the dark, instantly lit up.

Chang Zhi led Wen Yanxing into the house and brought out a medicine box.

Wen Yanxing sat on the sofa and watched her rummaging around, looking for the medicine box here and there, and finally found it and brought it over.

"Open your mouth," Chang Zhi sat next to Wen Yanxing with a spray of watermelon frost in her hand, legs touching.

Seeing Chang Zhi's serious face. Wen Yanxing opened his mouth obediently, and Chang Zhi realized how ruthless she was. She carefully squeezed the medicine on the wound she had bitten. Wen Yanxing made another "hiss" and closed his mouth.

Chang Zhi looked at him and said, "Is it useful? How about some more?"

Wen Yanxing frowned and shook his head. He finally squeezed out a word: "It hurts."

It really hurts. The stimulation of the medicine sprinkled on the wound is like alcohol sprinkled on it - stimulation,

Chang Zhi comforted him and said, "Good medicine tastes bitter?"

"...I don't think it's useful." Wen Yanxing said after relieving the stimulation.

Chang Zhi looked down at the watermelon frost in her hand, turned her back and read the instructions carefully, and asked, "What medicine should I use?"

Wen Yanxing thought about it and poked Chang Zhi, who was looking down at the instructions, with his finger.

Chang Zhi raised her eyes and Wen Yanxing pointed at her lips with one hand.

"What's wrong?" She looked confused.

"Hey," Wen Yanxing smiled, "Answer me first, did you bite it?"

Although she didn't want to admit it, Chang Zhi nodded: "...Yes."

"I think it's like this, the medicine is useless, I still feel pain," Wen Yanxing shook his head, paused and added, "The one who tied the bell must untie it... How about you kiss me again?"

Chang Zhi: "............Kiss you again???"

As Chang Zhi finished speaking, a pillow hit Wen Yanxing's face with a snap, and the pillow slid into his arms. Wen Yanxing hugged the pillow and looked at someone who got up and entered the house, smiling helplessly.

The day Wen Yanxing changed the live broadcast platform was Tuesday.

In the morning, Chang Zhi knocked on the door of Wen Yanxing's house, ready to watch his live broadcast starting at 1 pm.

Have lunch together by the way.

After guaranteeing that he would never make any noise during his live broadcast in the afternoon, Chang Zhi was allowed to enter Wen Yanxing's "studio".

A laptop, two desktop computers, and two chairs. The desktop computers were placed side by side, and the laptop was placed alone on another table.

Wen Yanxing turned on the laptop for Chang Zhi to play with, and sat at the table to complete the video to be released tonight.

Chang Zhi was curious, so she moved a small stool and sat next to Wen Yanxing, resting her chin on his arm, watching Wen Yanxing open the complex audio software on the computer.

Chang Zhi didn't understand, and she lost interest after watching for a few minutes. Wen Yanxing saw that she was bored to the point of being the tenth hot search on Weibo, and pointed his slender finger at the living room, "Do you want to play with Erqiu?"

"Erqiu?" Chang Zhi didn't react for a while, and only then did she realize that the Erqiu Wen Yanxing was talking about was the hedgehog.

Chang Zhi kicked Wen Yanxing's stool, "Are you sending me to play with small animals like this?"

"You look bored," Wen Yanxing said, "or you can bring it in and play together?"

Chang Zhi thought this was a good idea, and ran to the living room.

Chang Zhi was a little emotional when she stood in the living room, looking at the desk. When she came here a few months ago, she and Wen Yanxing were just neighbors, but now she is standing here in a different identity. This feeling is really amazing. Chang Zhi looked at the corner, the three-story "villa" of Erqiu that she saw when she came last time. Who knew that it had changed houses, from a three-story villa to a one-story big house. Chang Zhi stood in front of the table, looking at Erqiu under the transparent plastic on the top of the box. Erqiu lay on the roller inside, looking around, as if thinking about people. Chang Zhi opened the box, and Erqiu looked up in response, just meeting Chang Zhi's eyes. One person and one hedgehog looked at each other. Erqiu was so scared that he fell off the roller when he suddenly saw a stranger. Chang Zhi reached out and touched Erqiu, and the hedgehog's spines stood up. Wen Yanxing saw this scene when he finished editing the video. Chang Zhi walked into the door slowly while holding Erqiu's one-story big house that was much smaller than Erqiu. Fortunately, there were wheels, food bowls, nests and a hedgehog inside.

Wen Yanxing was startled and stood up quickly: "...What are you doing?"

Chapter 45 Hedgehogs prick your hands

Chang Zhi put the "house" on the table, raised her chin, pointed and said, "...Does it prick people?"

Wen Yanxing stopped the mouse, looked at Erqiu squatting in front of the water dispenser and licking the roller in the chocolate board, raised his head and asked Chang Zhi: "Did it prick you?"

"Yes," Chang Zhi knew that hedgehogs pricked people, but she didn't expect it to be so prickly. She stretched out her hand, her palm slightly red, "I wanted to catch it, but it pricked me and I almost dropped it. I quickly put it back... How do you usually play with Erqiu? Aren't you afraid of being pricked?"

Wen Yanxing recalled that when he brought Erqiu back from the pet store, its thorns hardened as soon as he touched it, and his hands were all red. He coughed lightly, "Erqiu may not be familiar with you. It will be fine once you are familiar with it."

After a pause, Wen Yanxing stood up and grabbed Chang Zhi's hand, "Let me see." As soon as the voice fell, He lowered his head and blew on Chang Zhi's slightly red palm, then looked up at her, "Does it hurt?"

His tone was low and gentle. Seeing her palm focused, Chang Zhi only felt that her palm was itchy, soft but very comfortable. Her face was slightly red, and she shook her head and said, "...Are you cheesy?"

Wen Yanxing let go, raised his eyebrows and said, "Where is this cheesy?"

Chang Zhi retracted her palm, put it behind her back, and pointed at Erqiu with her chin, "If you are not afraid of its thorns, catch Erqiu out. I think it is bored."

Erqiu in the hut had finished drinking water. It looked at the roller and was tired of playing. Then it looked at its soft bed and had slept enough. It shook its head for a long time, and the thorns on its back gradually softened-choosing to roll around in the same place.

Then it stopped again, and its originally bulging body shook up and down in a wave line.

Lowered its head to lick the hair on its belly to scratch its itch.

He kicked his legs like crazy pretending to be in danger...

He yawned at last, and expanded himself from "�_=" to "=�����=" to become a piece of "hedgehog cloth", looking up with an intoxicated look on his face.

Wen Yanxing: "............................" Why did he suddenly feel embarrassed? ?

Chang Zhi looked at him and laughed.

Erqiu was really bored.

Chang Zhi watched Wen Yanxing grab Erqiu from the house. Erqiu turned over and pressed his fleshy belly against Wen Yanxing's palm, looking very comfortable with his limbs spread out. Wen Yanxing put Erqiu next to the keyboard, and Erqiu climbed the number keys on the edge with ease.

Chang Zhi helped Wen Yanxing put Erqiu's house on the ground.

Erqiu was obviously much more obedient on the table. He lay there quietly watching Wen Yanxing typing on the keyboard. Chang Zhi sat next to Wen Yanxing, and Erqiu would occasionally look at her. As he watched, he ran to Chang Zhi's hand with his short legs and touched her with his head.

Chang Zhi had been watching Erqiu's every move. When Erqiu suddenly approached her, her heart melted. She poked Erqiu tentatively, and Erqiu nudged her finger.

So, when Wen Yanxing saved the officially finished video, he saw Chang Zhi teasing Erqiu beside him.

The pet and the person played very harmoniously, and it was obvious that they had become quite familiar with each other.

Wen Yanxing looked at the time displayed on the lower right corner of the computer, 11:35, it was lunch time, he turned around and asked Chang Zhi, "Are you hungry?"

Chang Zhi was having fun with Erqiu, Erqiu was so cute that she couldn't take her eyes off him, she said without raising her head, "It's already noon so soon? I'm fine, are you hungry?"

Wen Yanxing watched Chang Zhi devote herself to Erqiu, and for some reason felt that his position at the moment was a little delicate, he coughed lightly, "Why don't we go out to eat now, there are seats outside if we go early."

"...Why are you going out to eat at noon?" Chang Zhi finally looked up at Wen Yanxing, she looked a little confused, "We didn't eat enough outside last week, don't you feel sick? Cook at home."

Chang Zhi finally turned her attention to him, but Wen Yanxing was silent when he heard this question, and said for a long time, "Can you cook?"

"A little," Chang Zhi said, "not very good.

"I can't. "Wen Yanxing looked at Chang Zhi honestly, "Since moving here, I have eaten almost every meal outside."

Chang Zhi: "............What about outside of that?"

"Instant noodles, quick-frozen," Wen Yanxing was a little embarrassed when he said this, "...Simple, convenient and delicious, dumplings, ramen, glutinous rice, chicken pancakes, seafood noodles, spicy noodles... There are many flavors, but sometimes I get tired of them."

Chang Zhi: "......................."

"Do you want to eat at home? I seem to have a lot of vegetables in my refrigerator." Wen Yanxing suggested

Chang Zhi thought about her refrigerator, it seemed that there were not many vegetables in her refrigerator at home, she stood up and pointed at Erqiu, and said, "Then I'll go and take a look, you keep an eye on Erqiu and don't let it fall."

Wen Yanxing smiled, "I'm its owner, how could I let it fall? "

Chang Zhi then left with peace of mind.

Wen Yanxing and Erqiu, the "father and son", were left behind, staring at each other. Erqiu was very dissatisfied with Chang Zhi's departure. He turned around and watched Chang Zhi walk towards the door. He was about to follow her with his short legs, but was stopped by a finger.

He was stunned for two seconds, then changed direction and continued to walk, and was stopped by another finger.

Erqiu: "................."

After experiencing it several times, Erqiu finally got angry about it. His nose moved, and he was about to do something big when he was picked up by a big hand.

Then the whole hedgehog was lifted in front of a handsome face. He kicked his calves, and then the man looked at him and spoke——

"Did you have fun playing with the beautiful sister? Does she smell good? Is it comfortable to rub against her?" Wen Yanxing smiled, paused, and threatened in a serious tone, "Okay, there will be no next time. "

Erqiu: "............" What did this stupid shit shoveler say??

Before Erqiu could think about anything, Wen Yanxing held him back in his nest.

Wen Yanxing looked at Erqiu through the chocolate board and saw him barking at him angrily. He obviously hadn't had enough fun, and his claws were knocking on the plastic board——

Wen Yanxing felt much better, and he stood up and walked to the kitchen without looking back.

Chang Zhi walked to the kitchen and was stunned when she opened the refrigerator.

Wen Yanxing's refrigerator did have a lot of frozen foods as he said, in addition to drinks, such as Coke, Sprite, Fanta, Nestle, imported milk in cartons, and even five small bottles of childish AD calcium milk............

Then there was a bag of green lettuce.

A bag of thin and long bean sprouts.

A bag of round meatballs.

A bag of square tofu.

And a row of smooth and round eggs, arranged in a very neat row.

Chang Zhi: "..................."

There is no seasoning in the refrigerator, such as green peppers, onions, garlic, coriander, etc. -

Is this what is called a lot of dishes? ? ? ? Chang Zhi was confused.

Why does a grown man have such a simple appetite? ? ? ?

At this time, Wen Yanxing also caught up and saw Chang Zhi looking at the refrigerator with a strange look on his face.

"What's wrong?" Wen Yanxing stood behind Chang Zhi and looked at his refrigerator, "Is there a problem?"

Chang Zhi said with some difficulty, "You are a grown man, and your appetite... is so simple." All vegetarian, I still want to show off my skills?

Wen Yanxing took a closer look at the ingredients in the refrigerator, raised his eyebrows and explained, "I didn't buy this to cook, well, you can add it to the instant noodles when you eat it, especially the spicy instant noodles, the ingredients and these dishes are like hot pot, very delicious."

"What about the eggs? "

"Breakfast, just beat an egg and fry it in less than ten minutes, it's convenient."

"............"

Chang Zhi took out the lettuce and took a look. The lettuce looked fresh, so it must have been bought yesterday. She imagined the dishes that could be made in this refrigerator and said, "Then we'll eat stir-fried bean sprouts, stir-fried lettuce, eggs and tofu... so light."

Chang Zhi actually has a heavy taste, preferring chili or sour flavors, and sometimes even salty things...

It can be said that she has a heavy taste.

Wen Yanxing obviously doesn't like to eat such light food. He was silent for a while and suggested, "Why don't we go out to eat? "

"No, wait a minute," Chang Zhi really didn't want to go out to eat today. She had almost had difficulty making choices when eating out for a week. In addition, she had already made up her mind to show Wen Yanxing how to improve the food. She stepped out in her Minion slippers, "I'll go home and see what dishes I have, bring them over and cook them together. We should be able to make a table."

Wen Yanxing: "............"

She was very stubborn.

Chapter 46 Despair

Chang Zhi was surprised by more than that.

...She despairingly discovered that only a thin layer of salt was left in Wen Yanxing's house.

It might have been damp, and it couldn't be scraped off with a spoon.

As for the sauce and vinegar... well, let's not talk about it.

When Chang Zhi slowly brought meat, peppers, onions, garlic and other ingredients from home, Wen Yanxing and Erqiu were already sitting at the dining table, watching her quietly.

Chang Zhi glanced at Wen Yanxing who was sitting leisurely.

Erqiu, who had been through the □□, had obviously realized who the boss he was really facing was, and was gently rubbing Wen Yanxing's palm with his much softer thorns to tickle him.

Receiving Chang Zhi's gaze, Wen Yanxing sat up unconsciously, and then put Erqiu back into the house and stood up automatically.

Erqiu, who was put in solitary confinement again: "..................qaq"

Chang Zhi then walked to the kitchen with a bag of lettuce.

Wen Yanxing followed closely behind him and asked behind him, "Do you need my help?"

Chang Zhi paused, gently put the lettuce in his arms, looked up and smiled, "Wash the vegetables."

Wen Yanxing took the full arms of vegetables, was stunned for a moment, and nodded, "Okay."

In the kitchen, there was the sound of running water washing vegetables, and the sound of boiling oil in the pot. Chang Zhi looked over and looked at Wen Yanxing who was concentrating on washing vegetables. He lowered his head and rubbed and washed repeatedly, looking like he was doing something important, quite serious.

Chang Zhi turned around and fried the meat with confidence.

The meat slices turned in the pot, and they looked particularly good with the red peppers. The sizzling sound and the bursts of meat fragrance made people's appetites whetted. When Chang Zhi was putting the dishes on the plate, Wen Yanxing had just finished washing a basin of vegetables and put down the last green vegetable. Wen Yanxing sighed,

"I didn't expect that we would enter the life of firewood, rice, oil, salt, sauce, vinegar and tea so quickly."

Chang Zhi paused while putting the dishes on the plate, "So will I be disliked as a yellow-faced woman next?"

"... Let me make an analogy," Wen Yanxing said, "If you are a yellow-faced woman, then I might be a weird uncle with a beer belly and a big beard? Or the kind who is not doing his job properly."

Chang Zhi burst out laughing, and her hand shook and the spatula almost fell back into the pot. She stopped laughing and asked, "Are you nervous this afternoon?"

Wen Yanxing put the dish on the table next to Chang Zhi, wiped the counter with a rag, and said slowly, "It's okay, a little."

"Why?"

The rice cooker automatically jumped to the next gear with a snap, and the aroma of cooked rice spread in the air. Chang Zhi casually put the prepared dishes on the edge of the counter and looked up at Wen Yanxing who was wiping the counter with his head down.

"...There are so many whys," Wen Yanxing threw the rag into the sink and said lightly, "I'm worried that the fans are not as loyal as I thought. There are too few people coming."

Chang Zhi was stunned.

Is this... nervousness or lack of confidence? Should she do something?

She tapped her fingers on the corner of the table and thought for a long time before she comforted him, "No, your popularity... is really high." After saying that, she felt that it was not enough, so she reached out and patted Wen Yanxing's arm gently.

Wen Yanxing looked down at her white and tender arms, and asked with a curved corner of his lips, "Are you comforting me?"

Chang Zhi could not deny, "Hmm."

"...Old rules, you know, this is not enough."

Chang Zhi originally just patted him, but when she heard this, she immediately turned into a push, she snorted, "When was the old rule? Why don't I know? I don't understand, enough."

"Well, then I'll take it myself?" After he finished speaking, Chang Zhi watched him getting closer and closer to her. She blinked her eyelashes, closed her eyes, and her cheeks seemed to be numb for a moment of shyness.

There was a soft touch on her lips, and after his hand climbed up her waist, the place where he was touched felt sore and numb. He gently bit her lips, and gently tossed and turned.

It seemed like a long time had passed.

So long that the dish went from steaming hot to warm at the beginning, and Chang Zhi couldn't help but suck air from his mouth again. She stretched out her hand and pushed him, and he reluctantly let go and left.

Chang Zhi blushed, turned around and stuffed the dishes into his hands, "Go out, there's nothing for you to do here."

Wen Yanxing held the dishes and smiled, "You cook, I can just stand and watch."

"...Watching shit!"

"If you have such a heavy taste, it's not impossible."

"... There won't be a next time."

Wen Yanxing immediately changed his words, "I'll go put the dishes away first, I'll get the drinks outside and wait for you obediently."

At 3 pm, when Wen Yanxing started his first live broadcast on the Feiyun live broadcast platform, Chang Zhi sat next to Wen Yanxing.

Wen Yanxing turned on the camera for the first time during this live broadcast, but he didn't take pictures of his face, but clapped his hands.

His strength proved that he was not a substitute player or something like that.

Chang Zhi held the second ball and watched him start broadcasting. The number of people in the live broadcast room quickly jumped from 0 to four digits and five digits——

Wen Yanxing also didn't react. He raised his hand to adjust the microphone, coughed lightly and said, "Well... How to start? Hello everyone, I am Yan Zhi——"

The moment the voice fell, the five digits jumped to six digits, and the number of people increased by thousands of people every minute.

The number of viewers increased faster than when Wen Yanxing was broadcasting on Bilibili.

...Maybe it's because of the change of a formal live broadcast platform. After all, Bilibili is not a very professional live broadcast platform. It is more of a video sharing platform. Chang Zhi sat next to him and watched this scene, thinking.

The barrage also increased at a visible speed. In addition to the quick "666" and "2333" that come with the live broadcast platform, there are also those from the audience and fans——

Surprise.

[Yan Da, you actually turned on the camera? ? ?] [I always thought that Yan Da only broadcast games with the microphone, today... the benefits of the new platform are so exciting? ��Lick your hand, lick your hand, lick your hand, lick your hand, cry when your hand leaves your sight��Come from station B, download Feiyun on purpose? ...�

Wen Yanxing cleared his throat quietly, suppressed the joy on his lips, aimed at the microphone, and controlled the mouse on the screen to circle the key points, "Today is my first time to live broadcast on Feiyun. I am very grateful to the previous viewers for following me here... Without further ado, let's start the live broadcast directly. Everyone has seen today's content, PlayerUnknown's Battlegrounds... This game is very interesting. I started playing it about half a month ago, but I didn't play it for you -"

During Wen Yanxing's live broadcast, Chang Zhi quietly watched him speak seriously and watched him skillfully control the mouse and keyboard.

PlayerUnknown's Battlegrounds is a shooting online game. Players are airdropped to a random location with nothing on their bodies and start looking for supplies, avoiding and chasing other players until they win or die.

There will also be poison circles to increase the player's sense of urgency. If the player does not avoid the poison circles in time, the blood volume will continue to decrease until death. In short, this is a game with a sense of rhythm and tension. Wen Yanxing's game had only started for three minutes. The plane was flying in the air, and people kept jumping down to land. Wen Yanxing waited for a while and finally chose to land. The parachute was shaking, but

Wen Yanxing was surprised to find that there were still many enemies jumping down together. In fact, this was not a good thing. "Well, it's time to land now. Wait, there are three people here..." Wen Yanxing looked at the person on the screen who was shaking and pulling the parachute to descend, but was accidentally hit by another person's parachute and stuck on the roof. "... Wait, this person is too close to me and stuck me in the roof. What the hell? I got stuck in the roof in the first game, don't-" On the eaves of the screen, a female figurine with a long ponytail was stuck in it. The controlled dancing and dancing did not make any movement, not even a little movement, as if she was stuck in a quagmire. Wen Yanxing frowned and continued to control the character, trying to break free——

There were also a lot of people gloating in the barrage,

[Dream start] [Hahahaha, I like to see Yan Da's embarrassed look every time] [Exit and restart, I'm afraid you can't get out] [It's a bad luck to be stuck in a bug at the beginning]

However, the person who asked Wen Yanxing to restart a game was obviously disappointed. The little man on the screen moved again and staggered down from the eaves. At the same time, Wen Yanxing breathed a sigh of relief——

"I was scared to death. I thought I had to load and restart, and started picking up equipment, um, bandages——" Wen Yanxing searched all the way. Maybe it was too late to get a gun. He searched from the first floor to the second floor and then jumped down to an iron net. He controlled the little man to get out of the iron net, and then ran towards the factory in the distance. As soon as he entered the factory, he met an enemy girl with a gun.

Wen Yanxing: "Is there such a thing????"

With a bang, the gunshot was fired face to face. The little man on the screen controlled by Wen Yanxing instantly had no health bar, waved his fists weakly, and then fell to the ground and died. The game was over.

Wen Yanxing: "........................"

Strong.

Invincible.

He got stuck in the bug at the beginning, and finally broke free to make a big move, but he died before he could succeed. A gunshot shattered all his ambitions.

It's simply insane.

But everyone is a group of people who watch the fun and don't mind the big things. The number of live broadcasts continues to break through, and the barrage is also increasing. The barrage of gloating is even more piled up——

[666666][Real. Dreamy start][If God lets you start this game again, you have to start again][Meaa, I'm laughing to death hahahaha][Yan Da was silent, first the bug and then he was killed face to face, laughing and crying hahaha]

Wen Yanxing really didn't know whether to laugh or keep silent.

In short, he was now full of depression, because of the depression of being killed instantly by a single shot just now.

Chang Zhi sat next to him and watched all the time. She couldn't help laughing when he got stuck on the bug. Now seeing Wen Yanxing's black screen, she finally laughed a little.

But she quickly covered her mouth for fear of being heard by the audience in front of the screen. Her body was shaking slightly because of holding back laughter. Wen Yanxing, who was already speechless, took the time to look at Chang Zhi.

Wen Yanxing: "............Is it so funny?"

It seemed that he accidentally let slip that there was someone next to him. Wen Yanxing was stunned, and Chang Zhi also blinked.

"...Hey, don't gloat over other people's misfortunes," Wen Yanxing said in time, seemingly speaking to the audience and the comments, but in fact he was looking at Chang Zhi, accusing her, "I'm so miserable, it's rare to have a bug, shouldn't you feel sorry for me? What's the point of laughing so happily?"

Chang Zhi raised her eyebrows slightly with interest when she heard this, she casually put the second ball on her knees, lowered her head and silently took out her phone, opened the Feiyun Live app, quickly turned off the mute and entered the live broadcast room, and silently added a sentence among the many comments like [Give you some candles], [This opening style is so strange], [Hahahaha, I feel sorry for you for a second]—

[Sorry, I don't know why I don't feel sorry for you xd]

Chapter 47 Heartache

When Wen Yanxing was broadcasting live until 4pm, Erqiu had just woken up from a nap, and he had finished the water in the cup next to him.

Chang Zhi had been watching, and seeing this, she stood up and took the cup away and helped him pour water.

Wen Yanxing looked at Chang Zhi's back and felt very happy.

Erqiu and Wen Yanxing were the only ones left in the room.

Wen Yanxing had just started a new game of Jedi Escape, playing it with concentration, occasionally saying a few dirty words. Erqiu had just woken up, and after rolling around in a daze, he saw his master moving the mouse and typing on the keyboard very seriously.

It took one step forward, two steps... and just walked slowly into the camera range.

Wen Yanxing was used to it and didn't notice anything wrong.

However, a bunch of Erqiu fans exploded in the barrage -

[Ahhhhh, Hedgehog Highness] [Erqiu himself] [...Is this a moving ball? ? ��The thorn seems to be very prickly. Will it prick Yan Da and disturb him from playing games? 23333��Short legs are so cute——�

The comments were full of love. Erqiu certainly didn't know, and Wen Yanxing had no time to look at the comments on another machine.

The explorer. Wen. Non-fan. Erqiu's exploration of electronic devices began.

It first rubbed against Wen Yanxing's hand, looked up at the screen and camera, and the audience who were hit by this face said that they didn't want to watch Wen Yanxing play games, but Wen Yanxing still did his job conscientiously——

"I heard a sound,"

"Yes, I bet 50 cents that there must be someone behind that hill."

"Du is coming,"

"Hey, I don't have a car, it's a bit tiring to run to Du on foot..."

A burst of gunshot sound effects——

"Look, I told you, there's someone in that house!"

Audience: ... Erqiu looks at the camera, looks at the camera

When Wen Yanxing was unaware that he was satisfied with his words and deeds during the live broadcast, Erqiu had already become the anchor in the eyes of the one million viewers——

[A certain anchor made a million a month by live-streaming a hedgehog to be cute] [Yan Da, stop playing and let Ershu come] [666 malicious cute foul]

Erqiu has always been very interested in this square object, and the fast-moving things on it made it feel very novel.

Animals tend to get excited when they are excited. Erqiu yawned a lot, then jumped around excitedly while watching the screen, until——it jumped onto the keyboard.

Wen Yanxing: "................."

The "Start" shortcut key in the lower right corner was pressed, and the taskbar instantly appeared on the full-screen game on the screen. Wen Yanxing grabbed Erqiu expressionlessly.

"Why are you so noisy? Are you so excited today? Do you also want to watch my live broadcast?" Wen Yanxing said,

Erqiu thought he was in trouble.

The audience thought Erqiu was going to be banished to the cold palace.

However, Chang Zhi, who came in with a cup of water, also saw this scene——

She walked over quickly and knew that Erqiu was in trouble. She naturally reached out to take Erqiu. Erqiu, who escaped the disaster, lay docilely in Chang Zhi's palm.

Chang Zhi breathed a sigh of relief.

However, what she didn't know was that the camera had just honestly recorded this hand——

[Wow, is that a girl's hand?] [Ju Fucking white and thin? Does Yan Da have a woman in his family? ?] [Female, girlfriend's hand? ?] [Isn't Yan Da a virgin solo...] [Oh my god, oh my god, am I blind? I saw a third hand and it's a girl's? ? ? ? ?]

Chang Zhi didn't notice it and pushed the cup filled with water back to the keyboard, thinking she was considerate.

[............Did you see it, everyone?] [I saw it.] [It's impossible for a person to have three hands, right? Isn't Yan Da a deformed person? ��Ahhhhhhhhhhhhhh girlfriend? ? �

At this time, Chang Zhi was sitting down with two balls in her arms.

After handling the two balls, Wen Yanxing looked up and took the time to look at the screen, but was surprised to find that...

Wen Yanxing: "................."

His hand left the audience's sight. In reality, he didn't speak, but just poked Chang Zhi's arm with his hand.

Chang Zhi looked up with a confused look on her face, and saw Wen Yanxing pointing his hand high to another machine that was broadcasting live.

"What's wrong?" She said to Wen Yanxing silently.

Wen Yanxing also responded to her silently, "Your hand, go and see the barrage yourself."

Chang Zhi was really incompetent at lip reading. She looked at it for a long time and only understood the word "hand".

Wen Yanxing held his forehead, feeling very disappointed, and could only raise his hand and point to another computer screen, motioning her to look.

Hand? What's wrong with her hand? Chang Zhi grabbed the two balls, walked around from behind Wen Yanxing to the front of the machine, bent down slightly and looked at——

[Yan Daqiu, please explain who this girl is? ?] [Don't tell me that hand belongs to your mother...]

Chang Zhi: "???"

Before Chang Zhi could figure out the situation, there was silence behind her for a while, and Wen Yanxing, who hadn't even started the game, spoke, "Hand... do you believe me when I say it's mine?"

[Don't believe it] [Don't believe it 1] [No...]

"Okay," Wen Yanxing said helplessly, "You found out, so I have to confess?"

Chang Zhi turned around and looked at Wen Yanxing, her face full of surprise, and there was a hint of confusion between her eyebrows.

Is this going to...?

"Who just said that I was a soloist?" Wen Yanxing paused, and then said, "You are the one who is solo. I have recently formed a mixed male and female duo. Who wants to be single with you?!"

[66666666][woc which girl][broken heart, husband cheated][caught off guard...][Oh my god]

One minute after Wen Yanxing finished saying this, the number of viewers jumped from more than one million to one and a half million in just ten minutes at a speed visible to the naked eye.

This speed can be said to be very fast, and the results are also very good.

Wen Yanxing quickly jumped to the homepage ranking.

The official also secretly recommended it.

Chang Zhi stood by with a shocked face, and her heart was half surprised and half delighted.

She always thought that dating was a matter between two people, and there was no need to tell the fans. Telling them might hurt the other party.

She had already thought that she would tell the world when she was really stable in the future.

But now, although Wen Yanxing did not mention any names, he directly said that he had a girlfriend.

Although she was very surprised and secretly happy,

Will he lose fans like this?

After all, there are so many people who call him husband :)

Chang Zhi thought in her heart expressionlessly.

Also, she seemed to have thought that a small piece of news would appear on various websites tonight -

[Shocking, a certain anchor used hedgehog to stimulate the audience on the first day of live broadcast, and admitted that he already had a girlfriend...]

[Shocking, a certain anchor finally got rid of singleness after more than 20 years of solo...]

Chang Zhi: "................."

A bit funny.

Chapter 48 Is my girlfriend pretty?

Wen Yanxing glanced casually and picked a comment to respond to the audience's crazy enthusiasm——

[I just want to ask one question, is my girlfriend pretty?]

"Pretty, of course she is," Wen Yanxing looked up at Chang Zhi and chuckled. The voice was transmitted through the headset to the audience in front of the screen, and their hearts melted. "She is a beautiful person besides my mother and sister, in all senses. Of course, more importantly, I like her very much,"

Chang Zhi quietly watched his true confession to her, and her lips unconsciously raised.

[Please ask for photos, please ask for photos, I want to see——]

Wen Yanxing raised his eyebrows with interest, "Photos? If you say you want to see them, I will show them to you. Let's talk about it when there is a chance."

[Who is chasing who? ◈

"Who is chasing whom?" Wen Yanxing murmured and repeated the question. Chang Zhi was listening nervously. She put her hand on his shoulder and exerted a little force. Wen Yanxing smiled and said, "It must be me who chased her. I like her too much. There is nothing I can do."

[Ahhh, I ate a mouthful of dog food][Why do I have more gasoline and torches in my hands][Pah, I won't eat this dog food even if I starve to death...]

Wen Yanxing looked at these comments and laughed happily. He pressed Chang Zhi's hand on his shoulder with his right hand and said,

"Stop it."

The fans in front of the screen were very excited.

The reason was that Wen Yanxing's "Stop it" was too sweet ahh ... Gently stroking Erqiu, Chang Zhi looked at the teacup with dull eyes and asked Wen Yanxing, "Why did you suddenly tell the audience?"

Wen Yanxing lowered his head to talk to the executives and managers of Feiyun Live about the recommended positions. Hearing this, he did not look up and said lightly, "They asked."

"You answered it if they asked?"

"...It's hard to explain," Wen Yanxing finally raised his head after hearing this. He put his phone on the table, held Chang Zhi's arm and asked him to turn to him, with a serious expression, "I always feel that you are very scared."

"...Ah?" Chang Zhi unconsciously scratched Erqiu's thorns with her nails, "Is it?"

"Yeah," Wen Yanxing nodded, his eyes slightly sank, "You seem to be very afraid of others mentioning you."

Chang Zhi lowered her head, Erqiu lay comfortably in her palm, and felt her gaze, so he looked up at her.

Cute and irresistible.

"I'm not afraid of others mentioning me," Chang Zhi withdrew her hand, her voice a little vague, "I just think that if others know that I'm your girlfriend or you're my boyfriend, there will be some bad influence..."

"Why? I remember that we didn't set fire or kill anyone, right?" Wen Yanxing frowned and asked, "What's the impact?"

"No, it's not that exaggerated," Chang Zhi shook her head, "It's just that I was dissed by the whole nation before... I'm afraid of you..."

Chang Zhi has been like a frightened bird since the past.

Just a slight test will cause a conditioned reflex.

Even vigilance.

Although the matter has been clarified, those who believe will believe, and those who firmly don't believe will never believe.

She is really afraid that Wen Yanxing will lose fans because of her, be blackened, etc.

She is afraid that Wen Yanxing will feel that kind of isolated and helpless feeling.

It's so sad.

Wen Yanxing didn't know that Chang Zhi's thoughts were so boring. His voice sank. He bent down slightly to let Chang Zhi's eyes meet his. He said seriously, "What are you afraid of from me? Losing fans? I'm not afraid, so what are you afraid of?"

"Besides," he changed the subject, "Haven't you clarified it? Why do you care about those who don't believe it?"

"I want you, so I will accept everything about you. Good or bad influences have nothing to do with whether I like you or not. I'm not with you for other reasons, such as coveting you." Wen Yanxing said quietly.

The surroundings were suddenly very quiet, and Chang Zhi kept repeating what Wen Yanxing said in her mind.

Chang Zhi suddenly realized.

Yes. There's no need to care.

There's no need to care about how others see it. He originally cared about her, not others.

The person she likes is him, so let everything go naturally. Why hurt feelings for external things?

And, as far as it can be seen, the most likely person who can go to the end with her is Wen Yanxing.

What she should do is to treat him well, instead of hurting her feelings for other reasons.

His face was handsome, and his dark eyes looked at her like obsidian, as if he wanted to suck her in.

His lips were also red, just the right thickness, and looked very soft.

I really want to—

I don't know where the impulse came from, Chang Zhi's heart suddenly became full of heroic spirit, and the mood of wanting to do something surged up—

She leaned over slightly, raised her head and leaned over to kiss his lips before he could react.

Wen Yanxing's calm face fluctuated slightly, and his inner emotions were like the blue and calm sea that suddenly rolled up layers of waves, ups and downs.

She kissed his lips, with a small amplitude, vague, and in a voice that he could hear, lingeringly—

"I'm not new to being with you..."

The daze was only for a moment, and after Wen Yanxing reacted, Chang Zhi felt that her sore neck was finally relieved.

Because she was hugged into his arms, tightly as if the two were originally one.

His hands were around her slender waist, and her lips and tongue were found by him in a familiar way. He hooked her and entangled with him, like two little fish playing in the sea, happy and affectionate, full as if overflowing from the chest, and satisfied with his whole heart.

He held her in his mouth as if he was tasting some peerless delicacy, tasting it carefully, and then again, again... He was domineering and stingy and refused to share with others.

Chang Zhi raised her head, and her arms, as white and tender as lotus roots, unconsciously wrapped around his neck, and she stood on tiptoes to passively bear it.

His hand reached up from her wide T-shirt, and the warmth made her toes tremble and she was distracted for a moment. Suddenly, the tip of her tongue was lightly bitten, and Chang Zhi closed her eyes and her eyelashes trembled.

It was as if two legs of a person were walking on the line of her spine. I don't know when, the place where her chest was originally clamped loosened, and the buttons behind her were unbuttoned.

Chang Zhi opened her eyes and said indistinctly, "...Don't."

Wen Yanxing opened his eyes, suddenly bent down and picked her up horizontally.

Chang Zhi was startled. She was forced to hug his neck for fear of falling. The original restraint on her back was hanging there empty, which made her more majestic. Her heart beat very fast and she screamed, "What are you doing?!"

His eyes were slightly red, and he carried her out of the room, walked to the living room, and walked to the sofa.

Then he put her on the sofa, and he also got in the sofa, which was not wide to begin with, and insisted on hugging her.

Chang Zhi: "................."

The lights in the living room were not turned on. It was already night, and the sky was dark. The light in the room was cast into the living room through the door, bringing a little light. The living room was incredibly quiet, and only his and her breathing could be heard.

One after another, one rough and one thin, one fast and one slow.

Wen Yanxing held her like this, squeezing her to the inside of the sofa, with his lower back slightly bent, reaching his calves and then pressed against her.

No matter how dumb Chang Zhi was, she knew that he held her so tightly, but the gap left by the bend was...

Alas... She was not a girl who didn't know the world, and Chang Zhi's cheeks turned red again.

But even if the girl had studied biology, she would know what was there...

Chang Zhi seemed to raise her hand to cover her face.

Wen Yanxing held Chang Zhi, burying his head in her neck for a long time without moving. Chang Zhi thought he was beastly, but she didn't expect him to hold her like this.

She poked Wen Yanxing's back and asked knowingly, "... Why are you holding me like this... It's so tight." After saying that, she moved her body.

It was indeed uncomfortable. The sofa was so small, but he had to hold her over and then rub against her.

Can't he just sit down? Why did he have to lie down? And... Chang Zhi looked at the ceiling, and at this moment she wanted to button her clothes with her backhand.

It seems to be crooked...

Wen Yanxing rubbed her neck, and faced with Chang Zhi's struggle, he hugged her tighter.

Chang Zhi: "...why don't you get up first? I feel like I'm being squeezed to death."

Wen Yanxing spoke, his voice was unexpectedly hoarse,

"Don't move, I want to hug you like this... I can't hold it in."

I was holding it in.

Chapter 49 Don't dare to move

Chang Zhi didn't dare to move.

Wen Yanxing's words "I'm holding it in" seemed to still echo in her ears. Chang Zhi blushed and closed her eyes. His head buried deeper in her neck.

After a long time, Chang Zhi thought he would leave, but he rubbed her neck and said hoarsely,

"No, the more I think about it, the more..."

Chang Zhi pinched his shoulder, "Then don't think about it—"

"............" Wen Yanxing rubbed her again, "It's uncomfortable, I can't do it."

His voice was full of discomfort. Chang Zhi had never experienced such a thing. She just vaguely knew that men would feel uncomfortable if they held it in... Pinching the man's arm, Chang Zhi looked at the ceiling and blinked, and said hesitantly, "Or... I..."

"Come on."

Chang Zhi: "............"

Never seen Wen Yanxing's more magical side, Chang Zhi can't do it, and Wen Yanxing is also half-baked. He held her hand and put it into his pants, but men are a race that can learn without a teacher after all. After a long time, Chang Zhi felt that her hands were sore and sore, and he...

Wen Yanxing sat up suddenly.

Chang Zhi's cheeks were already red, and she didn't dare to look at him. She said goodbye quickly, and then left Wen Yanxing's house very quickly and ran back to her own home. Wen Yanxing didn't even have time to say anything.

After returning home, Chang Zhi leaned against the door and felt that her face was too hot.

As she was getting hotter, Chang Zhi remembered the scene just now. She pulled her hand out from her back and stared at her palm for a long time.

After a long while, she put her hand down and looked up, and suddenly felt sad.

So men are like this...?

Then what should she do in the future, in the future...

On the other side, Wen Yanxing looked at Chang Zhi who ran away, sat on the sofa, and stroked his forehead.

He didn't want to do it originally... It's just that,

It's said that men are easily provoked.

Wen Yanxing took out his mobile phone and was about to reply to Chang Zhi who ran away, when he saw a message from his sister.

[Lu Zhiyao]: Brother, I just watched the live broadcast!

�Lu Zhiyao��I saw that woman's hand!! Who! Tell me! I promise not to tell!

�ynzwyx7��.................

�ynzwyx7��Don't you usually not watch my live broadcast?

�Lu Zhiyao��Today, I heard that you changed the platform, so I watched it and threw a few rockets to support you...Oh, please tell me, for those rockets and because I am your sister, who made you tempted? ?

�ynzwyx7��Why are girls so gossipy? You don't know her even if I tell you.

�Lu Zhiyao��Then send me the picture, is it beautiful?

�ynzwyx7��Very beautiful.

Sister is showing off, Wen Yanxing found her photo from Chang Zhi's circle of friends and sent it to Wen Luying.

[ynzwyx7]: Your sister-in-law [Picture]

Wen Yanxing thought Wen Luying would sigh. In fact, he also looked at the screen and waited for the exclamation of amazement, ready to receive a wave of praise for Chang Zhi, but he didn't expect that after he sent this photo, Wen Luying was silent for a long time.

After three minutes, Wen Luying replied to him,

[Lu Zhiyao]: ... ... Tang Zhi?

[ynzwyx7]: ... How did you know?

[Lu Zhiyao]: Did you forget that I shared it with you before?

Wen Yanxing suddenly realized.

Yes, he knew Chang Zhi because of his sister's sharing. When he finished watching it, his mind was full of new topics, so...

[Lu Zhiyao]: I watched her dance video. She was on the hot search before. The milk tea shop manager that mgj has been working with and the dancer I like to watch are the same person. I was shocked.

[Lu Zhiyao]: Ah ah ah ah brother, how did you get together with her? It's not like them! ! ! !

�ynzwyx7��It's a neighbor...

�Lu Zhiyao��Wow, a match made in heaven, is it such a coincidence?

�ynzwyx7��She's very good, I'm always afraid she'll run away.

�Lu Zhiyao��Who's better than our mom?

Wen Yanxing and Wen Luying's mother was actually a first-class beauty when she was young. Even though she's middle-aged, she still looks like she's in her late thirties or early forties.

�ynzwyx7��They're all good, all beautiful, and I love them all.

�Lu Zhiyao��Speaking of our mom, I forgot to tell you one thing.

�Lu Zhiyao��At that time, I was just listening to your live broadcast while doing other things. The one who watched it very seriously was our mom. She asked if you would come back for the Mid-Autumn Festival and bring your girlfriend with you.

�ynzwyx7��..................

The days passed by with Wen Yanxing doing a stable live broadcast, Chang Zhi busy in the store, and occasionally dancing.

Chang Zhi wanted to shoot a video this day, but Jiang Huai was absent due to something. After Wen Yanxing knew about it, he offered to help her shoot.

Chang Zhi looked at him suspiciously, "Really?"

Wen Yanxing took out a dusty camera from the storage room at home and proved himself, "I've played with it before, so I can shoot a little bit."

Chang Zhi thought about it, if Wen Yanxing can't... just shoot it straight. With a little doubt in her heart, Chang Zhi took Wen Yanxing to the park where she had taken a good view before.

Wen Yanxing followed her with a lot of bags. It was the first time he did this, and he felt very curious looking at Chang Zhi's back.

Chang Zhi went to the bathroom to change clothes, and Wen Yanxing sat on a stone bench in the pavilion in the lake where they took the view and played with his mobile phone.

The scenery here is indeed beautiful, with a lake with occasional waves, lotus leaves on the lake, and fish floating on the water from time to time. Wen Yanxing thinks it can be regarded as one of the top three scenery in the parks he has visited.

He stood up, turned around and took the camera, stepped back a few steps, adjusted the position left and right, and finally pressed the shutter button.

After finishing, he lowered his head and was very satisfied with the photos he had just taken. He took a photo of the camera with his mobile phone and posted it on Weibo.

[Yan Zhi]: A rare time to relax, blowing the breeze, looking at the scenery and waiting for someone. [Picture]

[Comment]

[You'd better not mess with me]: Waiting for someone? Waiting for whom?

[Yan Zhi Fei Fu]: Jealousy made me deformed, and I tore this dog food apart viciously.

[The person I love most is...]: Waiting for my girlfriend? This is why you tuned your live broadcast to the evening today. Ah, I went on a date. I went on a date.

Wen Yanxing turned off his phone.

The bathroom is not far from here. Today is a weekday and there are not many people. Chang Zhi tried to wear such clothes outdoors for the first time, so when she came out of the cubicle in the bathroom, the first thing she met was the surprised look of a girl who was washing her hands.

Chang Zhi shyly raised her hand, and to avoid embarrassment, she touched her hair, then awkwardly leaned over to wash her hands, and left quickly in her high heels.

Facing the surprised or admiring eyes of passers-by along the way, Chang Zhi walked to the pavilion.

Because Wen Yanxing was carrying a lot of bags and taking pictures, no passers-by came to disturb him, so Wen Yanxing took pictures out of boredom, looked down at the photos he had just taken, and when he looked up again, Chang Zhi came from the path,

A touch of pink walked away from the end of the road, and the surroundings seemed to suddenly become quiet, leaving only the faint bird calls. Suddenly, there was nothing else in his eyes, only that beautiful figure.

She tied up her black hair, and a pink hairpin fixed her hairstyle. A strand of hair hung down, and she looked up at him with shyness and uneasiness. The exquisitely tailored custom cheongsam wrapped the owner's curvy figure. She held a fan in her hand, and slowly raised and lowered her high heels, stepping towards him step by step.

Chang Zhi always looks good when she walks. After years of dancing, she walks with a straight back, arms swinging naturally, steps evenly, and rhythmically. When she walks in a cheongsam, she looks even more charming.

She was like a fairy that suddenly appeared in the woods. She didn't move, but she made his heart flutter.

She was like a girl from the south of the Yangtze River in ancient times, whispering softly and gently invading people's hearts.

She walked towards him, and every step she took seemed to enter his heart.

Wen Yanxing was full of surprise, and Chang Zhi saw it when she approached him.

She pursed her lips, and the corners of her lips rose unconsciously. Her heart, which had been facing the attention of passers-by all the way, finally got affirmation.

She bent down slightly and sat back on the stone bench, looking up at his profile,

"Does it look good?"

Wen Yanxing put the camera aside and suddenly wanted to go on strike.

He didn't want to shoot anymore. Such a beautiful girl, it was enough for him to just look at her, but he had to shoot it for others to see? He also had to shoot her dancing? ?

No, no, no, he felt uncomfortable just thinking about it.

Wen Yanxing coughed lightly, raised his hand to tidy up Chang Zhi's hair, his eyes were gentle, and his voice was slightly deep, "It's beautiful, so beautiful."

"But, seriously, can I not take the photo?"

"...Why?"

"Because I don't want to take photos of you like this for others to see."

Chapter 50 Chang Zhi is also ready

Even if Wen Yanxing didn't want to shoot, he still had to shoot. After all, the purpose of their trip was for this, and Chang Zhi was also ready.

Wen Yanxing sighed while holding the camera, "I'm afraid I can't control myself and remember how many I want to count."

Chang Zhi came to his side and watched him adjust the camera position, "Hold steady, we can win."

Wen Yanxing looked at her sideways, and Chang Zhi smiled at him innocently.

So Wen Yanxing reluctantly took a step back with the camera.

Chang Zhi's cover dance this time was by2's peach blossom cheongsam, which was full of inexplicable feelings.

After all, by2 no longer had any particularly outstanding news, and the exposure rate was low, so that they gradually faded from the public's eyes, but in that era, they were also very popular and became a must-order singer in KTV.

This song is a duet dance, mixed with jazz elements. Chang Zhi turned her back to the camera, with her hands quietly placed on both sides.

The music started, starting with the opening of Peking Opera singing, accompanied by the melodious and elegant sound of the guzheng, and the novel sound of the snapping fingers, which was very catchy. Chang Zhi moved-

She turned around and took a step to the right. She looked up at the camera with her head lowered. She raised her arms and crossed them, stroking her waist like a wave. She naturally pressed her hands on her knees and squatted from right to left. She smiled at the camera with her lips pursed when she looked up.

There is no need to describe the charm in it.

Looking at Chang Zhi in the camera, Wen Yanxing's eyes suddenly deepened.

Especially to some of the movements-Chang Zhi turned her back to the camera, hugged her arms, twisted her waist to the beat, and then turned sideways to shake her hands.

Her legs were slightly tense, her lines were smooth and graceful, her waist was straight, her neck was slightly tilted, her beautiful collarbone was prominent, she was neat and gentle, and gentle and charming.

Wen Yanxing remembered some strange videos on Station B, and finally understood what the barrage said-

"I have to buy a few boxes of Nutri-Express again."

So, Nutri-Express has this meaning...

Wen Yanxing put his hand on his lips and coughed lightly.

Chang Zhi, who was dancing seriously, had no idea what Wen Yanxing was thinking.

Chang Zhi kept changing her arm movements to the beat, and her feet would step elsewhere from time to time, and finally she stopped at one place.

This place was the part of the original version of turning the handkerchief, and Chang Zhi was not very good at it, so she changed the movement to a fan without authorization.

Wen Yanxing paused the recording, and Chang Zhi walked up to take the fan from his hand. There was fine sweat on her forehead, but her eyes were sparkling, "Let's change to another place."

Wen Yanxing said "hmm", took out a pack of tissues from his trouser pocket, and took one out for her, "Wipe the sweat."

Chang Zhi followed suit.

The two walked out of the pavilion on the water and came to another place that Chang Zhi had scouted in advance.

Along the way, Chang Zhi lowered her head and held Wen Yanxing's arm, and there was no need to mention the gazes she met.

The fallen leaves all over the ground and the leaves that floated down from time to time were quite artistic in the camera, and Wen Yanxing played music again.

Wen Yanxing was fine when he looked ahead, and his mood did not fluctuate much compared to just now, until he saw Chang Zhi waving the fan again, half covering her face with a pair of curved eyebrows and eyes looking at the camera, and a gust of wind blew, her hair moved lightly, and the leaves were blown down. Chang Zhi was dressed in pink, like a fairy.

Wen Yanxing couldn't hold it in any longer.

What man could stand the person he loved, smiling at him, smiling so beautifully as if to seduce him——

So, when Chang Zhi finished filming this segment and was about to go forward to see the effect, she was stopped by Wen Yanxing.

"Don't move."

Chang Zhi stopped walking with the fan in hand, looked up and asked him, "What's wrong?"

Wen Yanxing strode to her side in two or three steps, lowered his head and looked at her, as if kindly reminding her, "Look up, there's something."

"...Ah? What's wrong???" Chang Zhi looked up blankly, letting him raise his big hand and move it on her head, pulling off a leaf, and then his fingers playfully passed through the hairpin-tightened hair.

With a slight force, Wen Yanxing pulled out the hairpin.

The hair loosened slightly and fell all down. Chang Zhi couldn't say anything she wanted to complain about him messing up her hair.

In her eyes, there was only the figure of Wen Yanxing getting closer and closer.

His lips were gently held and sucked, and he was already familiar with it.

The gentle wind blew, and the fallen leaves flew and fell on his shoulders.

Only tenderness remained.

On Saturday, Chang Zhi was still chatting with Wen Yanxing on WeChat before uploading the video at home. It was funny that the two of them lived across the street from each other, but every day, apart from meeting each other, they kept chatting on WeChat at home as long as they had nothing to do.

Chang Zhi told Wen Yanxing that this was because they were still in the passionate love period, and you would only find me annoying when you were in the fatigue period.

But Wen Yanxing said, I won't.

Chang Zhi asked why, and Wen Yanxing said, it's too late to find you talk too little.

After that, Chang Zhi told Wen Yanxing that her video had been uploaded. She had just logged into Weibo and saw a new Weibo status notification, saying that Wen Yanxing had transferred her video to Weibo.

Chang Zhi: "................."? ? ?

The content was like this.

[Feiyun Yanzhi v]: Good dancing, very memorable [Share: Tang Zhi's "Peach Blossom Cheongsam"]

And the style of the comment area is like this.

[You are my little luck]: Yan Da, your account has been hacked?

[Oh my god]: 66666 Yan Da, won't your girlfriend be jealous when she sees girls dancing? ?

[Yan Zhi is my husband]: Yan Da shared, I've finished watching it! It's good! I'll buy you a few boxes of Nutri-Express and send them to you! Send me the address in a private message!

[I am Yan Zhi's girlfriend]: I'm jealous.

[Hehehe]: Yan Zhi and Tang Zhi? Inexplicable CP.

Chang Zhi flipped through a few pages and went to private chat with Wen Yanxing.

[Tang Zhi]: You have a hole in your brain, why do you forward this?

[ynzwyx7]: I like it

[Tang Zhi]: Is it too late to delete it?

[ynzwyx7]: It's too late, it seems that I am trying to cover up.

�Tang Zhi��..................

�ynzwyx7��Keep it, just think of it as a VIP advertisement you paid for from me.

�Tang Zhi��Then I really thank you.

Chang Zhi casually captured a few comments and sent them over.

�Tang Zhi���Picture�Your wife said she would give you Nutri-Express, and your girlfriend said she was jealous.

�ynzwyx7��� � �

�ynzwyx7��You are jealous? �

Chang Zhi: "................."

�Tang Zhi��Don't misinterpret my meaning like this, okay!! It's not me! Don't look shocked.

�ynzwyx7��Okay, I'll go and clarify it right away.

�Tang Zhi��..................Don't? � Can I give you a doctorate degree from the Central Academy of Drama?

�ynzwyx7��I only have a master's degree. I'll go and clarify it.

...� � �

Chang Zhi looked confused. What did he clarify?

Wait... Weibo! ?

Chang Zhi quickly switched to the Weibo interface. Sure enough, Wen Yanxing had just updated a text-only Weibo.

[Feiyun Yanzhi]: She said she was jealous.

Chang Zhi: "........................" What kind of clarification is this? No, is there anything to clarify? This is all fake?

How could she be jealous?

Which eye of his saw that she was jealous?

[Comment]

[Your Little Luck]: Oh my god, you are feeding me dog food again.

[Flashing]: I won't eat this dog food.

[You'd better be careful]: You just said that Tang Zhi and Yan Da's imaginations were too big. Is Tang Zhi jealous of himself?

[Simple and hardworking Lou Che]: I am on the upper floor. I just saw that comment and almost laughed myself silly. Everyone knows that Yan Zhi has been a jerk to Tang Zhi. How could Tang Zhi be with such an idiot? Hahahahaha, unless she is also an idiot, hahahahahahaha

Chang Zhi: ".................." That's really embarrassing.

When Chang Zhi saw this message, Wen Yanxing also saw it.

Facing the comments full of diss atmosphere, Wen Yanxing, who was guilty of his crime, quietly opened the B station. He was planning to delete the jerk video with more than 10,000 comments in a few months. Wen Yanxing hesitated after watching this video and closed the interface again.

Forget it, I won't delete it. After all, it has a special meaning.

Idiots are idiots.

If you are not thick-skinned, you will not have a wife.

Just like the owner of this comment, you must be a single dog:)

Chapter 51 Live Platform

By mid-August, Wen Yanxing was already the third anchor on the Feiyun Live Platform. With his superb skills and dirty talk, he fought his way through a sea of internet celebrities and professional players.

Of course, it might also be because of his voice and hands.

After all, there are still many people who are hand-controlled and voice-controlled in this world.

There was a carnival on Feiyun Live in late August, and Wen Yanxing was also invited. He thought about it again and again and decided to go.

Wen Yanxing had not appeared in front of the public for so many years in live broadcasting. When the platform released the news that Wen Yanxing would show his face, his fans were all excited.

The tickets for the carnival were sold out.

Chang Zhi originally didn't want to go, but Wen Yanxing said that this was his second serious trip.

Chang Zhi looked at the situation and saw that she had nothing to do. The trip was only five days, and she also wanted to go to the scene to see it, so she agreed.

In the morning, the two dragged their luggage to the airport, and they arrived at the booked city in less than two hours. Feiyun platform arranged a hotel for the anchors, and Wen Yanxing led Chang Zhi to check in.

Chang Zhi then discovered that Feiyun platform only booked a king-size bed room for Wen Yanxing.

At the front desk, Chang Zhi stepped on Wen Yanxing, who had just smiled, and looked up and said, "How about I book another room?"

"Don't," Wen Yanxing's foot retracted, "It's inconvenient."

"...What's inconvenient?" Chang Zhi raised her eyebrows and looked at him with a smile.

"Just... meet," Wen Yanxing's expression was also very innocent. He raised his hands in surrender, "Can you trust me a little?"

After getting the room card, Chang Zhi said to Wen Yanxing when entering the elevator, "It depends on your performance today."

Wen Yanxing nodded, "Okay."

The two were still wearing the fake "couple hats" they wore last time in bw. This floor of the hotel was booked by Feiyun, so there were anchors and so on.

The real body of the sexy female anchor is actually 50-50, with short legs and long body. And the beautiful anchor actually has flaws all over her face, and she is dark... Wen Yanxing looked at it for a while and turned his head away.

It hurts the eyes.

Chang Zhi also saw it, and soon she lowered her head, her mind was full of this thick and exaggerated makeup, it was too terrible.

It will die in the light.

On the first night, Chang Zhi and Wen Yanxing had a regular meal. When they returned to the hotel, it was time to take a shower and go to bed. Wen Yanxing went to take a shower, and Chang Zhi sat in front of the mirror to remove her makeup. From time to time, she turned her head to look at the bathroom, wondering how she would wash it later...

She showed her boyfriend the way she just got out of the bath, and the atmosphere was a bit awkward.

Putting down the makeup removal cotton, Chang Zhi ran to the suitcase and started to look through her pajamas.

Because Wen Yanxing told her at the last minute, Chang Zhi didn't have that much time to clean up. The pajamas she wore before hadn't been washed yet, so she casually took a set of pajamas that she hadn't worn this year from the bottom of the closet. After flipping through it, Chang Zhi found that the set she took was a black silk pajamas with thin straps.

The fabric on the chest was very low.

Chang Zhi: "..........."

Chang Zhi squatted, holding the nightgown in her hands, looking at the bathroom with a desperate look on her face.

This nightgown is actually very comfortable. Chang Zhi liked it when she wore it alone at home before.

But today... The timing is wrong!

Chang Zhi usually doesn't wear underwear when she sleeps, but she plans to wear it today, but this thin strap low-cut... How can she wear it? Wouldn't it look weird? ?

She didn't bring anything like nipple covers...

Chang Zhi desperately put her head into the nightgown.

With a click, the door opened. Chang Zhi looked up and Wen Yanxing came out slowly in his nightgown with slightly wet hair.

He saw Chang Zhi squatting and pointed behind him, "Go wash up quickly, wash early and go to bed early."

Chang Zhi lowered her head and tried to find clothes that she usually wore during the day that she could wear at night.

After searching around, she found that either the T-shirts had embroidered prints on the chest that would make it uncomfortable to sleep, or they were made of chiffon fabric...

"Why don't you go?" Wen Yanxing looked at Chang Zhi, who was biting her lips and rummaging around, in confusion.

Chang Zhi stood up with a bath towel in her arms reflexively, and grabbed a pair of panties with her hand hidden in the bath towel, "Don't rush me, I'll go right away."

Chang Zhi thought, forget it, wait until she puts on the suspender nightgown and comes out with a bath towel wrapped around her, and gets into the quilt at lightning speed, and everything will be fine.

Wen Yanxing sat on the bed, got into the quilt to warm it up, and took out his mobile phone to check Weibo.

Maybe this trending search has nothing to do with him in the eyes of the outside world. Wen Yanxing clicked on the trending search and found out about this matter——

#Meng Xi's college girlfriend#

Seeing these two familiar words, Wen Yanxing frowned first, and then clicked in.

[Weibo]

[Laomao talks about gossip]: After the three episodes of Xun Jiao Ji were broadcast, the protagonist Meng Xi received a lot of attention. According to Meng Xi's college classmates, Meng Xi's girlfriend in college was Chang Zhi, who was called the most beautiful store manager some time ago. This is a youthful photo in college. Are you satisfied with the male god and the goddess? [Picture] [Picture]

[Comment]

[Oh, don't move]: Even if it is, it is also the ex, right?

[Zhang Fei is so voluptuous]: Another hype? It's eye-catching.

[There are beautiful grasses everywhere]: ... The photos are beautiful, but the CP is not accepted.

I don't know how other men feel when their girlfriends and exes are mentioned frequently.

Anyway, Wen Yanxing feels weird at the moment.

Although they are exes, why are the names Meng Xi and Chang Zhi so annoying when put together?

Wen Yanxing drew a circle on the screen with his thumb, then logged into WeChat and opened the family group.

�ynzwyx7��Brother, do you know Meng Xi?

�Wen Jinzhao��� � hm� �

�ynzwyx7��Is he famous?

�Wen Jinzhao��On Weibo, he has more than 10 million fans, so he is a new generation.

More than 10 million... Wen Yanxing thought about the fact that he had only recently reached 3.5 million fans.

�ynzwyx7��Does he make a lot of money?

�Wen Jinzhao��Why are you asking this...I am not sure, but in a month, he must have spent 10 million on variety shows, filming, and advertising.

�ynzwyx7��............

Wen Yanxing silently recalled his eight-digit income last month.

[ynzwyx7]: Many people like him?

[Wen Jinzhao]: In Tianyu? Right, I didn't pay much attention to him.

[ynzwyx77]: What's his personality like?

[Wen Yanxing]: I haven't had a deep contact with him. I heard that he is gentle, considerate and humble.

Wen Yanxing looked at the four words. So Chang Zhi used to like this kind of person?

Gentle? Wen Yanxing touched his face. He was okay. Considerate... It seems a little bit lacking. Humble? How can a broadcaster be humble? You must be able to brag to have fans...

Wen Yanxing looked at the screen expressionlessly and fell into deep thought.

He knew that there was nothing to mind about it. It was all in the past anyway, but his damn possessiveness was at work. Even this made him uncomfortable.

Jealous, he wanted to change Meng Xi's name on the hot search at the moment to his, so that it would be fair enough.

Chang Zhi came out of the shower, wrapped in a bath towel, and saw Wen Yanxing looking thoughtfully at the screen of his mobile phone.

She tiptoed and slowly approached, but Wen Yanxing seemed not to notice. Chang Zhi suddenly felt like playing a prank, pulled the bath towel tightly and pounced on the bed, and attacked his ticklish spot with her hand,

"What are you looking at?"

Wen Yanxing was ticklish, so he immediately shrank and held her hand, and faced Chang Zhi's smiling face.

Looking down, Chang Zhi tied a slipknot in front of her neck with the bath towel, which looked a little funny, but it blocked a large area of her chest.

Wen Yanxing's eyes darkened, and he handed the phone over, "Hot search."

"...Ah!" Chang Zhi immediately snatched the phone.

In fact, Chang Zhi has been very sensitive to these two words since the last time she was on the hot search.

Once bitten by a snake, you will be afraid of the rope for ten years.

After reading it quickly, Chang Zhi threw the phone back to Wen Yanxing and sat on the bed with no hope in life.

It's trending again.

And it's linked to Meng Xi.

What kind of bullshit marketing accounts are these? Chang Zhi leaned over and picked up her phone from the bedside table, and uninstalled Weibo neatly.

:)

She decided not to read it. Anyway, she and Meng Xi had broken up, and it was clear. It's better to leave this matter to them. She is no longer afraid.

After uninstalling Weibo, Chang Zhi found that someone had been staring at her with deep eyes.

Chang Zhi touched her arm, "Why are you looking at me like that?"

Wen Yanxing moved his lips, "Why are you on the hot search with him?"

"I don't know," Chang Zhi spread her hands, not understanding why she didn't report it before but now, she raised her eyebrows, "Wait... are you jealous?"

Wen Yanxing was silent for a while, and then a very low sound came out of his throat, "Yeah."

Chang Zhi couldn't help laughing, "Really? Why are you jealous?"

Wen Yanxing didn't answer her question, but pointed to the bath towel tied around her neck, "There's still water on the bath towel, why are you tying it like this? Do you still plan to sleep like this? Aren't you afraid of catching a cold?" While muttering like an old woman, Wen Yanxing reached out and untied the bath towel's slipknot with a flick of his finger.

Chang Zhi didn't even have time to grab it.

The speed at which the bath towel slid down was incredible.

In short, she felt that the area from her neck to her collarbone to her chest instantly became cold.

Chang Zhi's original smile immediately faded.

Chang's indifference.jpg

Chapter 52 Off-shoulder dress

Wen Yanxing had seen Chang Zhi wearing off-shoulder dresses, but they were just below the collarbone.

He had also seen Chang Zhi wearing cheongsam, but the collar of the cheongsam was too high.

This was the first time he saw Chang Zhi's chest showing a large area of skin.

The black suspenders formed a strong contrast with Chang Zhi's fair skin. The thin suspenders were almost negligible, and the round shoulders, delicate collarbones, and the faint cleavage when looking down were so tempting that people couldn't take their eyes off.

It seemed that she was not wearing... underwear.

Gulp - Wen Yanxing seemed to hear the sound of himself swallowing his saliva.

After Chang Zhi reacted, she lowered her head and quickly pulled up the quilt. He seemed to hear Wen Yanxing sighing.

Her face was as red as the sunset glow. Facing Wen Yanxing's regretful gaze, she said unconfidently, "What are you looking at..."

"...Looking at you," Wen Yanxing rubbed his forehead, "You are dressed like this, I am afraid I can't behave tonight, where is your blue nightgown?"

"I washed it," Chang Zhi pulled the quilt and said with her head down, "I didn't wear it on purpose for you to see, I was in a hurry, so I just picked it up."

"...Okay then," Wen Yanxing coughed lightly, and then asked her, "Do you want to go to bed?"

Chang Zhi: "..."

Chang Zhi's face turned red again, and she nodded, "Let's go to bed."

After that, she lay down obediently and wrapped herself up like a cicada pupa.

Wen Yanxing was helpless, "There's only one quilt, what should I cover myself with?"

Chang Zhi rubbed her legs in the quilt, and reluctantly gave Wen Yanxing half of the quilt, but the quilt was big enough, so she still covered herself tightly, and pressed the corners with her body, "Is this okay?" Chang Zhi asked?

Wen Yanxing nodded and got into the quilt, turning off the lights, leaving only a dim night light.

The dim light of the night light sprinkled on Chang Zhi's face. Chang Zhi grabbed the quilt with both hands, her body slightly tense, her eyes closed, her mouth pursed obediently, and felt the sound of turning off the lights, the sudden sinking of space beside her, and the breath of Wen Yanxing.

When people close their eyes, their sense of smell and hearing are particularly sensitive.

Chang Zhi heard the sound of him pulling the quilt, and smelled the faint smell of shower gel.

...Lemon? Or lavender?

Her eyes were dark, but she started to think wildly.

How should I sleep tonight? Is this it? Will he have anything?

Thinking of this, she was suddenly lifted up by an external force, and the quilt that she had tightly pressed to isolate Wen Yanxing straightened instantly. The warm body approached her, and Chang Zhi's body suddenly stiffened.

Wen Yanxing watched Chang Zhi's eyelashes under her eyelids move slightly under the light of the night light, like a frightened butterfly flapping its wings quickly.

"Are you asleep?" His voice unconsciously became softer, but it was already low and deep.

Chang Zhi pretended to sleep and didn't answer.

Wen Yanxing only laughed softly, and then Chang Zhi felt a warm arm on her waist. The place where she was pressed was numb and inexplicably softened. Chang Zhi told herself to pretend to sleep and pretend not to know.

But the man was even more aggressive and rubbed his legs against hers.

Chang Zhi was really numb all over now, and the unfamiliar feeling made her a little overwhelmed.

Wen Yanxing's lips were close to her ears, and he whispered to her: "Tangtang?"

Chang Zhi: "..........."

She opened her eyes helplessly, and then faced Wen Yanxing's handsome face.

His eyes were as bright as stars and looked at her, reflecting her appearance in his eyes.

"Goodnight kiss."

The next moment, he lowered his head and held her lips as she was about to speak, blocking all her words.

Holding her face gently, as if treating a princess, Chang Zhi was stunned at first, and then was taken away by Wen Yanxing.

Sucking, biting and licking, lips and tongues intertwined, his face was very close to her, her eyes blinked lightly, and when she was about to close them, her eyelashes seemed to sweep across his cheek, and the gentle kiss suddenly became a little radical.

His hand was originally supporting Chang Zhi's waist, but now it was restlessly upwards, exploring the treasure through the thin cloth.

After the first attempt was not blocked, Wen Yanxing became more and more unscrupulous.

Chang Zhi felt that her consciousness was about to leave. The double attack made her brain dizzy. She felt that this was wrong, but she couldn't help being carried away.

Her lips blocked by him made an unconscious warning, but she didn't realize it. But in the ears of the listeners, it was like the sound of nature and the horn of encouragement.

The soft voice seemed to tempt others to do something else.

One of the suspenders slipped off during the action. Someone was no longer satisfied with the cloth, and directly reached into the clothes, gently and tenderly.

Chang Zhi knew that she shouldn't do it, but she couldn't speak to stop it.

When she felt the edge of a rubber band and something was pressing against her thigh, she was suddenly kissed hard. The sound of mua was loud, and Chang Zhi opened her eyes...

Wen Yanxing grabbed her wrist, buried his head in her neck, bit her collarbone, and said in a muffled voice,

"Let you go, keep your promise."

Chang Zhi's eyes were still misty, and she seemed to understand, "...ah?"

Wen Yanxing was very disappointed with her, and held her wrist and pulled her under his already untied nightgown. Chang Zhi felt a thin layer of fabric and an unknown object, and was stunned for a moment.

She was kissed hard on the face again, "Silly, this is what you mean."

Um... eh? !

Chang Zhi widened her eyes in surprise, and when she came to her senses, she touched...

Ah ah ... A picture with thick mosaic flashed in her head, and the previous memory was still fresh. This is, this is...

"You won't..." She hesitated to speak.

Her other cheek was kissed again. Chang Zhi pursed her lips and was very shy. Wen Yanxing said, "It's so uncomfortable. I braked. Shouldn't you comfort me?"

But you didn't have to drive this car...

Chang Zhi wanted to refute, but Wen Yanxing grabbed her wrist and moved it closer.

Chang Zhi's face was so red that she could boil an egg, "You..." She didn't expect that Wen Yanxing on the bed would be so shameless? ?

"Really," Wen Yanxing's tone softened again, and his dark eyes looked at her expectantly, "I want to save it for after marriage, but now I can't help but react. If I hold it back...what will you do in the future?"

Chang Zhi was angry, "What does it have to do with me if you hold it back???"

"...You caused it."

"I can sleep well but I won't!"

"But the suspender skirt..."

"I said I didn't wear it for you! I accidentally! Just! Got it!!"

"...Okay, okay, I admit that I was plotting something bad and I have poor self-control, don't be angry."

"...That's more like it."

"Then do you agree?"

"Agree to what?"

"................."

Half an hour later, Chang Zhi felt that the skin on her palms was about to be worn out :)

Why did it take so long! Why did it take so long!

It shouldn't be like this!!

She was so tired... She had to deal with the symptoms of someone wanting to kiss her after just two glances.

Why did it feel more tormenting this time than the last time?

When Wen Yanxing dealt with the evidence and lay back on the bed, Chang Zhi had already turned her back to him.

He leaned over and hugged her.

Chang Zhi dodged, but he hugged her again and said, "The air conditioner is cold, I'm afraid you'll catch a cold, hold me."

Chang Zhi now knew that Wen Yanxing was the best at talking, and not only that, he was also flexible, so she just let him hold her.

It's actually pretty good to have a comfortable chest behind you.

Right?

Chang Zhi curled her lips.

Wen Yanxing went directly to the backstage for the anchors and staff, and Chang Zhi lined up in a proper manner with the first row ticket.

She was wearing a one-shoulder design T-shirt and denim shorts today, with her hair down and a baseball cap on her head. She looked youthful and invincible among a group of girls.

But the brim of the hat was too low.

When checking the tickets, the ticket inspector accidentally saw Chang Zhi's appearance, was stunned for a moment, and gave her the ticket stub three seconds later.

Chang Zhi said thank you and entered the venue.

After the ticket check was completed, the ticket inspector took the time to check Weibo and posted an instant Weibo.

[I am a staff member at Feiyun Carnival. Guess who I saw? ? ? Tang Zhi! The one who dances on B station. She is so beautiful in real life. There is no mistake. She actually came to watch Feiyun Carnival? ? What's going on? ? ? Which anchor is she following? ? ?]

Chang Zhi knew nothing about all this.

She sat in the first row, quietly waiting for the show to start.

Chapter 53 The Carnival officially begins

The host, dressed in a suit, announces the official start of the carnival.

This carnival is broadcast live online, mainly featuring competitions between game anchors and programs by beautiful anchors such as home dance and singing.

The entire platform invited the top ten anchors in each channel, a total of 200 anchors. Wen Yanxing was classified into the Honor of Kings area because he had basically played Honor of Kings except for the first day of live broadcasting PlayerUnknown's Battlegrounds, so he was classified into the Honor of Kings area.

The first program was a segment of LOL. Chang Zhi didn't understand it, so she lowered her head and pressed her hat to open her phone to chat with Wen Yanxing privately.

[Simple and hardworking Tang Zhi]: What are you doing now?

[Yan Zhi]: Backstage, waiting. Meet up with a few anchors I know and chat.

[Simple and hardworking Tang Zhi]: Chat with female anchors?

[Yan Zhi]: ...You want to trick me. There are no female anchors. The ones I meet up with are all in the game area. Let's go together.

Chang Zhi laughed softly.

[Simple and hardworking Tang Zhi]: Have you seen those female anchors? Are they pretty?

Wen Yanxing held his phone and looked around.

Some were playing with their phones, some were touching up their makeup with a mirror.

Some were wearing conservative or revealing clothes - he immediately lowered his head and typed on the screen:

[Yan Zhi]: I saw it, but not as pretty as you.

He understood Chang Zhi's words full of routines.

About an hour later, it was finally the turn of a certain honor zone.

Before going on stage, Wen Yanxing sent her a message,

[Yan Zhi]: I'm going on stage, look at me.

Chang Zhi raised her eyebrows slightly and looked up.

The host held the microphone and spoke in a rhythmic manner:

"With the recent popularity of a certain Honor, many excellent game anchors have emerged on our Feiyun platform. The following one has hundreds of thousands of fans on a famous bullet-screen website, and his Weibo fans have exceeded one million. Since joining our Feiyun platform, he has quickly become a popular anchor and is loved by everyone. Today is also his first appearance in front of the public. Let us invite—"

The host praised Wen Yanxing to the sky, but when he mentioned the bullet-screen website, there were faint screams from the girls in the audience. When it was time to invite him to come out, Chang Zhi looked back and found that many areas were holding signs with Yan Zhi printed on them.

Chang Zhi looked back in surprise and relief, and at this time the host also said Wen Yanxing's name:

"Let's invite Yan Zhi to the stage!"

When Wen Yanxing appeared on the right side of the stage in casual clothes, the whole venue instantly became boiling, with noise and screams mixed together. Some sharp-eyed people saw Wen Yanxing earlier and pointed at him and talked about him.

The live broadcast room of the Carnival also exploded, because the camera pulled a close-up, Wen Yanxing appeared on the screen, every move, even his side face was clearly captured.

[Woc, this is my Yan Da?]

[Ahhhhhhh so handsome, so handsome my husband is so handsome]

[Is Yan Zhi so handsome and masculine? ? ? I see he speaks in a coquettish way...]

[Obviously you can rely on your face but you rely on your talent...]

[I declare Yan Zhi to be my new boyfriend]

[666666 with this face, this height and this figure, go to the entertainment industry to be a game anchor ah ah ah ah]

Chang Zhi and Wen Yanxing, who were present, didn't know all this.

After Wen Yanxing stood on the stage, the noise from the audience finally died down a little, welcoming the first unimaginable enthusiasm of the Carnival so far, and the host was also a little grand.

But the host is the host after all, he quickly reacted and joked: "It seems that our Yan Zhi is really famous!"

Wen Yanxing smiled, took the microphone and waved to everyone, and bent down slightly: "Hello everyone, I am Yan Zhi."

He spoke clearly and in a low voice. He picked up the microphone and spoke unconsciously with a little broadcasting accent. As soon as he finished speaking, there was another scream from the audience.

The live broadcast room was full of bullet screens, and fans said it was too exciting.

[I am used to listening to it on the computer, but who can tell me why Yan Da's voice sounds better when he speaks live! !]

[My legs are weak...]

[Yan Da, sing for us]

[It's too exciting, I'm at the scene, in the first row, and I can see it clearly. The real person is taller and more handsome than the live broadcast! I want to climb the wall!]

[I am a man, I admit he is really handsome...]

In the live broadcast room, the cameraman aimed his lens at Wen Yanxing. In order to echo the host's words, the cameraman casually manipulated the camera to sweep from the first row to the back.

At this moment, Chang Zhi looked up at the stage, and her beautiful and delicate face appeared in the live broadcast room for a moment, but was not missed by the sharp-eyed people.

[Was that Tang Zhi just now? ?]

[... Damn, I recorded the live broadcast, I will watch the replay later]

[Just now I saw a staff member on Weibo saying that they saw Tang Zhi... Really]

[The tickets for the first row are so expensive, so willful]

[Whose is Tang Zhi coming to see? ?]

These online storms are a later story. Afterwards, the host invited several other anchors. The first link was a friendly match between the anchors and professional players.

When the professional players came out, there was a lot of cheering from the audience.

Several anchors held their mobile phones, and the pictures were played on the big screen.

In the sign mode, the profile of Wen Yanxing is shown on the big screen. He is discussing seriously with his teammates, and then he uses the jungler Li Yuanfang.

When Chang Zhi saw this scene, she almost immediately thought of the game she played with Wen Yanxing before.

She pursed her lips slightly, and opened her eyes slightly to watch seriously.

At the beginning, Luna was in the professional player team. If Luna was there, she must be targeted madly, so the five people of the anchor team set out towards the enemy's blue zone.

And it was obvious that the opponent was not jealous. The five people of the professional player team stood in the bushes, so the ten people of the two teams met here at the blue daddy.

The enemies were extremely jealous when they met, and they threw out skills one by one. Wen Yanxing was very wretched. Knowing that Luna was unwilling to give up the blue, he sold his teammates to dodge several skills by snake skin. Then he locked Luna directly with the first skill. The second skill tornado of the single Xiao Qiao helped control, and his teammates also assisted in consumption. He pressed his fingers on the screen quickly, and soon triggered the skill effect.

With a bang, the dart exploded, and Wen Yanxing got the first blood! By the way, he used the punishment to steal a wave of blue!

The first battle was a victory!

After reaching level 2 and quickly clicking the second skill, Wen Yanxing quickly ate other wild monsters, and his teammates returned to their respective lines to start snowballing.

After that, the anchor team frequently harassed the blue zone and stole the blue, and the professional team's Luna was very uncomfortable. But the professional team was not jealous. In a team battle, they accurately cut to the back row and wiped out the anchor team, and quickly took down the Overlord.

The anchor team calmly cleared the dragon, and the operations of the two sides' soldiers were comparable.

Time passed gradually, and more than 20 minutes later, there were already three Overlords, and the only defense towers left on both sides were the highland towers.

The last teamfight was with Xiao Qiao in the bottom lane. We were four against five, and Yan Zhi's Li Yuanfang was still in the red zone. He quickly took the red and rushed over. The opposite Luna was showing off, and his teammates were struggling to support. The four against five were also not in a good state. In the end, when the anchor team had only one low-health Zhang Fei left, there were still three people on the opposite side, and Wen Yanxing arrived at this time!

His ultimate skill threw away all the people, and his first skill quickly attacked. Zhang Fei finally took a lot of damage and died heroically. Only he and Luna were left on the screen.

When Luna wanted to mark him, he used the second skill's super long displacement and invincibility to dodge. Luna's ultimate was interrupted, and the screen showed the frustrated look of a professional player. Then, the next moment, the screen also belatedly showed a prompt-

"Li Yuanfang killed Damo"

"Li Yuanfang killed Taiyi Zhenren double kill!"

"Li Yuanfang killed Luna triple kill!"

"Team wiped out!"

At this point, only Wen Yanxing was left on the screen, and the mid-lane soldiers had reached the opponent's highland tower. The resurrection time was still 20-30 seconds. Wen Yanxing quickly rushed to the middle lane. As a shooter, his excellent tower-pushing ability allowed him to quickly demolish the highland tower.

Go straight to the crystal!

The opponent's Di Renjie was still five seconds away from resurrection. The soldiers arrived, Wen Yanxing was calm, and his teammates looked at him anxiously.

At the same time as the soldiers entered the crystal, Di Renjie had one second left to resurrect, and Wen Yanxing quickly hit the tower directly

Di Renjie resurrected, and he quickly used his third skill to slow down the enemy, while continuing to push the crystal.

The crystal attacked Wen Yanxing because he attacked Di Renjie, but Wen Yanxing was not in a hurry and continued to click.

Finally, when he was hit by the crystal and his health was low, and all the enemies were about to be resurrected, the crystal exploded.

This round, victory!

Everyone stood up.

Applause and cheers suddenly broke out from the audience.

Chapter 54 Shake hands

Applause sounded around them. Chang Zhi was originally focused on watching Wen Yanxing and had not yet reacted. Seeing this, she was stunned for a second before she started to applaud.

On the stage, the anchor team and the professional team stood up and shook hands with each other.

The settlement interface appeared on the big screen. Wen Yanxing's Li Yuanfang was the best MVP of the game. His output of 28.5% almost surpassed the professional team Luna's 28.1% to become the first in the game. His injury rate was 17.9%, the lowest in the team.

15-5-14.

Except for the slightly higher number of deaths, it was a very good result.

After Wen Yanxing left the field, a bunch of fans shouted reluctantly.

Chang Zhi suddenly had a bad heart and stood up and shouted "Don't leave". A girl next to her also shouted loudly. Seeing this, she took the opportunity to talk to Chang Zhi while taking a breath.

"Hey, so you are also a fan of Yan Da?"

Amidst the shouts, Chang Zhi heard this sentence suddenly. She was stunned for a moment and subconsciously looked at the owner who asked her the question.

The eyes under the baseball cap met the passerby girl. The girl saw Chang Zhi's whole face, opened her eyes wide in surprise, and opened her mouth slightly——

"Tang... Sister Tang?"

Chang Zhi's heart skipped a beat.

Her hands moved uncomfortably behind her back, and she coughed lightly: "Hmm..."

"Sister Tang, why are you here at the carnival!" Who knew that the girl directly grabbed her arm in a familiar way. Chang Zhi was stunned. The next moment, she heard the girl say, "I am Yuzi!!!!"

...Yuzi?

Who calls herself Yuzi... Wait!

Chang Zhi widened her eyes, no way?

"...Me, Yuzi in the management group?" Chang Zhi asked hesitantly.

"Yes, yes," Youzi nodded vigorously, "Sister Tang, I didn't expect that we would meet unexpectedly like this."

Chang Zhi: "..."

However, no matter how enthusiastically the fans shouted, Wen Yanxing still waved and left.

Youzi pulled Chang Zhi to sit down, and her attention had completely shifted from Wen Yanxing to Chang Zhi.

Chang Zhi felt mixed emotions. She never expected to meet Youzi in the group here.

She vaguely remembered that Youzi seemed to like Yan Zhi and Guichu very much, so it was reasonable for Youzi to appear here.

Youzi didn't expect to meet her goddess when she came to the carnival to see her idol. She was so excited, "Sister Tang, why did you come to the carnival? Are you here to see Yan Da?" When she said the second sentence, Youzi's tone was a little bit mean.

The tone of Yuzi's speech gave Chang Zhi a very familiar and natural feeling. Chang Zhi hesitated for a moment, and felt that this kind of thing could not be hidden from the girls in the management group. She nodded, "Well, let's see Yan Zhi."

Yuzi raised her eyebrows and smiled: "Sister Tang is also a fan of Yan Zhi? Speaking of which, Sister Tang, didn't you add Yan Da Penguin? Why don't you hook up with him... Oh, no, I was wrong. Yan Da got divorced a while ago..."

After that, Yuzi sighed again, "I didn't expect Yan Da to be so handsome. I don't know which girl is so lucky."

Chang Zhi lowered her eyes and looked at her knees. It was not easy to be honest. She said weakly, "Maybe... I am so lucky?"

Yuzi: "..................Huh???!!!"

Although Chang Zhi's voice was very low, the venue had already quieted down, and Yuzi heard Chang Zhi's shocking confession very clearly.

She almost thought that there was something wrong with her ears.

Youzi was speechless for a long time, and then she stammered, "Sister Tang, are you and Yan Da... together?"

"... right." Chang Zhi felt a little guilty at Youzi's shocked look.

After all, Wen Yanxing confessed that he was no longer single for a month, but she didn't tell anyone except her best friend Deng Jiadai, not even her close fans.

Uh...

It felt like an underground affair.

After getting the answer, Youzi was silent for a long time, lowering her head, and her hair covered her face so Chang Zhi couldn't see her expression clearly.

Chang Zhi said apologetically, "Yuzi, I'm sorry I told you now..."

But Yuzi looked up suddenly and shook her head vigorously when she heard this, "No, no, no, this is a good thing! Good things should be kept within the family, the idol and the goddess finally get married, perfect, very perfect!"

Yuzi kept calling Chang Zhi "goddess" and Chang Zhi felt embarrassed, and Yuzi continued to ask, "Sister Tang, you have kept it a secret from us for a long time, it turns out that the hand in that live broadcast was yours... Oh my God, are you living together? So soon? It's a bit exciting... When will you tell the world? Then everyone can have fun together..."

Chang Zhi blushed slightly, "We are not living together, we just met and found that we live very close to each other, so we told the world... I don't know either, let's see him."

After chatting with Yuzi for a while, Wen Yanxing sent a message to ask her to leave first and then sneak into the backstage to find her.

Chang Zhi lowered her head to reply to the message,

[Tang Zhi]: Are you sure?

[ynzwyx7]: Sure, there's nothing to be afraid of.

Chang Zhi glanced at Youzi, and seeing Youzi's gossipy eyes, she lowered her head and typed,

[Tang Zhi]: I ran into a girl in my fan management group. She's also your fan. I just told her that we're together.

[ynzwyx7]: ! ! !

What's the reaction? Chang Zhi stared at the screen.

After a few seconds, Wen Yanxing sent another message, his tone unquestionable.

[ynzwyx7]: Come backstage.

Chang Zhi held the phone and thought for a while, and briefly talked to Youzi. Youzi looked like "Go ahead, I know", and the two exchanged phone numbers, and Chang Zhi quietly left.

Following Wen Yanxing's instructions, she went to the backstage in many ways. Thinking that Wen Yanxing was waiting for her in the backstage and she didn't know what to do, Chang Zhi walked to Wen Yanxing's lounge with some trepidation, and opened the door carefully. There were five people sitting in the lounge.

They were the anchor team that was on the stage just now.

Wen Yanxing has become quite familiar with these anchors who used to know each other online but now meet in person. At first, the anchors didn't know what Chang Zhi did. When they saw Wen Yanxing going to greet her, they started to make a noise.

"Oh, girlfriend..."

"Sister-in-law is pretty!"

"Ah... OK, how could I know you!"

Chang Zhi was a little uneasy, and Wen Yanxing obviously noticed it. He first took Chang Zhi's hand, raised it and said, "Let me introduce you, this is my girlfriend."

Then he introduced the four anchors to Chang Zhi. Chang Zhi didn't know them at first, so she just listened. Then Wen Yanxing smiled and said to the anchors, "My girlfriend and I have something to do, so I'm leaving now. We can talk again next time. If you come to S City to play, you can find me."

"Ok, I'll definitely find you next time."

"Let's get together again when we're free."

"Let's make an appointment to play duo online when we're free. I'm really impressed today..."

The anchors were also very easy to talk to, so Wen Yanxing successfully pulled Chang Zhi out.

Chang Zhi was confused. He called her over and then pulled her away. What was he doing?

Wen Yanxing pulled her to a place, but he took out his phone first.

Chang Zhi watched him open Weibo, and then clicked on the private message.

[Yan Da, your girlfriend is not Tang Zhi, right?]

[Ahhhh, I saw Tang Zhi at the carnival...]

Chang Zhi pursed her lips, "What's going on?"

Wen Yanxing pointed at the phone and explained, "It seems that the camera of the carnival live broadcast accidentally captured you, and netizens saw it."

Chang Zhi was slightly stunned. She didn't expect that a flash of the camera could be recognized.

You know, she was wearing a hat!

Wen Yanxing's lips curved slightly, his eyes sparkling as he looked at her, and he said, "It's normal. Didn't you also meet your fans?"

After a pause, Wen Yanxing said, "Since everyone has seen it, why not..."

He held her hand and stretched it forward. The other hand holding the phone turned on the phone's camera mode and took a picture of the two people's interlocked hands.

"Why not... let's make it public."

Wen Yanxing held up his phone, and the photo in the phone was her and his hand holding. He looked at her with dark eyes and spoke seriously.

There were only him and her in the long corridor. He stood in front of the window sill, with light behind him.

Chang Zhi looked down at him holding her hand, warm and generous.

She held his hand tightly.

At this moment, it was probably the biggest gossip in the ghost animal circle, the dance circle, and the anchor circle.

Chapter 55

Fans on the Internet are all going crazy.

[Account hacked? ? ? ? ?]

[Word mom, I just saw someone on Weibo saying that they saw Tang Zhi at the carnival, and it hasn't even ended yet... I was caught off guard by the dog food]

[Lick my hand... I'm heartbroken]

[The wife ran off with someone, and the husband ran off with someone too]

[Ahhhh, I'm a fan of both of them and I'm satisfied with this dog food]

[Don't leave if you're satisfied! Please live stream the couple together!]

[This combination is totally unexpected... Their looks, um, so high...]

To be honest, no one expected it, and the two should have nothing in common.

But this happened.

Wen Yanxing flipped through the comments to see the reaction, and Chang Zhi leaned over to see.

Until he saw a particularly dirty comment, Wen Yanxing paused his finger sliding down the screen and read out the words word by word:

[My Tangtang's legs, Yan Da is so lucky——

"Hey, hey, hey?" Wen Yanxing calmly read out the last interjection of the comment, with a slight curve at the corner of his lips. Chang Zhi, whose chin was resting on his arm, had already blushed. She sat up straight and pushed Wen Yanxing.

"What are you laughing at?" She pretended to be fierce, "What do you want?"

Wen Yanxing slightly adjusted his eyebrows, glanced at her legs, shook his head, but raised the corner of his lips, "Nothing to laugh at, not very good, anyway, it's mine."

It was originally his, a previous brush.

He had touched it, rubbed it, and even... kissed it.

Chang Zhi always felt that Wen Yanxing's tone was malicious, and the picture appeared in her mind. She suddenly covered Wen Yanxing's mouth.

Wen Yanxing laughed out loud.

Chang Zhi was extremely ashamed and angry, "If you laugh again, I will, I will, I will..."

Wen Yanxing grabbed her wrist and pulled it down, freeing his mouth. He raised his eyebrows, "What?"

"...I don't want you anymore." Chang Zhi said harshly.

"It's okay," Wen Yanxing shook his head calmly, "I want you to do the same."

Chang Zhi: "............"

It was not until a week after the two-day carnival that the fans accepted the reality that Chang Zhi and Wen Yanxing were together, and then they were very happy... and urged the couple to live broadcast.

The style of Wen Yanxing's live broadcast room is like this every day——

[Did our Tangtang come to your house today?]

[Please turn on the camera for a couple live broadcast, it's pleasing to the eyes]

[Ahhhh I want to see the face, not the hands]

In the face of this situation, Wen Yanxing usually said calmly,

"Turn on the camera, it's impossible. Do you want to see the face or the live broadcast? To be honest, people can't be so superficial. Don't just look at the appearance, but also look at the inner qualities and talents. Be good and watch me play games carefully."

"Want to watch the couple live broadcast? Then what should we broadcast, double radio gymnastics or ice and fire?"

"Besides, I don't want to show her to you, I'll just watch."

No matter how deadly Wen Yanxing's words are, facts tell us that you will always have to pay for what you have done, and the fg you set up will always be broken.

The incident happened a week before the Mid-Autumn Festival. Wen Yanxing's desktop computer had some problems and was sent for repair, so he changed to a laptop for live broadcast.

At three o'clock in the afternoon, he had just turned on the live broadcast and had no time to debug. Chang Zhi had just returned from the milk tea shop. She now had the key to Wen Yanxing's house. In the afternoon, she brought two cups of milk tea to reward Wen Yanxing. As soon as she entered the house with milk tea, she saw Wen Yanxing frowning, with the screen of his laptop lowered, slightly bent over, and no one knew what he was doing.

"What's wrong?" Chang Zhi put the milk tea aside, and saw Wen Yanxing bending over to operate the computer with difficulty in the small space in the laptop. The USB camera was placed next to him, so she reached out and raised the screen a little, "Why is the screen so low? It's so tiring to watch?"

The tens of thousands of viewers who had just entered the screen first heard a female voice, and then saw Chang Zhi standing and Wen Yanxing bending over through the camera on the laptop.

[Woc what did I see!]

[Tangtang looks so good in this skirt! �

�Ahhhhh, the screenshots are as beautiful as a painting, hahahahaha, the appearance association is lucky�

�Remember someone said that he would never show his face hhhhh�

Wen Yanxing: "......................."

Chang Zhi saw herself on the screen almost the moment she saw the screen. Her eyes widened slightly, and then she heard Wen Yanxing's slightly helpless voice, "I haven't had time to turn it off yet, why are you in such a hurry to show your face?"

Chang Zhi instantly covered the small camera with her hand, and the audience's screens suddenly went dark.

�. . Turn off the camera? ? ? �

�Don't turn it off, it's so beautiful! �

The next moment, the audience heard the conversation between the two.

The female voice complained, "...You are the one who is in a hurry to show your face, how should I know!"

"...Okay, I am the one who is in a hurry to let you show your face," the man saw that the woman was angry, and gently coaxed her, then quietly changed the subject, "...Milk tea? For me?"

The girl was obviously still angry, "How about I drink two cups each?"

Then there was the sound of the straw piercing the cover of the cup, accompanied by the man's slightly gentle tone, "Okay, are you thirsty? You take a sip first."

"............"

[6666 This dog food caught me off guard]

[Ahhhhh gentle Yan Da hahahaha]

[Mom asked me why I laughed so pervertedly when I saw the black screen of my phone]

[Don't listen, don't listen to the bastard chanting]

[Let me see the screen, I will spend 10,000 yuan on gifts, okay]

However, they didn't feel proud for long, because Wen Yanxing acted quickly and simply interrupted the live broadcast.

He held the milk tea in his hand. Chang Zhi raised her eyes and glared at him. Then she lowered her eyes and grabbed the edge of the milk tea cup and drank two sips obediently as he said. When she looked up, she was kissed tightly.

She almost knocked over the milk tea in Wen Yanxing's hand.

After that, Wen Yanxing was still shameless, "Try it."

Chang Zhi's eyes were wet, staring at him, and her angry look was not convincing at all.

Instead, it made people want to bully her more - Wen Yanxing raised his hand and touched her head.

Thinking of the call from his mother the day before yesterday, he asked Chang Zhi, "Is it Mid-Autumn Festival next week?"

Chang Zhi was stunned by his question, thought about it and nodded, "It seems so, I forgot what day it was."

"...Do you want to go home with me?" Wen Yanxing suggested, paused and added, "My mother... cough, wants to see you."

Hearing that Wen Yanxing's mother wanted to see her, Chang Zhi's brain was suddenly confused.

Meet... meet the parents?

She was overwhelmed by these three words, but she didn't realize that she had said them in a surprised tone.

Wen Yanxing looked at her incredulous expression, "What's wrong, meeting a parent... is it scary?"

After thinking about it, Wen Yanxing rubbed Chang Zhi's head to comfort her, "Don't worry, my parents don't eat pretty girls."

"Or you don't want to?" Wen Yanxing asked again.

Chang Zhi's expression was a little stiff, and she said, "No, it's so fast, I..."

Chang Zhi hesitated to speak.

Meeting the parents is not a problem, it's her business. Once it comes to this kind of thing, Chang Zhi thought that she didn't have parents, would she be...

Chang Zhi lowered her eyes, her tone worried, "No, I didn't say I didn't want to, it's just that I... I heard that some families are very resistant to single-parent or "orphan" or something... Well, I..."

Wen Yanxing was silent, lowered his head and saw only Chang Zhi's pitiful head.

He sighed.

Then, Chang Zhi was hugged into someone's arms, with her right face pressed against his chest, feeling the vibration of his chest when he spoke.

"It's okay, my mother knew you before," Wen Yanxing patted her back and comforted her gently, "Our family is not that type."

"She will definitely like you very much when they meet." Wen Yanxing said with certainty.

Chang Zhi looked up and looked at his chin, "Why are you so sure?"

Wen Yanxing curled his lips, "First, you are very good."

"Second, you are someone her son likes very much."

"So... she will like you."

On the night of the Mid-Autumn Festival, Chang Zhi changed about five sets of clothes. After showing them to Wen Yanxing one by one, she finally wore a ladylike and gentle dress and followed Wen Yanxing to "meet the parents."

The so-called meeting the parents is actually having a meal together.

It can be regarded as a family dinner.

Holding the gift, Chang Zhi took a deep breath and told herself that it was just a meal, a smile, and it didn't matter.

However, when Wen Yanxing was about to press the doorbell when he stood at the door, Chang Zhi hugged his arm and tried to stop him.

"Wait a minute, I'm not ready yet..."

"What should I say when we meet later? Hello, auntie or something?"

"Don't press it, wait a minute, why are you in such a hurry..."

"I'm so nervous, is auntie really not fierce?"

"I'll prepare myself mentally..."

"My makeup is not smudged, eh... you!"

Before Chang Zhi finished speaking, Wen Yanxing's hand was finally annoyed by her and was about to press the doorbell, but the door clicked...

and opened.

Chapter 56 Chang Zhi Zhenren

It was under such circumstances that Wen Yanxing's mother first met Chang Zhi Zhenren.

Chang Zhi hugged her son's arm and almost threw herself into Wen Yanxing's arms, while her son raised his arms and looked at the woman in his arms helplessly with his head down.

When Chang Zhi saw the door slowly open, the middle-aged woman standing by the door had a brain freeze.

It was not until Wen Yanxing coughed lightly that she quickly stood up, her cheeks were already red, her arms were honestly placed in front of her, and she greeted him in a stammering manner.

In fact, when Wen's mother greeted her and Wen Yanxing pulled her into the house to sit down, she was still not in the right state.

So nervous, what should I say...

Wen Yanxing's father and his sister Wen Luying were sitting in the living room. The young girl lowered her head and crossed her legs to play with her mobile phone, while the middle-aged man looked at the advertisement of elderly health products on TV with a serious look.

The atmosphere was surprisingly weird.

It was not until Wen Luying looked up and saw Chang Zhi that her eyes lit up and she stood up and called out, "Sister-in-law?"

The air in the whole room seemed to flow again.

Mother Wen glanced at Father Wen.

Father Wen stared at the TV with a straight face, his expression unchanged.

Wen Yanxing looked at his sister with a teachable look on his face.

And Chang Zhi...

"Ah...ah?"

A voice of surprise and confusion at Wen Luying's address.

Wen Yanxing pulled Chang Zhi, "Sit down."

The five of them sat on the sofa together, and the topic was started by Mother Wen.

After all, they were two generations apart. Father Wen, who had been watching TV with a straight face, was very friendly to Chang Zhi, while Mother Wen was very concerned about her.

And Chang Zhi realized that Wen Luying was actually the author who had been writing articles for her milk tea shop...

Then, Mother Wen was going to make dinner, and Chang Zhi and Wen Luying took the initiative to help, leaving Father Wen and Wen Yanxing alone in the living room.

Wen Yanxing looked at the crowded and busy kitchen, listening to the faint discussion coming from it. There were three women closest to him in his life, and he felt an inexplicable satisfaction in his heart.

That's great.

He thought so and looked at his father again.

After the three women in the room left, Wen's father's kind expression was restrained.

And Wen Yanxing was also expressionless.

The father and son occupied both sides of the sofa, very far apart, and no one spoke.

The air seemed to stop flowing, and the atmosphere was quietly tense.

Then Wen's father spoke——

"You still remember to come back?"

Wen Yanxing's face sank.

In the kitchen, Wen Luying and Chang Zhi were already happily communicating.

Wen's mother went to the room to find something. Wen Luying was washing vegetables while complaining to Chang Zhi, "Sister-in-law, if it weren't for you, my brother might not have come back!"

Chang Zhi was still not used to the title of "sister-in-law", but when she heard Wen Luying's words, she asked with interest, "Why?"

"No, didn't my brother go live and make videos before?" Wen Luying paused and said, "My father didn't agree, and the two of them had a quarrel, so my brother moved out and didn't answer the phone at home."

"...Then the two of them are in the living room now," Chang Zhi's heart jumped, "Will they quarrel?"

"They..." Wen Luying poked her head and glanced at the living room, then shook her head, "They didn't say anything, I don't know, in fact, my brother and my father have quarreled since they were young, maybe it's the same sex that repels each other?"

Chang Zhi picked beans, absent-minded, a little worried.

Wen's mother came back soon.

Chang Zhi and Wen Luying helped with the preparations, and Wen's mother drove the two out when she was about to start cooking.

When they came out of the living room, Chang Zhi observed the father and son and found that they were both watching TV very seriously.

When Chang Zhi came, Wen Yanxing naturally sat inside to make room for her.

He also stuffed the pillow into her arms.

Chang Zhi tilted her head to look at him and asked in a low voice: "Are you okay?"

Wen Yanxing looked puzzled: "What's the matter?"

Chang Zhi pouted, but was too embarrassed to ask.

The dinner was very harmonious. In the evening, Wen Yanxing wanted to take Chang Zhi away, but Wen's mother said it was too late and stayed overnight.

Chang Zhi agreed.

There was another problem when assigning rooms. Wen Luying said she could sleep with Chang Zhi, but Wen Yanxing insisted——

"No." He looked very determined, "Tangtang, share a room with me."

Fortunately, Wen's father went to bed early. Wen's mother glared at her useless son, "You haven't married her yet, and you want her to sleep with you? What kind of ambition?"

Wen Luying smiled happily, "That's right, sister-in-law, sleep with me, the bed in my room is quite big."

Chang Zhi also wanted to be more reserved.

Although Wen Yanxing often stayed at his house these days, she was used to sleeping with him under the quilt.

It was a semi-cohabitation state.

But this was... Wen Yanxing's parents' house after all!

So, Chang Zhi slept with Wen Luying tonight.

After taking a shower and changing Wen Luying's clothes at night, Chang Zhi lay on the bed and took out her phone, and found that Wen Yanxing had sent her a message. The content was simply shameless.

�ynzwyx7�: Wait until my sister falls asleep.

�ynzwyx7�: Tell me, I'll wait for you next door.

�Tang Zhi�: ....

Chang Zhi glanced at Wen Luying and replied,

�Tang Zhi�: You're funny, just one night, your mother is right, what can I do if I go there.

�ynzwyx7�: I miss you, my heart is empty without you in my arms when I sleep.

Chang Zhi trembled with disgust.

�Tang Zhi�: ... This is not enough to convince me to do something bad.

�ynzwyx7�: Then... I'm happy tonight, and I have something good to share with you?

�ynzwyx7�: I'll let you go back in half an hour.

�Tang Zhi�: If I make any noise, your sister will find it, right?

[ynzwyx7]: No, she sleeps very soundly, like a pig, and can't be woken up unless there are firecrackers, alarm clocks and my mother.

[Tang Zhi]: ....

Under Wen Yanxing's attack, Chang Zhi agreed to his half-hour proposal.

After Wen Luying fell asleep, Chang Zhi got out of bed as he said, and looked back to see that Wen Luying was sleeping soundly with the quilt in her arms.

She went out quietly and knocked on Wen Yanxing's door.

The door was opened carefully, and Wen Yanxing's room was lit. He held the door and whispered to her, "Come in first."

The door was closed with a click, and Chang Zhi was held by Wen Yanxing, and her lips were kissed.

Chang Zhi raised her hand to touch her mouth.

Wen Yanxing looked at her, his eyes sparkling, and his face was sincere, "Really, after getting used to it, I can't sleep when you are not around."

He pointed to the clock hanging on the wall, pointing to zero o'clock, quite complaining.

Chang Zhi looked helpless, "... I feel like a thief."

Wen Yanxing put his arm around her waist and sat on the bed, "No, no, no, we are in our own home, we are family, how can we say we are thieves just by changing rooms."

"Then what do you want to tell me?" Chang Zhi lowered her head and played with his fingers, "You are so mysterious, why are you so happy?"

Wen Yanxing rested his chin on her shoulder, "I'm just taking you to meet my parents today, happy."

"... That's it?" Chang Zhi turned her head to look at him and raised her eyebrows, "I thought it was something else."

"... Don't you want to see me at night?" Wen Yanxing touched her hair and said with a smile, "Anyway, I have to watch you now to sleep well. You should be responsible for the habits you have developed, okay?"

The two talked about something else, Wen Yanxing put his arm around Chang Zhi and lay on the bed, Chang Zhi was also tired today, and she didn't know if she forgot to go back or something while chatting, leaning on the warm and broad chest, her eyelids became heavier, and then completely closed.

Wen Yanxing lowered his head and kissed her forehead, with a smile on his face.

In fact, he was not only happy because he brought Chang Zhi to meet his parents.

And...

A certain stubborn old man finally tried to agree with him.

Time went back to that time -

In the words of Wen's father that seemed full of sarcasm, Wen Yanxing chose to ignore him.

He knew that if he spoke, the two of them would quarrel again. Chang Zhi came today, and he didn't want to make trouble.

So Wen's father continued to talk to himself -

"I watched your live broadcast the day before yesterday," he said in a slightly slower tone, "I didn't expect you to be so popular."

Wen Yanxing still didn't speak, but just glanced at Wen's father.

"I heard that you are at the top of the list and you are a popular anchor," Wen's father said calmly, "How is it, can you support yourself with this?"

Wen Yanxing said, "Not bad."

Wen's father's tone suddenly became stern, and he asked again, "Can you support your girlfriend with this? Can you support your future family?"

"I think it's okay."

"...Okay," Wen's father's tone softened a little, "Then you can continue to do it."

Wen Yanxing suddenly opened his eyes wide, with a look of surprise.

"I am too lazy to interfere with you. I don't understand these new industries now. You have to fly when your wings are strong, and don't starve to death with your family." After a pause, Wen's father said, "Chang Zhi is a good girl, polite and well-educated. Live a good life in the future. Don't let her freeze and starve, and don't bully her because she has no support - your father will support her."

And the expression on Wen Yanxing's face also changed from surprise to joy -

Although Wen's father did not support, he just agreed.

At the end of the year, Wen Yanxing stopped broadcasting for one day and played with Chang Zhi for the whole six months and seventeen days he had been with Chang Zhi.

In the morning, he had a simple breakfast at McDonald's, a buffet at noon, a romantic movie in the afternoon, and a candlelight dinner at night.

He walked with Chang Zhi on a busy street. There was a large New Year's Eve event held in a shopping mall not far away.

Countdown to the end of the year, fireworks on time for the New Year.

Wen Yanxing pointed over there and asked Chang Zhi, "Do you want to go and see?"

Chang Zhi saw the crowd and thought it was okay, so she agreed.

At 23:59:50, the whole venue began to count down.

Chang Zhi leaned in Wen Yanxing's arms and looked up at the big clock hanging on the wall.

The crowd was shouting the countdown in her ears, and Chang Zhi was driven by the atmosphere and shouted along -

"Ten, nine, eight..."

"Five, four, three..."

"Two, one—"

On the clock, the minute hand and the second hand finally met the hour hand, and the fireworks suddenly rose into the night sky.

Before Chang Zhi finished her words, her hanging hand was suddenly lifted up by the person hugging her.

Then, a cold round object was put on her middle finger, the size was just right, not tight or loose.

Chang Zhi was slightly stunned, then opened her mouth in surprise, her eyes full of disbelief.

On the middle finger of her left hand, the diamond was still shining in the dark night.

The fireworks bloomed in the air, colorfully, embellishing the night sky.

"You..." Chang Zhi was speechless.

Wen Yanxing was close to her face, his breath surrounded her. He whispered nervously, "Agree?"

"Spend 2018, and even the next hundred years, spring, summer, autumn and winter with me. I want to see you every morning when I open my eyes."

Chang Zhi sniffed and looked at her hand, "When did you buy it?"

"Last week," Wen Yanxing said, looking at Chang Zhi staring at the ring and not answering whether he agreed or not, he coughed lightly, "Are you stupid?"

Chang Zhi didn't say anything, just looked at the ring. She wanted to say something, but she couldn't say it. She was afraid that as soon as she opened her mouth, tears would fall.

"Forget it," Wen Yanxing sighed and grabbed her hand, "Anyway, whether you agree or not, I'm going to put you on first, and you can't regret it."

There was another sound of fireworks rising and blooming in the air, and the light on her face was unpredictable.

Chang Zhi spoke, her voice hoarse, and as she expected, tears fell the moment she spoke.

"I didn't say I would regret it," she sniffed, turned around and buried herself in his arms, her snot and tears all rubbed on Wen Yanxing's clothes, "It was too sudden, I was scared."

She heard a laugh above her head, Wen Yanxing lifted her face and wiped her tears, "That's good... Don't cry, it hurts."

Chang Zhi blinked and nodded vigorously, "Yeah."

"Are you satisfied with the New Year's gift...?"

"... Quite satisfied." Very satisfied.

"Then tomorrow... No, that's wrong, is it this morning to register?"

"So soon, have you told your parents?"

"The household registration book is with me, what do you think?" He looked like he had already prepared it.

Sure enough, it was premeditated. Chang Zhi thought with tears and laughter.

"..."

"Okay then," Chang Zhi stretched out her arms and wrapped them around his neck, stood on tiptoe and kissed him, and smiled with tears on her face——

"Then, for the rest of my life... please give me more advice."

Just like what I said to you at the beginning, please give me more advice in the future.

I am so glad——

In the most turbulent time, I met the warmest you, and we will still depend on each other for the rest of our lives.

Chapter 57 A new storm has appeared in the anchor circle

On the first day of the new year, a new storm has appeared in the anchor circle——

[It is Tangzhi, not Tangzhi]: I was caught off guard... Please give me more advice! [Picture]

[Yanzhi]: Finally got her back... [Picture]

[Comment]

[tb coupon]: What the hell is a diamond ring! Send me a private message to get a coupon

[Tianlanlan]: Ah, he proposed after only six months of dating, and he broke up again

[hsisi]: Have a baby soon.

In addition to the enthusiasm of the fans, their friends also forwarded it.

Sister Qiao and Anan directly forwarded the congratulations and bombarded her with WeChat private messages. Chang Zhi woke up that day and kept replying with a mobile phone in her arms.

From Jiang Huai, Deng Jiadai, the management group, the fan group, and various friends...

This seems to be the feeling of being engaged to someone privately.

Chang Zhi looked at the person leaning on her and looking at the wedding process and the wedding company.

"Do I need to have an engagement party before getting married?"

"... It's not necessary. It's not a long time since the engagement, and I don't have any close relatives or anything like that. Don't waste the money, right?"

He looked up and pointed at his phone after a while, "Are the wedding photos taken in China or abroad?"

"Does it make a difference?"

"Yes, it seems to be more classy abroad."

"The places with scenery in China... are not bad either."

"The seaside, the beach, holding hands, drawing hearts. Parks, lawns, hugs, watching balloons?"

"Oh, and," Wen Yanxing added expressionlessly, "The red lip bridal makeup in the photo studio, and the background is a sticker bought from Taobao - an ancient castle?"

Chang Zhi: "................."

Chang Zhi didn't want to talk, so she lowered her head and continued to deal with Deng Jiadai's bombardment of "You actually accepted the ring" and "You are so unreserved".

However, Wen Yanxing seemed particularly excited and positive today. "I'll forget it. If it's fast, the money spent is enough, and it takes more than a month to prepare, it should be fine. Take the household registration book to get the certificate in the afternoon?"

"... Yeah."

"Do you want a girly or mature wedding?"

"Are you hungry?"

"???"

"Take a break."

"................."

....

Queue up in the afternoon, get the marriage certificate, and take pictures.

Wen Yanxing found a suit from the pile of cold, black, white and gray casual clothes in the closet. Chang Zhi was forced to cooperate and found a blue sleeveless dress.

Sitting on the chair when taking pictures, Wen Yanxing couldn't hide his smile, and the photographer praised him, "You smile so well."

Chang Zhi couldn't help laughing when she saw Wen Yanxing's silly look for the first time.

After getting the red book, the two people in the photo smiled like idiots. Wen Yanxing took a photo to show off and sent it to the family group.

[ynzwyx7]: [Picture]

[Sister]: Congratulations, sister-in-law 666666 is so beautiful. My brother is so stupid. Hahaha.

[Mom]: Silly son, your mouth is almost stretched to the back of your head.

[Dad]: Not bad.

[Dad]: [Congratulations on getting rich! Good luck!]

Wen Yanxing stretched out his hand and clicked. His father sent a red envelope of 1,000 yuan for four people. There were five people in this group, and he grabbed 77 yuan.

Chang Zhi was happy to see this number. She was also in this group and followed suit. She was the last one to grab it. Her luck was great. She grabbed more than 600 yuan.

Wen Luying grabbed 200 yuan, and Wen's mother grabbed more than 100 yuan.

[Sister]: Sister-in-law 6666 is so lucky!

[Wen's mother]: Well done!

Chang Zhi showed off the red envelope interface on her phone to Wen Yanxing, and said cheerfully, "The difference between three-digit and two-digit numbers... This is about looking at the face, you know?"

Wen Yanxing pretended not to hear and looked down at his phone.

[ynzwyx7]: It's really a red envelope from my father.

[Tangtang]: The family status is clear at a glance, I mean the lowest.

[Sister]: Just now, the lowest one sent a red envelope to celebrate!

It's obvious that he is talking about Wen Yanxing.

[ynzwyx7]: [mua]

After Wen Yanxing sent it, he quickly operated Chang Zhi's phone.

A "5200" on the screen scared Chang Zhi.

"So generous?" she asked.

"It's all yours." Wen Yanxing looked enthusiastic, took out the wallet from his pocket and put it in Chang Zhi's hand, "Take it."

Chang Zhi: "..." It feels like she will take it back soon.

But at the moment, she stuffed the wallet into her bag without any hesitation.

[Sister]: ....This is the same as not posting it.

[Mom]: You forgot about mom after you got a wife.

[Dad]: Please return the 77 yuan to me.

[ynzwyx7]: [Wish you good fortune and prosperity!]

So, everyone was happy.

Wen Yanxing sent the photo to his colleagues on the platform, a group of five anchors, and dissed the singles in the group.

[ynzwyx7]: Let me show you, it's true. Get rid of singleness, for life. [Picture]

[Xiao Kong]: Fuck you, this affection is showing off to me. 99.

[Shadow]: Young people still can't help but walk into the grave.

[ynzwyx7]: Lie down, luxurious grave, comfortable, I am willing.

[He Sheng]: Get out!

[Shadow]: Your skin must be itchy. Don't think that I won't do it just because you look good. Let's go solo and fight to the death.

[ynzwyx7]: Let's go buy a three-piece bedding set with my wife first.

[Shadow]: ....

After sending this line of words, Wen Yanxing held up the little red book and sighed to Chang Zhi: "Finally, we can live together legally."

Chang Zhi looked up and asked him: "So?"

"Let's buy bedding," Wen Yanxing curled his lips, "What color do you like? Red? Black?"

Chang Zhi shook her head, "Do I have to choose between these two? Isn't it better to go to the mall and choose slowly later?"

"It's not necessary to choose between these two," Wen Yanxing shook his head and said seriously, "It's just that I think red is festive and suitable for newlyweds, and black is dirt-resistant and suitable for..." Wen Yanxing stopped talking.

Chang Zhi: "................."

Chang Zhi had done many things with Wen Yanxing holding her hand, and she already understood.

So...

Chang Zhi covered her face.

What on earth was in his mind today?!

Chapter 58 Wen Yanxing smiled

Wen Yanxing said that he asked Chang Zhi for her opinion on the color of the sheets, but when he arrived at the mall, he directly asked the salesperson for the black set.

Then he hugged Chang Zhi, lowered his head and smiled, "You have one set and I have one set, it's convenient for changing and washing, you choose."

Chang Zhi: "............So you asked me before what was necessary?"

Wen Yanxing smiled, "It's whether this set is necessary or not."

Chang Zhi had long been led to be more and more dirty by Wen Yanxing. As the time spent with Wen Yanxing increased, Wen Yanxing's true nature was slowly exposed.

For example, as a otaku, the most basic entry... dirty.

And when playing online games, he especially likes to choose female characters, because... cough.

Chang Zhi was recently led by Wen Yanxing to play an online game. After all, Wen Yanxing mostly broadcasts King of Glory at night, and he also needs to play other games to relax.

So, in the game, Wen Yanxing's female character and Chang Zhi's beautiful female character even became sworn sisters...

He even developed the "hug" action to get close, and at a certain moment, it was like the two characters hugging and kissing.

In short, it can be said that he is quite good at developing special skills.

Pushing a cart full of household items to pay, Wen Yanxing took two boxes of mysterious cuboids at the counter in front of the cashier without changing his expression.

Chang Zhi watched him take them down and throw them into the shopping cart.

Her originally fair face turned red in an instant, and she gently pushed Wen Yanxing, "Why are you taking this?"

Wen Yanxing kept smiling, "Have you forgotten, the wedding night?"

Chang Zhi: "..."

It was really scary, her mind almost wanted her to say something like "In fact, we are a legal couple."

Ah... yes.

They got the marriage certificate today.

Chang Zhi touched her bag, which still contained the little red book.

It was almost six o'clock in the evening when she finished cleaning the house. This was the first time that Chang Zhi moved all her belongings to another person's house.

It was very familiar because she had come here frequently for more than half a year and even stayed overnight.

There was no sense of strangeness after moving.

It was just that the house was moved to the opposite side.

And the original owner of the house was the one who would spend the rest of her life with her in the future.

Chang Zhi stood at the door and looked at her locked home. Wen Yanxing looked at Chang Zhi standing in the entrance hall in a daze without closing the door, and asked loudly, "What are you looking at?"

"...My home," Chang Zhi paused, half-jokingly said, "Are you going to rent out the house opposite? I don't want to rent it...Landlord, I will continue to pay you rent in the future."

Wen Yanxing was slightly stunned, then stood up and walked over to help Chang Zhi close the door,

"Tomorrow, that room will be changed to your name."

"......?"

"That's your home, this is also your home," Wen Yanxing said softly, "Don't look at me like that, you are now a landlady, strictly speaking, it is considered the common property of the couple."

"...You don't do notarization, are you really not afraid that I will divorce you in the future." Chang Zhi said.

"Will you?"

Chang Zhi pursed her lips, thinking in her heart that she would not.

She was tired of walking, and the best safe haven was warm enough for a lifetime.

But Chang Zhi still said, "I don't know what I will think in the future."

Wen Yanxing pinched her nose, "You really dare to think."

When she shared a room with Wen Yanxing at night, Chang Zhi knew what would happen.

After all, it was a real wedding in all senses.

Although he was very familiar with her, she was also familiar with him.

Except for the last step.

Thinking of this, Chang Zhi lowered her head and stretched out her hand, looking at her palm, her face flushed.

Well...

She thought about herself.

I think it might be a little difficult.

Wen Yanxing just came out of the shower and saw Chang Zhi sitting on the bed, looking at her palm and lost in thought.

He walked over and sat next to her, interrupting her thoughts, "What are you thinking about?"

"... Thinking about whether it's too late to divorce now?"

Wen Yanxing: "..."

Wen Yanxing stretched out his hand and pinched Chang Zhi's face, "Are you going to piss me off to death?"

Chang Zhi grabbed it with her backhand, and the two began to quarrel.

Chang Zhi knew that Wen Yanxing was ticklish, so she raised her hand and thrust it straight into his vital point.

Wen Yanxing also knew Chang Zhi's routine, so he dodged to the side.

In the end, Chang Zhi's strength was certainly not as good as Wen Yanxing's. Wen Yanxing grabbed her wrists with one big hand, and she was pressed down on the bed.

The four looked at each other, and suddenly it was quiet.

It seemed that only the sound of breathing was heard, and someone moved secretly, as if teasing the heart.

Chang Zhi blinked, watching Wen Yanxing's face getting closer and closer to her.

Their soft lips pressed together, and the gentle lingering was intoxicating.

She closed her eyes obediently, and her arms, as slender and smooth as lotus roots, hugged his neck.

The warm body pressed on him, which was a bit heavy, but he quickly realized that he could hold it up a little with one hand, and the strength was reassuring.

Chang Zhi curled the corners of her mouth, but the satisfaction of this warmth soon disappeared.

As something entered a white-hot stage, Chang Zhi couldn't help but grab his back and shouted hoarsely,

"You... leave now! Right now... oooh, right now, right now... right now -"

The size is wrong, I strongly demand a refund!

In response to her, she suddenly vented her anger and exerted force. Chang Zhi couldn't help but scream, and then the man stopped. Her collarbone was bitten by him, and his low and restrained voice left no doubt, "No way."

Then her lips were kissed again, accompanied by vague instructions -

"You take it easy, I'm about to explode..."

Chang Zhi's mind suddenly exploded and nothing was left.

Later, she passively climbed his shoulders -

Like someone who is about to fall to the bottom of a cliff grabbing a life-saving branch, like a drowning person holding on to the only driftwood in the sea, like a person who is up and down like a bungee jumping machine and a roller coaster -

Stimulated, the brain is blank, until it finally turns into a dot.

Finally quiet.

Ending in fatigue and... satisfaction.

The next morning, Wen Yanxing was kicked out of the room with his pillow.

The reason was... he said something and wanted to do something else.

"Fortunately, I bought black sheets and... everything is ready..."

Chang Zhi was so tired that she was woken up by Wen Yanxing's kiss early in the morning. She took out her pillow and threw it directly at Wen Yanxing, and pushed him with all her strength.

Wen Yanxing was pushed off the bed without any preparation. Fortunately, there was a soft carpet under the bed, so he didn't suffer the tragedy of being killed by his wife by mistake.

Wen Yanxing rubbed his shoulder as a fulcrum, climbed up and looked at the instigator. Chang Zhi closed his eyes and mumbled in an incomprehensible language, and pulled the quilt and his pillow to continue sleeping.

Wen Yanxing: "................."

Chang Zhi woke up at noon, and kept silent while eating.

Last night, Wen Yanxing insisted on stopping... Chang Zhi coughed because his throat was uncomfortable, and his voice was hoarse when he spoke.

It's embarrassing to say... I cried out in pain.

Thinking of this, she looked up and glared at Wen Yanxing again. But her weak and limp appearance made her look like a spoiled child.

Wen Yanxing picked up a piece of green vegetable for her because Chang Zhi refused to speak, "Eat something light, it will heal faster."

Then he picked up some spicy fried beef for himself.

Chang Zhi spoke with a hoarse voice, "Aren't you tired?"

Wen Yanxing paused with his chopsticks, "Not bad..."

"I think I saw a treadmill in the guest room," Chang Zhi paused, drank a sip of water and continued, "You need to use your excess energy."

"...Don't, I have to live broadcast tonight."

Chang Zhi sneered, "You told me happily yesterday that you have seven days of wedding leave without live broadcast."

Wen Yanxing: "...I like to go to bed early."

"So I asked you to exercise more and go to bed earlier."

"...I won't touch you today, I swear."

"What about tomorrow?"

"No..."

"What about the day after tomorrow?"

"...Okay, have a good rest."

"What about next week?"

"...Don't, aren't you afraid that your husband will get angry and have a nosebleed?"

Chang Zhi handed him a whole pack of tissues.

"For you."

Wen Yanxing: "???"

Chang Zhi couldn't hold it back and said with a smile, "When you can't hold it anymore, cover your nose."

Wen Yanxing: "................."

THE END

Also by james

First Love a Rocky Road
Empress of The Ancient Tides
Sweet Surrender
Has The Idol Gone Crazy Today